AF147773

CLEEK:
The Man of
the Forty Faces

by

Thomas W. Hanshew

Double 9
BOOKS

CLEEK:
The Man of the Forty Faces
by Thomas W. Hanshew

Copyright © 2023

All Rights reserved.

No part of this publication may be reproduced, stored in a retrieval system, or transmitted in any form or by any means, electronic, mechanical, photocopying or Otherwise, without the written permission of the publisher.
The author/editor asserts the moral right to be identified as the author/editor of this work.

ISBN: 978-93-58593-00-6

Published by

DOUBLE 9 BOOKS

2/13-B, Ansari Road
Daryaganj, New Delhi – 110002
info@double9books.com
www.double9books.com
Tel. 011-40042856

This book is under public domain

ABOUT THE AUTHOR

Born in Brooklyn, New York, Thomas W. Hanshew was an American actor and playwright who lived from 1857 until 1914. When he was just 16 years old, Hanshew started his acting career by taking on small roles with Ellen Terry's company. He later played significant parts alongside Clara Morris and Adelaide Neilson. Later, in London, where he spent his final years, he was connected to a publishing business. He published more than 150 novels under various pen names, including "Charlotte May Kingsley," some of which he co-wrote with his wife Mary E. Hanshew. The consulting detective "Hamilton Cleek" (the assumed name of the King of Maurevania), a former thief who now works for law enforcement, was Hanshew's most well-known character. Cleek is referred to as "the man of the forty faces' ' for his extraordinary ability to pass for another person. Cleek, who is based in London's Clarges Street and who serves as the protagonist of dozens of short stories that were first published in 1910 and later compiled in a number of novels, is frequently consulted by Inspector Narkom of Scotland Yard.

CONTENTS

CHAPTER I

The sound came again—so unmistakably, this time, the sound of a footstep in the soft, squashy ooze on the Heath, there could be no question regarding the nature of it. Miss Lorne came to an instant standstill and clutched her belongings closer to her with a shake and a quiver; and a swift prickle of goose-flesh ran round her shoulders and up and down the backs of her hands. There was good, brave blood in her, it is true; but good, brave blood isn't much to fall back upon if you happen to be a girl without escort, carrying a hand-bag containing twenty-odd pounds in money, several bits of valuable jewellery—your whole earthly possessions, in fact—and have lost your way on Hampstead Heath at half-past eight o'clock at night, with a spring fog shutting you in like a wall and shutting out everything else but a "mackerel" collection of clouds that looked like grey smudges on the greasy-silver of a twilit sky.

She looked round, but she could see nothing and nobody. The Heath was a white waste that might have been part of the scenery in Lapland for all there was to tell that it lay within reach of the heart and pulse of the sluggish leviathan London. Over it the vapours of night crowded, an almost palpable wall of thick, wet mist, stirred now and again by some atmospheric movement which could scarcely be called a wind, although, at times, it drew long, lacey filaments above the level of the denser mass of fog and melted away with them into the calm, still upper air.

Miss Lorne hesitated between two very natural impulses—to gather up her skirts and run, or to stand her ground and demand an explanation from the person who was undoubtedly following her. She chose the latter.

"Who is there? Why are you following me? What do you want?" she flung out, keeping her voice as steady as the hard, sharp hammering of her heart would permit.

The question was answered at once—rather startlingly, since the footsteps which caused her alarm, had all the while proceeded from behind, and slightly to the left of her. Now there came a hurried rush and scramble on the right; there was the sound of a match being scratched, a blob of light in the grey of the mist, and she saw standing in front of her, a ragged, weedy, red-headed youth, with the blazing match in his scooped hands.

He was thin to the point of ghastliness. Hunger was in his pinched face, his high cheekbones, his gouged jaws; staring like a starved wolf, through the unnatural brightness of his pale eyes, from every gaunt feature of him.

"'Ullo!" he said with a strong Cockney accent, as he came up out of the fog, and the flare of the match gave him a full view of her, standing there with her lips shut hard, and, the hand-bag clutched up close to her with both hands. "You wot called, was it? Wot price me for arnswerin' of you, eh?"

"Yes, it was I that called," she replied, making a brave front of it. "But I do not think it was you that I called to. Keep away, please. Don't come any nearer. What do you want?" "Well, I'll take that blessed 'and-bag to go on with; and if there aren't no money in it—tumble it out—let's see—lively now! I'll feed for the rest of this week—Gawd, yuss!"

She made no reply, no attempt to obey him, no movement of any sort. Fear had absolutely stricken every atom of strength from her. She could do nothing but look at him with big, frightened eyes, and shake.

"Look 'ere, aren't you a-goin' to do it quiet, or are you a-goin' to mike me tike the blessed thing from you?" he asked.

"I'll do it if you put me to it—my hat! yuss! It aren't my gime—I'm wot you might call a hammer-chewer at it, but when there's summink inside you, wot tears and tears and tears, any gime's worth tryin' that pulls out the claws of it."

She did not move even yet. He flung the spent match from him, and made a sharp step toward her, and he had just reached out his hand to lay hold of her, when another hand—strong, sinewy, hard-shutting as an iron clamp—reached out from the mist, and laid hold of him; plucking him by the neckband and intruding a bunch of knuckles and shut fingers between that and his up-slanted chin.

"Now, then, drop that little game at once, you young monkey!" struck in the sharp staccato of a semi-excited voice. "Interfering with young ladies, eh? Let's have a look at you. Don't be afraid, Miss Lorne—nobody's going to hurt you."

Then a pocket torch spat out a sudden ray of light; and by it both the half-throttled boy and the wholly frightened girl could see the man who had thus intruded himself upon their notice.

"Oh, it is you—it is you again, Mr. Cleek?" said Ailsa with something between a laugh and a sigh of relief as she recognized him.

"Yes, it is I. I have been behind you ever since you left the house in Bardon Road. It was rash of you to cross the heath at this time and in this weather. I rather fancied that something of this kind would be likely to happen, and so took the liberty of following you."

"Then it was you I heard behind me?"

"It was I—yes. I shouldn't have intruded myself upon your notice if you hadn't called out. A moment, please. Let's have a look at this young highwayman, who so freely advertises himself as an amateur."

The light spat full into the gaunt, starved face of the young man and made it stare forth doubly ghastly. He had made no effort to get away from the very first. Perhaps he understood the uselessness of it, with that strong hand gripped on his ragged neckband. Perhaps he was, in his way, something of a fatalist—London breeds so many among such as he: starved things that find every boat chained, every effort thrust back upon them unrewarded. At any rate, from the moment he had heard the girl give to this man a name which every soul in England had heard at one time or another during the past two years, he had gone into a sort of mild collapse, as though realising the utter uselessness of battling against fate, and had given himself up to what was to be.

"Hello," said Cleek, as he looked the youth over. "Yours is a face I don't remember running foul of before, my young beauty. Where did you come from?"

"Where I seem like to be goin' now you've got your currant-pickers on me—Hell," answered the boy, with something like a sigh of despair. "Leastways, I been in Hell ever since I can remember anyfink, so I reckon I must have come from there."

"What's your name?"

"Dollops. S'pose I must a had another sometime, but I never heard of it. Wot's that? Yuss—most nineteen. *Wot?* Oh, go throw summink at yourself! I aren't too young to be 'ungry, am I? And where's a cove goin' to *find* this 'ere 'honest work' you're a-talkin' of? I'm fair sick of the gime of lookin' for it. Besides, you don't see parties as goes in for the other thing walkin' round with ribs on 'em like bed-slats, and not even the price of a cup of corfy in their pockets, do you? No fear! I wouldn't've 'urt the young lydie; but I tell you strite, I'd a took every blessed farthin' she 'ad on her if you 'adn't've dropped on me like this."

"Got down to the last ditch—down to the point of desperation, eh?"

"Yuss. So would you if you 'ad a fing inside you tearin' and tearin' like I 'ave. Aren't et a bloomin' crumb since the day before yesterday at four in the mawnin' when a gent in an 'ansom—drunk as a lord, he was—treated me and a parcel of others to a bun and a cup of corfy at a corfy stall over 'Ighgate way. Stood out agin bein' a crook as long as ever I could—as long as ever I'm goin' to, I reckon, now *you've* got your maulers on me. I'll be on the list after this. The cops 'ull know me; and when you've got the nime—well, wot's the odds? You might as well 'ave the gime as well, and git over goin' empty. All right, run me in, sir. Any'ow, I'll 'ave a bit to eat and a bed to sleep in to-night, and that's one comfort—"

Cleek had been watching the boy closely, narrowly, with an ever-deepening interest; now he loosened the grip of his fingers and let his hand drop to his side.

"Suppose I don't 'run you in,' as you put it? Suppose I take a chance and lend you five shillings, will you do some work and pay it back to me in time?" he asked.

The boy looked up at him and laughed in his face.

"Look 'ere, Gov'nor, it's playin' it low down to lark wiv a chap jist before you're goin' to 'ang 'im," he said. "You come off your blessed perch."

"Right," said Cleek. "And now you get up on yours and let us see what you're made of." Then he put his hand into his trousers pocket; there was a chink of coins and two half-crowns lay on his outstretched palm. "There you are—off with you now, and if you are any good, turn up some time to-night at No. 204, Clarges Street, and ask for Captain Horatio Burbage. He'll see that there's work for you. Toddle along now and get a meal and a bed. And mind you keep a close mouth about this."

The boy neither moved nor spoke nor made any sound. For a moment or two he stood looking from the man to the coins and from the coins back to the man; then, gradually, the truth of the thing seemed to trickle into his mind and, as a hungry fox might pounce upon a stray fowl, he grabbed the money and—bolted.

"Remember the name and remember the street," Cleek called after him.

"You take your bloomin' oath I will!" came back through the enfolding mist; "Gawd, yuss!"—Just that; and the youth was gone.

"I wonder what you will think of me, Miss Lorne," said Cleek, turning to her; "taking a chance like this; and, above all, with a fellow who would have stripped you of every jewel and every penny you have with you if things hadn't happened as they have?"

"And I can very ill afford to lose anything *now*—as I suppose you know, Mr. Cleek. Things have changed sadly for me since that day Mr. Narkom introduced us at Ascot," she said, with just a shadow of seriousness in her eyes. "But as to what I think regarding your action toward that dreadful boy.... Oh, of course, if there is a chance of saving him from a career of crime, I think one owes him that as a duty. In the circumstances, the temptation was very great. It must be a horrible thing to be so hungry that one is driven to robbery to satisfy the longing for food."

"Yes, very horrible—very, very indeed. I once knew a boy who stood as that boy stands—at the parting of the ways; when the good that was in him fought the last great fight with the Devil of Circumstances. If a hand had been stretched forth to help that boy at that time ... Ah, well! it wasn't. The Devil took the reins and the game went *his* way. If five shillings will put the reins into that boy's hands to-night and steer him back to the right path, so much the better for him and—for me. I'll know if he's worth the chance I took to-morrow. Now let us talk about something else. Will you allow me to escort you across the heath and see you safely on your way home? Or would you prefer that I should remain in the background as before?"

"How ungrateful you must think me, to suggest such a thing as that," she said with a reproachful smile. "Walk with me if you will be so kind. I hope you know that this is the third time you have rendered me a service since I had the pleasure of meeting you. It is very nice of you; and I am extremely grateful. I wonder you find the time or—well, take the trouble," rather archly; "a great man like you."

"Shall I take off my hat and say 'thank you, ma'am'; or just the hackneyed 'Praise from Sir Hubert is praise indeed'?" he said with a laugh as he fell into step with her and they faced the mist and the distance together. "I suppose you are alluding to my success in the famous Stanhope Case—the newspapers made a great fuss over that, Mr. Narkom tells me. But—please. One big success doesn't make a 'great man' any more than one rosebush makes a garden."

"Are you fishing for a compliment? Or is that really natural modesty? I had heard of your exploits and seen your name in the papers, oh, dozens of times before I first had the pleasure of meeting you; and since then ... No, I shan't flatter you by saying how many successes I have seen recorded to your credit in the past two years. Do you know that I have a natural predilection for such things? It may be morbid of me—is it?—but I have the strongest kind of a leaning toward the tales of Gaboriau; and I have always wanted to know a really great detective—like Lecocq, or Dupin. And that day at Ascot when Mr. Narkom told me that he would introduce me to the famous 'Man of the Forty Faces' ... Mr. Cleek, why do they call you 'the Man of the Forty Faces'? You always look the same to me."

"Perhaps I shan't, when we come to the end of the heath and get into the public street, where there are lights and people," he said. "That I always look the same in your eyes, Miss Lorne, is because I have but one face for you, and that is my real one. Not many people see it, even among the men of The Yard whom I occasionally work with. You do, however; so does Mr. Narkom, occasionally. So did that boy, unfortunately. I had to show it when I came to your assistance, if only to assure you that you were in friendly hands and to prevent you taking fright and running off into the mist in a panic and losing yourself where even I might not be able to find you. That is why I told the boy to apply for work to 'Captain Burbage of Clarges Street.' *I* am Captain Burbage, Miss Lorne. Nobody knows that but my good friend Mr. Narkom and, now, you."

"I shall respect it, of course," she said. "I hope I need not assure you of that, Mr. Cleek."

"You need assure me of nothing, Miss Lorne," he made reply. "I owe so much more to you than you are aware, that—Oh, well, it doesn't matter. You asked me a question a moment ago. If you want the answer to it—look here."

He stopped short as he spoke; the pocket-torch clicked faintly and from the shelter of a curved hand, the glow of it struck upward to his face. It was not the same face for ten seconds at a time. What Sir Horace Wyvern had seen in Mr. Narkom's private office at Scotland Yard on that night of nights more than two years ago, Sir Horace Wyvern's niece saw now.

"Oh!" she said, with a sharp intaking of the breath as she saw the writhing features knot and twist and blend. "Oh, don't! It is uncanny! It is amazing. It is awful!" And, after a moment, when the light had been shut off and the man beside her was only a shape in the mist: "I hope I may never see you do it again," she merely more than whispered. "It is the most appalling thing. I can't think how you do it—how you came by the power to do such a thing."

"Perhaps by inheritance," said Cleek, as they walked on again. "Once upon a time, Miss Lorne, there was a—er—lady of extremely high position who, at a time when she should have been giving her thoughts to—well, more serious things, used to play with one of those curious little rubber faces which you can pinch up into all sorts of distorted countenances—you have seen the things, no doubt. She would sit for hours screaming with laughter over the droll shapes into which she squeezed the thing. Afterward, when her little son was born, he inherited the trick of that rubber face as a birthright. It may have been the same case with me. Let us say it was, and drop the subject, since you have not found the sight a pleasing one. Now tell me something, please, that I want to know about you."

CHAPTER II

"About me, Mr. Cleek?"

"Yes. You spoke about there being a change in your circumstances—spoke as though you thought I knew. I do not; but I should like to if I may. It will perhaps explain why you are out alone and in this neighbourhood at this time of night."

"It will," she said, with just a shadow of deeper colour coming into her cheeks. "The house you saw me coming out of is the residence of a friend and former schoolmate. I went there to inquire if she could help me in any way to secure a position; and stopped later than I realised."

"Procure you a position, Miss Lorne? A position as what?"

"Companion, amanuensis, governess—anything that," with a laugh and a blush, "'respectable young females' may do to earn a living when they come down in the world. You may possibly have heard that my uncle, Sir Horace, has married again. I think you must have done so, for the papers were full of it at the time. But I forget"—quizzically—"you don't read newspapers, do you, even when they contain accounts of your own greatness."

"I wonder if I deserve that? At any rate, I got it," said Cleek with a laugh. "Yes, I heard all about Sir Horace's wedding. Some four or five months ago, wasn't it?"

"No, three—three, last Thursday, the fourteenth. A woman doesn't forget the date of her enforced abdication. The new Lady Wyvern soon let me know that I was a superfluous person in the household. To-day, I came to the conclusion to leave it; and have taken the first actual step toward doing so. A lucky step, too, I fancy; or, at least, it promises to be."

"As how?"

"My friend knows of two people who would be likely to need me: one, a titled lady here in England, who might be 'very glad to have me'—I am quoting that, please—as governess to her little boy. The other, a young French girl who is returning shortly to Paris, who also might be 'glad to have me' as companion. Of course, I would sooner remain in England, but—well, it is nicer to be a companion than a governess; and the young lady is very nearly my own age. Indeed, we were actually at the same school together when we were very little girls."

"I see," said Cleek, a trifle gloomily. "So then it is possible that it will, eventually, be the young French lady and—Paris, in future. When, do you fancy? Soon?"

"Oh, I don't know about that. I haven't quite made up my mind as yet which of the two it will be. And then there's the application to be sent afterwards."

"Still, it will be one of the two certainly?"

"Oh, yes. I shall have to earn my living in future, you know; so, naturally, of course—" She gave her shoulder an eloquent upward movement, and let the rest go by default.

Cleek did not speak for a moment: merely walked on beside her—a ridge between his eyebrows and his lower lip sucked in; as if he were mentally debating upon something and was afraid he might speak incautiously. But of a sudden:

"Miss Lorne," he said, in a curiously tense voice, "may I ask you something? Let us say that you had set your heart upon obtaining one or the other of these two positions—set it so entirely that life wouldn't be worth a straw to you if you didn't get it. Let us say, too, that there was something you had done, something in your past which, if known, might utterly preclude the possibility of your obtaining what you wanted—it is an absurd hypothesis, of course: but let us use it for the sake of argument. We will say you had done your best to live down that offensive 'something' done, and were still doing all that lay in your power to atone for it; that nobody but one person shared the knowledge of that 'something' with you, and upon his silence you could rely. Now tell me: would you feel justified in accepting the position upon which you had set your heart *without* confessing the thing; or would you feel in duty bound to speak, well knowing that it would in all human probability be the end of all your hopes? I should like to have your opinion upon that point, please."

"I can't see that I or anybody else could have other than the one," she replied. "It is an age-old maxim, is it not, Mr. Cleek, that two wrongs cannot by any possibility constitute a right? I should feel in duty bound, in honour bound, to speak, of course. To do the other would be to obtain the position by fraud—to steal it, as a thief steals things that *he* wants. No sort of atonement is possible, is even worth the name, if it is backed up by deceit, Mr. Cleek."

"Even though that deceit is the only thing that could give you your heart's desire? The only thing that could open the Gates of Heaven for you?"

"The 'Gates of Heaven,' as you put it, can never be opened with a lie, Mr. Cleek. They might be opened by the very thing of which you speak—confession. I think I should take my chances upon that. At any rate, if I failed, I should at least have preserved my self-respect and done more to merit what I wanted than if I had secured it by treachery. Think of the boy you helped a little while ago. How much respect will you have for him if he never lives up to his promise; never goes to Clarges Street at all? Yet if he does live up to it, will he not be doubly worth the saving? But please!" with a sudden change from seriousness to gaiety, "if I am to be led into sermonizing, might I not know what it is all about? I shall be right, shall I not, in supposing that all this is merely the preface to something else?"

"Either the Preface or—the Finis," said Cleek, with a deeply drawn breath. "Still, as you say, no atonement is worth calling an atonement if it is based upon fraud; and so—Miss Lorne, I am going to ask you to indulge in yet another little flight of fancy. Carry your mind back, will you, to the night when your cousin—to the night two years ago when Sir Horace Wyvern's daughter had her wedding presents stolen and you, I believe, had rather a trying moment with that fellow who was known as 'The Vanishing Cracksman.' You can remember it, can you not?"

"Remember it? I shall never forget it. I thought, when the police ran down stairs and left me with him, that I was talking to Mr. Narkom. I think I nearly went daft with terror when I found out that it was he."

"And you found it out only through his telling you, did you not? Afterward, I am told, the police found you lying fainting at the foot of the stairs. The man had touched you, spoken to you, even caught up your hand and put it to his lips? Can you remember what he said when he did that? Can you?"

"Yes," she answered, with a little shudder of recollection. "For weeks afterward I used to wake up in the middle of the night thinking of it and going cold all over. He said, 'You have come down into Hell and lifted me out. Under God, you shall lift me into Heaven as well!'"

"And perhaps you shall," said Cleek, stopping short and uncovering his head. "At any rate, I'll not attempt to win it by fraud. Miss Lorne, I am that man. I am the 'Vanishing Cracksman' of those other days. I've walked the 'straight path' since the moment I kissed your hand."

She said nothing, made no faintest sound. She couldn't—all the strength, all the power to do anything but simply stand and look at him had gone out of her. But even so, she was conscious—dimly but yet conscious—of a feeling of relief that they had come at last close to the end of the heath, that there was the faint glow of lights dimly observable through the enfolding mist, and that there was the rumble of wheels, the pulse of life, the law-guarded paths of the city's streets beyond.

CHAPTER III

She could not herself have been more conscious of that feeling of relief than he was of its coming. It spoke to him in the swift glance she gave toward those distant, fog-blurred lights, in the white, drained face of her, in the shrinking backward movement of her body when he spoke again; and something within him voiced "the exceeding bitter cry."

"I am not sure that I even hoped you would take the revelation in any other way than this," he said. "A hawk—even a tamed one—must be a thing of terror in the eyes of a dove. Still, I am not sorry that I have made the confession, Miss Lorne. When the worst has been told, a burden rolls away."

"Yes," she acquiesced faintly, finding her voice; but finding it only to lose it again. "But that you—that *you*...." And was faint and very still again.

"Shall we go on? It isn't more than fifty paces to the road; and you may rely upon finding a taxicab there. Would you like me to show you the way?"

"Yes, please. I—oh, don't think me unsympathetic, unkind, severe. It is such a shock; it is all so horrible—I mean—that is.... Let me get used to it. I shall never tell, of course—no, never! Now, please, may we not walk faster? I am very, very late as it is; and they will be worrying at home."

They did walk faster, and in a minute more were at the common's end. Cleek stopped and again lifted his hat.

"We will part here, Miss Lorne," he said. "I won't force my company on you any further. From here, you are quite beyond all danger, and I am sure you would rather I left you to find a taxi for yourself. Good night." He did not even offer to put out his hand. "May I say again, that I am not sorry I told you? Nor did I ever expect you would, take it other than like this. It is only natural. Try to forgive me; or, at the least, believe that I have not tried to keep your friendship by a lie, or to atone in seeming only. Good night."

He gave her no chance to reply, no time to say one single word. Deep wounds require time in which to heal. He knew that he had wounded the white soul of her so that it was sick with uncertainty, faint with dread; and, putting on his hat, stepped sharply back and let the mist take him and hide him from her sight.

But, though she did not see, he was near her even then.

He knew when she walked out into the light-filled street; he knew when she found a taxicab; and he did not make an effort to go his way until he was sure that she was safely started upon hers. Then he screwed round on his heel and went back into the mist and loneliness of the heath, and walked, and walked, and walked. Afterward—long afterward: when the night was getting old and the town was going to sleep, he, too, fared forth in quest of a taxi, and finding one went *his* way as she had gone hers.

In the neighbourhood of Bond Street—now a place of darkness and slow-tramping policemen—he dismissed the taxi and continued the journey along Piccadilly afoot. It was close to one o'clock when he came at length to Clarges Street and swung into it from the Piccadilly end, and moved on in the direction of the house which sheltered him and his secrets together. But, though he walked with apparent indifference, his eye was ever on the lookout for some chance watcher in the windows of the other houses; for "Captain Horatio Burbage" was supposed, in the neighbourhood, to be a superannuated seaman who maintained a bachelor establishment with the aid of an elderly housekeeper and a deaf-and-dumb maid of all work.

But no one was on the watch to-night; and it was only when he came at last to the pillared portico of his own residence that he found any sign of life from one end of the street to the other. He did find it then, however; for the boy, Dollops, was sitting huddled up on the top step with the thick shadow of the portico making a safe screen for him.

He had made good use of the two half-crowns, for he had not only feasted—and was feasting still: on a bag of winkles and a saveloy—but was washed and brushed and had gone to the length of a shoe-shine and a collar.

"Been waitin' since eleven o'clock, sir," he said, getting up and pulling his forelock as Cleek appeared. "Didn't knock and arsk for no one, though—not me. Twigged as it would be you, sir, on account of your sayin' to-night. I've read summink of the ways of 'tecs. Wot ho!"

"You seem a sharp little customer, at all events," said Cleek with a curious one-sided smile—a smile that was peculiar to him. "I somehow fancy that I've made a good investment, Dollops. Filled up, eh?"

"No, sir—never filled. Born 'ungry, I reckon. But filled as much as you could fill me, bless your 'eart. I aren't never goin' to forget that, Gov'nor—no fear. An eater and a scrapper I am, sir; and I'll scrap for *you*, sir, while there's a bloomin' breff left in my blessed body! Gimme the tip wot kind of work I *can* do for you, Gov'nor, will you? I want to get them two 'arf-crowns off my conscience as quick as I can."

Cleek looked at him and smiled again.

"Yes, I'm *sure* I made a good bargain, Dollops," he said. "Come in." And in this way the attachment which existed between them ever afterward had its beginning.

He took the boy in and up to the little room on the second floor which he called his den; and, turning on the light, motioned him to a chair, laid aside his hat and gloves, and was just about to pull up a chair for himself when he caught sight of an unstamped letter lying upon his writing-table.

"Sit down there and wait a moment until I read this, my lad," he said; and forthwith tore the letter open.

It was from Superintendent Narkom. He had known that from the first, however. No one but Narkom ever wrote him letters. This one was exceedingly brief. It simply contained these two lines:

"My dear Cleek. The Three Jolly Fishermen, Richmond, at tea-time to-morrow. An astonishing affair. Yours, M. N."

"Dollops, my lad, I think I'm going to make a man of you," he said as he tore the letter into a dozen pieces and tossed the fragments into a waste-basket. "At any rate, I'm going to have a try. Know anything about Richmond?"

"Yuss, sir."

"Good. Well, we'll have a half-hour's talk and then I'll find a temporary bed for you for the night, and to-morrow we'll take a pull on the river at Richmond and see what we shall see."

The half-hour, however, developed into a full one; for it was after two o'clock when the talk was finished and a bed improvised for the boy; but Cleek, saying good night to him at last and going to his own bedroom, felt that it was a long, long way from being time wasted.

What Dollops thought is, perhaps, best told by the fact that he burst out crying when Cleek came in in the morning to ask how he had slept.

"Slept, Gov'nor!" he said. "Why, bless your 'eart, sir, I couldn't a slept better on a bed of roses, nor 'ad 'arf such comfort. Feel like I needed someone to lend me a biff on the coco, sir, to make sure as I aren't a dreamin'—it's so wot a cove fancies 'Eaven to be like, sir."

And afterward, when the day was older, and they had gone to Richmond, and Cleek—in his boating flannels—was pulling him up the shining river and talking to him again as he had talked last night, he felt that it was even more like Heaven than ever.

It was after four—long after—when they finally separated and Cleek, leaving the boy in charge of the boat, stepped ashore in the neighbourhood of the inn of the Three Jolly Fishermen and went to keep his appointment with Narkom.

He found him enjoying tea at a little round table in the niche of a big bay window in the small private parlour which lay immediately behind the bar-room.

"My dear chap, do forgive me for not waiting," said the superintendent contritely, as Cleek came in, looking like a college-bred athlete in his boating-flannels and his brim-tilted panama. "But the fact is you are a little later than I anticipated; and I was simply famishing."

"Share the blame of my lateness with me, Mr. Narkom," said Cleek as he tossed aside his hat and threw the fag-end of his cigarette through the open window. "You merely said 'tea-time,' not any particular hour; and I improved the opportunity to take another spin up the river and to talk like a Dutch uncle to a certain young man whom I shall introduce to your notice in due time. It isn't often that duty calls me to a little Eden like this. The air is like balm to-day; and the river—oh, the river is a sheer delight."

Narkom rang for a fresh pot of tea and a further supply of buttered toast, and, when these were served, Cleek sat down and joined him.

"I dare say," said the superintendent, opening fire at once, "that you wonder what in the world induced me to bring you out here to meet me, my dear fellow, instead of following the usual course and calling at Clarges Street? Well, the fact is, Cleek, that the gentleman with whom I am now about to put you in touch lives in this vicinity, and is so placed that he cannot get away without running the risk of having the step he is taking discovered."

"Humph! He is closely spied upon, then?" commented Cleek. "The trouble arises from someone or something in his own household?"

"No—in his father's. The 'trouble,' so far as I can gather, seems to emanate from his stepmother, a young and very beautiful woman, who was born on the island of Java, where the father of our client met and married her some two years ago, whither he had gone to probe into the truth of the amazing statement that a runic stone had been unearthed in that part of the globe."

"Ah, then you need not tell me the gentleman's name, Mr. Narkom," interposed Cleek. "I remember perfectly well the stir which that ridiculous and unfounded statement created at the time. Despite the fact that scholars of all nations scoffed at the thing, and pointed out that the very term 'rune' is of Teutonic origin, one enthusiastic old gentleman—Mr. Michael Bawdrey, a retired brewer, thirsting for something more enduring than malt to carry his name down the ages—became fired with enthusiasm upon the subject, and set forth for Java 'hot foot,' as one might say. I remember that the papers made great game of him; but I heard, I fancy, that, in spite of all, he was a dear, lovable old chap, and not at all like the creature the cartoonists portrayed him."

"What a memory you have, my dear Cleek. Yes, that is the party; and he *is* a dear, lovable old chap at bottom. Collects old china, old weapons, old armour, curiosities of all sorts—lots of 'em bogus, no doubt; catch the charlatans among the dealers letting a chance like that slip them—and is never so happy as when showing his 'collection' to his friends and being mistaken by the ignorant for a man of deep learning."

"A very human trait, Mr. Narkom. We all are anxious that the world should set the highest possible valuation upon us. It is only when we are underrated that we object. So this dear, deluded old gentleman, having failed to secure a 'rune' in Java, brought back something equally cryptic—a woman? Was the lady of his choice a native or merely an inhabitant of the island?"

"Merely an inhabitant, my dear fellow. As a matter of fact, she is English. Her father, a doctor, long since deceased, took her out there in her childhood. She was none too well off, I believe; but that did not prevent her having many suitors, among whom was Mr. Bawdrey's own son, the gentleman who is anxious to have you take up this case."

"Oho!" said Cleek, with a strong, rising inflection. "So the lady was of the careful and calculating kind? She didn't care for youth and all the rest of it when she could have papa and the money-chest without waiting. A common enough occurrence. Still, this does not make up an 'affair,' and especially an 'affair' which requires the assistance of a detective, and you spoke of 'a case.' What is the case, Mr. Narkom?"

"I will leave Mr. Philip Bawdrey himself to tell you that," said Narkom, as the door opened to admit a young man of about eight-and-twenty, clothed in tennis flannels, and looking very much perturbed, a handsome, fair-haired, fair-moustached young fellow, with frank, boyish eyes and that unmistakable something which stamps the products of the 'Varsities. "Come in, Mr. Bawdrey. You said we were not to wait tea, and you see that we haven't. Let me have the pleasure of introducing Mr.—"

"Headland," put in Cleek adroitly, and with a look at Narkom as much as to say, "Don't give me away. I may not care to take the case when I hear it, so what's the use of letting everybody know who I am?" Then he switched round in his chair, rose, and held out his hand. "Mr. George Headland, of the Yard, Mr. Bawdrey. I don't trust Mr. Narkom's proverbially tricky memory for names. He introduced me as Jones once, and I lost the opportunity of handling the case because the party in question couldn't believe that anybody named Jones would be likely to ferret it out."

"Funny idea, that!" commented young Bawdrey, smiling, and accepting the proffered hand. "Rum lot of people you must run across in your line, Mr. Headland. Shouldn't take you for a detective myself, shouldn't even in a room full of them. College man, aren't you? Thought so. Oxon or Cantab?"

"Cantab—Emmanuel."

"Oh, Lord! Never thought I'd ever live to appeal to an Emmanuel man to do anything brilliant. I'm an Oxon chap; Brasenose is my alma mater. I say, Mr. Narkom, do give me a cup of tea, will you? I had to slip off while the others were at theirs, and I've run all the way. Thanks very much. Don't mind if I sit in that corner and draw the curtain a little, do you?" his frank, boyish face suddenly clouding. "I don't want to be seen by anybody passing. It's a horrible thing to feel that you are being spied upon, at every turn, Mr. Headland, and that want of caution may mean the death of the person you love best in all the world."

"Oh, it's that kind of case, is it?" queried Cleek, making room for him to pass round the table and sit in the corner, with his back to the window and the loosened folds of the chintz curtain keeping him in the shadow.

"Yes," answered young Bawdrey, with a half-repressed shudder and a deeper clouding of his rather pale face. "Sometimes I try to make myself believe that it isn't, that it's all fancy, that she never could be so inhuman, and yet how else is it to be explained? You can't go behind the evidence; you can't make things different simply by saying that you will not believe." He stirred his tea nervously, gulped down a couple of mouthfuls of it, and then set the cup aside. "I can't enjoy anything; it takes the savour out of everything when I think of it," he added, with a note of pathos in his voice. "My dad, my dear, bully old dad, the best and dearest old boy in all the world! I suppose, Mr. Headland, that Mr. Narkom has told you something about the case?"

"A little—a very little indeed. I know that your father went to Java, and married a second wife there; and I know, too, that you yourself were rather taken with the lady at one time, and that she threw you over as soon as Mr. Bawdrey senior became a possibility."

"That's a mistake," he replied. "She never threw me over, Mr. Headland; she never had the chance. I found her out long before my father became anything like what you might call a rival, found her out as a mercenary, designing woman, and broke from her voluntarily. I only wish that I had known that he had one serious thought regarding her. I could have warned him; I could have spoken then. But I never did find out until it was too late. Trust her for that. She waited until I had gone up-country to look after some fine old porcelains and enamels that the governor had heard about; then she hurried him off and tricked him into a hasty marriage. Of course, after that I couldn't speak—I wouldn't speak. She was my father's wife, and he was so proud of her, so happy, dear old boy, that I'd have been little better than a brute to say anything against her."

"What could you have said if you had spoken?"

"Oh, lots of things—the things that made me break away from her in the beginning. She'd had more love affairs than one; her late father's masquerading as a doctor for another. They had only used that as a cloak. They had run a gambling-house on the sly—he as the card-sharper, she as the decoy. They had drained one poor fellow dry, and she had thrown him over after leading him on to think that she cared for him and was going to marry him. He blew out his brains in front of her, poor wretch. They say she never turned a hair. You wouldn't believe it possible, if you saw her; she is so sweet and caressing, and so young and beautiful, you'd almost believe her an angel. But there's Travers in the background—always Travers."

"Travers! Who is he?"

"Oh, one of her old flames, the only one she ever really cared for, they say. She was supposed to have broken with him out there in Java, because they were too poor to marry; and now he's come over to England, and he's there, in the house with the dear old dad and me, and they are as thick as thieves together. I've caught them whispering and prowling about together, in the grounds and along the lanes, after she has said 'Good night,' and gone to her room and is supposed to be in bed. There's a houseful of her old friends three parts of the time. They come and they go, but Travers never goes. I know why"—waxing suddenly excited, suddenly vehement—"yes! I know why. He's in the game with her!"

"Game! What game, Mr. Bawdrey? What is it that she is doing?"

"She's killing my old dad!" he answered, with a sort of sob in his excited voice. "She's murdering him by inches, that's what she's doing, and I want you to help me bring it home to her. God knows what it is she's using or how she uses it; but you know what demons they are for secret poisons, those Javanese, what means they have of killing people without a trace. And she was out there for years and years. So, too, was Travers, the brute! They know all the secrets of those beastly barbarians, and between them they're doing something to my old dad."

"How do you know that?"

"I don't know it—that's the worst of it. But I couldn't be surer of it if they took me into their secrets. But there's the evidence of his condition; there's the fact that it didn't begin until after Travers came. Look here, Mr. Headland, you don't know my dad. He's got the queerest notions sometimes. One of his fads is that it's unlucky to make a will. Well, if he dies without one, who will inherit his money, as I am an only child?"

"Undoubtedly you and his widow."

"Exactly. And if I die at pretty nearly the same time—and they'll see to that, never fear; it will be my turn the moment they are sure of him—she will inherit everything. Now, let me tell you what's happening. From being a strong, healthy man, my father has, since Travers's arrival, begun to be attacked by a mysterious malady. He has periodical fainting-fits, sometimes convulsions. He'll be feeling better for a day or so; then, without a word of warning, whilst you're talking to him, he'll drop like a shot bird and go into the most horrible convulsions. The doctors can't stop it; they don't even know what it is. They only know that he's fading away—turning from a strong, virile old man into a thin, nervous, shivering wreck. But I know! I know! They're dosing him somehow with some diabolical Javanese thing, those two. And yesterday—God help me!—yesterday, I, too, dropped like a shot bird; I, too, had the convulsions and the weakness and the fainting-fit. My time has begun also!"

"Bless my soul! what a diabolical thing!" put in Narkom agitatedly. "No wonder you appealed to me!"

"No wonder!" Bawdrey replied. "I felt that it had gone as far as I dared to let it; that it was time to call in the police and to have help before it was too late. That's the case, Mr. Headland. I want you to find some way of getting at the truth, of looking into Travers's luggage, into my stepmother's effects, and unearthing the horrible stuff with which they are doing this thing; and perhaps, when that is known, some antidote may be found to save the dear old dad and restore him to what he was. Can't you do this? For God's sake, say that you can."

"At all events, I can try, Mr. Bawdrey," responded Cleek.

"Oh, thank you, thank you!" said Bawdrey gratefully. "I don't care a hang what it costs, what your fees are, Mr. Headland. So long as you run those two to earth, and get hold of the horrible stuff, whatever it is, that they are using, I'll pay any price in the world, and count it cheap as compared with the life of my dear old dad. When can you take hold of the case? Now?"

"I'm afraid not. Mysterious things like this require a little thinking over. Suppose we say to-morrow noon? Will that do?"

"I suppose it must, although I should have liked to take you back with me. Every moment's precious at a time like this. But if it must be delayed until to-morrow—well, it must, I suppose. But I'll take jolly good care that nobody gets a chance to come within touching distance of the pater—bless him!—until you do come, if I have to sit on the mat before his door until morning. Here's the address on this card, Mr. Headland. When and how shall I expect to see you again? You'll use an alias, of course?"

"Oh, certainly! Had you any old friend in your college days whom your father only knew by name and who is now too far off for the imposture to be discovered?"

"Yes. Jim Rickaby. We were as inseparable as the Siamese twins in our undergrad days. He's in Borneo now. Haven't heard from him in a dog's age."

"Couldn't be better," said Cleek. "Then 'Jim Rickaby' let it be. You'll get a letter from him first thing in the morning saying that he's back in England, and about to run down and spend the week-end with you. At noon he will arrive, accompanied by his Borneo servant, named—er—Dollops. You can put the 'blackie' up in some quarter of the house where he can move about at will without disturbing any of your own servants, and can get in and out at all hours; he will be useful, you know, in prowling about the grounds at night and ascertaining if the lady really does go to bed when she retires to her room. As for 'Jim Rickaby' himself—well, you can pave the way for his operations by informing your father, when you get the letter, that he has gone daft on the subject of old china and curios and things of that sort, don't you know."

"What a ripping idea!" commented young Bawdrey. "I twig. He'll get chummy with you, of course, and you can lead him on and adroitly 'pump' him regarding her, and where she keeps her keys and things like that. That's the idea, isn't it?"

"Something of that sort. I'll find out all about her, never fear," said Cleek in reply. Then they shook hands and parted, and it was not until after young Bawdry had gone that either he or Narkom recollected that Cleek had overlooked telling the young man that Headland was not his name.

"Oh, well, it doesn't matter. Time enough to tell him that when it comes to making out the cheque," said Cleek, as the superintendent remarked upon the circumstance. Then he pushed back his chair and walked over to the window, and stood looking silently out upon the flowing river. Narkom did not disturb his reflections. He knew from past experience, as well as from the manner in which he took his lower lip between his teeth and drummed with his finger-tips upon the window-ledge, that some idea relative to the working out of the case had taken shape within his mind, and so, with the utmost discretion, went on with his tea and refrained from speaking. Suddenly Cleek turned. "Mr. Narkom, do me a favour, will you? Look me up a copy of Holman's 'Diseases of the Kidneys' when you go back to town. I'll send Dollops round to the Yard to-night to get it."

"Right you are," said Narkom, taking out his pocket-book and making a note of it. "But, I say, look here, my dear fellow, you can't possibly believe that it's anything of that sort—anything natural, I mean—in the face of what we've heard?"

"No, I don't. I think it's something confoundedly unnatural, and that that poor old chap is being secretly and barbarously murdered. I think that— and—I think, too—" His voice trailed off. He stood silent and preoccupied for a moment, and then, putting his thoughts into words, without addressing them to anybody: "Ayupee!" he said reflectively; "Pohon-Upas, Antjar, Galanga root, Ginger and Black Pepper—that's the Javanese method of procedure, I believe. Ayupee!—yes, assuredly, Ayupee!"

"What the dickens are you talking about, Cleek? And what does all that gibberish and that word 'Ayupee' mean?"

"Nothing—nothing. At least, just yet. I say, put on your hat, and let's go for a pull on the river, Mr. Narkom. I've had enough of mysteries for to-day and am spoiling for another hour in a boat."

Then he screwed round on his heel and walked out into the brilliant summer sunshine.

CHAPTER IV

Promptly, at the hour appointed, "Mr. Jim Rickaby" and his black servant arrived at Laburnam Villa; and certainly the former had no cause to complain of the welcome he received at the hands of his beautiful young hostess.

He found her not only an extremely lovely woman to the eye, but one whose gentle, caressing ways, whose soft voice and simple girlish charm were altogether fascinating, and, judging from outward appearances, from the tender solicitude for her elderly husband's comfort and well-being, from the look in her eyes when she spoke to him, the gentleness of her hand when she touched him, one would have said that she really and truly loved him, and that it needed no lure of gold to draw this particular May to the arms of this one December.

He found Captain Travers a laughing, rollicking, fun-loving type of man—at least, to all outward appearances—who seemed to delight in sports and games and to have an almost childish love of card tricks and that species of entertainment which is known as parlour magic. He found the three other members of the little house-party—to wit: Mrs. Somerby-Miles, Lieutenant Forshay, and Mr. Robert Murdock—respectively, a silly, flirtatious, little gadfly of a widow; a callow, love-struck, lap-dog, young army officer, with a budding moustache and a full-blown idea of his own importance; and a dour Scotchman of middle age, with a passion for chess, a glowering scorn of frivolities, and a deep and abiding conviction that Scotland was the only country in the world for a self-respecting human being to dwell in, and that everything outside of the Established Church was foredoomed to flames and sulphur and the perpetual prodding of red-hot pitchforks. And last, but not least by any means, he found Mr. Michael Bawdrey just what he had been told he would find him, namely, a dear, lovable, sunny-tempered old man, who fairly idolised his young wife and absolutely adored his frank-faced, affectionate, big boy of a son, and who ought not, in the common course of things, to have an enemy or an evil wisher in all the world.

The news, which, of course, had preceded Cleek's arrival, that this whilom college chum of his son's was as great an enthusiast as he himself on the subject of old china, old porcelain, bric-à-brac and curios of every sort, filled him with the utmost delight, and he could scarcely refrain from rushing him off at once to view his famous collection.

"Michael, dear, you mustn't overdo yourself just because you happen to have been a little stronger these past two days," said his wife, laying a gentle hand upon his arm. "Besides, we must give Mr. Rickaby time to breathe. He has had a long journey, and I am sure he will want to rest. You can take him in to see that wonderful collection after dinner, dear."

"Humph! Full of fakes, as I supposed—and she knows it," was Cleek's mental comment upon this. And he was not surprised when, finding herself alone with him a few minutes later, she said, in her pretty, pleading way:

"Mr. Rickaby, if you are an expert, don't undeceive him. I could not let you go to see the collection without first telling you. It is full of bogus things, full of frauds and shams that unscrupulous dealers have palmed off on him. But don't let him know. He takes such pride in them, and—and he's breaking down—God pity me, his health is breaking down every day, Mr. Rickaby, and I want to spare him every pang, if I can, even so little a pang as the discovery that the things he prizes are not real."

"Set your mind at rest, Mrs. Bawdrey," promised Cleek. "He will not find it out from me. He will not find anything out from me. He is just the kind of man to break his heart, to crumple up like a burnt glove, and come to the end of all things, even life, if he were to discover that any of his treasures, anything that he loved and trusted in, is a sham and a fraud."

His eyes looked straight into hers as he spoke, his hand rested lightly on her sleeve. She sucked in her breath suddenly, a brief pallor chased the roses from her cheeks, a brief confusion sat momentarily upon her. She appeared to hesitate, then looked away and laughed uneasily.

"I don't think I quite grasp what you mean, Mr. Rickaby," she said.

"Don't you?" he made answer. "Then I will tell you—some time—to-morrow, perhaps. But if I were you, Mrs. Bawdrey—well, no matter. This I promise you: that dear old man shall have no ideal shattered by me."

And, living up to that promise, he enthused over everything the old man had in his collection when, after dinner that night, they went, in company with Philip, to view it. But bogus things were on every hand. Spurious porcelains, fraudulent armour, faked china were everywhere. The loaded cabinets and the glazed cases were one long procession of faked Dresden and bogus faience, of Egyptian enamels that had been manufactured in Birmingham, and of sixth-century "treasures" whose makers were still plying their trade and battening upon the ignorance of such collectors as he.

"Now, here's a thing I am particularly proud of," said the gulled old man, reaching into one of the cases and holding out for Cleek's admiration an irregular disc of dull, hammered gold that had an iridescent beetle embedded in the flat face of it. "This scarab, Mr. Rickaby, has helped to make history, as one might say. It was once the property of Cleopatra. I was obliged to make two trips to Egypt before I could persuade the owner to part with it. I am always conscious of a certain sense of awe, Mr. Rickaby, when I touch this wonderful thing. To think, sir, to think! that this bauble once rested on the bosom of that marvellous woman; that Mark Antony must have seen it, may have touched it; that Ptolemy Auletes knew all about it, and that it is older, sir, than the Christian religion itself!"

He held it out upon the flat of his palm, the better for Cleek to see and to admire it, and signed to his son to hand the visitor a magnifying glass.

"Wonderful, most wonderful!" observed Cleek, bending over the spurious gem and focussing the glass upon it; not, however, for the purpose of studying the fraud, but to examine something just noticed—something round and red and angry-looking which marked the palm itself, at the base of the middle finger.

"No wonder you are proud of such a prize. I think I should go off my head with rapture if I owned an antique like that. But, pardon me, have you met with an accident, Mr. Bawdrey? That's an ugly place you have on your palm."

"That? Oh, that's nothing," he answered, gaily. "It itches a great deal at times, but otherwise it isn't troublesome. I can't think how in the world I got it, to tell the truth. It came out as a sort of red blister in the beginning, and since it broke it has been spreading a great deal. But, really, it doesn't amount to anything at all."

"Oh, that's just like you, dad," put in Philip, "always making light of the wretched thing. I notice one thing, however, Rickaby, it seems to grow worse instead of better. And dad knows as well as I do when it began. It came out suddenly about a fortnight ago, after he had been holding some green worsted for my stepmother to wind into balls. Just look at it, will you, old chap?"

"Nonsense, nonsense!" chimed in the old man, laughingly. "Don't mind the silly boy, Mr. Rickaby. He will have it that that green worsted is to blame, just because he happened to spy the thing the morning after."

"Let's have a look at it," said Cleek, moving nearer the light. Then, after a close examination, "I don't think it amounts to anything, after all," he added, as he laid aside the glass. "I shouldn't worry myself about it if I were you, Phil. It's just an ordinary blister, nothing more. Let's go on with the collection, Mr. Bawdrey; I'm deeply interested in it, I assure you. Never saw such a marvellous lot. Got any more amazing things—gems, I mean—like that wonderful scarab? I say!"—halting suddenly before a long, narrow case, with a glass front, which stood on end in a far corner, and, being lined with black velvet, brought into ghastly prominence the suspended shape of a human skeleton contained within—"I say! What the dickens is this? Looks like a doctor's specimen, b'gad. You haven't let anybody—I mean, you haven't been buying any prehistoric bones, have you, Mr. Bawdrey?"

"Oh, that?" laughed the old man, turning round and seeing to what he was alluding. "Oh, that's a curiosity of quite a different sort, Mr. Rickaby. You are right in saying it looks like a doctor's specimen. It is—or, rather, it was. Mrs. Bawdrey's father was a doctor, and it once belonged to him. Properly, it ought to have no place in a collection of this sort, but—well, it's such an amazing thing I couldn't quite refuse it a place, sir. It's a freak of nature. The skeleton of a nine-fingered man."

"Of a what?"

"A nine-fingered man."

"Well, I can't say that I see anything remarkable in that. I've got nine fingers myself, nine and one over, when it comes to that."

"No, you haven't, you duffer!" put in young Bawdrey, with a laugh. "You've got eight fingers—eight fingers and two thumbs. This bony johnny has nine fingers and two thumbs. That's what makes him a freak. I say, dad, open the beggar's box, and let Rickaby see."

His father obeyed the request. Lifting the tiny brass latch which alone secured it, he swung open the glazed door of the case, and, reaching in, drew forward the flexible left arm of the skeleton.

"There you are," he said, supporting the bony hand upon his palm, so that all its fingers were spread out and Cleek might get a clear view of the monstrosity. "What a trial he must have been to the glove trade, mustn't he?" laughing gaily. "Fancy the confusion and dismay, Mr. Rickaby, if a fellow like this walked into a Bond Street shop in a hurry and asked for a pair of gloves."

Cleek bent over and examined the thing with interest. At first glance, the hand was no different from any other skeleton hand one might see any day in any place where they sold anatomical specimens for the use of members of the medical profession; but as Mr. Bawdrey, holding it on the palm of his right hand, flattened it out with the fingers of his left, the abnormality at once became apparent. Springing from the base of the fourth finger, a perfectly developed fifth appeared, curling inward toward what had once been the palm of the hand, as though, in life, it had been the owner's habit of screening it from observation by holding it in that position. It was, however, perfectly flexible, and Mr. Bawdrey had no difficulty in making it lie out flat after the manner of its mates.

The sight was not inspiring—the freaks of mother Nature rarely are. No one but a doctor would have cared to accept the thing as a gift, and no one but a man as mad on the subject of curiosities and with as little sense of discrimination as Mr. Bawdrey would have dreamt for a moment of adding it to a collection.

"It's rather uncanny," said Cleek, who had no palate for the abnormal in Nature. "For myself, I may frankly admit that I don't like things of that sort about me."

"You are very much like my wife in that," responded the old man. "She was of the opinion that the skeleton ought to have been destroyed or else handed over to some anatomical museum. But—well, it is a curiosity, you know, Mr. Rickaby. Besides, as I have said, it was once the property of her late father, a most learned man, sir, most learned, and as it was of sufficient interest for him to retain it—oh, well, we collectors are faddists, you know, so I easily persuaded Mrs. Bawdrey to allow me to bring it over to England with me when we took our leave of Java. And now that you have seen it, suppose we have a look at more artistic things. I have some very fine specimens of neolithic implements and weapons which I am most anxious to show you. Just step this way, please."

He let the skeleton's hand slip from his own, swing back into the case, and forthwith closed the glass door upon it; then, leading the way to the cabinet containing the specimens referred to, he unlocked it, and invited Cleek's opinion of the flint arrow-heads, stone hatchets, and granite utensils within.

For a minute they lingered thus, the old man talking, laughing, exulting in his possessions, the detective examining and pretending to be deeply impressed. Then, of a sudden, without hint or warning to lessen the shock of it, the uplifted lid of the cabinet fell with a crash from the hand that upheld it, shivering the glass into fifty pieces, and Cleek, screwing round on his heel with a "jump" of all his nerves, was in time to see the figure of his host crumple up, collapse, drop like a thing shot dead, and lie foaming and writhing on the polished floor.

"Dad! Oh, heavens! Dad!" The cry was young Bawdrey's. He seemed fairly to throw himself across the intervening space and to reach his father in the instant he fell. "Now you know! Now you know!" he went on wildly, as

Cleek dropped down beside him and began to loosen the old man's collar. "It's like this always; not a hint, not a sign, but just this utter collapse. My God, what are they doing it with? How are they managing it, those two? They're coming, Headland. Listen! Don't you hear them?"

The crash of the broken glass and the jar of the old man's fall had swept through all the house, and a moment later, headed by Mrs. Bawdrey herself, all the members of the little house-party came piling excitedly into the room.

The fright and suffering of the young wife seemed very real as she threw herself down beside her husband and caught him to her with a little shuddering cry. Then her voice, uplifting in a panic, shrilled out a wild appeal for doctor, servants—help of any kind. And, almost as she spoke, Travers was beside her, Travers and Forshay and Robert Murdock—yes, and silly little Mrs. Somerby-Miles, too, forgetting in the face of such a time as this to be anything but helpful and womanly—and all of these gave such assistance as was in their power.

"Help me get him up to his own room, somebody, and send a servant post-haste for the doctor," said Captain Travers, taking the lead after the fashion of a man who is used to command. "Calm yourself as much as possible, Mrs. Bawdrey. Here, Murdock, lend a hand and help him."

"Eh, mon, there is nae help but Heaven's in sic a case as this," dolefully responded Murdock, as he came forward and solemnly stooped to obey. "The puir auld laddie! The Laird giveth and the Laird taketh awa', and the weel o' mon is as naething."

"Oh, stow your croaking, you blundering old fool!" snapped Travers, as Mrs. Bawdrey gave a heart-wrung cry and hid her face in her hands. "You and your eternal doldrums! Here, Bawdrey, lend a hand, old chap. We can get him upstairs without the assistance of this human trombone, I know."

But "this human trombone" was not minded that they should; and so it fell out that, when Lieutenant Forshay led Mrs. Somerby-Miles from the room, and young Bawdrey and Captain Travers carried the stricken man up the stairs to his own bed-chamber, his wife flying in advance to see that everything was prepared for him, Cleek, standing all alone beside the shattered cabinet, could hear Mr. Robert Murdock's dismal croakings rumbling steadily out as he mounted the staircase with the others.

For a moment after the closing door of a room overhead had shut them from his ears, he stood there, with puckered brows and pursed-up lips, drumming with his finger-tips a faint tattoo upon the framework of the shattered lid; then he walked over to the skeleton case, and silently regarded the gruesome thing within.

"Nine fingers," he muttered sententiously, "and the ninth curves inward to the palm!" He stepped round and viewed the case from all points—both sides, the front, and even the narrow space made at the back by the angle of the corner where it stood. And after this he walked to the other end of the room, took the key from the lock, slipped it in his pocket, and went out, closing the door behind him, that none might remember it had not been locked when the master of the place was carried above.

It was, perhaps, twenty minutes later that young Bawdrey came down and found him all alone in the smoking-room, bending over the table whereon the butler had set the salver containing the whiskey decanter, the soda siphon, and the glasses that were always laid out there, that the gentlemen might help themselves to the regulation "night-cap" before going to bed.

"I've slipped away to have a word in private with you, Headland," he said, in an agitated voice, as he came in. "Oh, what consummate actors they are, those two. You'd think her heart was breaking, wouldn't you? You'd think—Hullo! I say! What on earth are you doing?" For, as he came nearer, he could see that Cleek had removed the glass stopper of the decanter, and was tapping with his finger-tips a little funnel of white paper, the narrow end of which he had thrust into the neck of the bottle.

"Just adding a harmless little sleeping-draught to the nightly beverage," said Cleek, in reply, as he screwed up the paper funnel and put it in his pocket. "A good sound sleep is an excellent thing, my dear fellow, and I mean to make sure that the gentlemen of this house-party have it—one gentleman in particular: Captain Travers."

"Yes; but—I say! What about me, old chap? I don't want to be drugged, and you know I have to show them the courtesy of taking a 'night-cap' with them."

"Precisely. That's where you can help me out. If any of them remark anything about the whiskey having a peculiar taste, you must stoutly assert that you don't notice; and, as they've seen you drinking from the same decanter—why, there you are. Don't worry over it. It's a very, very harmless draught; you won't even have a headache from it. Listen here, Bawdrey. Somebody is poisoning your father."

"I know it. I told you so from the beginning, Headland," he answered, with a sort of wail. "But what's that got to do with drugging the whiskey?"

"Everything. I'm going to find out to-night whether Captain Travers is that somebody or not. Sh-h-h! Don't get excited. Yes, that's my game. I want to get into his rooms whilst he is sleeping, and be free to search his effects. I want to get into every man's room here, and wherever I find poison—well, you understand?"

"Yes," he replied, brightening as he grasped the import of the matter. "What a ripping idea! And so simple."

"I think so. Once let me find the poison, and I'll know my man. Now one other thing: the housekeeper must have a master-key that opens all the bedrooms in the place. Get it for me. It will be easier and swifter than picking the locks."

"Right you are, old chap. I'll slip up to Mrs. Jarret's room and fetch it to you at once."

"No; tuck it under the mat just outside my door. As it won't do for me to be drugged as well as the rest of you. I shan't put in an appearance when the rest come down. Say I've got a headache, and have gone to bed. As for my own 'night-cap'—well, I can send Dollops down to get the butler to pour me one out of another decanter, so that will be all right. Now, toddle off and get the key, there's a good chap. And, I say, Bawdrey, as I shan't see you again until morning—good-night."

"Good-night, old chap!" he answered in his impulsive, boyish way. "You are a friend, Headland. And—you'll save my dad, God bless you! A true, true friend—that's what you are. Thank God I ran across you."

Cleek smiled and nodded to him as he passed out and hurried away; then, hearing the other gentlemen coming down the stairs, he, too, made haste to get out of the room and to creep up to his own after they had assembled, and the cigar cabinet and the whiskey were being passed round, and the doctor was busy above with the man who was somebody's victim.

* * * * *

The big old grandfather clock at the top of the stairs pointed ten minutes past two, and the house was hushed of every sound save that which is the evidence of deep sleep, when the door of Cleek's room swung quietly open, and Cleek himself, in dressing-gown and wadded bedroom slippers, stepped out into the dark hall, and, leaving Dollops on guard, passed like a shadow over the thick, unsounding carpet.

The rooms of all the male occupants of the house, including that of Philip Bawdrey himself, opened upon this. He went to each in turn, unlocked it, stepped in, closed it after him, and lit the bedroom candle.

The sleeping-draught had accomplished all that was required of it; and in each and every room he entered—Captain Travers's, Lieutenant Forshay's, Mr. Robert Murdock's—there lay the occupant thereof stretched out at full length in the grip of that deep and heavy sleep which comes of drugs.

Cleek made the round of the rooms as quietly as any shadow, even stopping as he passed young Bawdrey's on his way back to his own to peep in there. Yes; he, too, had got his share of the effective draught, for there he lay snarled up in the bed-clothes, with his arms over his head and his knees drawn up until they were on a level with his waist, and his handsome, boyish face a little paler than usual.

Cleek didn't go into the room, simply looked at him from the threshold, then shut the door, and went back to Dollops.

"All serene, Gov'nor?" questioned that young man, in an eager whisper.

"Yes, quite," his master replied, as he turned to a writing-table whereon there lay a sealed note, and, pulling out the chair, sat down before it and took up a pen. "Wait a bit, and then you can go to bed. I'll give you still another note to deliver. While I'm writing it you may lay out my clothes."

"Slipping off, sir?"

"Yes. You will stop here, however. Now, then, hold your tongue; I'm busy."

Then he pulled a sheet of paper to him and wrote rapidly:

"DEAR MR. BAWDREY:

"I've got my man, and am off to consult with Mr. Narkom and to have what I've found analysed. I don't know when I shall be back—probably not until the day after to-morrow. You are right. It is murder, and Java is at the bottom of it. Dollops will hand you this. Say nothing—just wait till I get back."

This he slipped, unsigned in his haste, into an envelope, handed it to Dollops, and then fairly jumped into his clothes. Ten minutes later, he was out of the house, and—the end of the riddle was in sight.

CHAPTER V

On the morrow, Mrs. Bawdrey made known the rather surprising piece of news that Mr. Rickaby had written her a note to say that he had received a communication of such vital importance that he had been obliged to leave the house that morning before anybody was up, and might not be able to return to it for several days.

"No very great hardship in that, my dear," commented Mrs. Somerby-Miles, "for a more stupid and uninteresting person I never encountered. Fancy! he never even offered to assist the gentlemen to get poor Mr. Bawdrey upstairs last night. How is the poor old dear this morning, darling? Better?"

"Yes—much," said Mrs. Bawdrey, in reply. "Doctor Phillipson came to the house before four o'clock, and brought some wonderful new medicine that has simply worked wonders. Of course, he will have to stop in bed and be perfectly quiet for three or four days; but, although the attack was by far the worst he has ever had, the doctor feels quite confident that he will pull him safely through."

Now although, in the light of her apparent affection for her aged husband, she ought, one would have thought, to be exceedingly happy over this, it was distinctly noticeable that she was nervous and ill at ease, that there was a hunted look in her eyes, and that, as the day wore on, these things seemed to be accentuated. More than that, there seemed added proof of the truth of young Bawdrey's assertion that she and Captain Travers were in league with each other, for that day they were constantly together, constantly getting off into out-of-the-way places, and constantly talking in an undertone of something that seemed to worry them.

Even when dinner was over, and the whole party adjourned to the drawing-room for coffee, and the lady ought, in all conscience, to have given herself wholly up to the entertainment of her guests it was observable that she devoted most of her time to whispered confidences with Captain Travers, that they kept going to the window and looking up at the sky, as if worried and annoyed that the twilight should be so long in fading and the night in coming on. But worse than this, at ten o'clock Captain Travers made an excuse of having letters to write, and left the room, and it was scarcely six minutes later that she followed suit.

But the Captain had not gone to write letters, as it had happened. Instead, he had gone straight to the morning-room, an apartment immediately behind that in which the elder Mr. Bawdrey's collection was housed, and from which a broad French window opened out upon the grounds, and it might have caused a scandal had it been known that Mrs. Bawdrey joined him there one minute after leaving the drawing-room.

"It is the time, Walter, it is the time!" she said, in a breathless sort of way, as she closed the door and moved across the room to where he stood, a dimly seen figure in the dim light. "God help and pity me! but I am so nervous, I hardly know how to contain myself. The note said at ten to-night in the morning-room, and it is ten now. The hour is here, Walter, the hour is here!"

"So is the man, Mrs. Bawdrey," answered a low voice from the outer darkness; then a figure lifted itself above the screening shrubs just beyond the ledge of the open window, and Cleek stepped into the room.

She gave a little hysterical cry and reached out her hands to him.

"Oh, I am so glad to see you, even though you hint at such awful things, I am so glad, so glad!" she said. "I almost died when I read your note. To think that it is murder—murder! And but for you he might be dead even now. You will like to know that the doctor brought the stuff you sent by him—brought it at once—and my darling is better—better."

Before Cleek could venture any reply to this, Captain Travers stalked across the room and gripped his hand.

"And so you are that great man Cleek, are you?" he said. "Bully boy! Bully boy! And to think that all the time it wasn't some mysterious natural affliction; to think that it was crime—murder—poison. What poison, man, what poison—what?"

"Ayupee, or, as it is variously called in the several islands of the Eastern Archipelago, Pohon-Upas, Antjar, and Ipo," said Cleek, in reply. "The deadly venom which the Malays use in poisoning the heads of their arrows."

"What! that awful stuff!" said Mrs. Bawdrey, with a little shuddering cry. "And someone in this house—" Her voice broke. She plucked at Cleek's sleeve and looked up at him in an agony of entreaty. "Who?" she implored. "Who in this house could? You said you would tell to-night—you said you would. Oh, who could have the heart? Ah! Who? It is true, if you have not heard it, that once upon a time there was bad blood between Mr. Murdock and him—that Mr. Murdock is a family connection; but even he, oh, even he—Tell me—tell me, Mr. Cleek!"

"Mrs. Bawdrey, I can't just yet," he made reply. "In my heart I am as certain of it as though the criminal had confessed; but I am waiting for a sign, and, until that comes, absolute proof is not possible. That it will come, and may, indeed, come at any moment now that it is quite dark, I am very certain. When it does—"

He stopped and threw up a warning hand. As he spoke a queer thudding sound struck one dull note through the stillness of the house. He stood, bent forward, listening, absolutely breathless; then, on the other side of the wall, there rippled and rolled a something that was like the sound of a struggle between two voiceless animals, and—the sign that he awaited had come!

"Follow me—quickly, as noiselessly as you can. Let no one hear, let no one see!" he said in a breath of excitement. Then he sprang cat-like to the door, whirled it open, scudded round the angle of the passage to the entrance of the room where the fraudulent collection was kept, and went in with the silent fleetness of a panther. And a moment later, when Captain Travers and Mrs. Bawdrey swung in through the door and joined him, they came upon a horrifying sight.

For there, leaning against the open door of the case where the skeleton of the nine-fingered man hung, was Dollops, bleeding and faint, and with a score of tooth-marks on his neck and throat, and on the floor at his feet Cleek was kneeling on the writhing figure of a man, who bit and tore and snarled like a cornered wolf and fought with teeth and feet and hands alike in the wild effort to get free from the grip of destiny. A locked handcuff clamped one wrist, and from it swung, at the end of the connecting chain, its unlocked mate; the marks of Dollops' fists were on his lips and cheeks, and at the foot of the case, where the hanging skeleton doddered and shook to the vibration of the floor, lay a shattered phial of deep-blue glass.

"Got you, you hound!" said Cleek, through his teeth as he wrenched the man's two wrists together and snapped the other handcuff into place. "You beast of ingratitude—you Judas! Kissing and betraying like any other Iscariot! And a dear old man like that! Look here, Mrs. Bawdrey; look here Captain Travers; what do you think of a little rat like this?"

They came forward at his word, and, looking down, saw that the figure he was bending over was the figure of Philip Bawdrey.

"Oh!" gulped Mrs. Bawdrey, and then shut her two hands over her eyes and fell away weak and shivering. "Oh, Mr. Cleek, it can't be—it can't! To do a thing like that?"

"Oh, he'd have done worse, the little reptile, if he hadn't been pulled up short," said Cleek in reply. "He'd have hanged you for it, if it had gone the way he planned. You look in your boxes; you, too, Captain Travers. I'll wager each of you finds a phial of Ayupee hidden among them somewhere. Came in to put more of the cursed stuff on the ninth finger of the skeleton, so that it would be ready for the next time, didn't he, Dollops?"

"Yes, Gov'nor. I waited for him behind the case just as you told me to, sir, and when he ups and slips the finger of the skilligan into the neck of the bottle, I nips out and whacks the bracelet on him. But he was too quick for me, sir, so I only got one on; and then, the hound, he turns on me like a blessed hyena, sir, and begins a-chawin' of me windpipe. I say, Gov'nor, take off his silver wristlets, will you, sir, and lemme have jist ten minutes with him on my own? Five for me, sir, and five for his poor old dad!"

"Not I," said Cleek. "I wouldn't let you soil those honest hands of yours on his vile little body, Dollops. Thought you had a noodle to deal with, didn't you, Mr. Philip Bawdrey? Thought you could lead me by the nose, and push me into finding those phials just where you wanted them found, didn't you? Well, you've got a few more thoughts coming. Look here, Captain Travers: what do you think of this fellow's little game? Tried to take me in about you and Mrs. Bawdrey being lovers, and trying to do away with him and his father to get the old man's money."

"Why, the contemptible little hound! Bless my soul, man, I'm engaged to Mrs. Bawdrey's cousin. And as for his stepmother—why, she threw the little worm over as soon as he began making love to her, and tried to make her take up with him by telling her how much he'd be worth when his father died."

"I guessed as much. I didn't fancy him from the first moment; and he was so blessed eager to have me begin by suspecting you two, that I smelt a rat at once. Oh, but he's been crafty enough in other things. Putting that devilish stuff on the ninth finger of the skeleton, and never losing an opportunity to get his poor old father to handle it and show it to people. It's a strong, irritant poison—sap of the upas-tree is the base of it—producing first an irritation of the skin, then a blister, and, when that broke, communicating the poison directly to the blood every time the skeleton hand touched it. A weak solution at first, so that the decline would be natural, the growth of the malady gradual. But if I'd found that phial in your room last night, as he hoped and believed I had done—well, look for yourself. The finger of the skeleton is thick with the beastly, gummy stuff to-night. Double strength, of course. The next time his father touched it he'd have died before morning. And the old chap fairly worshipping him. I suspected him, and suspected what the stuff that was being used really was from the beginning. Last night I drugged him, and then—I knew."

"Knew, Mr. Cleek? Why, how could you?"

"The most virulent poisons have their remedial uses, Captain," he made reply. "You can kill a man with strychnine; you can put him in his grave with arsenic; you can also use both these powerful agents to cure and to save, in their proper proportions and in the proper way. The same rule applies to Ayupee. Properly diluted and properly used, it is one of the most powerful agents for the relief, and, in some cases, the cure, of Bright's disease of the kidneys. But the Government guards this unholy drug most carefully. You can't get a drop of it in Java for love or money, unless on the order of a recognized physician; and you can't bring it into the ports of England unless backed by that physician's sworn statement and the official stamp of the Javanese authorities. A man undeniably afflicted with Bright's disease could get these things—no other could. Well, I wanted to know who had succeeded in getting Ayupee into this country and into this house. Last night I drugged every man in it, and—I found out."

"But how?"

"By finding the one who could not sleep stretched out at full length. One of the strongest symptoms of Bright's disease is a tendency to draw the knees up close to the body in sleep, Captain, and to twist the arms above the head. Of all the men under this roof, this man here was the only one who slept like that last night!" He paused and looked down at the scowling, sullen creature on the floor. "You wretched little cur!" he said, with a gesture of unspeakable contempt. "And all for the sake of an old man's money! If I did my duty, I'd gaol you. But if I did, it would be punishing the innocent for the crimes of the guilty. It would kill that dear old man to learn this; and so he's not going to learn it, and the law's not going to get its own." He twitched out his hand, and something tinkled on the floor. "Get up!" he said sharply. "There's the key of the handcuffs; take it and set yourself free. Do you know what's going to happen to you? To-morrow morning Dr. Phillipson is going to examine you, and to report that you'll be a dead man in a year's time if you stop another week in this country. You are going out of it, and you are going to stop out of it. Do you understand? *Stop* out of it to the end of your days. For if ever you put foot in it again I'll handle you as a terrier handles a rat! Dollops!"

"Yes, Gov'nor?"

"My things packed and ready?"

"Yes, sir. And all waitin' in the arbour, sir, as you told me to have 'em."

"Good lad! Get them, and we'll catch the first train back. Mrs. Bawdrey, my best respects. Captain, all good luck to you," said Cleek—and swung out into the darkness and the moist, warm fragrance of the night; his mental poise a bit unsteady, his nerves raw. It was not in him to have stopped longer, to have remained under the same roof with a monster like young Bawdrey and keep his temper in check.

CHAPTER VI

The stillness, the balm, the soothing influences of the night worked their own spell; and, after a time, rubbed out the mental wrinkles and brought a sense of restfulness and peace. It could not well do otherwise with such a nature as his. The night was all a-musk with mignonette and roses, the sky all a-glitter with stars. A gunshot distant the river ran—a silver thing ribboning along between the dark of bending trees; somewhere in the darkness a nightingale shook out the scale of Nature's Anthem to the listening Night, and, farther afield, others took up the chorus of it and sang and sang with the sheer joy of living.

What a world—God, what a world for parricides to exist in, and for the sons of men to forget the Fifth Commandment!

He walked on faster, and made his way to the arbour where Dollops waited. The boy rose to meet him.

"Everythink all ready, sir—see!" he said, holding up a kit bag. "Wot's it now, Gov'nor?—the railway station? Good enough. Shall I nip off ahead or keep with you till we get there?"

"Suit yourself, my lad."

"Thanky, sir; then I'll walk at your heels, if you don't mind. I'd like to walk at your heels all the rest of my blessed life. Did I carry it off all right, Gov'nor? Did I do it jist as you wanted of it done?"

"To a T, my lad," said Cleek, smiling and patting him on the shoulder. "You'll do, Dollops—you'll do finely. I think I did a good job for the pair of us, my boy, when I gave you those two half-crowns."

"Advanced, Gov'nor, advanced," corrected Dollops, with a look of sheer affection. "Let me work 'em off, sir, like you said I might. I don't want nothin' but wot I earns, Gov'nor; nothin' but wot I've got a right to have; for when I sees wot wantin' money as don't belong to you leads to; when I thinks wot that young Bawdrey chap was willin' to do for the love of havin' it—"

"Don't!" struck in Cleek, a trifle roughly. "Drop the man's name—I can't trust myself to think of it. That the one world, the one self-same world, could hold two such widely dissimilar creations of God as that monster and ... No matter. Thank God, I've been able to do something to-night for a good woman—I owe so much to another of her kind. No; don't speak— just walk quietly and"—jerking his thumb in the direction of the fluting nightingales—"listen to that. God! the man who could think evil things when a nightingale sings, isn't fit to stand even in the Devil's presence."

Dollops looked at him—half-puzzled, half-awed. He could not understand the character of the man: there were so many sides to it; and they came and went so oddly. One minute, a very brute-beast in his ferocity, the next, a woman in his tenderness and a poet in his thoughts. But if the boy was puzzled, he was, at least, discreet. He put nothing into words: merely walked on in silence, and left the man to his thoughts and the nightingales to their melody.

And Cleek was unusually thoughtful from that period onward; speaking hardly a word through all the journey home. For now that the events which had occupied his mind for the past two or three days were over and done with, his memory harked back to those things which had to do with his own affairs, and he caught himself wondering how matters had gone with Ailsa Lorne; which of the two positions—the English one or the French—she had finally elected to apply for; and if time had as yet softened the shock of that disclosure made in the mist and darkness at Hampstead Heath.

He had, of course, heard nothing of her since that time; and the days he had spent at Richmond had utterly precluded the possibility of giving himself that small pleasure—so often indulged in—of adopting a safe disguise, prowling about the neighbourhood where she lived until she should come forth upon one errand or another, and then following her, unsuspected.

That she could have taken the knowledge of what he once had been in no other way than she had done; that to such a woman, such a man must at the first blush be an object of abhorrence—a thing to be put out of her life as completely and as expeditiously as possible—he fully realised; yet, at bottom, he was conscious of a hope that Time—even so little as had passed—might lend a softening influence that should lead eventually to Pity, and from that to a day when the word Forgiveness might be spoken.

He wanted that forgiveness—the soul of the man needed it, as parched plants need water. He had not climbed up out of himself without some struggle, some moments when he wavered between what he had become, and what Nature had written that he was meant to be; for no Soul is purged all in a moment, no man may conquer himself with just one solitary fight. He needed her forgiveness, the thought of her, the hope of her, to rivet his armour for the long, brave fight. He needed her Friendship—if he might never have her love he needed *that*. And if she were to pass like this from his life.... If the Light were to go out ... and all the long, dark way of the Future still to be faced.... Something within him seemed to writhe. He took his lower lip between his thumb and forefinger and squeezed it hard.

That he had hoped for some token, some word—forwarded through Mr. Narkom—he did not quite realise until he got back to Clarges Street and found that there was none.

Followed a sense of despair, a moment of deep dejection, that passed in turn and gave place to a feeling of personal injury, of savage resentment, and of the ferocity which comes when the half-tamed wolf wakes to the realisation that here is nothing before it evermore, but the bars of the cage and the goad of the keeper; and that far and away in the world there are still the free woods, the naked body of Nature, and the savage company of its kind.

Under the stress of that gust of passion, he sent Dollops flying from the room. He wrenched open the drawer of his writing-table, and scooped up in his hands some trifles of faded ribbon and trinkets of gold—things that he treasured, none knew why or for what—and holding them thus, looked down on them and laughed, bitterly and savagely, as though a devil were within him.

"Me! She scorns me!" he said, and laughed again, and flung them all back and shut the drawer upon them. And presently he knew that he held her all the higher because she did scorn him; because her life was such that she *could* scorn him; and the bitterness dropped out of him, his eyes softened, and though he still laughed, it was for an utterly different reason, and in a wholly different way.

Some pots of tulips and mignonette stood on the ledge of his window. He walked over to see that they were watered before he went to bed. And between the time when he got down on his knees to fish out his bath-slippers from beneath the bed-stead and the creak of the springs when he lay down for the night, he was so long and so still that one might have believed he was doing something else.

He slept long, and rose in the morning soothed and subdued in spirit— better and brighter in every way; for now no affair, for The Yard hampered his movements and claimed his time. He was free; he was back in the Town— beautiful because it contained her—and he might hark back to the old trick of watching and following and being close to her without her knowledge.

It was a vain hope that, however. For, although he dressed and went out and haunted the neighbourhood of Sir Horace Wyvern's house for hours on end, he saw nothing of her that day. Nor did he see her the next, nor the next, nor yet the next again. At first, he began to think that she must come out and return during the times when he was obliged to go off guard and get his meal—for he could not bring himself to play the part of the spy or the common policeman, and filch news from the servants—but when a week had gone by in this manner, he set all question upon that point at rest by remaining at his post from sunrise to ten o'clock at night. She did not appear. He wondered what that meant—whether it indicated that she had already accepted one of the two positions, or had gone to stop with her friend on the other side of Hampstead Heath.

The result of that wondering was that, for the next five days, the gentleman who was known in Clarges Street as "Captain Horatio Burbage," became a regular visitor to the neighbourhood of the house in Bardon Road. The issue was exactly the same. Miss Lorne did not appear.

He could no longer doubt that she had accepted one or other of the two positions; but steadfastly refrained from making any personal inquiry. She would hear of it if anybody called to inquire her whereabouts; and she would guess who had done it. He would not have her feel that he was thrusting himself upon her, inquiring about her as one might inquire about a common servant. If it was her will that he should know, then that knowledge should come from her, not be picked up as one picks up clues to missing people of the criminal class.

So then, it was good-bye to Bardon Road, just as it had been good-bye to Mayfair. He turned his back upon it in the very moment he came to that conclusion, and had just set his face in the direction of the heath when he was brought to a standstill by the sound of someone calling out sharply: "Burbage—I say, Captain Burbage: stop a moment, please." And, screwing round instantly, he saw a red limousine pelting toward him, and an excited chauffeur waving a gloved hand.

He knew that red limousine, and he knew that chauffeur. Both belonged to Mr. Maverick Narkom.

He stood waiting until the motor was abreast of him—had, in fact, come to a standstill—then spoke in a guarded tone:

"What is it, Lennard?" he asked. "The Yard?"

"Yessir. Young Dollops told us where to look for you. Hop in quickly, sir. Superintendent inside."

Cleek opened the door of the vehicle at once, stepped in, shut it after him, and sat down beside Mr. Narkom with the utmost composure.

"My dear fellow, I *have* had a chase!" said the superintendent, with a long deep breath of relief, as the limousine swung out into the roadway, and pelted off westward at a pace that brushed the very fringes of the speed limit. "I made certain I should find you at home. Fairly floored when I discovered that you weren't. If it hadn't been for that boy, Dollops—bright young button, that Dollops, Cleek; exceedingly bright, b'gad."

"Yes," agreed Cleek, quietly. "Bright, faithful, and—inventive."

"Really? What has the young beggar invented, then?"

"An original appliance which may possibly be of a good deal of service one of these days. But, never mind that at present. It is fair to suppose, from your rushing out here in quest of me, that you've got something on hand, isn't it?"

"Yes—rather! An amazing 'something,' old chap. It's a letter. Arrived at headquarters about an hour and a half ago. Not an affair for The Yard this time, Cleek, but a thing you must take up on your own, if you take it up at all; and I tell you frankly, I don't like it."

"Why?"

"For one thing, it's from Paris; and—well, you know what dangers Paris would have for *you*. There's that she-devil you broke with—that woman Margot. You know what she swore, what she wrote when you sent her that letter telling her that you were done with her and her lot, and warning her never to set foot on English soil again? If you were to run foul of her—if she were ever to get any hint of your real identity—"

"She can't. She knows no more of my real history than you do; no more than I actually know of hers. Our knowledge of each other began when we started to 'pal' together—it ended when we split, eighteen months ago. But about that letter? What is it? Why do you say that you don't like it?"

"Well, to begin with, I'm afraid it is some trap of hers to decoy you over there—get you into some unknown place—"

"There are no 'unknown places' in Paris so far as I am concerned. I know every hole and corner of it, from the sewers on. I know it as well as I know London, as well as I know Berlin—New York—Vienna—Edinburgh—Rome. You couldn't lose me or trap me in any one of them. Is that the letter in your hand? Good—then read it, please."

"To the Superintendent of Police, Scotland Yard," read Narkom, obeying the request.

"'DISTINGUISHED MONSIEUR:

"'Of your grace and pity, I implore you to listen to the prayer of an unhappy man whose honour, whose reason, whose very life are in deadly peril, not alone of "The Red Crawl," but of things he may not even name, dare not commit to writing, lest this letter should go astray. It shall happen, monsieur, that the whole world shall hear with amazement of that most marvellous "Cleek"—that great reader of riddles and unmasker of evildoers who, in the past year, has made the police department of England the envy of all nations; and it shall happen also that I who dare not appeal to the police of France appeal to the mercy, the humanity, of this great man, as it is my only hope. Monsieur, you have his ear, you have his confidence, you have the means at your command. Ah! ask him, pray him, implore him for the love of God, and the sake of a fellow-man, to come alone to the top floor of the house number 7 of the Rue Toison d'Or, Paris, at nine hours of the night of Friday, the 26th inst., to enter into the darkness and say but the one word "Cleek" as a signal it is he, and I may come forward and throw myself upon his mercy. Oh, save me, Monsieur Cleek—save me! save me!'

"There, that's the lot, and there's no signature," said Narkom, laying down the letter. "What do you make of it, Cleek?"

CHAPTER VII

"A very real, a very moving thing, Mr. Narkom," he replied. "The cry of a human heart in deep distress; the agonised appeal of a man so wrought up by the horrors of his position that he forgets to offer a temptation in the way of reward, and speaks of outlandish things as though they must be understood of all. As witness his allusion to something which he calls 'The Red Crawl,' without attempting to explain the meaningless phrase. Whatever it is, it is so real to him that it seems as if everybody must understand."

"You think, then, that the thing is genuine?"

"So genuine that I shall answer its call, Mr. Narkom, and be alone in the dark on the top floor of No. 7, Rue Toison d'Or, to-morrow night as surely as the clock strikes nine."

And that was how the few persons who happened to be in the quiet upper reaches of the Rue Bienfaisance at half-past eight o'clock the next evening came to see a fat, fussing, red-faced Englishman in a grey frock-coat, white spats, and a shining topper, followed by a liveried servant with a hat-box in one hand and a portmanteau in the other—so conspicuous, the pair of them, that they couldn't have any desire to conceal themselves—cross over the square before the Church of St. Augustine, fare forth into the darker side passages, and move in the direction of the street of the Golden Fleece.

They were, of course, Cleek and the boy Dollops.

"Lumme, Gov'nor," whispered he, as they turned at last into the utter darkness and desertion of the narrow Rue Toison d'Or, "if this is wot yer calls Gay Paree—this precious black slit between two rows of houses—I'll take a slice of the Old Kent Road with thanks. Not even so much as a winkle-stall in sight, and me that empty my shirt-bosom's a-chafing my blessed shoulder-blades!"

"You'll see plenty of life before the game's over, I warrant you, Dollops. Now then, my lad, here's a safe spot. Sit down on the hat-box and wait. That's No. 7, that empty house with the open door, just across the way. Keep your eye on it. I don't know how long I'll be, but if anybody comes out before I do, mind you don't let him get away."

"No fear!" said Dollops sententiously. "I'll be after him as if he was a ham sandwich, sir. Look out for my patent 'Tickle Tootsies' when you come out, Gov'nor. I'll sneak over and put 'em round the door as soon as you've gone in." For Dollops, who was of an inventive turn of mind, had an especial "man-trap" of his own, which consisted of heavy brown paper, cut into squares, and thickly smeared over with a viscid varnish-like substance that would adhere to the feet of anybody incautiously stepping upon it, and so interfere with flight that it was an absolute necessity to stop and tear the papers away before running with any sort of ease and swiftness was possible. This was the "invention" to which Cleek had alluded. Dollops, who was rather proud of the achievement, carried with him a full supply of ready-cut papers and a big collapsible tube of the viscid, ropy, varnish-like glue.

Meantime, Cleek, having left the boy sitting on the hat-box in the darkness, crossed the narrow street to the open doorway of No. 7, and, without hesitation, stepped in. The place was as black as a pocket, and had that peculiar smell which belongs to houses that have long stood vacant. The house, nevertheless, was a respectable one, and, like all the others, fronted on another street—this dark Toison d'Or being merely a back passage used principally by the tradespeople for the delivery of supplies. Feeling his way to the first of the three flights of stairs which led upward into the stillness and gloom above, Cleek mounted steadily until he found himself at length in a sort of attic—quite windowless, and lit only by a skylight through which shone the ineffectual light of the stars. It was the top at last. Bracing his back against the wall, so that nobody could get behind him, and holding himself ready for any emergency, he called out in a clear, calm voice: "Cleek!"

Almost simultaneously there was a sharp metallic "snick," an electric bulb hanging from the ceiling flamed out luminously, a cupboard door flashed open, a voice cried out in joyous, perfect English: "Thank God for a man!" And, switching round with a cry of amazement, he found himself looking into the face and eyes of a woman.

And of all women in the world—Ailsa Lorne!

He sucked in his breath and his heart began to hammer.

"Miss Lorne!" he exclaimed, so carried out of himself that he scarcely knew what he did. "It was the French position that you chose, then? It is you—*you*—that calls upon me?"

"No, it is not," she made reply, a rush of colour reddening her cheeks, a feeling of embarrassment and of a natural restraint making her shake visibly. "I am merely the envoy of another. I should not know you, disguised as you are, but for that. Yes, I chose the French position, as you see, Mr. Cleek. I am now the companion to Mademoiselle Athalie, daughter of the Baron de Carjorac."

"Baron de Carjorac? Do you mean the French Minister of the Interior, the President of the Board of National Defences, Miss Lorne—that enthusiastic old patriot, that rabid old spitfire, whose one dream is the wresting back of Alsace-Lorraine, the driving of the hated Germans into the sea? Do you mean that ripping old firebrand?"

"Yes. But you'd not call him that if you were to see him now; if you could see the wreck, the broken and despairing wreck, that six weeks of the Château Larouge, six weeks of that horrible 'Red Crawl' have made of him."

"'The Red Crawl'! Good heavens! then that letter, that appeal for help—"

"Came from him!" she finished excitedly. "It was he who was to have met you here to-night, Mr. Cleek. This house is one he owns; he thought he might with safety risk coming here, but—he can't! he can't! He knows now that there is danger for him everywhere; that his every step is tracked; that the snare which is about him has been about him, unsuspected, for almost a year; that he dare not, absolutely dare not, appeal to the French police, and that if it were known he had appealed to you, he would be a dead man inside of twenty-four hours, and not only dead, but—disgraced. Oh, Mr. Cleek!"—she stretched out two shaking hands and laid them on his arm, lifted a white, imploring face to his—"save him! save that dear broken old man! Ah, think! think! They are our friends, our dear country's friends, these French people. Their welfare is our welfare, ours is theirs. Oh, help him, save him, Mr. Cleek—for his own sake—for mine—for France. Save him, and win my gratitude for ever!"

"That is a temptation that would carry me to the ends of the earth, Miss Lorne. Tell me what the work is, and I will carry it through. What is this incomprehensible thing of which both you and Baron de Carjorac have spoken—this thing you allude to as 'The Red Crawl'?"

She gave a little shuddering cry and fell back a step, covering her face with both hands.

"Oh!" she said, with a shiver of repulsion. "It is loathly—it is horrible—it is necromancy—beyond belief! Why, oh, why were we ever driven to that horrible Château Larouge! Why could not fate have spared the Villa de Carjorac? It could not have happened then!"

"Villa de Carjorac? That was the name of the baron's residence, I believe. I remember reading in the newspapers some five or six weeks ago that it was destroyed by fire, which originated—nobody knew how—in the apartments of the late baroness in the very dead of the night. I thought at the time it read suspiciously like the work of an incendiary, although nobody hinted at such a thing. The Château Larouge I also have a distinct memory of, as an old historic property in the neighbourhood of St. Cloud. Speaking from past experience, I know that, although it is in such a state of decay, and supposed to be uninhabitable, it has, in fact, often been occupied at a period when the police and the public believed it to be quite empty. Gentlemen of the Apache persuasion have frequently made it a place of retreat. There is also an underground passage—executed by those same individuals—which connects with the Paris sewers. That, too, the police are unaware of. What can the ruined Château Larouge possibly have to do with the affairs of the Baron de Carjorac, Miss Lorne, that you connect them like this?"

"They have everything to do with them—everything. The Château is no longer a ruin, however. It was purchased, rebuilt, refitted by the Comtesse Susanne de la Tour, Mr. Cleek, and she and her brother live there. So do we—Athalie, Baron de Carjorac, and I. So, also, does the creature—the thing—the abominable horror known as 'The Red Crawl.'"

"My dear Miss Lorne, what are you saying?"

"The truth, nothing but the truth!" she answered hysterically. "Oh, let me begin at the beginning—you'll never understand unless I do. I'll tell you in as few words as possible—as quickly as I can. It all began last winter, when Athalie and her father were at Monte Carlo. There they met Madame la Comtesse de la Tour and her brother, Monsieur Gaston Merode. The baron has position but he has not wealth, Mr. Cleek. Athalie is ambitious. She loves luxury, riches, a life of fashion—all the things that boundless money can give; and when Monsieur Merode—who is young, handsome, and said to be fabulously wealthy—showed a distinct preference for her over all the other marriageable girls he met, she was flattered out of her silly wits. Before they left Monte Carlo for Paris everybody could see that he had only to ask her hand, to have it bestowed upon him. For although the baron never has cared for the man, Athalie rules him, and her every caprice is humoured.

"But for all he was so ardent a lover, Monsieur Merode was slow in coming to the important point. Perhaps his plans were not matured. At any rate, he did not propose to Athalie at Monte Carlo; and, although he and his sister returned to Paris at the same time as the baron and his daughter, he still deferred the proposal."

"Has he not made it yet?"

"Yes, Mr. Cleek. He made it six weeks ago—to be exact, two nights before the Villa de Carjorac was fired."

"You think it was fired, then?"

"I do now, although I had no suspicion of it at the time. Athalie received her proposal on the Saturday, the baron gave his consent on the Sunday, and on Monday night the villa was mysteriously burnt, leaving all three of us without an immediate refuge. In the meantime, Madame la Comtesse had purchased the ruin of the Château Larouge, and during the period of her brother's deferred proposal was engaged in fitting it up as an abode for herself and him. On the very day it was finished, Monsieur Merode asked for Athalie's hand."

"Oho!" said Cleek, with a strong rising inflection. "I think I begin to smell the toasting of the cheese. Of course, when the villa was burnt out, Madame la Comtesse insisted that, as the *fiancée* of her brother, Mlle. de Carjorac must make her home at the Château until the necessary repairs could be completed; and, of course, the baron had to go with her?"

"Yes," admitted Ailsa. "The baron accepted—Athalie would not have allowed him to decline had he wished to—so we all three went there and have been residing there ever since. On the night after our arrival an alarming, a horrifying thing occurred. It was while we were at dinner that the conversation turned upon the supernatural—upon houses and places that were reputed to be haunted—and then Madame la Comtesse made a remarkable statement. She laughingly asserted that she had just learned that, in purchasing the Château Larouge, she had also become the possessor of a sort of family ghost. She said that she had only just heard—from an outside source—that there was a horrible legend connected with the place; in short, that for centuries it had been reputed to be under a sort of spell of evil and to be cursed by a dreadful visitant known as 'The Red Crawl'—a hideous and loathsome creature, neither spider nor octopus, but horribly resembling both—which was supposed to 'appear' at intervals in the middle of the night, and, like the fabled giants of fairy tales, carry off 'lovely maidens and devour them.'"

"Who is responsible for that ridiculous assertion, I wonder? I think I may say that I know as much about the Château Larouge and its history as anybody, Miss Lorne, but I never heard of this supposed 'legend' before in all my life."

"So the baron, too, declared, laughing as derisively as any of us over the story, although it is well known that he has a natural antipathy to all crawling things—an abhorrence inherited from his mother—and has been known to run like a frightened child from the appearance of a mere garden spider."

"Oho!" said Cleek again. "I see! I see! The toasted cheese smells stronger, and there's a distinct suggestion of the Rhine about it this time. There's something decidedly German about that fabulous 'monster' and that haunted château, Miss Lorne. They are clever and careful schemers, those German Johnnies. Of course, this amazing 'Red Crawl' was proved to have an absolute foundation in fact, and equally, of course, it 'appeared' to the Baron de Carjorac?"

"Yes—that very night. After we had all gone to bed, the house was roused by his screams. Everybody rushed to his chamber, only to find him lying on the floor in a state of collapse. The thing had been in his room, he said. He had seen it—it had even touched him—a horrible, hideous red reptile, with squirming tentacles, a huge, glowing body, and eyes like flame. It had crept upon him out of the darkness—he knew not from where. It had seized him, resisted all his wild efforts to tear loose from it, and when he finally sank, overcome and fainting, upon the floor, his last conscious recollection was of the loathsome thing settling down upon his breast and running its squirming 'feelers' up and down his body."

"Of course! Of course! That was part of the game. It was after something. Something of the utmost importance to German interests. That's why the Château Larouge was refitted, why the Villa de Carjorac was burnt down, and why this Monsieur Gaston Merode became engaged to Mademoiselle Athalie."

"Oh, how could you know that, Mr. Cleek? Nobody ever suspected. The baron never confessed to any living soul until he did so to me, to-day—and then only because he had to tell somebody, in order that the appointment with you might be kept. How, then, could you guess?"

"By putting two and two together, Miss Lorne, and discovering that they do not make five. The inference is very clear: Baron de Carjorac is President of the Board of National Defences; Germany, in spite of its public assurances to the contrary, is known by those who are 'on the inside' to harbour a very determined intention of making a secret attack, an unwarned invasion, upon England. France is the key to the situation. If, without the warning that must come through the delay of picking a quarrel and entering into an open war with the Republic, the German army can swoop down in the night, cross the frontier, and gain immediate possession of the ports of France, in five hours' time it can be across the English Channel, and its hordes pouring down upon a sleeping people. To carry out this programme, the first step would, of course, be to secure knowledge of the number, location, manner of the secret defences of France—the plans of fortification, the maps of the 'danger zone,' the documentary evidence of her strongest and weakest points—and who so likely to be the guardian of these as the Baron de Carjorac? That is how I know that 'The Red Crawl' was after something of vital importance to German interests, Miss Lorne. That he got it, I know from the fact that the baron, while hinting at disgrace and speaking of peril to his own life, dared not confide in the French authorities and ask the assistance of the French police. Moreover, if 'The Red Crawl' had failed to secure anything, the baron, with his congenital loathing of all crawling things, would have left the Château Larouge immediately."

"Oh, to think that you guessed it so easily—and it was all such a puzzle to me. I could not think, Mr. Cleek, why he did remain—why he would not be persuaded to go, although every night was adding to the horror of the thing and it seemed clear to me that he was going mad. Of course, Madame la Comtesse and her brother tried to reason him out of what he declared, tried to make him believe that it was all fancy—that he did not really see the fearful thing; it was equally in vain that I myself tried to persuade him to leave the place before his reason became unsettled. Last night"—she paused, shuddered, put both hands over her face, and drew in a deep breath—"last night, I, too, saw 'The Red Crawl,' Mr. Cleek—I, too!"

"You, Miss Lorne?"

"Yes. I made up my mind that I would—that, if it existed, I would have absolute proof of it. The countess and her brother had scoffed so frequently, had promised the baron so often that they would set a servant on guard in the corridor to watch, and then had said so often to poor, foolish, easily persuaded Athalie that it was useless doing anything so silly, as it was absolutely certain that her father only imagined the thing, that I—I determined to take the step myself, unknown to any of them. After everybody had gone to bed, I threw on a loose, dark gown, crept into the corridor, and hid in a niche from which I could see the door of the baron's room. I waited until after midnight—long after—and then—and then—"

"Calm yourself, Miss Lorne. Then the thing appeared, I suppose?"

"Yes; but not before something equally terrible had happened. I saw the door of the countess's room open; I saw the countess herself come out, accompanied by the man who up till then I had believed, like everybody else, was her brother."

"And who is not her brother, after all?"

"No, he is not. Theirs is a closer tie. I saw her kiss him. I saw her go with him to an angle of the corridor, lift a rug, and raise a trap in the floor."

"Hullo! Hullo!" ejaculated Cleek. "Then she, too; knows of the passage which leads to the sewers. Clearly, then, this Countess de la Tour is not what she seems, when she knows secrets that are known only to the followers of—well, never mind. Go on, Miss Lorne, go on. You saw her lift that trap; and—what then?"

"Then there came up out of it—oh, the most loathsome-looking creature I ever saw; a huge, crawling, red shape that was like a blood-red spider, with the eyes, the hooked beak, and the writhing tentacles of an octopus. It made no sound, but it seemed to know her, to understand her, for when she waved her hand toward the open door of her own room it crawled away and, obeying that gesture, dragged its huge bulk over the threshold, and passed from sight. Then the man she called her brother kissed her again, and as he descended into the darkness below the trap I heard her say quite distinctly: 'Tell Marise that I will come as soon as I can; but not to delay the revel. If I am compelled to forego it to-night, there shall be a wilder one to-morrow, when Clodoche arrives.'"

"Clodoche! By Jupiter!" Cleek almost jumped as he spoke. "Now I know the 'lay'! No; don't ask me anything yet. Go on with the story, please. What then, Miss Lorne, what then?"

"Then the man below said something which I could not hear—something to which she answered in these words: 'No, no; there is no danger. I will guard it safely, and it shall go into no hands but Clodoche's. He and Count von Hetzler will be there about midnight to-morrow to complete the deal and pay over the money. Clodoche will want the fragment, of course, to show to the count as a proof that it is the right one, as "an earnest" of what the remainder is worth. And you must bring me that "remainder" without fail, Gaston—you hear me?—without fail! I shall be there, at the rendezvous, awaiting you, and the thing must be in our hands when von Hetzler comes. The thing must be finished to-morrow night, even if you and Serpice have to throw all caution to the winds and throttle the old fool.' Then, as if answering a further question, she laughingly added: 'Oh, get that fear out of your head. I'm not a bat, to be caught napping. I'll give it to no one but Clodoche—and not even to him until he gives the secret sign.' And then, Mr. Cleek, as she closed the trap I heard the man call back to her 'Good night' and give her a name I had not heard before. We had always supposed that she had been christened 'Suzanne,' but as that man left he called her—"

"I know before you tell me—'Margot'!" interjected Cleek. "I guessed the identity of this 'Countess de la Tour' from the moment you spoke of Clodoche and that secret trap. Her knowledge of those two betrayed her to me. Clodoche is a renegade Alsatian, a spy in the pay of the German Government, and an old *habitué* of 'The Inn of the Twisted Arm,' where the Queen of the Apaches and her pals hold their frequent revels. I can guess the remainder of your story now. You carried this news to the Baron de Carjorac, and he, breaking down, confessed to you that he had lost something."

"Yes, yes—a dreadful 'something,' Mr. Cleek: the horrible thing that has been making life an agony to him ever since. On the night when that abominable 'Red Crawl' first overcame him, there was upon his person a most important document—a rough draft of the maps of fortification and the plan of the secret defences of France, the identical document from which was afterwards transcribed the parchment now deposited in the secret archives of the Republic. When Baron de Carjorac recovered his senses after his horrifying experience—"

"That document was gone?"

"Part of it, Mr. Cleek—thank God, only a part! If it had been the parchment itself, no such merciful thing could possibly have happened. But the paper was old, much folding and handling had worn the creases through, and when, in his haste, the secret robber grabbed it, whilst that loathsome creature held the old man down, it parted directly down the middle, and he got only a vertical section of each of its many pages."

"Victoria! 'And the fool hath said in his heart, There is no God,'" quoted Cleek. "So, then, the hirelings of the enemy have only got half what they are after; and, as no single sentence can be complete upon a paper torn like that, nothing can be made of it until the other half is secured, and—our German friends are still 'up a gum-tree.' I know now why the baron stayed on at the Château Larouge, and why 'The Red Crawl' is preparing to pay him another visit to-night: he hoped, poor chap, to find a clue to the whereabouts of the fragment he had lost; and that thing is after the fragment he still retains. Well, it will be a long, long day before either of those two fragments fall into German hands."

"Oh, Mr. Cleek, you think you can get the stolen paper back? You believe you can outwit those dreadful people and save the Baron de Carjorac's honour and his life?"

"Miss Lorne"—he took her hand in his and lifted it to his lips—"Miss Lorne, I thank you for giving me the chance! If you will do what I ask you, be where I ask you in two hours' time, so surely as we two stand here this minute, I will put back the German calendar by ten years at least. They drink 'To the day,' those German Johnnies, but by to-morrow morning the English hand you are holding will have given them reason to groan over the night!"

CHAPTER VIII

It was half-past eleven o'clock. Madame la Comtesse, answering a reputed call to the bedside of a dying friend, had departed early, and was not to be expected back, she said, until to-morrow noon. The servants—given permission by the gentleman known in the house as Monsieur Gaston Merode, and who had graciously provided a huge char-à-banc for the purpose—had gone in a body to a fair over in the neighbourhood of Sèvres, and darkness and stillness filled the long, broad corridor of the Château Larouge. Of a sudden, however, a mere thread of sound wavered through the silence, and from the direction of Miss Lorne's room a figure in black, with feet muffled in thick, woollen stockings, padded to an angle of the passage, lifted a trap carefully hidden beneath a huge tiger-skin rug, and almost immediately Cleek's head rose up out of the gap.

"Thank God you managed to do it. I was horribly afraid you would not," said Ailsa in a palpitating whisper.

"You need not have been," he answered. "I know a dozen places beside 'The Inn of the Twisted Arm' from which one can get into the sewers. I've screwed a bolt and socket on the inner side of this trap in case of an emergency, and I've carried a few things into the passage for 'afterwards.' I suppose that fellow Merode, as he calls himself, is in his room, waiting?"

"Yes; and, although he pretends to be alone to-night, he—he has other men with him, hideous, ruffianly looking creatures, whom I saw him admit after the servants had gone. The countess has left the house and gone I don't know where."

"I do, then. Make certain she's at 'The Twisted Arm,' waiting, first, for the coming of Clodoche, and, second, for the arrival of this precious 'Merode' with the remaining half of the document. I've sent Dollops there to carry out his part of the programme, and when once I get the password Margot requires before she will hand over the paper, the game will be in my hands entirely. They are desperate to-night, Miss Lorne, and will stop at nothing—not even murder. There! the rug's replaced. Quick! lead me to the baron's room—there's not a minute to waste."

She took his hand and led him tiptoe through the darkness, and in another moment he was in the Baron de Carjorac's presence.

"Oh, monsieur, God for ever bless you!" exclaimed the broken old man, throwing himself on his knees before Cleek.

"Out with the light—out with the light!" exclaimed he, ducking down suddenly. "Were you mad to keep it burning till I came, with that"—pointing to a huge bay window opening upon a balcony—"uncurtained and the grounds, no doubt, alive with spies?"

Miss Lorne sprang to the table where the baron's reading-lamp stood, jerked the cord of the extinguisher, and darkness enveloped the room, darkness tempered only by the faint gleams of the moon streaming over the balcony, and through the panes of the uncurtained window.

Cleek, on his knees beside the kneeling baron, whipped a tiny electric torch from his pocket, and, shielding its flare with his scooped hands, flashed it upon the old man's face.

"Simple as rolling off a log—exactly like your pictures," he commented. "I'll 'do' you as easily as I 'do' Clodoche—and I could 'do' him in the dark from memory. Quick"—snicking off the light of the electric torch and rising to his feet—"into your dressing-room, baron. I want that suit of clothes; I want that ribbon, that cross—and I want them at once. You're a bit thicker-set than me, but I've got my Clodoche rig on underneath this, and it will fill out your coat admirably and make us as like as two peas. Give me five minutes, Miss Lorne, and I promise you a surprise."

He flashed out of sight with the baron as he ceased speaking; and Ailsa, creeping to the window and peering cautiously out, was startled presently by a voice at her elbow saying, in a tone of extreme agitation: "Oh, mademoiselle, I fear, even yet I fear, that this Anglais monsieur attempts too much, and that the papier he is gone for ever."

"Oh, no, baron, no!" she soothed, as she laid a solicitous hand upon his arm. "Do believe in him; do have faith in him. Ah, if you only knew—"

"Thanks. I reckon I shall pass muster!" interposed Cleek's voice; and it was only then she realised. "You'll find the baron in the other room, Miss Lorne, looking a little grotesque in that grey suit of mine. In with you, quickly; go with him through the other door, and get below before those fellows begin to stir. Get out of the house as quietly and as expeditiously as you can. With God's help, I'll meet you at the Hôtel du Louvre in the morning, and put the missing fragment in the baron's hands."

"And may God give you that help!" she answered fervently as she moved towards the dressing-room door. "Ah, what a man! what a man!"

Then, in a twinkling she was gone, and Cleek stood alone in the silent room. Giving her and the baron time to get clear of the other one, he went in on tiptoe, locked the door through which they had passed, put the key in his pocket, and returned. Going to the door which led from the main room into the corridor, he took the key from the lock of that, too, replacing it upon the outer side, and leaving the door itself slightly ajar.

"Now then for you, Mr. 'The Red Crawl,'" he said, as he walked to the baron's table, and, sinking down into a deep chair beside it, leaned back with his eyes closed as if in sleep, and the faint light of the moon half-revealing his face. "I want that password, and I'll get it, if I have to choke it out of your devil's throat! And she said that she would be grateful to me all the rest of her life! Only 'grateful,' I wonder? Is nothing else possible? What a good, good thing a real woman is!"

* * * * *

How long was it that he had been reclining there waiting before his strained ears caught the sound of something like the rustling of silk shivering through the stillness, and he knew that at last it was coming? It might have been ten minutes, it might have been twenty—he had no means of determining—when he caught that first movement, and, peering through the slit of a partly opened eye, saw the appalling thing drag its huge bulk along the balcony, and, with squirming tentacles writhing, slide over the low sill of the window, and settle down in a glowing red heap upon the floor; and—fake though he knew it to be—he could not repress a swift rush and prickle of "goose-flesh" at sight of it.

For a few seconds it lay dormant; then one red feeler shot out, then another, and another, and it began to edge its way across the carpet to the chair. Cleek lay still and waited, his heavy breathing sounding regularly, his head thrown back, his limp hands lying loosely, palms upward, beside him; and nearer and nearer crept the loathsome, red, glowing thing.

It crawled to his feet, and still he was quiet; it slid first one tentacle, and then another, over his knees and up toward his breast, and still he made no movement; then, as it rose higher—rose until its hideous beaked countenance was close to his own, his hands flashed upward and clamped together like a vice—clamped on a palpitating human throat—and in the twinkling of an eye the tentacles were wrapped about him, and he and "The Red Crawl" were rolling over and over on the floor and battling together.

"Serpice, you low-bred hound, I know you!" he whispered, as they struggled. "You can't utter a cry—you shan't utter a cry—to bring help. I'll throttle you, you beastly renegade, that's willing to sell his own country—throttle you, do you hear?—before you shall bring any of your mates to the rescue. Oh, you've not got a weak old man to fight with this time! Do you know me? It's the 'cracksman'—the 'cracksman' who went over to the police. If you doubt it, now that we're in the moonlight, look up and see my face. Oho! you recognise me, I see. Well, you will die looking at me, you dog, if you deny me what I'm after. I'll loosen my grip enough for you to whisper, and no more. Now what's the password that Clodoche must give to Margot to-night at 'The Twisted Arm'? Tell me what it is; if you want your life, tell me what it is."

"I'll see you dead first!" came in a whisper from beneath the hideous mask. Then, as Cleek's fingers clamped tight again and the battle began anew, one long, thin arm shot out from amongst the writhing tentacles, one clutching hand gripped the leg of the table, and, with a wrench and a twist, brought it crashing to the ground with a sound that a deaf man might have heard.

And in an instant there was pandemonium.

A door flung open, and clashing heavily against the wall, sent an echo reeling along the corridor; then came a clatter of rushing feet, a voice cried out excitedly: "Come on! come on! He's had to kill the old fool to get it!" and Cleek had just time to tear loose from the shape with which he was battling, and dodge out of the way when the man Merode lurched into the room, with half a dozen Apaches tumbling in at his heels.

"Serpice!" he cried, rushing forward, as he saw the gasping red shape upon the floor; "Serpice! Mon Dieu! what is it?"

"The cracksman!" he gulped. "Cleek!—
the cracksman who went against us!
Catch him! stop him!"

"The cracksman!" howled out Merode, twisting round in the darkness and reaching blindly for the haft of his dirk. "Nom de Dieu! Where?"

And almost before the last word was uttered a fist like a sledge-hammer shot out, caught him full in the face, and he went down with a whole smithy of sparks flashing and hissing before his eyes.

"There!" answered Cleek, as he bowled him over. "Gentlemen of the sewers, my compliments. You'll make no short cut to 'The Twisted Arm' to-night!"

Then, like something shot from a catapult, he sprang to the door, whisked through it, banged it behind him, turned the key, and went racing down the corridor like a hare.

"It must be sheer luck now!" he panted, as he reached the angle and, kicking aside the rug, pulled up the trap. "They'll have that door down in a brace of shakes, and be after me like a pack of ravening wolves. The race is to the swift this time, gentlemen, and you'll have to take a long way round if you mean to head me off."

Then he passed down into the darkness, closed the trap-door after him, shot into its socket the bolt he had screwed there, flashed up the light of his electric torch, and, *without* the password, turned toward the sewers, and ran, and ran, and ran!

CHAPTER IX

It lacked but a minute of the stroke of twelve, and the revels at "The Twisted Arm"—wild at all times, but wilder to-night than ever—were at their noisiest and most exciting pitch. And why not? It was not often that Margot could spend a whole night with her rapscallion crew, and she had been here since early evening—was to remain here until the dawn broke grey over the house-tops and the murmurs of the workaday world awoke anew in the streets of the populous city. It was not often that each man and each abandoned woman present knew to a certainty that he or she would go home through the mists of the grey morning with a fistful of gold that had been won without labour or the taking of any personal risk; and to-night the half of four hundred thousand francs was to be divided among them.

No wonder they had made a carnival of it, and tricked themselves out in gala attire; no wonder they had brought a paste tiara and crowned Margot—Margot, who was in flaming red to-night, and looked a devil's daughter indeed, with her fire-like sequins and her red ankles twinkling as she threw herself into the thick of the dance and kicked, and whirled, and flung her bare arms about to the lilt of the music and the fluting of her own happy laughter.

"Per Bacco! The devil's in her to-night!" grinned old Marise, the innkeeper, from her place behind the bar, where the lid of the sewer-trap opened. "She has not been like it since the cracksman broke with her, Toinette. But that was before your time, *ma fille.* Mother of the heavens! but there was a man for you! There was a king that was worthy of such a queen. Name of disaster! that she could not hold him, that the curse of virtue sapped such a splendid tree, and that she could take up with another after him!"

"Why not?" cried Toinette, as she tossed down the last half of her absinthe and twitched her flower-crowned head. "A kingdom must have a king, *ma mère;* and Dieu: but he is handsome, this Monsieur Gaston Merode! And if he carries out his part of the work to-night he will be worthy of the homage of all."

"'If' he carries it out—'if'!" exclaimed Marise, with a lurch of the shoulders and a flirt of her pudgy hand. "Soul of me! that's where the difference lies. Had it been the cracksman, there would have been no 'if'—it were done as surely as he attempted it. Name of misfortune! I had gone into a nunnery had I lost such a man. But she—"

The voice of Margot shrilled out and cut into her words. "Absinthe, Marise, absinthe for them all—and set the score down to me!" she cried. "Drink up, my bonny boys; drink up, my loyal maids. Drink—drink till your skins will hold no more. No one pays to-night but me!"

They broke into a cheer, and bearing down in a body upon Marise, threw her into a fever of haste to serve them.

"To Margot!" they shouted, catching up the glasses and lifting them high. "*Vive la Reine des Apaches! Vive la compagnie!* To Margot! To Margot!"

She swept them a merry bow, threw them a laughing salute, and drank the toast with them.

"Messieurs, my love—mesdames et mademoiselles, my admiration," she cried, with a ripple of joy-mad laughter. "To the success of the Apaches, to the glory of four hundred thousand francs, and to the quick arrival of Serpice and Gaston!" Then, her upward glance catching sight of the musicians sipping their absinthe in the little gallery above, she flung her empty glass against the wall behind them, and shook with laughter as they started in alarm and spilled the green poison when they dodged aside. "Another dance, you dawdlers!" she cried. "Does Marise pay you to sit there like mourners? Strike up, you mummies, or you pay yourselves for what you drink to-night. Soul of desires!"—as the musicians grabbed up their instruments, and a leaping, lilting, quick-beating air went rollicking out over the hubbub—"a quadrille, you angels of inspiration! Partners, gentlemen! Partners, ladies! A quadrille! A quadrille!"

They set up a many-throated cheer and flocked out with her upon the floor; and in one instant feet were flying, skirts were whirling, laughter and jest mingling with waving arms and kicking toes, and the whole place was in one mad riot of delirious joy.

And in the midst of this there rolled up suddenly a voice crying, as from the bowels of the earth, "Hola! Hola! La la! loi!" the cry of the Apache to his kind.

"Mother of delights! It is one of us, and it comes from the sewer passage—from the sewer!" shrilled out Marise, as the dancers halted and Margot ran, with fleet steps, towards the bar. "Listen! listen! They come to you, Margot—Serpice and Gaston. The work is done."

"And before even Clodoche or von Hetzler have arrived!" she replied excitedly. "Give them light, give them welcome. Be quick!"

Marise ducked down, loosened the fastenings of the trap-door, flung it back, and, leaning over the gap with a light in her hand, called down into the darkness, "Hola! Hola! La! la! loi! Come on, comrades, come on!"

The caller obeyed instantly. A hand reached up and gripped the edge of the flooring, and out of the darkness into the light emerged the figure of a man in a leather cap and the blue blouse of a mechanic—a pale, fox-faced, fox-eyed fellow, with lank, fair hair, a brush of ragged, yellow beard, and with the look and air of the sneak and spy indelibly branded upon him.

It was Cleek.

"Clodoche!" exclaimed Marise, falling back in surprise.

"Clodoche!" echoed Margot. "Clodoche—and from the sewers?"

"Yes—why not?" he answered, his tongue thick-burred with the accent of Alsace, his shifting eyes flashing toward the huge window behind the bar, where, in the moonlight, the narrow passage leading down to the door of "The Twisted Arm" gaped evilly between double rows of scowling, thief-sheltering houses. "Name of the fiend! Is this the welcome you give the bringer of fortune, Margot?"

"But from the sewer?" she repeated. "It is incomprehensible, *cher ami.* You were to pilot von Hetzler over from the Café Dupin to the square beyond there"—pointing to the window—"to leave him waiting a moment while you came on to see if it were safe for him to enter; and now you come from the sewer—from the opposite direction entirely!"

"Mother of misfortunes! You had done the same yourself—you, Lantier; you, Clopin; you, Cadarousse; any of you—had you been in my boots," he made answer. "I stole a leaf from your own book, earlier in the evening. Garotted a fellow with jewels on him—in the Rue Noir, near the Market Place—and nearly got into 'the stone bottle' for doing it. He was a decoy, set there by the police for some of you fellows, and there was a sergeant de ville after me like a whirlwind. I was not fool enough to turn the chase in this direction, so I doubled and twisted until it was safe to dive into the tavern of Fouchard, and lay in hiding there. Fouchard let his son carry a message to the count for me, and will guide him to the square. When it grew near the time to come, Fouchard let me down into the sewer passage from there. Get on with your dance—silence is always suspicious. An absinthe, Marise! Have Gaston and Serpice arrived yet with the rest of the document, Margot la reine?"

"Not yet," she answered. "But one may expect them at any minute."

"Where is the fragment we already possess?"

"Here," tapping her bodice and laughing, "tenderly shielded, *mon ami*, and why not? Who would not mother a thing that is to bring one four hundred thousand francs?"

"Let me see it. It must be shown to the count, remember. He will take no risks, come not one step beyond the square, until he is certain that it is the paper his Government requires. Let me have it—let me take it to him—quick!"

She waved aside airily the hand he stretched toward her, and danced into the thick of the resumed quadrille.

"Ah, non! non! non!" she laughed, as he came after her. "The conditions were of your own making, *cher ami*; we break no rules even among ourselves."

"Soul of a fool! But if the count comes to the square—he is due there now, mignonne—and I am not there to show him the thing—Margot, for the love of God, let me have the paper!"

"Let me have the sign, the password!"

Cleek snapped at a desperate chance because there was nothing else to do, because he knew that at any moment now the end might come.

"'When the purse will not open, slit it!'" he hazarded, desperately—choosing, on the off-chance of its correctness, the password of the Apache.

"It is not the right one! It is by no means the right one!" she made reply, backing away from him suddenly, her absinthe-brightened eyes deriding him, her absinthe-sharpened laughter mocking him. "Your thoughts are in the Bois, *cher ami*. What is the password of the brotherhood to the cause of Germany, stupid? It is not right, non! non! It is not right!"

The cause of Germany! At the words the truth rushed like a flash of inspiration across Cleek's mind. The cause of Germany! What a dolt he was not to have thought of that before! There was but one phrase ever used for that among the Kaiser's people, and that phrase—

"'To the day!'" he said, with a burst of sudden laughter. "My wits are in the moon to-night, *la reine*. 'To the day,' of course—'To the day!'" And even before she replied to him, he knew that he had guessed aright.

"Bravo!" she said, with a little hiccough—for the absinthe, of which she had imbibed so freely to-night, was beginning to take hold of her. "A pretty conspirator to forget how to open the door he himself locked! It is well I know thee—it is well it was the word of les Apaches in the beginning, or I had been suspicious, silly! Wait but a moment!"—putting her hand to her breast and beginning to unfasten her bodice—"wait but a moment, Monsieur Twitching-Fingers, and the thing shall be in your hand."

The strain, the relief, were all too great for even such nerves as Cleek's, and if he had not laughed aloud, he knew that he must have cheered.

"Oho! you grin because one's fingers blunder with eagerness," hiccoughed Margot, thinking his laughter was for the trouble she had in getting the fastenings of her bodice undone. "Peste, monsieur! may not a lady well be modestly careful, when—Name of the devil! what's that?"

It was the note of a whistle shrilling down the narrow passage without— the passage where Dollops, in Apache garb, had been set on watch; and, hearing it, Cleek clamped his jaws together and breathed hard. A single whistle—short and sharp, such as this one was—was the signal agreed upon that the real Clodoche was coming, and that he and Count von Hetzler had already appeared in the square beyond.

"Soul of a sloth! Will not that hurry you, *la reine*?" he said excitedly, in reply to Margot's startled question. "It is the signal Fouchard's son was to give when he and von Hetzler arrived at the place where I am to meet them. Give me the paper—quick! quick! Tear the fastenings, if they will not come undone else. One cannot keep a von Hetzler waiting like a lackey for a scrap of ribbon and a bit of lace."

"Pardieu! they have kept better men than he waiting many an hour before this," she made reply. "But you shall have the thing in a twinkling now. There! but one more knot, and then it is in your hands."

And, had the fates not decreed otherwise, so, indeed, it would have been. But then, just then, when another second would have brought the paper into view, another moment seen it shut tight in the grip of his itching fingers, disaster came and blotted out his hopes!

Without hint or warning, without sign or sound to lessen the shock of it, the trap-door behind the bar flew up and backward with a crash that sent Marise and her assistants darting away from it in shrieking alarm; a babel of excited voices sounded, a scurry of rushing feet scuffled and flashed along the shaking floor, and Merode and his followers tumbled helter-skelter into the room.

Cleek, counting on the bolt which kept them from entering the passage from the corridor of the Château Larouge—forcing them to take a long, roundabout journey to "The Twisted Arm"—had not counted on their shortening that journey by entering the passage from Fouchard's tavern, doing, in fact, the very thing which he had declared to Margot he himself had done. And lo! here they were, howling and crowding about him—dirks in their hands and devils in their eyes and hearts—and the paper not his yet!

A clamour rose as they poured in; the dancers ceased to dance; the music ceased to play; and Margot, shutting a tight clutch on the loosened part of her half-unfastened bodice, swung away from Cleek's side, and flew in a panic to Merode.

"Gaston!" she cried, knowing from his wild look and the string of oaths and curses his followers were blurting out that something had gone amiss. "Gaston, *mon coeur*! Name of disaster! what is wrong?"

"Everything is wrong!" he flung back excitedly. "That devil—that renegade—that fury, Cleek, the cracksman, is here. He came to the rescue—came out of the very skies—and all but killed Serpice!"

"Cleek!" Fifty shrill voices joined Margot's in that screaming cry; fifty more dirks flashed into view. "Cleek in France? Cleek? Where is he? Which way did he go? Where's the narker—where—where?"

"Here, if anywhere!"

"Here?"

"Yes—unless you've been fooled, and let him get away. He knows about the paper, and is after it, Margot; and if anyone has come up from the sewers within the past twenty minutes—"

They knew—they grasped the situation instantly—and a roar of excited voices yelled out: "Clodoche! Clodoche! Clodoche!" as, snarling and howling like a pack of wolves, they bore down with a rush on the blue-bloused figure that was creeping towards the door.

But as they sprang it sprang also! It was neck or nothing now. Cleek realised it, and, throwing himself headlong over the bar, clutched frantically at the lever which he knew controlled the flow of gas, jammed it down with all his strength, shut off the light, and, grabbing up a chair, sent it crashing through the window.

The crowd surged on towards the wrecked bar with a yell, surged from all directions, and then abruptly stopped and huddled together in one. For the sudden flashing down of the darkness within, had made more prominent, the moon-lighted passage without; and there, scuttling away in alarm from this sudden uproar, and the outward flying of that hurled chair, a figure which but a moment before had come skulking to the window, could now be seen.

"There he goes—there! there!" shrilled out a chorus of excited voices, as the yellow-bearded, blue-bloused figure came into view. "After him! Catch him! Knife him!"

In an instant they were at the door, tumbling out into the darkness, pouring up the passage in hot pursuit. And it was at that moment the balance changed again. Those who were in the front rank of the pursuers were in time to see a lithe, thin figure—dressed as one of their own kind—spring up in the path of that other figure, jump on it, grip it, clap a huge square of sticky brown paper over the howling mouth of it, and bear it, struggling and kicking, to the ground.

In another second they, too, were upon it—swarming over it like rats, and digging and hacking at it with their dirks. And so they were still hacking at it—although it had long since ceased to move, or to make any sound—when Merode came up and called them to a halt.

"Drag it inside; let Margot have a thrust at it—it is her right. Pull off the dog's disguise, and bring me the plucky one that captured him. He shall have absinthe enough to swim in, the little king! Off with it all, Lanchere. First, the plaster—that's right. Now, the wig and beard, and after that—What's that you say? The beard is real? The hair is real? They will not come off? Name of the devil! what are you saying?"

"The truth, *mon roi*, the truth! Mother of disasters! It is not the cracksman—it is the real Clodoche we have killed!"

For one moment a sort of panic held them, swayed them, befogged the brains of them; then, of a sudden, Merode howled out, "Get back! Get back! The fellow's in there still!" and led a blind race down the passage to the bar, where they had seen Cleek last. It was still in darkness; but an eager hand gripping the lever, turned on the gas again, and matches everywhere were lifted to the jets.

And when the light flamed out and the room was again ablaze they knew that they might as well hope to call back yesterday as dream of finding Cleek again. For there on the floor, her limp hands turned palms upward, a chloroformed cloth folded over her mouth and nose, lay, in a deep stupor, the figure of Margot, her bodice torn wide open and the paper forever gone!

* * * * *

It was five minutes later when the Count von Hetzler, crouching back in the shadow of the square and waiting for the return of Clodoche, heard a dull, whirring sound that was unmistakably the purr of a motor throb through the stillness; and, leaning forward, saw an automobile whirl up out of the darkness, cut across the square, and dash off westward like a flash.

Yet in the brief instant it took to go past the place where he waited there was time for him to catch the sharp click of a lowered window, see the clear outlines of a man's face looking out, and to hear a voice from within the vehicle speak.

"Herr Count," it said in clear, incisive tones. "A positively infallible recipe for the invasion of England: Wait until the Channel freezes and then skate over. Good night!"

"One for his nob that, Gov'nor—my hat, yuss!" said Dollops, with a shrill laugh, as he stuck a red head and a face all shiny with cocoa butter and half-removed grease-paint out of the window, and, despite the fact that the swift pace of the automobile had already carried it far past the place where the count had been in hiding, made a fan of his five fingers and his snub nose. "Oh, Mother 'Ubbard! Did you see him, sir? Bunked back in his 'ole like somebody had 'give him the hook,' and cleared the blessed stage before the eggs began to fly. I don't think them Germans 'ull be sittin' on the steps of St. Paul's this year, sir—not them!"

Cleek laughed; and, ordering the boy to shut down the window and get on with the work of changing his clothes, set about doing the same thing himself.

"I suppose you know, you clever little monkey, that I should have been floating down the Seine with a slit throat and enough lead in me to sink a barrel by this time, if it hadn't been for you," he said, as he pushed the outward semblance of Clodoche into the kit-bag, and began to get into ordinary civilian's dress as expeditiously as possible. "If you had slipped up—if you had been one-half minute late—or if that fellow had had a chance to make one cry before you covered his mouth—"

"Please, sir—don't!" interposed Dollops, with a sort of shiver. "If anythink had've happened to you, Gov'nor ..." Then stopped short and made a sound as if he were swallowing something, and then grew very, very still.

Cleek looked at him out of the corner of his eye—moved in spite of himself—hesitated a moment and then, obeying an impulse, leaned over and gently tapped him on the shoulder.

"Dollops, shake hands," he said.

"Sir!"

"Shake hands."

"Gawd, Gov'nor! You don't never *mean* that, sir?"

"Shake hands," said Cleek for the third time. "Do you know, you little monkey, that you're the only soul in all God's world that could ever muster up a tear for me? Thank you, my lad—you're a brick!"—then gripped the grimy hand that was reached out with a sort of awe, wrung it heartily, patted the astonished boy on the shoulder; and fell to whistling merrily as he went on with his dressing.

"Sir, you do lick me, you fair do," said Dollops, laughing unsteadily, and drawing his sleeve across his eyes. "Arfter wot you've been and went through, a-sittin' there and whistlin' as merry as can be—like as if life was all beer and skittles, and you hadn't a care in the world."

"I haven't—for the minute, my lad," said Cleek with a laugh of utter happiness. "Beer and skittles? Lord, it's all roses my boy, roses! I've had the good luck to accomplish a thing that's going to give me—well, at least one moment in Paradise—and when a man has a prospect like that in view ..." His voice trailed off; he laughed again; then fell to whistling once more— noisily, joyously, as if some schoolboy sort of madness was in his blood to-night—and was still whistling when the automobile pulled up sharply in front of the Hôtel du Louvre.

CHAPTER X

By this time he had concluded the alteration in his toilet which was necessary to assure his entrance into the hotel without occasioning comment; and as Dollops had followed suit they readily passed muster, when they alighted, for an ordinary English gentleman accompanied by an ordinary English manservant.

"What was the charge at the garage?" inquired Cleek of Dollops just previously to alighting.

"I dunno wot it runs to in this 'ere rum lingo of francs and sous, sir," said Dollops, "but the garage gent he said it would amount to two pounds ten in English money, so I'll have to leave you to work it out for yourself. The shuvver, he said sommink about 'poor boars'—which I've heard is wot you has to give 'em as a tip to themselves, Gov'nor—so I promised him 'arf a crown to stop at 'tother end of that passage leadin' up from The Twisted Arm till he was wanted, sir. Made it a good tip because I wanted him to be there sure—it would have been a case of 'nab' for us if he hadn't. Wasn't too much, was it, sir?"

"No," said Cleek—and let him see that it wasn't by giving the chauffeur a pourboire of ten francs and sending him back to the garage with the impression that he had had dealings with a millionaire.

Ten minutes later the hotel register bore the record of the arrival of "Mr. Philip Barch and servant"; and one attendant was engaged in showing the servant into a neat little bedroom which was to be his resting-place until morning while another was ushering the master into the suite engaged by the Baron de Carjorac.

Three persons were there: the Baron, his daughter, and his daughter's companion; but Cleek saw but one—and that the only one who made no movement, uttered no sound, when he came into the room. Curiously pale and curiously quiet, she stood with one arm resting on the mantelpiece and the other hanging by her side, looking at him—looking *for* him, in fact—but not saying one word, not making one sound. That she left wholly to the baron and his daughter.

They, too, maintained, although with an effort, an appearance of composure so long as the hotel servant was present; but in the moment the door closed and the man was gone an overpowering excitement seized and mastered them.

"Monsieur, for the love of God, don't tell me you have failed," implored the baron. "I have died a hundred deaths of torture and suspense since your card was carried up. But if I am to hear bad news ... Oh, my country!"

"Don't cross bridges, baron, until you come to them," said Cleek composedly. "I gave Miss Lorne my promise that I would not leave France until I had done what she asked me to do; and—I am returning to England to-morrow by the noon boat. I have had an exciting evening, but it has had its compensation. Here is something for you. I had a bit of a fight for it, baron—look out that it doesn't get into the wrong hands again."

He had taken a small packet of torn papers from his pocket while he was speaking; now he put it into the baron's hand—not wholly without a certain sense of gratification, however, in the excitement and delight which the act called forth; for no man is utterly devoid of personal vanity, personal pride in his achievements, and this man was no less human than his kind.

He let the tumult of excitement and joy wear itself out; he suffered the baron's embraces—even the two rapturous kisses the man planted upon first one and then the other of his cheeks—he endured Mlle. Athalie's exuberant hand-clapping and hand-shaking and the cyclonic and wholly Gallic manner in which she deported herself when comparison with the fragments which the baron had still retained proved beyond all question that these were indeed the missing portions of the all-important document; and not until these things were over did he so much as look at Ailsa Lorne again.

She had taken no part in the general excitement, moved not one foot from where she had been standing from the first. Even when Athalie danced over and hugged her and showed the important fragments; even when she reproved her with a wondering, "Ah, you strange Anglais—you stone-cold Anglais! Is it possible that you can have blood in your veins and yet take wondrous things like this so calmly?"—even then, she merely smiled and remained standing just as she still was; her pallor not one whit lessened, her reserve but the merest shadow less apparent than it had been before.

Cleek chose that moment to walk over to her, to lift his eyes to hers, and to stand looking at her questioningly. For now that he was close to her he could see that she was trembling nervously; that her calmness was merely an outward thing, and that under it nerves writhed and a frightened heart was beating thick and fast.

Was even the fancied moment in Paradise to be denied him then? That such a woman could not, all in a moment—could not by just one act of heroism on his part—be won over and lured into complete forgetfulness of such a past as his, he realized to the fullest extent. Always he had been conscious of that; but even so ... Ah, well, the meanest may hope, the lowest may at least look up; and even saints and angels were not above saying, "Well done!" to a soul that had struggled, to a sinner that had done his best.

"I managed it, you see, Miss Lorne," he said, in a slightly lowered voice, while the baron busied himself in looking for his cheque-book and Athalie bustled about in quest of ink and a pen. "It wasn't an easy night's work, and I'm a bit fagged out. So, as I leave in the morning, it will be good-bye as well as good-night."

She moved for the first time. The hand that lay upon the shelf of the mantelpiece shook and closed quickly. She lifted up her head and looked at him. Her eyes were misty and faint clouds of color were coming and going over her face.

"What is it?" he asked. "Surely, Miss Lorne, you—are not afraid of me?"

"No," she said, averting her face again. "Not of you but of myself. That is—I—" trying to laugh, but making a parody of it—"I was always more or less of a coward, Mr. Cleek, but ..." She faced round again sharply and held out her hand to him. "Will you let me thank you? Will you let me say that I must be merely a little child in intellect since it is only now that I have begun to understand how natural it is that a pound of gold should inevitably outweigh an ounce of dirt? And will you please understand that I am trying to thank you, trying to let you know that I am very, very sorry if I ever hurt your feelings. I don't think I meant to. I couldn't see then so clearly as I do now. Please forgive me."

He took the hand she held out to him; and so had his moment in Paradise after all.

"Hurt me as often as you like, if it will always end like this," he said with a queer little laugh that seemed to come from the very depths of his chest. "As for that other time ... How could I have expected that you would take it in any other way, being what you are and I what I had been? I am glad I told you. You could never have respected me for an instant if you had found it out in any other way; and I want your respect: I want it very, very earnestly, Miss Lorne. If you can ever give it to me I'll do my best to be worthy of it."

She had withdrawn her hand from his and was drumming with her finger-tips upon the mantelshelf. A little pucker was between her eyebrows, she was biting her under lip perplexedly, and appeared to be hesitating. But of a sudden she twitched round her head sharply and a sweep of red went up over her face.

"Shall I show you how much I do respect you, then?" she said. "One may ask of a friend things one would not dream of asking of a mere acquaintance, and so—Mr. Cleek, this night of horror has been too much for me. I know now that I can no longer remain in this position in this dreadful city. I have already resigned my post, and will return to England, and—if I am not too late for it—make an effort to secure the post of governess to Lady Chepstow's little son. I shall start in the morning. Will you play the part of friend and guide and see me safely across the Channel?"

"Do you mean that?" he asked, his face alight, his eyes shining. "You will let me have the privilege, the honour? What a queen you are! You give largesse with both hands when a simple coin would have been enough. Shall I secure your tickets? When will you have your luggage ready? Is there anything you will need before you leave?"

She smiled at his enthusiasm, coloured anew, and again held out her hand.

"We will talk of all that in the morning," she said. "There will be plenty of time. Mlle. de Carjorac has promised to look after my effects and to see that they are shipped on to me in due course. But now it really must be good-night. I shall see you again at breakfast."

"At breakfast?" repeated Cleek, with a happy laugh. "I wonder if you understand that I shall be kicking my heels on my bedside until it is ready?—that I shan't sleep a wink all night?"

And as events proved he came respectably close to living up to that exuberant assertion—merely napping now and again, to wake up suddenly and "moon" for an hour or so; and, between periodical inspections of his watch, to wonder if God ever made a night so long and slow-dragging as this one.

It had its recompense, however; for all—or nearly all—the next day was passed in company with *her*; and more than that he would not have asked of Heaven. Long before she rose he had made all arrangements for the journey to Calais; and she was not a little gratified—yes, and touched if the truth must be told—on arriving at the train, to find that he had made no effort to secure accommodations which would compel her to endure his companionship alone from the Gare du Nord to the steamer, but had considerately reserved seats in a compartment containing other travellers, and had done everything in his power to relieve her of any possible embarrassment and to insure her all possible comforts. Even magazines and pictorial papers were not omitted, but were there for her in plenty lest she might prefer an excuse for not indulging much in conversation; and there was also a huge bunch of La France roses bought at the temporary flower market beside the Madeleine at daybreak that morning.

"They are beautiful, aren't they?" he said, as he laid them in her lap. "Will it surprise you to learn that flowers are a passion with me, and that I am a living refutation of the fallacy that 'there can be nothing very wrong about a man who can cultivate a garden'?"

She looked up at him and smiled.

"I think nothing about you will surprise me—you are so many-sided and—if you will pardon me saying it—so different from what one imagines men of—of your calling to be," she said; and laughed a little, colouring divinely until her face was like the roses themselves. "You treat me as if I were a queen; and I am not used to Court manners. Where, if you please, did you acquire yours?"

"In the vast Kingdom of the World," he made answer, with just a momentary change of countenance—a mere suspicion of embarrassment: laughed off before she could be quite sure that it had had any real existence. "Please remember that to appear to be what one is not, and to ape manners foreign to one's real self is part of what you have so nicely, so euphemistically, termed 'my calling.' I am an Actor on the World's Stage, Miss Lorne; I should be but a very poor one if I could not accommodate myself to many rôles."

"If you play them all so well as you do that of the *preux chevalier*, it is no wonder you are a success," she replied gaily, slipping thus into easy conversation with him.

And so it fell out that the magazines and the illustrated papers were not so much of a boon as both had fancied they might be when Cleek brought them to her; for they had not even been opened when the train ran up to the quay side at Calais and brought them almost abreast of the channel steamer.

CHAPTER XI

It was not until they were aboard the boat and the shores of France were slipping off into the distance that Miss Lorne saw anything at all of Dollops. As he had travelled down from Paris to Calais in a separate compartment there had been no opportunity to do so. He had, too, held himself respectfully aloof even after they had boarded the steamer; and, but that once, when a lurch of the vessel had unexpectedly disturbed Cleek's equilibrium and knocked his hat off, she might not have seen him even then.

But the manner in which he pounced upon that hat, the tender care with which he brushed it, and the affectionate interest in both voice and eyes when he handed it back and inquired eagerly, "Didn't hurt yourself, Gov'nor, did you, sir?" compelled her to take notice of him, and, in doing so, to understand the position in which they stood to each other.

"You are travelling with a servant?" she enquired.

"More than a servant—a devoted henchman, Miss Lorne. They say you can't purchase fidelity for all the money in the world, but I secured the finest brand of it in the Universe by the simple outlay of two half crowns. It is the boy of that night on Hampstead Heath—the boy who stood at the turning point. The Devil didn't get him, you see. He kept his promise and has been walking the straight road ever since."

She turned round and looked at him; realizing more of the man's character in that moment than a hundred deeds of bravery, a thousand acts of gentle courtesy, could ever have made her understand.

"And you took him in?" she said slowly. "You gave him a chance? You helped him to redeem himself? How good of you."

"How good *for* me, you mean," he laughed, "It was 'bread on the waters' with a vengeance, Miss Lorne. I should have lost my life last night but for that boy."—And told her briefly and airily how the thing had come to pass.

"Don't think it vindictive of me, but I am sorry, I am very, very sorry you were not able to hand that dreadful woman, Margot, over to the authorities, Mr. Cleek," she said, with an expression of great seriousness.

"She is not likely to forget or to forgive what you have done; and some day, perhaps ... Oh, do be on your guard. It was really foolhardy to have attempted the thing alone. Surely you might have appealed for assistance to the Paris police and not only have minimised your personal risk but made sure of the woman's arrest."

"Not without allowing the authorities to learn exactly what the Baron de Carjorac was so anxious to keep them *from* learning, Miss Lorne. They must have found out what I was after, what really had been lost, if I had applied to them for assistance. I had either to do the thing alone or drop the case entirely. And drop it I would not after *you* had asked me to accept it, and—Pardon? No, Miss Lorne, I do not know who the woman Margot really is. Even that name may be fictitious, as was the one of 'Comtesse de la Tour.' I only know of her that she is one of the great figures of the Underworld; that money is her game—money alone; money first, last, and all the time; that her personal history is as much of a mystery to her closest associates as was—well, no matter; people of that ilk are not fit subjects to discuss with you. All that I know of the woman is that she has travelled pretty well over the world; that some six or eight months ago she was in Ceylon with a—er—a certain member of her crew, and came within an ace of falling foul of the law. She had put up a plan to loot the depository of the Pearl Fisheries Company at a period when there were thousands of pounds worth of gems awaiting transport. With her usual luck she slipped out of the net and left the country before she could be arrested. But she will have found something there that will repay her for the visit in one way or another. Luck of that kind seems to follow her always."

And a long time afterward he had reason to remember what he said. For the present, however, he had banished from his mind all things but the happiness which was his to-day; and gave himself up to that happiness with his whole heart.

Not once did he again intrude anything that had to do with himself, his exploits, or his future upon Ailsa's attention until all the voyage across the channel and all the journey from Dover up to London had come to an end; and even then, eager though he was to know how matters might shape themselves for *her* future—he was tactful, considerate, careful not to force her into any embarrassing position or to claim from her more than the merest acquaintance might.

"You are going to your friend at Hampstead, I suppose," he said as he handed her into a taxicab at Charing Cross. "I shall like to know if you succeed in getting the position with Lady Chepstow; and if you send no word to Mr. Narkom, I shall take silence as an assent and know that you have."

And afterward, when the days grew in number and late April merged into early May and no word came, he knew that she had succeeded; and was comforted, thinking of her safely housed and perhaps in a position more congenial than the last. At any rate, she was in England, she was again in the same land with him; and that of itself was comfort.

But other comforts were not wanting. The full glory of tulip time was here; The Yard had no immediate occasion for his services, and time was his to dawdle in the public parks among the children, the birds, and the flowers.

"And, lord, how he do love 'em all, bless his heart!" commented Dollops in confidence to himself as he bustled about, putting the Den in order, watering the plants and touching lovingly the things that belonged to the master he adored—his daily task when Cleek was in the Park and had no need for his services. It was a pleasure to the boy, that service. His whole heart was in it. He resented anything that interfered with it even for an instant; and as at this particular time he was in the very midst of preparing a small surprise against his master's return, he was by no means pleased when a sharp whirring sound of a telephone bell shrilled out from the adjoining room and called him from his labour of love.

"Oh, blow that thing! A body don't have a minute to call his own since it's been put in," he blurted out disgustedly, and answered the call. "'Ullo! Yuss; this is Cap'n Burbage's. Wot? No, he aren't in. Dunno when he will be. Dunno where he is. But if there's any messidge—I say, who wants him? Wot? Oh, s'elp me. You, is it, Mr. Narkom? Yuss, it's me, sir—Dollops. Wot? No, sir. Went out two hours ago. Gone to Kensington Palace Gardens. Tulips is in full bloom and you couldn't hold him indoors with a chain at tulip-time, bless his heart. Yuss, sir. Top hat, white spats—same as the 'Cap'n' always wears, sir."

Narkom, at the other end of the line, called back: "If I miss him, if he comes in without seeing me, tell him to wait; I'll be round before three. Good-bye!" then hung up the receiver and turned to the gentleman who stood by the window on the other side of the private office, agitatedly twirling the end of his thick grey-threaded moustache with one hand, while with the other he drummed a nervous tattoo upon the broad oaken sill. "Not at home, Sir Henry; but, fortunately, I know where to find him with but little loss of time," he said, and pressed twice upon an electric button beside his desk. "My motor will be at the door in a couple of minutes, and with ordinary luck we ought to be able to pick him up inside of the next half-hour."

Sir Henry—Sir Henry Wilding, Bart., to give him his full name and title—a handsome, well-set-up man of about forty years of age, well groomed, and with the upright bearing which comes of military training, twisted round on his heel at this and gave the superintendent an almost grateful look.

"I hope so—God knows I hope so, Mr. Narkom," he said agitatedly. "Time is the one important thing at present. The suspense and uncertainty are getting on my nerves so horribly that the very minutes seem endless. Remember, there are only three days before the race, and if those rascals, whoever they are, get at Black Riot before then, God help me—that's all! And if this man Cleek can't probe the diabolical mystery, they *will* get at her, too, and put Logan where they put Tolliver, the brutes!"

"You may trust Cleek to see that they don't, Sir Henry. It is just the kind of case he will glory in; and if Black Riot is all that you believe her, you'll carry off the Derby in spite of these enterprising gentry who—Hallo! here's the motor. Clap on your hat, Sir Henry, and come along. Mind the step! Kensington Palace Gardens, Lennard—and as fast as you can streak it."

CHAPTER XII

The chauffeur proved that he could "streak it" as close to the margin of the speed limit as the law dared wink at, even in the case of the well-known red limousine, and in a little over ten minutes pulled up before the park gates. Narkom jumped out, beckoned Sir Henry to follow him, and together they hurried into the grounds in quest of Cleek.

Where the famous tulip beds made splotches of brilliant colour against the clear emerald of the closely clipped grass they came upon him—a solitary figure in the garb of the elderly seaman, "Captain Burbage, of Clarges Street"—seated on one of the garden benches, his hands folded over the knob of his thick walking-stick and his chin resting upon them, staring fixedly at the gorgeous flowers and apparently deaf and blind to all else.

He was not, however; for as the superintendent approached he, without altering his gaze or his attitude in the slightest particle, said with the utmost calmness: "Superb, are they not, my friend? What a pity they should be scentless. It is as though Heaven had created a butterfly and deprived it of the secret of flight. Walk on, please, without addressing me. I am quite friendly with that policeman yonder and I do not wish him to suspect that the elderly gentleman he is so kind to is in any way connected with The Yard. Examine the tulips. That's right. You came in your limousine, of course? Where is it?"

"Just outside the gates, at the end of the path on the right," replied Narkom, halting with Sir Henry and appearing to be wholly absorbed in pointing out the different varieties of tulips.

"Good," replied Cleek, apparently taking not the slightest notice. "I'll toddle on presently, and when you return from inspecting the flowers you will find me inside the motor awaiting you."

"Do, old chap—and please hurry; time is everything in this case. Let me introduce you to your client. (Keep looking at the flowers, please, Sir Henry.) I have the honour to make you acquainted with Sir Henry Wilding, Cleek; he needs you, my dear fellow."

"Delighted—in both instances. My compliments, Sir Henry. By any chance that Sir Henry Wilding whose mare, Black Riot, is the favourite for next Wednesday's Derby?"

"Yes—that very man, Mr. Cleek; and if—"

"Don't get excited and don't turn, please; our friend the policeman is looking this way. What's the case? One of 'nobbling'? Somebody trying to get at the mare?"

"Yes. A desperate 'somebody,' who doesn't stop even at murder. A very devil incarnate who seems to possess the power of invisibility, and who strikes in the dark. Save me, Mr. Cleek! All I've got in the world is at stake, and if anything happens to Black Riot, I'm a ruined man."

"Yar-r-r!" yawned the elderly sea captain, rising and stretching. "I do believe, constable, I've been asleep. Warm weather, this, for May. A glorious week for Epsom. Shan't see you to-morrow, I'm afraid. Perhaps shan't see you until Thursday. Here, take that, my lad, and have half-a-crown's worth on Black Riot for the Derby; she'll win it, sure."

"Thanky, sir. Good luck to you, sir."

"Same to you, my lad. Good day." Then the old gentleman in the top hat and white spats moved slowly away, passed down the tree-shaded walk, passed the romping children, passed the Princess Louise's statue of Queen Victoria, and, after a moment, vanished. Ten minutes later, when Narkom and Sir Henry returned to the waiting motor, they found him seated within it awaiting them, as he had promised. Giving Lennard orders to drive about slowly in the least frequented quarters, while they talked, the superintendent got in with Sir Henry, and opened fire on the "case" without further delay.

"My dear Cleek," he said, "as you appear to know all about Sir Henry and his famous mare, there's no need to go into that part of the subject, so I may as well begin by telling you at once that Sir Henry has come up to town for the express purpose of getting you to go down to his place in Suffolk to-night in company with him, as his only hope of outwitting a diabolical agency which has set out to get at the horse and put it out of commission before Derby Day, and in the most mysterious, the most inscrutable manner ever heard of, my dear chap. Already one groom who sat up to watch with her has been killed, another hopelessly paralysed, and to-night Logan, the mare's trainer, is to sit up with her in the effort to baulk the almost superhuman rascal who is at the bottom of it all. Conceive if you can, my dear fellow, a power so crafty, so diabolical, that it gets into a locked and guarded stable, gets in, my dear Cleek, despite four men constantly pacing back and forth before each and every window and door that leads into the place and with a groom on guard inside, and then gets out again in the same mysterious manner without having been seen or heard by a living soul. In addition to all the windows being small and covered with a grille of iron, a fact which would make it impossible for anyone to get in or out once the doors were closed and guarded, Sir Henry himself will tell you that the stable has been ransacked from top to bottom, every hole and every corner probed into, and not a living creature of any sort discovered. Yet only last night the groom, Tolliver, was set upon inside the place and killed outright in his efforts to protect the horse; killed, Cleek, with four men patrolling outside, and willing to swear—each and every one of them—that nothing and no one, either man, woman, child or beast, passed them going in or getting out from sunset until dawn."

"Hum-m-m!" said Cleek, sucking in his lower lip. "Mysterious, to say the least. Was there no struggle? Did the men on guard hear no cry?"

"In the case of the first groom, Murple, the one that was paralysed—no," said Sir Henry, as the question was addressed to him. "But in the case of Tolliver—yes. The men heard him cry out, heard him call out 'Help!' but by the time they could get the doors open it was all over. He was lying doubled up before the entrance to Black Riot's stall, with his face to the floor, as dead as Julius Caesar, poor fellow, and not a sign of anybody anywhere."

"And the horse? Did anybody get at that?"

"No; for the best of reasons. As soon as these attacks began, Mr. Cleek, I sent up to London. A gang of twenty-four men came down, with steel plates, steel joists, steel posts, and in seven hours' time Black Riot's box was converted into a sort of safe, to which I alone hold the key the instant it is locked up for the night. A steel grille about half a foot deep, and so tightly meshed that nothing bigger than a mouse could pass through, runs all round the enclosure close to the top of the walls, and this supplies ventilation. When the door is closed at night, it automatically connects itself with an electric gong in my own bedroom, so that the slightest attempt to open it, or even to touch it, would hammer out an alarm close to my head."

"Has it ever done so?"

"Yes—last night, when Tolliver was killed."

"How killed, Sir Henry? Stabbed or shot?"

"Neither. He appeared to have been strangled, poor fellow, and to have died in most awful agony."

"Strangled? But, my dear sir, that would hardly have been possible in so short a time. You say your men heard him call out for help. Granted that it took them a full minute—and it probably did not take them half one—to open the doors and come to his assistance, he would not be stone dead in so short a time; and he was stone dead when they got in, I believe you said?"

"Yes. God knows what killed him—the coroner will find that out, no doubt—but there was no blood shed and no mark upon him that I could see."

"Hum-m-m! Was there any mark on the door of the steel stall?"

"Yes. A long scratch, somewhat semi-circular, and sweeping downwards at the lower extremity. It began close to the lock and ended about a foot and a half lower."

"Undoubtedly, you see, Cleek," put in Narkom, "someone tried to force an entrance to the steel room and get at the mare, but the prompt arrival of the men on guard outside the stable prevented his doing so."

Cleek made no response. Just at that moment the limousine was gliding past a building whose courtyard was one blaze of parrot tulips, and, his eye caught by the flaming colours, he was staring at them and reflectively rubbing his thumb and forefinger up and down his chin. After a moment, however:

"Tell me something, Sir Henry," he said abruptly. "Is anybody interested in your not putting Black Riot into the field on Derby Day? Anybody with whom you have a personal acquaintance, I mean, for of course I know there are other owners who would be glad enough to see him scratched. But is there anybody who would have a particular interest in your failure?"

"Yes—one. Major Lambson-Bowles, owner of Minnow. Minnow's second favourite, as perhaps you know. It would delight Lambson-Bowles to see me 'go under'; and as I'm so certain of Black Riot that I've mortgaged every stick and stone I have in the world to back her, I should go under if anything happened to the mare. That would suit Lambson-Bowles down to the ground."

"Bad blood between you, then?"

"Yes—very. The fellow's a brute, and—I thrashed him once, as he deserved, the bounder. It may interest you to know that my only sister was his first wife. He led her a dog's life, poor girl, and death was a merciful release to her. Twelve months ago he married a rich American woman— widow of a man who made millions in hides and leather. That's when Lambson-Bowles took up racing, and how he got the money to keep a stud.

Had the beastly bad taste, too, to come down to Suffolk—within a gunshot of Wilding Hall—take Elmslie Manor, the biggest and grandest place in the neighbourhood, and cut a dash under my very nose, as it were."

"Oho!" said Cleek; "then the major is a neighbour as well as a rival for the Derby plate. I see! I see!"

"No, you don't—altogether," said Sir Henry quickly. "Lambson-Bowles is a brute and a bounder in many ways, but—well, I don't believe he is low-down enough to do this sort of thing—and with murder attached to it, too—although he did try to bribe poor Tolliver to leave me. Offered my trainer double wages, too, to chuck me and take up his horses."

"Oh, he did that, did he? Sure of it, Sir Henry?"

"Absolutely. Saw the letter he wrote to Logan."

"Hum-m-m! Feel that you can rely on Logan, do you?"

"To the last gasp. He's as true to me as my own shadow. If you want proof of it, Mr. Cleek, he's going to sit in the stable and keep guard himself to-night—in the face of what happened to Murple and Tolliver."

"Murple is the groom who was paralysed, is he not?" said Cleek, after a moment. "Singular thing, that. What paralysed him, do you think?"

"Heaven knows. He might just as well have been killed as poor Tolliver was, for he'll never be any use again, the doctors say. Some injury to the spinal column, and with it a curious affection of the throat and tongue. He can neither swallow nor speak. Nourishment has to be administered by tube, and the tongue is horribly swollen."

"I'm of the opinion, Cleek," put in Narkom, "that strangulation is merely part of the procedure of the rascal who makes these diabolical nocturnal visits. In other words, that he is armed with some quick-acting infernal poison, which he forces into the mouths of his victims. That paralysis of the muscles of the throat is one of the symptoms of prussic acid poisoning, you must remember."

"I do remember, Mr. Narkom," replied Cleek enigmatically. "My memory is much stimulated by these details, I assure you. I gather from them that, whatever is administered, Murple did not get quite so much of it as Tolliver, or he, too, would be dead. Sir Henry"—he turned again to the baronet—"do you trust everybody else connected with your establishment as much as you trust Logan?"

"Yes. There's not a servant connected with the hall that hasn't been in my service for years, and all are loyal to me."

"May I ask who else is in the house besides the servants?"

"My wife, Lady Wilding, for one; her cousin, Mr. Sharpless, who is on a visit to us, for another; and, for a third, my uncle, the Rev. Ambrose Smeer, the famous revivalist."

"Mr. Smeer does not approve of the race track, of course?"

"No, he does not. He is absurdly 'narrow' on some subjects, and 'sport' of all sorts is one of them. But, beyond that, he is a dear, lovable old fellow, of whom I am amazingly fond."

"Hum-m-m! And Lady Wilding and Mr. Sharpless—do they, too, disapprove of racing?"

"Quite to the contrary. Both are enthusiastic upon the subject, and both have the utmost faith in Black Riot's certainty of winning. Lady Wilding is something more than attached to the mare; and as for Mr. Sharpless, he is so upset over these rascally attempts that every morning when the steel room is opened and the animal taken out, although nothing ever happens in the daylight, he won't let her get out of his sight for a single instant until she is groomed and locked up for the night. He is so incensed, so worked up over this diabolical business, that I verily believe if he caught any stranger coming near the mare he'd shoot him in his tracks."

"Hum-m-m!" said Cleek abstractedly, and then sat silent for a long time, staring at his spats and moving one thumb slowly round the breadth of the other, his fingers interlaced and his lower lip pushed upwards over the one above.

"There, that's the case, Cleek," said Narkom, after a time. "Do you make anything out of it?"

"Yes," he replied; "I make a good deal out of it, Mr. Narkom, but, like the language of the man who stepped on the banana skin, it isn't fit for publication. One question more, Sir Henry. Heaven forbid it, of course, but if anything should happen to Logan to-night, whom would you put on guard over the horse to-morrow?"

"Do you think I could persuade anybody if a third man perished?" said the baronet, answering one question with another. "I don't believe there's a groom in England who'd take the risk for love or money. There would be nothing for it but to do the watching myself. What's that? Do it? Certainly, I'd do it! Everybody that knows me knows that."

"Ah, I see!" said Cleek, and lapsed into silence again.

"But you'll come, won't you?" exclaimed Sir Henry agitatedly. "It won't happen if you take up the case; Mr. Narkom tells me he is sure of that. Come with me, Mr. Cleek. My motor is waiting at the garage. Come back with me, for God's sake—for humanity's sake—and get to the bottom of the thing."

"Yes," said Cleek in reply. "Give Lennard the address of the garage, please; and—Mr. Narkom!"

"Yes, old chap?"

"Pull up at the first grocer's shop you see, will you, and buy me a couple of pounds of the best white flour that's milled; and if you can't manage to get me either a sieve or a flour dredger, a tin pepper-pot will do!"

CHAPTER XIII

It was two o'clock when Sir Henry Wilding's motor turned its back upon the outskirts of London, and it was a quarter past seven when it whirled up to the stables of Wilding Hall, and the baronet and his grey-headed, bespectacled and white-spatted companion alighted, having taken five hours and a quarter to make a journey which the trains which run daily between Liverpool Street and Darsham make in four.

As a matter of fact, however, they really had outstripped the train, but it had been Cleek's pleasure to make two calls on the way, one at Saxmundham, where the paralysed Murple lay in the infirmary of the local practitioner, the other at the mortuary where the body of Tolliver was retained, awaiting the sitting of the coroner. Both the dead and the still living man Cleek had subjected to a critical personal examination, but whether either furnished him with any suggested clue he did not say; indeed, the only remark he made upon the subject was when Sir Henry, on hearing from Murple's wife that the doctor had said he would probably not last the week out, had inquired if the woman knew where to "put her hand on the receipt for the payment of the last premium, so that her claim could be sent into the life assurance company without delay when the end came."

"Tell me something, Sir Henry," said Cleek when he heard that, and noticed how gratefully the woman looked at the baronet when she replied, "Yes, Sir Henry, God bless you, sir!" "Tell me, if it is not an impertinent question, did you take out an insurance policy on Murple's life and pay the premium on it yourself? I gathered the idea that you did from the manner in which the woman spoke to you."

"Yes, I did," replied Sir Henry. "As a matter of fact, I take out a similar policy—payable to the widow—for every married man I employ in connection with my racing stud."

"May I ask why?"

"Well, for one thing, they usually are too poor and have too many children to support to be able to take it out for themselves, and exercising racers has a good many risks. Then, for another thing, I'm a firm believer in the policy of life assurance. It's just so much money laid up in safety, and one never knows what may happen."

"Then it is fair," said Cleek, "to suppose, in that case, that you have taken out one on your own life?"

"Yes—rather! And a whacking big one, too."

"And Lady Wilding is, of course, the beneficiary?"

"Certainly. There are no children, you know. As a matter of fact, we have been married only seven months. Before the date of my wedding the policy was in my uncle Ambrose's—the Rev. Mr. Smeer's—favour."

"Ah, I see!" said Cleek reflectively. Then fell to thinking deeply over the subject, and was still thinking of it when the motor whizzed into the stable yard at Wilding Hall and brought him into contact for the first time with the trainer, Logan. He didn't much fancy Logan at first blush—and Logan didn't fancy him at all at any time.

"Hur!" he said disgustedly, in a stage aside to his master, as Cleek stood on the threshold of the stable, with his head thrown back and his chin at an angle, sniffing the air somewhat after the manner of a bird-dog. "Hur! If un's the best Scotland Yard could let out to ye, sir—a half-baked old softy like that!—the rest of 'em must be a blessed poor lot, Ah'm thinkin'. What's un doin' now, the noodle?—snuffin' the air like he did not understand the smell of it! He'd not be expectin' a stable to be scented with eau de cologne, would he? What's un name, sir?"

"Cleek."

"Hur! Sounds like a golf-stick—an' Ah've no doubt he's got a head like one: main thick and with a twist in un. I dunna like 'tecs, Sir Henry, and I dunna like this one especial. Who's to tell as he aren't in with they devils as is after Black Riot? Naw! I dunna like him at all."

Meantime, serenely unconscious of the displeasure he had excited in Logan's breast, Cleek went on sniffing the air and "poking about," as he phrased it, in all corners of the stable; and when, a moment later, Sir Henry went in and joined him, he was standing before the door of the steel room examining the curving scratch of which the baronet had spoken.

"What do you make of it, Mr. Cleek?"

"Not much in the way of a clue, Sir Henry—a clue to any possible intruder, I mean. If your artistic soul hadn't rebelled against bare steel— which would, of course, have soon rusted in this ammonia-impregnated atmosphere—and led you to put a coat of paint over the metal, there would have been no mark at all, the thing is so slight. I am of the opinion that

Tolliver himself caused it. In short, that it was made by either a pin or a cuff button in his wristband when he was attacked and fell. But, enlighten me upon a puzzling point, Sir Henry: What do you use coriander and oil of sassafras for in a stable?"

"Coriander? Oil of sassafras? I don't know what the dickens they are. Have you found such things here?"

"No; simply smelt them. The combination is not usual—indeed, I know of but one race in the world who make any use of it, and they merely for a purpose which, of course, could not possibly exist here, unless—"

He allowed the rest of the sentence to go by default, and turning, looked all round the place. For the first time he seemed to notice something unusual for the equipment of a stable, and regarded it with silent interest. It was nothing more nor less than a box, covered with sheets of virgin cork, and standing on the floor just under one of the windows, where the light and air could get to a weird-looking, rubbery-leaved, orchid-like plant, covered with ligulated scarlet blossoms which grew within it.

"Sir Henry," he said, after a moment, "may I ask how long it is since you were in South America?"

"I? Never was there in my life, Mr. Cleek—never."

"Ah! Then who connected with the hall has been?"

"Oh, I see what you are driving at," said Sir Henry, following the direction of his gaze. "That Patagonian plant, eh? That belonged to poor Tolliver. He had a strange fancy for ferns and rock plants and things of that description, and as that particular specimen happens to be one that does better in the atmosphere of a stable than elsewhere, he kept it in here."

"Who told him that it does better in the atmosphere of a stable?"

"Lady Wilding's cousin, Mr. Sharpless. It was he who gave Tolliver the plant."

"Oho! Then Mr. Sharpless has been to South America, has he?"

"Why, yes. As a matter of fact, he comes from there; so also does Lady Wilding. I should have thought you would have remembered that, Mr. Cleek, when—But perhaps you have never heard? She—they—that is," stammering confusedly and colouring to the temples, "up to seven months ago, Mr. Cleek, Lady Wilding was on the—er—music-hall stage. She and Mr. Sharpless were known as 'Signor Morando and La Belle Creole'—they did a living statue turn together. It was highly artistic; people raved; I—er— fell in love with the lady and—that's all!"

But it wasn't; for Cleek, reading between the lines, saw that the mad infatuation which had brought the lady a title and an over-generous husband had simmered down—as such things always do sooner or later—and that the marriage was very far from being a happy one. As a matter of fact, he learned later that the county, to a woman, had refused to accept Lady Wilding; that her ladyship, chafing under this ostracism, was for having a number of her old professional friends come down to visit her and make a time of it, and that, on Sir Henry's objecting, a violent quarrel had ensued, and the Rev. Ambrose Smeer had come down to the hall in the effort to make peace. And he learned something else that night which gave him food for deep reflection: the Rev. Ambrose Smeer, too, had been to South America, and when he met that gentleman—well, in spite of the fact that Sir Henry thought so highly of him, and it was known that his revival meetings had done a world of good, Cleek did not fancy the Rev. Ambrose Smeer any more than he fancied the trainer, Logan.

But to return to the present. By this time the late falling twilight of May had begun to close in, and presently—as the day was now done and the night approaching—Logan led in Black Riot from the paddock, followed by a slim, sallow-featured, small-moustached man, bearing a shotgun, and dressed in grey tweeds. Sir Henry, who, it was plain to see, had a liking for the man, introduced this newcomer to Cleek as the South American, Mr. Andrew Sharpless.

"That's the English of it, Mr. Cleek," said the latter jovially, but with an undoubted Spanish twist to the tongue. "I wouldn't have you risk breaking your jaw with the Brazilian original. Delighted to meet you, sir. I hope to Heaven you will get at the bottom of this diabolical thing. What do you think, Henry? Lambson-Bowles's jockey was over in this neighbourhood this afternoon. Trying to see how Black Riot shapes, of course, the bounder! Fortunately I saw him skulking along on the other side of the hedge, and gave him two minutes in which to make himself scarce. If he hadn't, if he had come a step nearer to the mare, I'd have shot him down like a dog. That's right, Logan, put her up for the night, old chap, and I'll get out your bedding."

"Aye," said Logan, through his clamped teeth, "and God help man or devil that comes a-nigh her this night—God help him, Lunnon Mister, that's all Ah say!" Then he passed into the steel room with the mare, attended her for the night, and coming out a minute or two later, locked her up and gave Sir Henry the key.

"Broke her and trained her, Ah did; and willin' to die for her, Ah am, if Ah can't pull un through no other way," he said, pausing before Cleek and giving him a black look, "A Derby winner her's cut out for, Lunnon Mister, and a Derby winner her's goin' to be, in spite of all the Lambson-Bowleses and the low-down horse-nobblers in Christendom!" Then he switched round and walked over to Sharpless, who had taken a pillow and a bundle of blankets from a convenient cupboard, and was making a bed of them on the floor at the foot of the locked steel door.

"Thanky, sir, 'bliged to un, sir," said Logan as Sharpless hung up the shotgun and, with a word to the baronet, excused himself and went in to dress for dinner. Then he faced round again on Cleek, who was once more sniffing the air, and pointed to the rude bed: "There's where Ted Logan sleeps this night—there!" he went on suddenly; "and them as tries to get at Black Riot comes to grips with me first, me and the shotgun Mr. Sharpless has left Ah. And if Ah shoot, Lunnon Mister, Ah shoot to kill!"

"Do me a favour, Sir Henry," said Cleek. "For reasons of my own, I want to be in this stable alone for the next ten minutes, and after that let no one come into it until morning. I won't be accountable for this man's life if he stops in here to-night, and for his sake, as well as for your own, I want you to forbid him to do so."

Logan seemed to go nearly mad with rage at this.

"Ah won't listen to it! Ah will stop here—Ah will! Ah will!" he cried out in a passion. "Who comes ull find Ah here waitin' to come to grips with un. Ah won't stop out—Ah won't! Don't un listen to Lunnon Mister, Sir Henry—for God's sake, don't!"

"I am afraid I must in this instance, Logan. You are far too suspicious, my good fellow. Mr. Cleek doesn't want to 'get at' the mare; he wants to protect her; to keep anybody else from getting at her, so—join the guard outside if you are so eager. You must let him have his way." And, in spite of all Logan's pleading, Cleek did have his way.

Protesting, swearing, almost weeping, the trainer was turned out and the doors closed, leaving Cleek alone in the stable; and the last Logan and Sir Henry saw of him until he came out and rejoined them he was standing in the middle of the floor, with his hands on both hips, staring fixedly at the impromptu bed in front of the steel-room door.

"Put on the guard now and see that nobody goes into the place until morning, Sir Henry," he said when he came out and rejoined them some minutes later. "Logan, you silly fellow, you'll do no good fighting against Fate. Make the best of it and stop where you are."

CHAPTER XIV

That night Cleek met Lady Wilding for the first time. He found her what he afterwards termed "a splendid animal," beautiful, statuesque, more of Juno than of Venus, and freely endowed with the languorous temperament and the splendid earthy loveliness which grows nowhere but under tropical skies and in the shadow of palm groves and the flame of cactus flowers. She showed him but scant courtesy, however, for she was but a poor hostess, and after dinner carried her cousin away to the billiard-room, and left her husband to entertain the Rev. Ambrose and the detective as best he could. Cleek needed but little entertaining, however, for in spite of his serenity he was full of the case on hand, and kept wandering in and out of the house and upstairs and down until eleven o'clock came and bed claimed him with the rest.

His last wakeful recollection was of the clock in the lower corridor striking the first quarter after eleven; then sleep claimed him, and he knew no more until all the stillness was suddenly shattered by a loud-voiced gong hammering out an alarm and the sound of people tumbling out of bed and scurrying about in a panic of fright. He jumped out of bed, pulled on his clothing, and rushed out into the hall, only to find it alive with people, and at their head Sir Henry, with a dressing-gown thrown on over his pyjamas and a bedroom candle in his shaking hand.

"The stable!" he cried out excitedly. "Come on, come on, for God's sake! Someone has touched the door of the steel room; and yet the place was left empty—empty!"

But it was no longer empty, as they found out when they reached it, for the doors had been flung open, the men who had been left on guard outside the stables were now inside it, the electric lights were in full blaze, the shotgun still hanging where Sharpless had left it, the impromptu bed was tumbled and tossed in a man's death agony, and at the foot of the steel door Logan lay, curled up in a heap and stone dead!

"He would get in, Sir Henry, he'd have shot one or the other of us if we hadn't let him," said one of the outer guards as Sir Henry and Cleek appeared. "He would lie before the door and watch, sir—he simply would; and God have mercy on him, poor chap; he was faithful to the last!"

"And the last might not have come for years, the fool, if he had only obeyed," said Cleek; then lapsed into silence and stood staring at a dust of white flour on the red-tiled floor and at a thin wavering line that broke the even surface of it.

It was perhaps two minutes later when the entire household—mistress, guests, and servants alike—came trooping across the open space between the hall and the stables in a state of semi-deshabille, but in that brief space of time friendly hands had reverently lifted the body of the dead man from its place before the steel door, and Sir Henry was nervously fitting the key to the lock in a frantic effort to get in and see if Black Riot was safe.

"Dios! what is it? What has happened?" cried Lady Wilding as she came hurrying in, followed closely by Sharpless and the Rev. Ambrose Smeer. Then, catching sight of Logan's body, she gave a little scream and covered her eyes. "The trainer, Andrew, the trainer now!" she went on half hysterically. "Another death—another! Surely they have got the wretch at last?"

"The mare! The mare, Henry! Is she safe?" exclaimed Sharpless excitedly as he whirled away from his cousin's side and bore down upon the baronet. "Give me the key—you're too nervous." And, taking it from him, unlocked the steel room and passed swiftly into it.

In another instant Black Riot was led out—uninjured, untouched, in the very pink of condition—and, in spite of the tragedy and the dead man's presence, one or two of the guards were so carried away that they essayed a cheer.

"Stop that! Stop it instantly!" rapped out Sir Henry, facing round upon them. "What's a horse—even the best—beside the loss of an honest life like that?" and flung out a shaking hand in the direction of dead Logan. "It will be the story of last night over again, of course? You heard his scream, heard his fall, but he was dead when you got to him—dead—and you found no one here?"

"Not a soul, Sir Henry. The doors were all locked; no grille is missing from any window; no one is in the loft; no one in any of the stalls; no one in any crook or corner of the place."

"Send for the constable—the justice of the peace—anybody!" chimed in the Rev. Ambrose Smeer at this. "Henry, will you never be warned, never take these awful lessons to heart? This sinful practice of racing horses for money—"

"Oh, hush, hush! Don't preach me a sermon now, uncle," interposed Sir Henry. "My heart's torn, my mind crazed by this abominable thing. Poor old Logan! Poor, faithful old chap! Oh!" He whirled and looked over at Cleek, who still stood inactive, staring at the flour-dusted floor. "And they said that no mystery was too great for you to get to the bottom of it, no riddle too complex for you to find the answer! Can't you do something? Can't you suggest something? Can't you see any glimmer of light at all?"

Cleek looked up, and that curious smile which Narkom knew so well— and would have known had he been there was the "danger signal"—looped up one corner of his mouth.

"I fancy it is all 'light,' Sir Henry," he said. "I may be wrong, but I fancy it is merely a question of comparative height. Do I puzzle you by that? Well, let me explain. Lady Wilding there is one height, Mr. Sharpless is another, and I am a third; and if they two were to place themselves side by side and, say, about four inches apart, and I were to stand immediately behind them, the difference would be most apparent. There you are. Do you grasp it?"

"Not in the least."

"Bothered if I do either," supplemented Sharpless. "It all sounds like tommy rot to me."

"Does it?" said Cleek. "Then let me explain it by illustration"—and he walked quietly towards them. "Lady Wilding, will you oblige me by standing here? Thank you very much. Now, if you please, Mr. Sharpless, will you stand beside her ladyship while I take up my place here immediately behind you both? That's it exactly. A little nearer, please—just a little, so that your left elbow touches her ladyship's right. Now then"—his two hands moved briskly, there was a click-click, and after it: "There you are— that explains it, my good Mr. and Mrs. Filippo Bucarelli; that explains it completely!"

And as he stepped aside on saying this, those who were watching, those who heard Lady Wilding's scream and Mr. Sharpless's snarling oath and saw them vainly try to spring apart and dart away, saw also that a steel handcuff was on the woman's right wrist, its mate on the man's left one, and that they were firmly chained together.

"In the name of Heaven, man," began Sir Henry, appalled by this, and growing red and white by rapid turns.

"I fancy that Heaven has very little to do with this precious pair, Sir Henry," interposed Cleek. "You want the two people who are accountable for these diabolical crimes, and—there they stand."

"What! Do you mean to tell me that Sharpless, that my wife—"

"Don't give the lady a title to which she has not and never had any legal right, Sir Henry. If it had ever occurred to you to emulate my example to-night and search the lady's effects, you would have found that she was christened Enriqua Dolores Torjado, and that she was married to Señor Filippo Bucarelli here, at Valparaiso, in Chili, three years ago, and that her marriage to you was merely a clever little scheme to get hold of a pot of money and share it with her rascally husband."

"It's a lie!" snarled out the male prisoner. "It's an infernal policeman's lie! You never found any such thing!"

"Pardon me, but I did," replied Cleek serenely. "And what's more, I found the little phial of coriander and oil of sassafras in your room, señor, and—I shall finish off the Mynga Worm in another ten minutes!"

Bucarelli and his wife gave a mingled cry, and, chained together though they were, made a wild bolt for the door; only, however, to be met on the threshold by the local constable, to whom Cleek had dispatched a note some hours previously.

"Thank you, Mr. Philpotts; you are very prompt," he said. "There are your prisoners nicely trussed and waiting for you. Take them away—we are quite done with them here. Sir Henry"—he turned to the baronet—"if Black Riot is fitted to win the Derby she will win it, and you need have no more fear for her safety. No one has ever for one moment tried to get at her. You yourself were the one that precious pair were after, and the bait was your life assurance. By killing off the watchers over Black Riot one by one they knew that there would come a time when, being able to get no one else to take the risk of guarding the horse and sleeping on that bed before the steel-room door, you would do it yourself; and when that time came they would have had you."

"But how? By what means?"

"By one of the most diabolical imaginable. Among the reptiles of Patagonia, Sir Henry, there is one—a species of black adder, known in the country as the Mynga Worm—whose bite is more deadly than that of the rattler or the copperhead, and as rapid in its action as prussic acid itself. It has, too, a great velocity of movement and a peculiar power of springing and hurling itself upon its prey. The Patagonians are a barbarous people in the main and, like all barbarous people, are vengeful, cunning, and subtle. A favourite revenge of theirs upon unsuspecting enemies is to get within touch of them and secretly to smear a mixture of coriander and oil of sassafras upon some part of their bodies, and then either to lure or drive them into the forest; for by a peculiar arrangement of Mother Nature this mixture has a fascination, a maddening effect upon the Mynga Worm—just as a red rag has on a bull—and, enraged by the scent, it finds the spot smeared with it and delivers its deadly bite."

"Good heaven! How horrible! And you mean to tell me—"

"That they employed one of these deadly reptiles in this case? Yes, Sir Henry. I suspected it the very moment I smelt the odour of the coriander and sassafras; but I suspected that an animal or a reptile of some kind was at the bottom of the mystery at a prior period. That is why I wanted the flour. Look! Do you see where I sifted it over this spot near the Patagonian plant? And do you see those serpentine tracks through the middle of it? The Mynga Worm is there—in that box, at the roots of that plant. Now see!"

He caught up a horse blanket, spread it on the floor, lifted the box and plant, set them down in the middle of it, and with a quick gathering up of the ends of the blanket converted it into a bag and tied it round with a hitching strap.

"Get spades, forks, anything, and dig a hole outside in the paddock," he went on. "A deep hole—a yard deep at the least—then get some straw, some paraffin, turpentine—anything that will burn furiously and quickly—and we will soon finish the little beast."

The servants flew to obey, and when the hole was dug he carried the bag out and lowered it carefully into it, covered it with straw, drenched this with a gallon or more of lamp oil, and rapidly applied a match to it and sprang back.

A moment later those who were watching saw a small black snake make an ineffectual effort to leap out of the blazing mass, fall back into the flames and disappear for ever.

"The method of procedure?" said Cleek, answering the baronet's query as the latter was pouring out what he called "a nerve settler," prior to following the Rev. Ambrose's example and going to bed. "Very cunning, and yet very, very simple, Sir Henry. Bucarelli made a practice, as I saw this evening, of helping the chosen watcher to make his bed on the floor in front of the door to the steel room, but during the time he was removing the blankets from the cupboard his plan was to smear them with the coriander and sassafras and so arrange the top blanket that when the watcher lay down the stuff touched his neck or throat and made that the point of attack for the snake, whose fangs make a small round spot not bigger than a knitting needle, which is easily passed over by those not used to looking for such a thing. There was such a spot on Tolliver's throat; such another at the base of Murple's skull, and there is a third in poor Logan's left temple. No, thank you—no more to-night, Sir Henry. Alcohol and I are never more than speaking acquaintances at the best of times. But if you really wish to do me a kindness—"

"I don't think there is room to doubt that, Mr. Cleek. If I am certain of anything in this world I am certain of Black Riot's success on Wednesday; and that success I feel I shall owe to you. Money can't offset some debts, you know; and if there is anything in the world I can do, you have only to let me know."

"Thank you," said Cleek. "Then invite me to spend to-morrow here, and give me the freedom of those superb gardens. My senses are drunk already with the scent of your hyacinths; and if I might have a day among them, I should be as near happy as makes no difference."

He had his day—breaking it only to 'phone up to Clarges Street and quiet any possible fears upon Dollops's part—and if ever man was satisfied, that man was he.

CHAPTER XV

It was late on the afternoon of the day following when he turned up at Clarges Street and threw Dollops into a very transport of delight at the bare sight of him.

"Crumbs, Gov'nor, but I am glad to see you, sir!" said the boy, with a look of positive adoration. "A fish out o' water ain't a patch to wot I've felt like—Lord, no! Why, sir, it's the first time you've ever been away from me since you took me on; and the dreams I've had is enough to drive a body fair dotty. I've seen parties a-stickin' knives in your back and puttin' poison in your food and doin' the Lord knows wot not to you, sir; and every blessed nerve in my body has been a doin' of a constant shake—like a jelly-fish on a cold day."

Cleek laughed, and catching him by the shoulder whirled him round, looked at him, and then clapped him on the back.

"Look here, don't you get to worrying and to developing nerves, young man," he said, "or I shall have to ship you off somewhere for a long rest; and I'm just beginning to feel as if I couldn't do without you. What you want is a change; and what I want is the river, so, if there is no message from The Yard—"

"There isn't, sir."

"Good. Then 'phone through to Mr. Narkom and tell him that you and I are going for a few days up the river as far as Henley, and that we are going to break it on Wednesday to go to the Derby."

"Gov'nor! Gawd's truth, sir, you aren't never a-goin' to give me two sich treats as that? From now till Thursday with jist you—jist *you*, sir? I'll go balmy on the crumpet—I'll get to stickin' straws in my bloomin' 'air!"

"You 'get to' the telephone and send that message to The Yard, if you know when you're well off," said Cleek, laughing. "And, after that, out with the kit bag and in with such things as we shall need; and—Hullo! what's this thing?"

"A necktie and a rose bush wot I took the liberty of buyin' for you, sir, bein' as you give me ten shillin's for myself," said Dollops sheepishly. "I been a-keepin' of my eye on that rose bush and that necktie for a week past, sir. I 'ope you'll take 'em, Gov'nor, and not think me presumin', sir."

Cleek faced round and looked at him—a long look—without saying anything, then he screwed round on his heel and walked to the window.

"It is very nice and very thoughtful of you, Dollops," he said presently, his voice a little thick, his tones a little uneven. "But don't be silly and waste your money, my lad. Lay it by. You may need it one day. Now toddle on and get things ready for our outing." But afterwards—when the boy had gone and he was alone in the room—he walked back to the potted rose bush and touched its buds lovingly, and stood leaning over it and saying nothing for a long time. And though the necktie that hung on its branches was a harlequin thing of red and green and violent purple, when he came to dress for that promised outing he put it on and adjusted it as tenderly, wore it as proudly as ever knight of old wore the colours of his lady.

"You look a fair treat in it, sir," said Dollops, delightedly and admiringly, when he came in later and saw that he had it on. And if anything had been wanting to make him quite, quite happy, it was wanting no more. Or, if it had been, the night that came down and found them housed in a little old-world inn, with a shining river at its door and the hush and the odorous darkness of the country lanes about it, must of itself have supplied the omission; for when all the house was still and all the lights were out, he crept from his bed and curled up like a dog on the mat before Cleek's door, and would not have changed places with an emperor.

They were up and on the river, master and man, almost as soon as the dawn itself; taking their morning plunge under a sky that was but just changing the tints of rose to those of saffron before they merged into the actual light of day; and to the boy the man seemed almost a god in that dim light, which showed but an ivory shoulder lifting now and again as he struck outwards and deft his way through a yielding, yellow-grey waste that leaped in little lilac-hued ripples to his chin, and thence wavered off behind him in dancing lines of light. And once, when he heard him lift up his voice and sing as he swam, he felt sure that he *must* be a god—that that alone could explain why he had found him so different from other men, and cared for him as he had never cared for any human thing before.

From dawn to dark that day was one of unalloyed delight to him. Never before had the starved soul of him—fed, all his life, when it was fed at all, from the drippings of the flesh-pots and the "leavings" of the City—found any savour in the insipid offerings of the Country; never before had he known what charms lie on a river's breast, what spells of magic a blossoming hedge and the white "candles" of a horse-chestnut tree may weave, and never before had a meadow been anything to him but a simple grass-grown field. To-day Nature—through this man who was so essentially bred in the very womb of her—spoke to his understanding and found her words not lost on air. The dormant things within the boy had awakened. Life spoke; Hope sang; and between them all the world was changed. Yesterday, he had looked upon this day of idling in the country as a pleasant interlude, as a happy prologue to those greater delights that would come when he at last went to Epsom and really saw the famous race for the Derby. To-day, he was sorry that anything—even so great a thing as that—must come to disturb such placid happiness as this.

And yet, when the wondrous "Wednesday" came and he was actually on his way to Epsom Downs at last ... Ah, well, Joy is elastic; Youth is a time of many dreams, and who blames a boy for being delighted that one of them is coming true at last?

Cleek did not, at all events. Indeed, Cleek aided and abetted him in all his boisterous outbursts from first to last; and was quite as excited as he when the event of the meeting—the great race for the famous Derby Stakes—was put up at last. Indeed, he was a bit wilder, if anything, than the boy himself when the flag fell and the whole field swept by in one thunderous rush, with Minnow in the lead and Black Riot far and away behind. Nor did his excitement abate when, as the whole cavalcade swung onwards over the green turf with the yelling thousands waving and shouting about it, Sir Henry Wilding's mare began to lessen that lead, and foot by foot to creep up towards the head.

He shouted then—as wildly as Dollops himself, as wildly as any man present. He jumped up on his seat and waved his hat; he thumped Dollops on the back and cried: "She's creeping up! She's creeping up! Stick to it, old chap, stick to it! Give her her head, you fool! She'll do it—by God, she'll do it! Hurrah! Hurrah!" And was shouted down, and even seized and pulled down by others whose view he obstructed, and whose interest and excitement were as great as his.

Onwards they flew, horses and riders, the whole pounding, mixing, ever-changing mass of them; jackets and caps of every hue flashing here and there—now in a huddled mass, now with this one in the lead, and again with that: a vast, ever-moving, ever-altering kaleidoscope that was, presently, hidden entirely from the main mass of the onlookers, by the surging crowd, the mass of drags and carriages of all sorts in the huge square of the central enclosure, and most of all by the people who stood up on seats and wheels and even the tops of the vehicles. Then, for a little time, the roars came from a distance only—from those in the enclosure who alone could see—

then neared and neared and grew in volume, as the unseen racers pounded onward and came pelting up the long stretch toward Tattenham Corner. And by and bye they swung into view again—still a huddled mass, still so closely packed together that the positions of the individual horses was a matter of uncertainty—but always the roaring sound went on and always it came nearer and nearer, until a thousand voices took it up at the foot of the grand stand, and other thousands bellowed it up and up from tier to tier to the very roof.

For, of a sudden, that blaze of caps and jackets, that huddle of horses red and horses grey, horses black and horses roan, piebald, white—every colour that a horse may be—had come at last to Tattenham Corner and burst into the full view of everybody. Yet, as they came, a black mare, hugging the railed enclosure on the inner side of the sweep, arrowed forward with a sudden spurt, came like a rocket to the fore, and all the earth and all the sky seemed to ring with the cry: "Wilding! Wilding! Black Riot leads! Black Riot leads!"

She did—and kept it to the end!

In half a minute her number was up, yelling thousands were tumbling out upon the field to cheer her, to cheer her rider, to cheer her proud owner when he came out to lead her to the paddock and the weighing room, and to feel in that moment the proudest and the happiest man in England; and of those, not the least excited and delighted was Cleek.

Carried away by enthusiasm, he had risen again in his seat and, with his hat held aloft upon a walking stick, was waving and stamping and shouting enthusiastically: "Black Riot wins! Black Riot! Black Riot! Bully boy! Bully boy!"

And so he was still shouting when he felt a hand touch him, and looking round saw Mr. Narkom.

"Ripping, wasn't it, old chap?" said the superintendent. "No wonder you are excited, considering what interest you have. Been looking for you, my dear fellow. Knew of course, from your telling me, that you would be here to-day, but shouldn't have been able to identify you but for the presence of young Dollops here. I say: you're not going to stop now that the great race is over, are you? The rest won't amount to anything."

"No, I shall not stop," said Cleek. "Why? Do you want me?"

"Yes. Lennard's outside with the limousine. Hop into it, will you, and meet me at the Fiddle and Horseshoe, between Shepherd's Bush and Acton?

It's only half-past three and the limousine can cover the distance in less than no time. Can't go with you. Got to round up my men here, first. Join you shortly, however. McTavish has a sixty-horse-power Mercedes, and he'll rush me over almost on your heels. Let Dollops go home by train, and you meet me as I've asked, will you?"

"Yes," said Cleek.

And so the joyous holiday came to an unexpected end.

Parting from Dollops, and leaving the boy to journey on to Clarges Street alone, he fared forth to find Lennard and the red limousine, and was whirled away in record time to the inn of the Fiddle and Horseshoe.

CHAPTER XVI

It had but just gone five when Narkom walked into the little bar parlour and found him standing there, looking out on the quaint, old-fashioned bowling green that lay all steeped in sunshine and zoned with the froth of pear and apple blossoms thick piled above the time-stained bricks of an enclosing wall.

"What a model of punctuality you are, old chap," the superintendent said, nodding approvingly. "Wait a moment while I go and order tea, and then we will get down to business in real earnest. Shan't be long."

"Pray, don't hurry yourself on my account, Mr. Narkom," returned Cleek, "coming down to earth" out of a mental airship. "I could do with another hour of that"—nodding toward the view—"and still wonder where the time had gone. These quaint old inns, which the march of what we are pleased to call 'Progress' is steadily crowding off the face of the land, are always deeply interesting to me; I love them. What a day! What a picture! What a sky! As blue as what Dollops calls the 'Merry Geranium Sea.' I'd give a Jew's eye for a handful of those apple blossoms—they are divine!"

Narkom hastened from the room without replying. The strain of poetry underlying the character of this strange, inscrutable man, his amazing love of Nature, his moments of almost womanish weakness and sentiment, astonished and mystified him. It was as if a hawk had acquired the utterly useless trick of fluting like a nightingale, and being himself wholly without imagination, he could not comprehend it in the smallest degree.

When he returned a few minutes later, however, the idealist seemed to have simmered down into the materialist, the extraordinary to have become merged in the ordinary, for he found his famous ally no longer studying the beauties of Nature, but giving his whole attention to the sordid commonplaces of man, for he was standing before a glaringly printed bill one of many that were tacked upon the walls, which set forth in amazing pictures and double-leaded type the wonders that were to be seen daily and nightly at Olympia, where, for a month past, "Van Zant's Royal Belgian Circus and World-famed Menagerie" had been holding forth to "Crowded and delighted audiences." Much was made of two "star turns" upon this lurid bill: "Mademoiselle Marie de Zanoni, the beautiful and peerless bareback equestrienne, the most daring lady rider in the universe," for the one; and for the other, "Chevalier Adrian di Roma, king of the animal world, with his great aggregation of savage and ferocious wild beasts, including the famous man-eating African lion, Nero, the largest and most ferocious animal of its species in captivity." And under this latter announcement there was a picture of a young and handsome man, literally smothered with medals, lying at full length, with his arms crossed and his head in the wide-open jaws of a snarling, wild-eyed lion.

"My dear chap, you really do make me believe that there actually is such a thing as instinct," said Narkom, as he came in. "Fancy your selecting that particular bill out of all the others in the room! What an abnormal individual you are!"

"Why? Has it anything to do with the case you have in hand?"

"Anything to do with it? My dear fellow, it *is* 'the case.' I can't imagine what drew your attention to it."

"Can't you?" said Cleek, with a half-smile. Then he stretched forth his hand and touched the word "Nero" with the tip of his forefinger. "That did. Things awaken a man's memory occasionally, Mr. Narkom, and—Tell me, isn't that the beast there was such a stir about in the newspapers a fortnight or so ago—the lion that crushed the head of a man in full view of the audience?"

"Yes," replied Narkom, with a slight shudder. "Awful thing, wasn't it? Gave me the creeps to read about it. The chap who was killed, poor beggar, was a mere boy, not twenty, son of the Chevalier di Roma himself. There was a great stir about it. Talk of the authorities forbidding the performance, and all that sort of thing. They never did, however, for on investigation— Ah, the tea at last, thank fortune. Come, sit down, my dear fellow, and we'll talk whilst we refresh ourselves. Landlady, see that we are not disturbed, will you, and that nobody is admitted but the parties I mentioned?"

"Clients?" queried Cleek, as the door closed and they were alone together.

"Yes. One, Mlle. Zelie, the 'chevalier's' only daughter, a slack-wire artist; the other, Signor Scarmelli, a trapeze performer, who is the lady's fiancé."

"Ah, then our friend the chevalier is not so young as the picture on the bill would have us believe he is."

"No, he is not. As a matter of fact, he is considerably past forty, and is—or, rather, was, up to six months ago, a widower with three children, two sons and a daughter."

"I suppose," said Cleek, helping himself to a buttered scone, "I am to infer from what you say that at the period you mentioned, six months ago, the intrepid gentleman showed his courage yet more forcibly by taking a second wife? Young or old?"

"Young," said Narkom in reply. "Very young, not yet four-and-twenty, in fact, and very, very beautiful. That is she who is 'featured' on the bill as the star of the equestrian part of the programme: 'Mlle. Marie de Zanoni.' So far as I have been able to gather, the affair was a love match. The lady, it appears, had no end of suitors, both in and out of the profession; it has even been hinted that she could, had she been so minded, have married an impressionable young Austrian nobleman of independent means who was madly in love with her; but she appears to have considered it preferable to become 'an old man's darling,' so to speak, and to have selected the middle-aged chevalier rather than someone whose age is nearer her own."

"Nothing new in that, Mr. Narkom. Young women before Mlle. Marie de Zanoni's day have been known to love elderly men sincerely: young Mrs. Bawdrey, in the case of 'The Nine-fingered Skeleton,' is an example of that. Still, such marriages are not common, I admit, so when they occur one naturally looks to see if there may not be 'other considerations' at the bottom of the attachment. Is the chevalier well-to-do? Has he expectations of any kind?"

"To the contrary; he has nothing but the salary he earns—which is by no means so large as the public imagines; and as he comes of a long line of circus performers, all of whom died early and poor, 'expectations,' as you put it, do not enter into the affair at all. Apparently the lady did marry him for love of him, as she professes and as he imagines; although, if what I hear is true, it would appear that she has lately outgrown that love; in short, that a Romeo more suitable to her age has recently joined the show in the person of a rider called Signor Antonio Martinelli; that he has fallen desperately in love with her, and that—"

He bit off his words short and rose to his feet. The door had opened suddenly to admit a young man and a young woman, who entered in a state of nervous excitement. "Ah, my dear Mr. Scarmelli, you and Miss Zelie are most welcome," continued the superintendent. "My friend and I were this moment talking about you."

Cleek glanced across the room, and, as was customary with him, made up his mind instantly. The girl, despite her association with the arena, was a modest, unaffected little thing of about eighteen; the man was a straight-looking, clear-eyed, boyish-faced young fellow of about eight-and-twenty; well, but by no means flashily, dressed, and carrying himself with the air of one who respects himself and demands the respect of others. He was evidently an Englishman, despite his Italian *nom de théâtre*, and Cleek decided out of hand that he liked him.

"We can shelve 'George Headland' in this instance, Mr. Narkom," he said, as the superintendent led forward the pair for the purpose of introducing them, and suffered himself to be presented in the name of Cleek.

The effect of this was electrical; would, in fact, had he been a vain man, have been sufficient to gratify him to the fullest, for the girl, with a little "Oh!" of amazement, drew back and stood looking at him with a sort of awe that rounded her eyes and parted her lips, while the man leaned heavily upon the back of a convenient chair and looked and acted as one utterly overcome.

"Cleek!" he repeated, after a moment's despairful silence. "You, sir, are that great man? This is a misfortune, indeed."

"A misfortune, my friend? Why a 'misfortune,' pray? Do you think the riddle you have brought is beyond my powers?"

"Oh, no; not that—never that!" he made reply. "If there is any one man in the world who could get at the bottom of it, could solve the mystery of the lion's change, the lion's smile, you are that man, sir, you. That is the misfortune: that you could do it, and yet—I cannot expect it, cannot avail myself of this great opportunity. Look! I am doing it all on my own initiative, sir—all for the sake of Zelie and that dear, lovable old chap, her father. I have saved fifty-eight pounds, Mr. Cleek. I had hoped that that might tempt a clever detective to take up the case; but what is such a sum to such a man as you?"

"If that is all that stands in the way, don't let it worry you, my good fellow," said Cleek, with a smile. "Put your fifty-eight pounds in your pocket against your wedding-day, and—good luck to you. I'll take the case for nothing. Now then, what is it? What the dickens did you mean just now when you spoke about 'the lion's change' and 'the lion's smile'? What lion— Nero? Here, sit down and tell me all about it."

"There is little enough to tell, Heaven knows," said young Scarmelli, with a sigh, accepting the invitation after he had gratefully wrung Cleek's hand, and his fiancée, with a burst of happy tears, had caught it up as it slipped from his and had covered it with thankful kisses. "That, Mr. Cleek, is where the greatest difficulty lies—there is so little to explain that has any bearing upon the matter at all. It is only that the lion—Nero, that is, the chevalier's special pride and special pet—seems to have undergone some great and inexplicable change, as though he is at times under some evil spell, which lasts but a moment and yet makes that moment a tragical one. It began, no one knows why nor how, two weeks ago, when, without hint or warning, he killed the person he loved best in all the world—the chevalier's eldest son. Doubtless you have heard of that?"

"Yes," said Cleek. "But what you are now telling me sheds a new light upon the matter. Am I to understand, then, that all that talk, on the bills and in the newspapers, about the lion being a savage and a dangerous one is not true, and that he really is attached to his owner, and his owner's family?"

"That is the truth," replied Scarmelli; "Nero is, in fact, the gentlest, most docile, most intelligent beast of his kind living. In short, sir, there's not a 'bite' in him; and, added to that, he is over thirty years old. Zelie—Miss di Roma—will tell you that he was born in captivity; that from his earliest moment he has been the pet of her family; that he was, so to speak, raised with her and her brothers; that, as children, they often slept with him; that he will follow those he loves like any dog, fight for them, protect them, let them tweak his ears and pull his tail without showing the slightest resentment, even though they may actually hurt him. Indeed, he is so general a favourite, Mr. Cleek, that there isn't an attendant connected with the show who would not, and, indeed, has not at some time, put his head in the beast's mouth, just as the chevalier does in public, certain that no harm could possibly come of the act.

"You may judge, then, sir, what a shock, what a horrible surprise it was when the tragedy of two weeks ago occurred. Often, to add zest to the performance, the chevalier varies it by allowing his children to put their heads into Nero's mouth instead of doing so himself, merely making a fake of it that he has the lion under such control that he will respect any command given by him. That is what happened on that night. Young Henri was chosen to put his head into Nero's mouth, and did so without fear or hesitation. He took the beast's jaws and pulled them apart, and laid his head within them, as he had done a hundred times before; but of a sudden an appalling, an uncanny, thing happened. It was as though some supernatural power laid hold of the beast and made a thing of horror of what a moment before had been a noble-looking animal; for suddenly a strange hissing noise issued from its jaws, its lips curled upward until it smiled—smiled, Mr. Cleek!—oh, the ghastliest, most awful, most blood-curdling smile imaginable—and then, with a sort of mingled snarl and bark, it clamped its jaws together and crushed the boy's head as though it were an egg-shell!"

He put up his hands and covered his eyes as if to shut out some appalling vision, and for a moment or two nothing was heard but the low sobbing of the victim's sister.

"As suddenly as that change had come over the beast, Mr. Cleek," Scarmelli went on presently, "just so suddenly it passed, and it was the docile, affectionate animal it had been for years. It seemed to understand that some harm had befallen its favourite—for Henri was its favourite—and, curling itself up beside his body, it licked his hands and moaned disconsolately in a manner almost human. That's all there is to tell, sir, save that at times the horrid change, the appalling smile, repeat themselves when either the chevalier or his son bend to put a head within its jaws, and but for their watchfulness and quickness the tragedy of that other awful night would surely be repeated. Sir, it is not natural; I know now, as surely as if the lion itself had spoken, that someone is at the bottom of this ghastly thing, that some human agency is at work, some unknown enemy of the chevalier's is doing something, God alone knows what or why, to bring about his death as his son's was brought about."

And here, for the first time, the chevalier's daughter spoke.

"Ah, tell him all, Jim, tell him all," she said, in her pretty broken English. "Monsieur, may the good God in heaven forgive me, if I wrong her; but—but—Ah, Monsieur Cleek, sometimes I feel that she, my stepmother, and that man, that 'rider' who knows not how to ride as the artist should—monsieur, I cannot help it, but I feel that they are at the bottom of it."

"Yes, but why?" queried Cleek. "I have heard of your father's second marriage, mademoiselle, and of this Signor Antonio Martinelli, to whom you allude. Mr. Narkom has told me. But why should you connect these two persons with this inexplicable thing? Does your father do so, too?"

"Oh, no! Oh, no!" she answered excitedly. "He does not even know that we suspect, Jim and I. He loves her, monsieur. It would kill him to doubt her."

"Then why should you?"

"Because I cannot help it, monsieur. God knows, I would if I could, for I care for her dearly—I am grateful to her for making my father happy. My brothers, too, cared for her. We believed she loved him; we believed it was because of that she married him. And yet—and yet—Ah, monsieur, how can I fail to feel as I do when this change in the lion came with that man's coming? And she—ah, monsieur, she is always with him. Why does she curry favour of him and his rich friend?"

"He has a rich friend, then?"

"Yes, monsieur. The company was in difficulties; Monsieur van Zant, the proprietor, could not make it pay, and it was upon the point of disbanding. But, suddenly, this indifferent performer, this rider who is, after all, but a poor amateur and not fit to appear with a company of trained artists, suddenly this Signor Martinelli comes to Monsieur van Zant to say that, if he will engage him, he has a rich friend—one Señor Sperati, a Brazilian coffee planter—who will 'back' the show with his money and buy a partnership in it. Of course, M. van Zant accepted; and since then this Señor Sperati has travelled everywhere with us, has had the entrée like one of us, and his friend, the bad rider, has fairly bewitched my stepmother, for she is ever with him, ever with them both, and—and—Ah, mon Dieu! the lion smiles, and my people die! Why does it 'smile' for no others? Why is it only they—my father, my brother—they alone?"

"Is that a fact?" said Cleek, turning to young Scarmelli. "You say that all connected with the circus have so little fear of the beast that even attendants sometimes do this foolhardy trick. Does the lion never 'smile' for any of those?"

"Never, Mr. Cleek—never under any circumstances. Nor does it always smile for the chevalier and his son. That is the mystery of it. One never knows when it is going to happen—one never knows why it does happen. But if you could see that uncanny smile—"

"I should like to," interposed Cleek. "That is, if it might happen without any tragical result. Hum-m-m! Nobody but the chevalier and the chevalier's son! And when does it happen in their case—during the course of the show, or when there is nobody about but those connected with it?"

"Oh, always during the course of the entertainment, sir. Indeed, it has never happened at any other time—never at all."

"Oho!" said Cleek. "Then it is only when they are dressed and made up for the performance, eh? Hum-m-m! I see." Then he relapsed into silence for a moment, and sat tracing circles on the floor with the toe of his boot. But, of a sudden: "You came here directly after the matinee, I suppose?" he queried, glancing up at young Scarmelli.

"Yes; in fact, before it was wholly over."

"I see. Then it is just possible that all the performers have not yet got into their civilian clothes. Couldn't manage to take me round behind the scenes, so to speak, if Mr. Narkom will lend us his motor to hurry us there? Could, eh? That's good. I think I'd like to have a look at that lion and, if you don't mind, an introduction to the parties concerned. No! don't fear; we won't startle anybody by revealing my identity or the cause of the visit. Let us say that I'm a vet, to whom you have appealed for an opinion, regarding Nero's queer conduct. All ready, Mr. Narkom? Thanks—then let's be off."

Two minutes later the red limousine was at the door, and, stepping into it with his two companions, he was whizzed away to Olympia and the first step towards the solution of the riddle.

CHAPTER XVII

As it is the custom of those connected with the world of the circus to eat, sleep, have their whole being, as it were, within the environment of the show, to the total exclusion of hotels, boarding-houses, or outside lodgings of any sort, he found on his arrival at his destination the entire company assembled in what was known as the "living-tent," chatting, laughing, reading, playing games, and killing time generally whilst waiting for the call to the "dining-tent," and this gave him an opportunity to meet all the persons connected with the "case," from the "chevalier" himself to the Brazilian coffee planter who was "backing" the show.

He found this latter individual a somewhat sullen and taciturn man of middle age, who had more the appearance of an Austrian than a Brazilian, and with a swinging gait and an uprightness of bearing which were not to be misunderstood.

"Humph! Known military training," was Cleek's mental comment as soon as he saw the man walk. "Got it in Germany, too; I know that peculiar 'swing.' What's his little game, I wonder? And what's a Brazilian doing in the army of the Kaiser? And, having been in it, what's he doing dropping into this line—backing a circus, and travelling with it like a Bohemian?"

But although these thoughts interested him, he did not put them into words nor take anybody into his confidence regarding them.

As for the other members of the company, he found "the indifferent rider," known as Signor Antonio Martinelli, an undoubted Irishman of about thirty years of age, extremely handsome, but with a certain "shiftiness" of the eye which was far from inspiring confidence, and with a trick of the tongue which suggested that his baptismal certificate probably bore the name of Anthony Martin. He found, too, that all he had heard regarding the youth and beauty of the chevalier's second wife was quite correct, and although she devoted herself a great deal to the Brazilian coffee planter and the Irish-Italian "Martinelli," she had a way of looking over at her middle-aged spouse, without his knowledge, that left no doubt in Cleek's mind regarding the real state of her feelings towards the man. And last, but not least by any means, he found the chevalier himself a frank, open-minded, open-hearted, lovable man who ought not, in the natural order of things, to have an enemy in the world. Despite his high-falutin' *nom de théâtre*, he was Belgian—a big, soft-hearted, easy-going, unsuspicious fellow, who worshipped his wife, adored his children, and loved every creature of the animal world.

How well that love was returned, Cleek saw when he went with him to that part of the building where his animals were kept, and watched them "nose" his hand or lick his cheek whenever the opportunity offered. But Nero, the lion, was perhaps the greatest surprise of all, for so tame, so docile, so little feared was the animal, that its cage-door was open, and they found one of the attendants squatting cross-legged inside and playing with it as though it were a kitten.

"There he is, doctor," said the chevalier, waving his hand towards the beast. "Ah, I will not believe that it was anything but an accident, sir. He loved my boy. He would hurt no one that is kind to him. Fetch him out, Tom, and let the doctor see him at close quarters."

Despite all these assurances of the animal's docility, Cleek could not but remember what the creature had done, and, in consequence, did not feel quite at ease when it came lumbering out of the cage with the attendant and ranged up alongside of him, rubbing its huge head against the chevalier's arm after the manner of an affectionate cat.

"Don't be frightened, sir," said Tom, noticing this. "Nothing more'n a big dog, sir. Had the care of him for eight years, I have—haven't I, chevalier?—and never a growl or scratch out of him. No 'smile' for your old Tom, is there, Nero, boy, eh? No fear! Ain't a thing as anybody does with him, sir, that I wouldn't do off-hand and feel quite safe."

"Even to putting your head in his mouth?" queried Cleek.

"Lord yes!" returned the man, with a laugh. "That's nothing. Done it many a day. Look here!" With that he pulled the massive jaws apart, and, bending down, laid his head within them. The lion stood perfectly passive, and did not offer to close his mouth until it was again empty. It was then that Cleek remembered and glanced round at young Scarmelli.

"He never 'smiles' for any but the chevalier and his son, I believe you said," he remarked. "I wonder if the chevalier himself would be as safe if he were to make a feint of doing that?" For the chevalier, like most of the other performers, had not changed his dress after the matinee, since the evening performance was soon to begin; and if, as Cleek had an idea, that the matter of costume and make-up had anything to do with the mystery of the thing, here, surely, was a chance to learn.

"Make a feint of it? Certainly I will, doctor," the chevalier replied. "But why a feint? Why not the actual thing?"

"No, please—at least, not until I have seen how the beast is likely to take it. Just put your head down close to his muzzle, chevalier. Go slow, please, and keep your head at a safe distance."

The chevalier obeyed. Bringing his head down until it was on a level with the animal's own, he opened the ponderous jaws. The beast was as passive as before; and, finding no trace of the coming of the mysterious and dreaded "smile," he laid his face between the double row of gleaming teeth, held it there a moment, and then withdrew it uninjured. Cleek took his chin between his thumb and forefinger and pinched it hard. What he had just witnessed would seem to refute the idea of either costume or make-up having any bearing upon the case.

"Did you do that to-day at the matinee performance, chevalier?" he hazarded, after a moment's thoughtfulness.

"Oh, yes," he replied. "It was not my plan to do so, however. I alter my performance constantly to give variety. To-day I had arranged for my little son to do the trick; but somehow—Ah! I am a foolish man, monsieur; I have odd fancies, odd whims, sometimes odd fears, since—since that awful night. Something came over me at the last moment, just as my boy came into the cage to perform the trick I changed my mind. I would not let him do it. I thrust him aside and did the trick myself."

"Oho!" said Cleek. "Will the boy do it to-night, then, chevalier?"

"Perhaps," he made reply. "He is still dressed for it. Look, here he comes now, monsieur, and my wife, and some of our good friends with him. Ah, they are so interested, they are anxious to hear what report you make upon Nero's condition."

Cleek glanced round. Several members of the company were advancing towards them from the "living-tent." In the lead was the boy, a little fellow of about twelve years of age, fancifully dressed in tights and tunic. By his side was his stepmother, looking pale and anxious. But although both Signor Martinelli and the Brazilian coffee planter came to the edge of the tent and looked out, it was observable that they immediately withdrew, and allowed the rest of the party to proceed without them.

"Dearest, I have just heard from Tom that you and the doctor are experimenting with Nero," said the chevalier's wife, as she came up with the others and joined him. "Oh, do be careful, do! Much as I like the animal, doctor, I shall never feel safe until my husband parts with it or gives up that ghastly 'trick.'"

"My dearest, my dearest, how absurdly you talk!" interrupted her husband. "You know well that without that my act would be commonplace, that no manager would want either it or me. And how, pray, should we live if that were to happen?"

"There would always be my salary; we could make that do."

"As if I would consent to live upon your earnings and add nothing myself! No, no! I shall never do that—never. It is not as though that foolish dream of long ago had come true, and I might hope one day to retire. I am of the circus, and of it I shall always remain."

"I wish you might not; I wish the dream might come true, even yet," she made reply. "Why shouldn't it? Wilder ones have come true for other people; why should they not for you?"

Before her husband could make any response to this, the whole trend of the conversation was altered by the boy.

"Father," he said, "am I to do the trick to-night? Señor Sperati says it is silly of me to sit about all dressed and ready if I am to do nothing, like a little super, instead of a performer and an artist."

"Oh, but that is not kind of the señor to say that," his father replied, soothing his ruffled feelings. "You are an artist, of course; never super—no, never. But if you shall do the trick or not, I cannot say. It will depend, as it did at the matinee. If I feel it is right, you shall do it; but if I feel it is wrong, then it must be no. You see, doctor," catching Cleek's eye, "what a little enthusiast he is, and with how little fear."

"Yes, I do see, chevalier; but I wonder if he would be willing to humour me in something? As he is not afraid, I've an odd fancy to see how he'd go about the thing. Would you mind letting him make the feint you yourself made a few minutes ago? Only, I must insist that in this instance it be nothing more than a feint, chevalier. Don't let him go too near at the time of doing it. Don't let him open the lion's jaws with his own hands. You do that. Do you mind?"

"Of a certainty not, monsieur. Gustave, show the good doctor how you go about it when papa lets you do the trick. But you are not really to do it just yet, only to bend the head near to Nero's mouth. Now then, come, see."

As he spoke he divided the lion's jaws and signalled the child to bend. He obeyed. Very slowly the little head drooped nearer to the gaping, full-fanged mouth, very slowly and very carefully, for Cleek's hand was on the boy's shoulder, Cleek's eyes were on the lion's face. The huge brute was as meek and as undisturbed as before, and there was actual kindness in its fixed eyes. But of a sudden, when the child's head was on a level with those gaping jaws, the lips curled backward in a ghastly parody of a smile, a weird, uncanny sound whizzed through the bared teeth, the passive body bulked as with a shock, and Cleek had just time to snatch the boy back when the great jaws struck together with a snap that would have splintered a skull of iron had they closed upon it.

The hideous and mysterious "smile" had come again, and, brief though it was, its passing found the boy's sister lying on the ground in a dead faint, the boy's stepmother cowering back, with covered eyes and shrill, affrighted screams, and the boy's father leaning, shaken and white, against the empty case and nursing a bleeding hand.

In an instant the whole place was in an uproar. "It smiled again! It smiled again!" ran in broken gasps from lip to lip; but through it all Cleek stood there, clutching the frightened child close to him, but not saying one word, not making one sound. Across the dark arena came a rush of running footsteps, and presently Señor Sperati came panting up, breathless and pale with excitement.

"What's the matter? What's wrong?" he cried. "Is it the lion again? Is the boy killed? Speak up!"

"No," said Cleek very quietly, "nor will he be. The father will do the trick to-night, not the son. We've had a fright and a lesson, that's all." And, putting the sobbing child from him, he caught young Scarmelli's arm and hurried him away. "Take me somewhere that we can talk in safety," he said. "We are on the threshold of the end, Scarmelli, and I want your help."

"Oh, Mr. Cleek, have you any idea—any clue?"

"Yes, more than a clue. I know how, but I have not yet discovered why. Now, if you know, tell me what did the chevalier mean, what did his wife mean, when they spoke of a dream that might have come true, but didn't? Do you know? Have you any idea? Or, if you have not, do you think your fiancée has?"

"Why, yes," he made reply. "Zelie has told me about it often. It is of a fortune that was promised and never materialized. Oh, such a long time ago, when he was quite a young man, the chevalier saved the life of a very great man, a Prussian nobleman of great wealth. He was profuse in his thanks and his promises, that nobleman; swore that he would make him independent for life, and all that sort of thing."

"And didn't?"

"No, he didn't. After a dozen letters promising the chevalier things that almost turned his head, the man dropped him entirely. In the midst of his dreams of wealth a letter came from the old skinflint's steward enclosing him the sum of six hundred marks, and telling him that as his master had come to the conclusion that wealth would be more of a curse than a blessing to a man of his class and station, he had thought better of his rash promise. He begged to tender the enclosed as a proper and sufficient reward for the service rendered, and 'should not trouble the young man any further.' Of course, the chevalier didn't reply. Who would, after having been promised wealth, education, everything one had confessed that one most desired? Being young, high-spirited, and bitterly, bitterly disappointed, the chevalier bundled the six hundred marks back without a single word, and that was the last he ever heard of the Baron von Steinheid from that day to this."

"The Baron von Steinheid?" repeated Cleek, pulling himself up as though he had trodden upon something. "Do you mean to say that the man whose life he saved—Scarmelli—tell me something: Does it happen by any chance that the 'Chevalier di Roma's' real name is Peter Janssen Pullaine?"

"Yes," said Scarmelli, in reply. "That is his name. Why?"

"Nothing, but that it solves the riddle, and—the lion has smiled for the last time! No, don't ask me any questions; there isn't time to explain. Get me as quickly as you can to the place where we left Mr. Narkom's motor. Will this way lead me out? Thanks! Get back to the others, and look for me again in two hours' time; and—Scarmelli!"

"Yes, sir?"

"One last word—don't let that boy get out of your sight for one instant, and don't, no matter at what cost, let the chevalier do his turn to-night before I get back. Good-bye for a time. I'm off."

Then he moved like a fleetly-passing shadow round the angle of the building, and two minutes later he was with Narkom in the red limousine.

"To the German embassy as fast as we can fly," he said as he scrambled in. "I've something to tell you about that lion's smile, Mr. Narkom, and I'll tell it while we're on the wing."

CHAPTER XVIII

It was nine o'clock and after. The great show at Olympia was at its height; the packed house was roaring with delight over the daring equestrianship of "Mlle. Marie de Zanoni," and the sound of the cheers rolled in to the huge dressing-tent, where the artists awaited their several turns, and the chevalier, in spangled trunks and tights, all ready for his call, sat hugging his child and shivering like a man with the ague.

"Come, come, buck up, man, and don't funk it like this," said Señor Sperati, who had graciously consented to assist him with his dressing because of the injury to his hand. "The idea of you losing your nerve, you of all men, and because of a little affair like that. You know very well that Nero is as safe as a kitten to-night, that he never has two smiling turns in the same week, much less the same day. Your act's the next on the programme. Buck up and go at it like a man."

"I can't, señor, I can't!" almost wailed the chevalier. "My nerve is gone. Never, if I live to be a thousand, shall I forget that awful moment, that appalling 'smile.' I tell you, there is wizardry in the thing; the beast is bewitched. My work in the arena is done—done for ever, señor. I shall never have courage to look into the beast's jaws again."

"Rot! You're not going to ruin the show, are you, and after all the money I've put into it? If you have no care for yourself, it's your duty to think about me. You can at least try. I tell you you must try! Here, take a sip of brandy, and see if that won't put a bit of courage into you. Hello!" as a burst of applause and the thud of a horse's hoofs down the passage to the stables came rolling in, "there's your wife's turn over at last; and there—listen! the ringmaster is announcing yours. Get up, man; get up and go out."

"I can't, señor—I can't! I can't!"

"But I tell you you must."

And just here an interruption came.

"Bad advice, my dear captain," said a voice—Cleek's voice—from the other end of the tent; and with a twist and a snarl the "señor" screwed round on his heel in time to see that other intruders were putting in an appearance as well as this unwelcome one.

"Who the deuce asked you for your opinion?" rapped out the "señor" savagely. "And what are you doing in here, anyhow? If we want the service of a vet., we're quite capable of getting one for ourselves without having him shove his presence upon us unasked."

"You are quite capable of doing a great many things, my dear captain, even making lions smile!" said Cleek serenely. "It would appear that the gallant Captain von Gossler, nephew, and, in the absence of one who has a better claim, heir to the late Baron von Steinheid—That's it, nab the beggar. Played, sir, played! Hustle him out and into the cab, with his precious confederate, the Irish-Italian 'signor,' and make a clean sweep of the pair of them. You'll find it a neck-stretching game, captain, I'm afraid, when the jury comes to hear of that poor boy's death and your beastly part in it."

By this time the tent was in an uproar, for the chevalier's wife had come hurrying in, the chevalier's daughter was on the verge of hysterics, and the chevalier's prospective son-in-law was alternately hugging the great beast-tamer and then shaking his hand and generally deporting himself like a respectable young man who had suddenly gone daft.

"Governor!" he cried, half laughing, half sobbing. "Bully old governor. It's over—it's over. Never any more danger, never any more hard times, never any more lion's smiles."

"No, never," said Cleek. "Come here, Madame Pullaine, and hear the good news with the rest. You married for love, and you've proved a brick. The dream's come true, and the life of ease and of luxury is yours at last, Mr. Pullaine."

"But, sir, I—I do not understand," stammered the chevalier. "What has happened? Why have you arrested the Señor Sperati? What has he done? I cannot comprehend."

"Can't you? Well, it so happens, chevalier, that the Baron von Steinheid died something like two months ago, leaving the sum of sixty thousand pounds sterling to one Peter Janssen Pullaine and the heirs of his body, and that a certain Captain von Gossler, son of the baron's only sister, meant to make sure that there was no Peter Janssen Pullaine and no heirs of his body to inherit one farthing of it."

"Sir! Dear God, can this be true?"

"Perfectly true, chevalier. The late baron's solicitors have been advertising for some time for news regarding the whereabouts of Peter

Janssen Pullaine, and if you had not so successfully hidden your real name under that of your professional one, no doubt some of your colleagues would have put you in the way of finding it out long ago. The baron did not go back on his word and did not act ungratefully. His will, dated twenty-nine years ago, was never altered in a single particular. I rather suspect that that letter and that gift of money which came to you in the name of his steward, and was supposed to close the affair entirely, was the work of his nephew, the gentleman whose exit has just been made. A crafty individual that, chevalier, and he laid his plans cleverly and well. Who would be likely to connect him with the death of a beast-tamer in a circus, who had perished in what would appear an accident of his calling? Ah, yes, the lion's smile was a clever idea—he was a sharp rascal to think of it."

"Sir! You—you do not mean to tell me that he caused that? He never went near the beast—never—even once."

"Not necessary, chevalier. He kept near you and your children; that was all that he needed to do to carry out his plan. The lion was as much his victim as anybody else—you or your children. What it did it could not help doing. The very simplicity of the plan was its passport to success. All that was required was the unsuspected sifting of snuff on the hair of the person whose head was to be put in the beast's mouth. The lion's smile was not, properly speaking, a smile at all, chevalier; it was the torture which came of snuff getting into its nostrils, and when the beast made that uncanny noise and snapped its jaws together, it was simply the outcome of a sneeze. The thing would be farcical if it were not that tragedy hangs on the thread of it, and that a life, a useful human life, was destroyed by means of it. Yes, it was clever, it was diabolically clever; but you know what Bobby Burns says about the best laid schemes of mice and men. There's always a Power—higher up—that works the ruin of them."

With that he walked by, and, going to young Scarmelli, put out his hand.

"You're a good chap and you've got a good girl, so I expect you will be happy," he said; and then lowered his voice so that the rest might not reach the chevalier's ears. "You were wrong to suspect the little stepmother," he added. "She's true blue, Scarmelli. She was only playing up to those fellows because she was afraid the 'señor' would drop out and close the show if she didn't, and that she and her husband and the children would be thrown out of work. She loves her husband—that's certain—and she's a good little woman; and, Scarmelli!"

"Yes, Mr. Cleek?"

"There's nothing better than a good woman on this earth, my lad. Always remember that. I think you, too, have found one. I hope you have. I hope you'll be happy. What's that? Owe me? Not a rap, my boy. Or, if you feel that you must give me something, give me your prayers for equal luck, and—send me a slice of the wedding cake. Good-night!"

And twisted round on his heel and walked out; making his way out to the streets and facing the journey to Clarges Street afoot. For to be absolutely without envy of any sort is not given to anything born of woman; and the sight of this man's happiness, the knowledge of this man's reward, brought upon him a bitter recollection of how far he still was from his own.

Would he ever get that reward? he wondered. Would he ever be nearer to it than he was to-night? It hurt—yes, it hurt horribly, sometimes, this stone-cold silence, this walking always in shadowed paths without a ray of light, without the certainty of arriving *anywhere*, though he plod onward for a lifetime—and the old feeling of savage resentment, the old sense of self-pity—the surest thing on God's earth to blaze a trail for the oncoming of the worst that is in a man—bit at the soul of him and touched him on the raw again.

He knew what that boded; and he also knew the antidote.

"Dollops, they broke into our holiday—they did us out of a part of it, didn't they, old chap?" he said, when he reached home at last and found the boy anxiously awaiting him. "Well, we'll have a day for every hour they deprived us of, a whole day, bonny boy. Pack up again and we'll be off to the land as God made it, and where God's things still live; and we'll have a fortnight of it—a whole blessed fortnight, my boy, with the river and the fields and the flowers and the dreams that hide in trees."

Dollops made no reply. He simply bolted for the kit-bag and began to pack at once. And the morrow, when it came, found these two—the servant who was still a boy, and the master who had discovered the way back to boyhood's secrets—forging up the shining river and seeking the Land of Nightingales again.

CHAPTER XIX

The spring had blossomed itself out and the summer had bloomed itself in. The holiday up the river was a thing of the past; the dreams of the Dreamer had given place to those sterner phases of life which must be coped with by the Realist; and Cleek was "back in harness" again.

A half-dozen more or less important cases had occupied his time since his return; but, although he had carried these to a successful issue and had again been lauded to the skies by the daily papers, the one word of praise from the one quarter whence he so earnestly desired to hear was never forthcoming.

Of Ailsa Lorne he had heard not a solitary thing, either directly or indirectly, since that day when he had put her into the taxicab at Charing Cross Station and saw her safely on her way to Hampstead before he went his own.

True, her silence was, as he had agreed, an admission that all was well with her and that she had secured the position in question; true it was also that it was not for her to take the initiative and break that silence; that he fully realised how impossible, for a girl born and bred as she had been, to voluntarily open up a correspondence with a man who was as yet little more than a mere acquaintance; but, all the same, he chafed under that silence and spent many a wakeful hour at night brooding on it.

In his heart he knew that if any advance was to be made, that advance was the man's duty, not the woman's; but the fear that she would think he was thrusting himself upon her, the dread that even yet the white soul of her could not but shrink from a closer association with him, kept him from taking one step towards breaking the silence he deplored.

The French have a proverb which says: "It is always the unexpected that happens." And it was the unexpected that happened in this case.

In the midst of his dejection, in the very depths of returning despair, there came to him this note from Mr. Narkom:

"My Dear Cleek,

"Kindly refrain from going out this evening. I shall call about nine o'clock, bringing with me Miss Ailsa Lorne, whom you doubtless remember, and her present patron, Angela, Countess Chepstow, the young widow of that ripping old warhorse, who, as you may recall, quelled that dangerous and fanatical rising of the Cingalese at Trincomalee. These ladies wish to see you with reference to a most extraordinary case, an inexplicable mystery, which both they and I believe no man but yourself can satisfactorily probe.

"Yours in haste,

"Maverick Narkom."

So, then, he was to see her again, to touch her hand, hear her voice, look into the eyes that had lighted him back from the path to destruction! Cleek's heart began to hammer and his pulses to drum. Needless to say, he took extraordinary care with his toilet that evening, with the result that when the ladies arrived there was nothing even vaguely suggestive of the detective about him.

"Oh, Mr. Cleek, do help us—please do," implored Ailsa, after the first greetings were over. "Lady Chepstow is almost beside herself with dread and anxiety over the inexplicable thing, and I have persuaded her that if anybody on earth can solve the mystery of it, avert the new and appalling danger of it, it is you! Oh, say that you will take the case, say that you will save little Lord Chepstow and put an end to this maddening mystery!"

"Little Lord Chepstow?" repeated Cleek, glancing over at the countess, who stood, a very Niobe in her grief and despair, holding out two imploring hands in silent supplication. "That is your ladyship's son, is it not?"

"Yes," she answered, with a sort of wail; "my only son—my only child. All that I have to love—all that I have to live for in this world."

"And you think the little fellow is in peril?"

"Yes—in deadly peril."

"From what source? From whose hand?"

"I don't know—I don't know!" she answered, distractedly. "Sometimes I am wild enough to suspect even Captain Hawksley, unjust and unkind as it seems."

"Captain Hawksley? Who is he?"

"My late husband's cousin; heir, after my little son, to the title and estates. He is very poor, deeply in debt, and the inheritance would put an end to all his difficulties. But he is fond of my son; they seem almost to worship each other. I, too, am fond of him. But, for all that, I have to remember that he and he alone would benefit by Cedric's death, and—and—wicked as it seems—Oh, Mr. Cleek, help me! Direct me! Sometimes I doubt him. Sometimes I doubt everybody. Sometimes I think of those other days, that other mystery, that land which reeks of them; and then—and then—Oh, that horrible Ceylon! I wish I had never set foot in it in all my life!"

Her agitation and distress were so great as to make her utterances only half coherent; and Ailsa, realising that this sort of thing must only perplex Cleek, and leave him in the dark regarding the matter upon which they had come to consult him, gently interposed.

"Do try to calm yourself and to tell the story as briefly as possible, dear Lady Chepstow," she advised. Then, taking the initiative, added quietly, "It begins, Mr. Cleek, at a period when his little lordship, whose governess I have the honour to be, was but two years old, and at Trincomalee, where his late father was stationed with his regiment four years ago. Somebody, for some absurd reason, had set afoot a ridiculous rumour that the English had received orders from the Throne to stamp out every religion but their own—in short, if the British were not exterminated, dreadful desecrations would occur, as they were determined—"

"To loot all the temples erected to Buddha, destroy the images, and make a bonfire of all the sacred relics," finished Cleek himself. "I rarely forget history, Miss Lorne, especially when it is such recent history as that memorable Buddhist rising at Trincomalee. It began upon an utterly unfounded, ridiculous rumour; it terminated, if my memory serves me correctly, in something akin to the very thing it was supposed to avert. That is to say, during the outburst of fanaticism, that most sacred of all relics—the holy tooth of Buddha—disappeared mysteriously from the temple of Dambool, and in spite of the fact that many lacs of rupees were offered for its recovery, it has never, I believe, been found, or even traced, to this day, although a huge fortune awaits the restorer, and, with it, overpowering honours from the native princes. Those must have been trying times, Lady Chepstow, for the commandant's wife, the mother of the commandant's only child?"

"Horrible! horrible!" she answered, with a shudder, forgetting for an instant the dangers of the present in the recollection of the tragical past. "For a period, our lives were not safe; murder hid behind every bush, skulked in the shadow of every rock and tree, and we knew not at what minute the little garrison might be rushed under cover of the darkness and every soul slaughtered before the relief force could come to our assistance. I died a hundred deaths in a day in my anxiety for husband and child. And once the very zealousness of our comrades almost brought about the horror I feared. Oh!"—with a shudder of horrified recollection and a covering of the eyes, as if to shut out the memory of it—"Oh! that night—that horrible night! Unknown to any of us, my baby, rising from the bed where I had left him sleeping, whilst I went outside to stand by Lord Chepstow, wandered beyond the line of defence, and, before anybody realised it, was out in the open, alone and unprotected.

"Ferralt, the cook, saw him first; saw, too, the crouching figure of a native, armed with a gun, in the shadow of the undergrowth. Without hesitation the brave fellow rushed out, fell upon the native before he could dart away, wrenched the gun from him, and brained him with the butt. A cry of the utmost horror rang out upon the air, and, uttering it, another native bounded out from a hiding-place close to where the first had been killed, and flew zigzagging across the open, where Cedric was. Evidently he had no intention of molesting the little fellow, for he fled straight on past him, still shrieking after the accident occurred; but to Ferralt it seemed as if his intention were to murder the boy, and, clapping the gun to his shoulder, in a panic of excitement, he fired. If it had been one of the soldiers, someone—anyone—who understood marksmanship and was not likely to be in a nervous quake over the circumstances, the thing could not have happened, although the fugitive was careering along in a direct line with my precious little one. But, with Ferralt—Oh, Mr. Cleek, can you imagine my horror when I saw the flash of that shot, heard a shrill cry of pain, and saw my child drop to the ground?"

"Good heaven!" exclaimed Cleek, agitated in spite of himself. "Then the blunderer shot the child instead of the native?"

"Yes; and was so horrified by the mishap that, without waiting to learn the result, he rushed blindly to the brink of a deep ravine, and threw himself headlong to death. But the injury to Cedric was only a trifling one after all. The bullet seemed merely to have grazed him in passing, and, beyond a ragged gash in the fleshy part of the thigh, he was not harmed at all. That I myself dressed and bandaged, and in a couple of weeks it was quite healed. But it taught me a lesson, that night of horror, and I never let my baby out of my sight for one instant from that time until the rising was entirely quelled.

"As suddenly as it had started, the trouble subsided. Native priests came under a flag of truce to Lord Chepstow, and confessed their error, acknowledged that they had never any right to suspect the British of any design upon their gods, for the loot of the temple had actually taken place in the midst of the rising, and they knew that it could not have come from the hands of the soldiers, for they had had them under surveillance all the time, and not one person of the race had ventured within a mile of the temple.

"Yet the tooth of Buddha had been taken, the sacred tooth which is more holy to Buddhists than the statue of Gautama Buddha itself. Their remorse was very real, and after that, to the day of his death from fever, eighteen months afterward, they could never show enough honour to Lord Chepstow. And even then their favour continued. They transferred to the little son the homage they had done the father, but in a far, far greater degree. If he had been a king's son they could have shown him no greater honour. Native princes showered him with rich gifts; if he walked out, his path was strewn with flowers by bowing maidens; if he went into the market-place, the people prostrated themselves before him.

"When I questioned Buddhist women of this amazing homage to Cedric, they gave me a full explanation. My son was sacred, they said. Buddha had withdrawn his favour from his people because of the evil they had done in suspecting the father and of the innocent life—Ferralt's—which had been sacrificed, and they had been commanded of the priests to do homage to the child and thereby appease the offended god, who, doubtless, had himself spirited away the holy tooth, and would not restore it until full recompense was made to the sacred son of the sacred dead.

"When it became known that I had decided to return to England with my boy, native princes offered me fabulous sums to remain, and when they found that I could not be tempted to stay, the populace turned out in every town and village through which we passed on our way to the ship, and bowing multitudes followed us to the very last. Nor did it cease with that, for in all the years that have followed, even here in London, the homage and worship have continued. My son can go nowhere but that he is followed by Cingalese; can see no man or woman of the race, but he or she prostrates herself before him and murmurs, 'Holy, most holy!' And daily, almost hourly, rich gifts are showered upon him from unknown hands, and he is watched over and guarded constantly. I tell you all this, Mr. Cleek, that you may the better understand how appalling is the horror which now assails us, how frightful is the knowledge that someone now seeks his life, and is using every means to take it."

"In other words, my dear Cleek," put in Narkom, as her ladyship, overcome with emotion, broke down suddenly, "there appears to be a sudden and inexplicable change of front on the part of these fanatics, and they now seem as anxious to bring evil to his little lordship as they formerly were to protect and cherish him. At any rate, someone of their order has, upon three separate occasions within the last month, endeavoured to kidnap him, and, in one instance, even attempted to murder him."

"Is that a fact?" queried Cleek sharply, glancing over at Miss Lorne. "You are certain it is not a fancy, but an absolute fact?"

"Yes; oh, yes!" she made answer, agitatedly. "Twice when I have gone into the Park with him, attempts have been made to separate us, to get him away from me; and once they did get him away—so swiftly, so adroitly, that he had vanished before I could turn round. But, although a bag had been thrown over his head to stifle his cries, he managed to make a very little one. I plunged screaming into the undergrowth from which that cry had come, and was just in time to save him. He was lying on the ground all bundled up in a bag, and his assailant, who must have heard me coming, had gone as if by magic. His little lordship, however, was able to tell me that the man was a Cingalese, and that he had 'tried to cut him with a knife.'"

"Cut him with a knife?" repeated Cleek in a reflective tone, and blew out a long, low whistle.

"Oh! but that is not the worst, Mr. Cleek," went on Ailsa. "Three days ago a woman—a very beautiful and distinguished-looking woman—called to see Lady Chepstow regarding the reference of a former servant, one Jane Catherboys, who used to be her ladyship's maid. After the caller left, a box of sugared violets was found lying temptingly open on a table in the main hall. Little Cedric is passionately fond of sugared violets, and, had he happened to pass that way before the box was discovered, he surely would have yielded to the temptation and eaten some. In removing the box the parlour-maid accidentally upset it, and before she could gather all the violets up her ladyship's little Pomeranian dog snapped up one and ate it. It was dead in six minutes' time! The sweets were simplý loaded with prussic acid. When we came to inquire into the matter in the hope of tracing the mysterious caller, we found that Jane Catherboys was no longer in need of a position; that she had been married for eight months; that she knew nothing whatever of the woman, and had sent no one to inquire into her references."

"All of which shows, my dear Cleek," put in Narkom significantly, "that, whatever hand is directing these attempts, it belongs to one who knows more than a mere outsider possibly could: in short, to one who is aware of his little lordship's excessive fondness for sugared violets, and is aware that Lady Chepstow once did have a maid named Jane Catherboys."

"If," said Cleek, "you mean to suggest by that that this points suspiciously in Captain Hawksley's direction, Mr. Narkom, permit me to say that it does not necessarily follow. The clever people of the under-world do nothing by halves nor without careful inquiry beforehand; that is what makes the difference between the common pickpocket and the brilliant swindler." He turned to Ailsa. "Is that all, Miss Lorne, or am I right in supposing that there is even worse to come?"

"Oh, much worse—much, Mr. Cleek! The knowledge that these would-be murderers, whoever they are, whatever may be their mysterious motive, have grown desperate enough to invade the house itself has driven Lady Chepstow well-nigh frantic. Of course, orders were immediately given to the servants that no stranger, no matter how well dressed, how well seeming, nor what the plea, was, from that moment, to be allowed past the threshold. We felt secure in that, knowing that no servant of the household would betray his or her trust, and that all would be on the constant watch for any further attempt. The unknown enemy must have found out about these precautions, for no stranger came again to the door. But last night a thing we had never counted upon happened. In the dead of the night the unknown broke into the house—into the very nursery itself—and but that Lady Chepstow, impelled she does not know by what, only that she was nervous and wakeful, and felt the need of some companionship, rose and carried the sleeping child into her own bed, he would assuredly have been murdered. The nurse, awakened by a horrible suffocating sensation, opened her eyes to find a man bending over her with a chloroform-soaked cloth, which he was about to lay over her face. She shrieked and fainted, but not before she saw the man spring to the little bed on the other side of her own, hack furiously at it with a long, murderous knife, then dart to the window and vanish. In the darkness he had not, of course, been able to see that that little bed was empty, for its position kept it in deep shadow, and hearing the household stir at the sound of the nurse's shriek, he struck out blindly and flew to save himself from detection. The nurse states that he was undoubtedly a foreigner—a dark-skinned Asiatic—and her description of him tallies with that his little lordship gave of the man who attempted to kill him that day in the Park. There, Mr. Cleek," she concluded, "that's the whole story. Can't you do something to help us—something to lift this constant state of dread and to remove this terrible danger from little Lord Chepstow's life?"

"I'll try, Miss Lorne; but it is a most extraordinary case. Where is the boy, now?"

"At home, closely guarded. We appealed to Mr. Narkom, and he generously appointed two detective officers to sit with his little lordship and keep constant watch over him whilst we are away."

"And in the meantime," added Mr. Narkom, "I've issued orders for a general rounding-up of all the Cingalese who can be traced or are known to be in town. Petrie and Hammond have that part of the job in hand, and if they hit upon any Asiatic who answers to the description of this murderous rascal—"

"I don't believe they will," interposed Cleek; "or, if they do, I don't for a moment believe he will turn out to be the guilty party. In other words, I have an idea that the fellow will prove to be a European."

"But, my dear fellow, both his little lordship and the nurse saw the man, and, as you have heard, they both agree that he was dark-skinned and quite Oriental in appearance."

"One of the easiest possible disguises, Mr. Narkom. A wig, a stick of grease-paint, a threepenny twist of crepe hair, and there you are! No, I do not believe that the man is a Cingalese at all; and, far from his having any connection with what you were pleased to term just now a change of front on the part of the Buddhists who have so long held the little chap as something sacred, I don't believe that they know anything about him. I base that upon the fact that the child is still treated with homage whenever he goes out, according to what Miss Lorne says, and that, with the single exception of that one woman who tried to poison him, nobody but just one man—this particular one man—has ever made any attempt to harm the boy. Fanatics, like those Cingalese, cleave to an idea to the end, Mr. Narkom; they don't cast it aside and go off at another tangent. You have heard what Lady Chepstow says the native women told her; the boy was sacred; their priests had commanded them to appease Buddha by doing homage to him until the tooth was found, and the tooth has not been found up to the present day! That means that nothing on earth could change their attitude toward him, that not one of the Buddhist sect would harm a solitary hair of his head for a king's ransom; so you may eliminate the Cingalese from the case entirely so far as the attempts upon the child's life are concerned. Whoever is making the attempts is doing so without their knowledge and for a purely personal reason."

"Then, in that case, this Captain Hawksley—"

"I'll have a look at that gentleman before I tumble into bed to-night, and you shall have my views upon that point to-morrow morning, Mr. Narkom. Frankly, things point rather suspiciously in the captain's direction, since he is apparently the only person likely to be benefited by the boy's death, and if a motive cannot be traced to some other person—" He stopped abruptly and held up his hand. Outside in the dim halls of the house a sudden noise had sprung into being, the noise of someone running upstairs in great haste, and, stepping quickly to the door, Cleek drew it sharply open. As he did so, Dollops came puffing up out of the lower gloom, a sheep's trotter in one hand, and a letter in the other.

"Law, Gov'nor!" groaned he, from midway on the staircase, "I don't believe as I'm ever goin' to be let get a square tuck-in this side of the buryin' ground! Jist finished wot was left of that there steak and kidney puddin', sir, and started on my seckint trotter, when I sees a pair o' legs nip parst the area railin's to the front door, and then nip off again like greased lightnin', and when I ups and does a flyin' leap up the kitchen stairs, there was this here envellup in the letter-box, and them there blessed legs nowheres in sight. I say, sir," agitatedly, "look wot's wrote on the envellup, will yer? And us always keepin' of it so dark."

Cleek plucked the letter from his extended hand, glanced at it, and puckered up his lips; then, with a gesture, he sent Dollops back below stairs, and, returning to the room, closed the door behind him.

"The enemy evidently knows all Lady Chepstow's movements, Mr. Narkom," he said. "I expect she and Miss Lorne have been under surveillance all day and have been followed here. Look at that!" He flung the letter down on a table as he spoke, and Narkom, glancing at it, saw printed in rude, illiterate letters upon the envelope the one word "Cleek." The identity of "Captain Burbage" was known to someone, and the secret of the house in Clarges Street was a secret no longer!

"Purposely disguised, you see. No one, not even a little child, would make such a botch of copying the alphabet as that," Cleek said, as he took the letter up and opened it. The sheet it contained was lettered in the same uncouth manner, and bore these words:

"Cleek, take a fool's advice and don't accept the Chepstow case. Be warned. If you interfere, somebody you care about will pay the price. You'll find it more satisfactory to buy a wedding bouquet than a funeral wreath!"

"Oh!" shuddered the two ladies in one breath. "How horrible! How cowardly!" And then, feeling that her last hope had gone, Lady Chepstow broke into a fit of violent weeping and laid her head on Ailsa's shoulder.

"Oh, my baby! My darling baby boy!" she sobbed. "And now they are threatening somebody that you, too, love. Of course, Mr. Cleek, I can't expect you to risk the sacrifice of your own dear ones for the sake of me and mine, and so—and so—Oh, take me away, Miss Lorne! Let me go back to my baby and have him while I may."

"Good-night, Mr. Cleek!" said Ailsa, stretching out a shaking hand to him. "Thank you so much for—for what you would have done but for this. And you were our last hope, too!"

"Why give it up then, Miss Lorne?" he said, holding her hand and looking into her eyes. "Why not go on letting me be your last hope—your only hope?"

"Yes, but they—they spoke of a funeral wreath."

"And they also spoke of a wedding bouquet! I am going to take the case, Miss Lorne—take it, and solve it, as I'm a living man. Thank you!" as her brimming eyes uplifted in deep thankfulness and her shaking hand returned the pressure of his. "Now, just give me five minutes' time in the next room—it's my laboratory, Lady Chepstow—and I'll tell you whether I shall begin with Captain Hawksley or eliminate him from the case entirely. You might go in ahead, Mr. Narkom, and get the acid bath and the powder ready for me. We'll see what the finger-prints of our gentle correspondent have to tell, and, if they are not in the records of Scotland Yard or down in my own private little book, we'll get a sample of Captain Hawksley's in the morning."

Then, excusing himself to the ladies, he passed into the inner room in company with Narkom, and carried the letter with him. When he returned it was still in his hand, but there were greyish smudges all over it.

"There's not a finger-print in the lot that is worth anything as a means of identification, Miss Lorne," he said. "But you and Lady Chepstow may accept my assurance that Captain Hawksley is not the man. The writer of this letter belongs to the criminal classes; he is on his guard against the danger of finger-prints, and he wore rubber gloves when he penned this message. When I find him, rest assured I shall find a man who has had dealings with the police before and whose finger-prints are on their records. I don't know what his game is nor what he's after yet, but I will inside of a week. I've an idea; but it's so wild a thing I'm almost afraid to trust myself to believe it possible until I stumble over something that points the same way. Now, go home with Lady Chepstow, and begin the work of helping me."

"Helping you? Oh, Mr. Cleek, can we? Is there anything we can do to help?"

"Yes. When you leave the house, act as though you are in the utmost state of dejection—and keep that up indefinitely. Make it appear, for I am certain you will be followed and spied upon, as if I had declined the case. But don't have any fear about the boy. The two constables will sleep in the room with him to-night and every night until the thing is cleared up and the danger past. To-morrow about dusk, however, you, personally, take him for a walk near the Park, and if, among the other Cingalese you may meet, you should see one dressed as an Englishman, and wearing a scarlet flower in his buttonhole, take no notice of how often you see him nor of what he may do."

"It will be you, Mr. Cleek?"

"Yes. Now go, please; and don't forget to act as if you and her ladyship were utterly broken-hearted. Also" —his voice dropped lower, his hand met her hand, and in the darkness of the hall a little silver-plated revolver was slipped into her palm —"also, take this. Keep it always with you, never be without it night or day, and if any living creature offers you violence, shoot him down as you would a mad dog. Good-night, and —remember!"

And long after she and Lady Chepstow had gone down and passed out into the night he stood there, looking the situation straight in the face and thinking his own troubled thoughts.

"A wedding bouquet! A threat against her, and the mention of a wedding bouquet!" he said, as he went back into the room and sat down to figure the puzzle out. "Only one creature in the world knows of my feelings in that direction, and only one creature in the world would be capable of that threat—Margot! But what interest could she or any of her tribe have in the death of Lady Chepstow's little son? Her game is always money. If she were after a ransom she would try to abduct the child, not to kill him, and if" —A sudden thought came and wrenched away his voice. He sat a moment twisting his fingers one through the other and frowning at the floor; then, of a sudden, he gave a cry and jumped to his feet. "Five lacs of rupees—a fortune! By George, I've got it!" he fairly shouted. "The wild guess was a correct one, I'll stake my life. Let's put it to the test."

CHAPTER XX

The summer twilight was deepening into the summer dusk when Ailsa, acting upon Cleek's advice, set forth with his little lordship the following evening, and turned her steps in the direction of the Park; but although, on her way there, she observed more than once that a swarthy-skinned man in European dress who wore a scarlet flower in his coat, and was so perfect a type of the Asiatic that he would have passed muster for one even among a gathering of Cingalese, kept appearing and disappearing at irregular intervals, it spoke well for the powers of imitation and self-effacement possessed by Dollops, that she never once thought of associating that young man with the dawdling messenger boy who strolled leisurely along with a package under his arm and patronised every bun-shop, winkle-stall, and pork-pie purveyor on the line of march.

For upward of an hour this sort of thing went on without any interruption or any solitary thing out of the ordinary, Ailsa strolling along leisurely, with the boy's hands in hers and his innocent prattle running on ceaselessly; then, of a sudden, whilst they were moving along close to the Park railings and in the shadow of the overhanging trees, the figure of an undersized man in semi-European costume, but wearing on his head the twisted turban of a Cingalese, issued from one of the gates, and well-nigh collided with them.

He drew back, murmuring an apology in pidgin-English, then, seeing the child, he salaamed profoundly and murmured in a voice of deep reverence, "Holy, most holy!" and prostrated himself, with his forehead touching the ground, until Ailsa and the child had passed on. But barely had they taken five steps before Cleek appeared upon the scene, and did exactly the same thing as the Cingalese.

"All right. You may go home now. I've got my man," he whispered, as Ailsa and the boy passed by. "Look for me at Chepstow House some time to-night." Then rose, as she walked on, and went after the man who first had prostrated himself before the child.

He had risen and gone on his way, but not before witnessing Cleek's obeisance, and flashing upon him a sharp, searching look. Cleek quickened his steps and shortened the distance between them. Now or never was the time to put to the test that wild thought which last night had hammered on his brain, for it was certain that this man was in very truth a Cingalese, and, as such, must know! He stretched forth his hand and touched the man, who drew back sharply, half indignantly, but changed his attitude entirely when Cleek, who knew Hindustani more than well, spoke to him in the native tongue.

"Unto thee, oh, brother!" Cleek said. "Thou, too, art of us, for thou, too, dost acknowledge the sacred shrine. These eyes have beheld thee."

All his hopes rested on the slim pillar of that one word, "shrine," and his heart almost ceased to beat as he watched to see how it was received. It broke, however, into a very tumult of disturbance in the next instant, for the man positively beamed as he gave reply.

"Sacred be the shrine!" he answered in Hindustani. "Clearly thou art of us—not of those others."

"Others? What others? I am but newly come to this country."

"Walk with me, then, to my abode, sup with me, eat of my salt, and I will tell thee then, oh, brother. But I forget: thou hast no knowledge of me. Listen, then. I am Arjeeb Noosrut, father of the High Priest Seydama, and it is among the people of my house that the gun is yet preserved. Nor has the blood of Seydama been ever washed from the wood of it. Come."

All in a moment a light seemed to break over Cleek's brain. The missing link had been supplied—the one thing that could make possible the wild thought which had come to him last night had been given into his hands, and here at last was the key to the amazing mystery! He turned without a word and went with Arjeeb Noosrut.

"What an ass!" he said to himself in the soundless words of thought "What an ass never to have suspected it when it is all so clear!"

Meantime Ailsa and the boy, dismissed from any further need of service, walked on through the deepening dusk and turned their faces homeward. But they had not gone twenty yards from the spot where Cleek had seen them last when his little lordship set up a joyful cry and pointed excitedly to a claret-coloured limousine which at that moment swung in from the middle of the roadway and slowed down as it neared the kerb.

"Oh, look, Miss Lorne; here's mummie's motor car; and I do believe that's Bimbi peeping out of it!" exclaimed the child—"Bimbi" being his pet name for Captain Hawksley—then broke, in wild excitement, from Ailsa's detaining hand and fled to a tall, military-looking man with a fair beard and moustache who had just that moment alighted from the vehicle. "It is Bimbi—it is!—it is!" he shouted as he ran. "Oh, Bimbi, I *am* glad!"

"Ceddie, dear, you mustn't be so boisterous!" chided Ailsa, coming up with him at the kerb. "How fond he is of you to be sure, Captain Hawksley. You've come for us, I suppose? Ceddie recognised the car at once."

"Yes; jump in," he answered. "Lady Chepstow sent me after you. She's nervous, poor soul, every moment the boy's away from her. Jump in, old chap!"—catching up his little lordship and swinging him inside. "Better take the back seat, Miss Lorne; it's more comfortable. Quite settled, both of you? That's good. All right, chauffeur—Home!"

Then he jumped in after them, closed the door, dropped into a seat, and the motor, making a wide curve out into the road, pelted away into the fast-gathering darkness.

"Bimbi says maybe he's going to be my daddy one day—didn't you, Bimbi?" said his little lordship, climbing up on to "Bimbi's" knee and snuggling close to him.

"I say, you know, you mustn't tell secrets, old chap!" was the laughing response. "Miss Lorne will hand you over to Nursie with orders to put you to bed if you do, *I* know—won't you, Miss Lorne?"

"He ought to be in bed, anyhow," responded Ailsa gaily; and then, this giving the conversation a merry turn, they talked and laughed and kept up such a chatter that three-quarters of an hour went like magic and nobody seemed aware of it. But suddenly Ailsa thought, and then put her thoughts into words.

"What a long time we are in getting home," she said, and bent forward so that the light from the window might fall upon the dial of her wrist watch, then gave a little startled cry and half rose from her seat. For the darkness was now tempered by moonlight, and she could see that they were no longer in the populous districts of the town, but were speeding along past woodlands and open fields in the very depths of the country. "Good gracious! Johnston must have lost his senses!" she exclaimed agitatedly. "Look where we are, Captain Hawksley!—out in the country with only a farmhouse or two in sight. Johnston! Johnston!" She bent forward and rapped wildly on the glass panel. "Johnston, stop!—turn round!—are you out of your head? Captain Hawksley, stop him—stop him for pity's sake!"

"Sit down, Miss Lorne." He made reply in a low, level voice, a voice in which there was something that made her pluck the child to her and hold him right to her breast. "You are not going home to-night. You are going for a ride with me; and if—Oh, that's your little game, is it?" lurching forward as she made a frantic clutch at the handle of the door. "Sit down, do you hear me?—or it will be worse for you! There!"—the cold bore of a revolver barrel touched her temple and wrung a quaking gasp of terror from her—"Do you feel that? Now you sit down and be quiet! If you make a single move, utter a single cry, I'll blow your brains out before you've half finished it. Look here, do you know who you're dealing with now? See!"

His hand reached up and twitched away the fair beard and moustache; he bent forward so that the moonlight through the glass could fall on his face. It had changed as his voice had now changed, and she saw that she was looking at the man who in those other days of stress and trial had posed as "Gaston Merode," brother to the fictitious "Countess de la Tour."

"You!" she said in a bleak voice of desolation and fright. "Dear heaven, that horrible Margot's confederate, the King of the Apaches!"

"Yes!" he rapped out. "You and that fellow Cleek came between us in one promising game, but I'm hanged if you shall do it in this one! I want this boy, and—I've got him. Now, you call off Cleek and tell him to drop this case—to make no effort to follow us or to come between us and the kid—or I'll slit your throat after I've done with his little lordship here. Lanisterre!"—to the chauffeur—"Lanisterre, do you hear?"

"Oui, monsieur."

"Give her her head—full speed—and get to the mill as fast as you can. Margot will be with us in another two hours' time."

CHAPTER XXI

Through the ever-deepening dusk Cleek and Arjeeb Noosrut moved onward together; and onward behind them moved, too, the same dilatory messenger boy who had loitered about in the neighbourhood of the park, squandering his halfpence now as then, leaving a small trail of winkle shells and trotter bones to mark the record of his passage, and never seeming to lose one iota of his appetite, eat as much and as often as he would.

The walk led down into the depths of Soho, that refuge of the foreign element in London; but long before they halted at the narrow doorway of a narrow house in a narrow side street—a street that seemed to have gone to sleep in an atmosphere of gloom and smells—Cleek had adroitly "pumped" Arjeeb Noosrut dry, and the riddle of the sacred son was a riddle to him no longer. He was now only anxious to part from the man and return with the news to Lady Chepstow, and was casting round in his mind for some excuse to avoid going indoors with him and wasting precious time in breaking bread and eating salt, when there lurched out of an adjoining doorway an ungainly figure in turban and sandals and the full flower of that grotesque regalia which passes muster at cheap theatres and masquerade balls for the costume of a Cingalese. The fellow had bent forward out of the deeper darkness of the house-passage into the murk and gloom of the ill-lit street, and was straining his eyes as if in search for someone long expected.

"Dog of an infidel!" exclaimed Arjeeb Noosrut, speaking in Hindustani, and spitting on the pavement as he caught sight of the man. "See, well-beloved, he is of those 'others' of which I spoke when I first met thee. There are many of them, but true believers none. They dwell in a room huddled up as unclean things in the house there; they drink and make merry far into the night, and a woman veiled and in European garb comes to them and drinks with them sometimes—and sometimes a man of her kind with her; and they speak a tongue that is not the tongue of our people; yet have I seen them go forth into the city and do homage as we to the sacred son."

Cleek sucked in his breath and, twitching round, stared at the dim figure leaning forward in the dim light.

"By George!" he said to himself; "if I know anything, I ought to know the slouch and the low-sunk head of the Apache! And the woman comes!—

And a man comes!—And there are five lacs of rupees! I wonder! I wonder! But no—she wouldn't come here, to a place like this, if she had ventured back into England and had called some of the band over to help. She'd go to the old spot—to the old haunt where she and I used to lie low and laugh whilst the police were hunting for me. She'd go there, I'm sure, to the old Burnt Acre Mill, where, if you were 'stalked,' you could open the sluice gates and let the Thames and the mill stream rush in and meet, and make a hell of whirling waters that would drown a fish. She would go there if it were she. And yet—it is an Apache: I swear it is an Apache!"

He turned and looked back at Arjeeb Noosrut, then raised his hand and brushed it down the back of his head, which was always the sign "Wait!" to Dollops—and then spoke as calmly as he could.

"Brother, I will go in and break bread and eat salt with thee," he said. "But I may do no more, for to-night I am in haste."

"Come then," the man answered; and taking him by the hand, led him in and up to a room at the back of the second storey, where, hot as the night was, the windows were closed and a woman squatted before a lighted brasier, was dripping the contents of an oil cruse over the roasting carcass of a young kid.

"It is to shut out the sounds of the vile infidel orgies from the house adjoining," explained Arjeeb Noosrut, as Cleek walked to the tightly closed window and leant his forehead against it. "Yet, if the heat oppresses thee—"

"It does," interposed Cleek, and leant far out into the darkness as though sucking in the air when the sash was raised and the thing which had been only a dim babel of wordless sounds a moment before, became now the riotous laughter and the ribald comments of men upon the verses of a comic song which one of their number was joyously singing.

"French!" said Cleek under his breath, as he caught the notes of the singer and the words of his audience—"French—I knew it!"

Then he drew in his head, and having broken of the bread and eaten of the salt which, at a word from Arjeeb Noosrut, the woman brought on a wicker tray and laid before them, he moved hastily to the door.

"Brother and son of the faithful, peace be with thee—I must go," he said. "But I come again; and it is written that thou shalt be honoured above all men when I return to thee, and that the true believers—the true sons of Holy Buddha—shall have cause to set thy name at the head of the records of those who are most blest of him!"

Then he salaamed and passed out; and, closing the door behind him, ran like a hare down the narrow stairs. At the door Dollops rose up like the imp in a pantomime and jumped toward him.

"Law, Gov'nor, I'm nigh starved a-waitin' for yer!" he said in a whisper. "Wot's the lay now? A double-quick change? I've got the stuff here, look!" — holding up the package he was carrying — "or a chance for me to do some fly catchin' with me bloomin' tickle tootsies?"

The man in the Cingalese costume had vanished from the doorway of the adjoining house, and, catching the boy by the arm, Cleek hurried him to it and drew him into the dark passage.

"I'm going to the back; I'm going to climb up to the windows of the second storey and see who's there and what's going on," he whispered. "Lie low and watch. I think it's Margot's gang."

"Oh, colour me blue! Them beauties? And in London? I'd give a tanner for a strong cup o' tea!"

"Sh-h-h! Be quiet—speak low. Don't be seen, but keep a close watch; and if anybody comes downstairs—"

"He's mine!" interjected Dollops, stripping up his sleeves. "Glue to the eyebrows and warranted to stick! Nip away, Gov'nor, and leave it to the tickle tootsies and me!" Then, as Cleek moved swiftly and silently down the passage and slipped out into a sort of yard at the back of the house, he pulled out his roll of brown paper squares and his tube of adhesive, and crawling upstairs on his hands and knees, began operations at the top step. But he had barely got the first "plaster" fairly made and ready to apply when there came a rush of footsteps behind him and he was obliged to duck down and flatten himself against the floor of the landing to escape being run down by a man who dashed in through the lower floor, flew at top speed up the stairs, and, with a sort of blended cheer and yell, whirled open a door on the landing above and vanished. In a twinkling other cheers rang out, there was the sound of hastily moving feet and the uproar of general excitement.

"Oh, well, if you won't stop to be waited on, gents, help yourselves!" said Dollops with a chuckle. Then he began backing hastily down the stairs, squirting the contents of the tube all over the steps, and concluded the operation by scattering all the loose sheets of paper on the floor at the foot of them before slipping out into the street and composedly waiting.

Meantime Cleek, sneaking out through the rear door, found himself in a small, brick-paved yard hemmed in by a high wall thickly fringed on the top with a hedge of broken bottles. At one time in its history the house had been occupied by a catgut maker, and the rickety shed in which he had carried on his calling still clung, sagging and broken-roofed, to the building itself, its rotten slates all but vanished, and its interior piled high with mildewed bedding, mouldy old carpet, broken furniture, and refuse of every sort.

A foot or two above the roof-level of this glowed—two luminous rectangles in the blackness of darkness—the windows of the back room on the second storey; and out of these came floating still the song, the laughter, and the jabbered French he had heard in the house next door. It did not take him long to make up his mind. Gripping the swaying supports of the sagging shed, he went up it with the agility of a monkey, crawled to the nearer of the two windows, and, cautiously raising himself, peeped in. What he saw made him suck in his breath sharply and sent his heart hammering hard and fast.

A dozen men were in the room—men whose faces, despite an inartistic attempt to appear Oriental, he recognized at a glance and knew better than he knew his own. About them lay discarded portions of Cingalese attire, thrown off because of the heat, and waiting to be resumed at any moment. The air was thick with tobacco smoke and rank with spirituous odours. Sprawled figures were everywhere, and on a sort of couch against the opposite wall, a cigarette between her fingers, a glass of absinthe at her elbow, her laughter and badinage ringing out as loudly as any, lay the lissom figure of Margot!

But even as Cleek looked in upon it the picture changed. Swift, sharp, and sudden came the rattle of flying feet on the outer stairs. Margot flung aside her cigarette and jumped up, the song and the laughter came to an abrupt end, the door flew open, and with a shout and a cheer a man bounced into the room.

"Serpice! Ah, *le bon Dieu!* it is Serpice at last!" cried out Margot in joyous excitement, as she and the others crowded round him. "Soul of a sluggard, don't waste time in laughing and capering like this! Speak up, speak up, you hear? Are we to fly at once to the mill and join him? Has he succeeded? Is it done?"

"Yes, yes, yes!" shouted back Serpice, throwing up his cap and capering. "It is done! It is done! Under the very nose of the cracksman, too! Merode's got them—got them both! The little lordship and the Mademoiselle Lorne, too! They took the bait like gudgeons; they stepped into the automobile without a fear, and—whizz! it was off to the mill like that! La, la, la! We win, we win, we win!"

The shock of the thing was too much for Cleek. Carried out of himself by the knowledge that the woman he loved was now in peril of her life, discretion forsook him, blind rage mastered him, and he did one of the few foolish things of his life.

"You lie, you brute—you lie!" he shouted, jumping up into full view. "God help the man who lays a hand on her! Let him keep his life from me if he can!"

"The cracksman!" yelled out Serpice. "The cracksman! The cracksman!" echoed Margot and the rest. Then a pistol barked and spat, the light was swept out, a bullet sang past Cleek's ear, and he realised how foolish he had been. For part of the crowd came surging to the window, part went in one blind rush for the door to head him off and hem him in, and, through the din and hubbub rang viciously the voice of Margot shrilling out: "Kill him! Kill him!" as though nothing but the sight of his blood would glut the malice of her.

It was neck or nothing now, and the race was to the swift. He dropped through a gap in the ragged roof—sheer down, like a shot—into the rubble and refuse below; he lurched through the shed to the door, and through that to the black passage leading to the street—the clatter on the higher staircase giving warning of the crowd coming after him—and flew like a hare hard pressed toward the outer door, and then—just then, when every little moment counted—there was a scrambling sound, a chorus of oaths, a slipping, a sliding, a bang on one step and a bump on another; and, as he darted by, and sprang out into the street, the hall was filled with a writhing, scuffling, swearing mass of glue-covered men struggling in a whirling waste of loose brown paper.

"This way! come quickly, for your life!" he shouted to Dollops, as he came plunging out into the street. "They've got them—got his little lordship! Got Miss Lorne—in spite of me. Come on! come on! come on!"—and flew like an arrow from crossing to crossing and street to street with Dollops, like a shadow, at his heels.

A sudden swerve to the right brought them into a lighted and populous thoroughfare. Italian restaurants, German delicatessen shops, eating places of a dozen other nationalities lined the pavements on both sides of the street, and, in front of these a high-power motor stood, protected by the watchful eye of an accommodating policeman while the chauffeur sampled Chianti in a wine-shop close by. With a rush and a leap Cleek was upon it, and with another rush and a leap the constable was upon him, only to be greeted with the swift flicking open of a coat and the gleam of a badge that every man in the force knew.

"Cleek?"

"Yes! In the name of The Yard; in the name of the king! get out of the way! In with you, Dollops! We'll get the brutes yet!"

Then he bent over, threw in the clutch, and discarding all speed laws, sent the car humming and tearing away.

"Hold tight!" he said, through his teeth. "Whatever comes, we've got to get to Burnt Acre Mill inside of an hour. If you know any prayers, Dollops, say them."

"The Lord fetch us home in time for supper!" gulped the boy obediently. "S'help me, Gov'nor, the wind's goin' through my teeth like I was a mouth organ—and I'm hollow enough for a flute!"

CHAPTER XXII

It is strange how, in moments of stress and trial, even in times of tragedy, the most commonplace thoughts will intrude themselves and the mind separate itself from the immediate events. As Merode put the cold muzzle of the revolver to Ailsa's temple and she ought, one would have supposed, to have been deaf and blind to all things but the horror of her position, one of these strange mental lapses occurred, and her mind, travelling back over the years of her early schooldays, dwelt on a punishment task set her by her preceptress—the task of copying three hundred times the phrase "Discretion is the better part of valour."

As the recollection of that time rose before her mental vision, the value of the phrase itself forced its worth upon her and, huddling back in the corner of the limousine, she clutched the frightened child to her and gave implicit obedience to Merode's command to make no effort to attract attention either by word or deed. And he, fancying that he had thoroughly cowed her, withdrew the touch of the weapon from her temple, but held it ready for possible use in the grip of his thin, strong hand.

For a time the limousine kept straight on in its headlong course, then, of a sudden, it swerved to the left, the gleam of a river—all silver with moonlight—struck up through a line of trees on one side of the car, the blank unbroken dreariness of a stretch of waste land spread out upon the other; and presently, by the slowing down of the motor, Ailsa guessed that they were nearing their destination. They reached it a few moments later, and a peep from the window, as the vehicle stopped, showed her the outlines of a ruined watermill—ghostly, crumbling, owl-haunted—looming black against the silver sky.

A crumbled wheel hung, rotten and moss-grown, over a dry water-course, where straggling willows stretched out from the bank and trailed their long, feathery ends a yard or so above the level of the weeds and grasses that carpeted the sandy bed of it, and along its edge—once built as a protection for the heedless or unwary, but now a ruin and a wreck—a moss-grown wall with a narrow, gateless archway made an irregular shadow on the moon-drenched earth. She saw that archway and that dry water-course, and a new, strong hope arose within her. Discretion had played its part; now it was time for Valour to take the stage.

"Come, get out—this is the end," said Merode, as he unlatched the door of the limousine and alighted. "You may yell here until your throat splits, for all the good it will do you. Lanisterre, show us a light; the path to the door is uncertain, and the floor of the mill is unsafe. This way, if you please, Miss Lorne. Let me have the boy—I'll look after him!"

"No, no!—not yet! Please, not yet!" said Ailsa, with a little catch in her voice as she plucked his little lordship to her and smothered his frightened cries against her breast. "Let me have him whilst I may—let me hold him to—the last, Monsieur Merode. His mother trusts me. She will want to know that I—I stood by him until I could stand no longer. Please!—we are so helpless—I am so fond of him, and—he is such a very little boy. Listen! You want me to write to Mr. Cleek; you want me to ask something of him. I won't do it for myself—no, not if you kill me for refusing. I'll never do it for myself; but—but I will do it if you won't separate us until he has had time to say his prayers."

"Oh, all right, then," he agreed. "If it's any consolation doing a fool's trick like that, why—do it! Now come along, and let's get inside the mill without any more nonsense. Lanisterre, bring that lantern here so that mademoiselle can see the path to the door. This way, if you please, Miss Lorne."

"Thank you," she said as she alighted and moved slowly in the direction of the door, soothing the child as they crept along almost within touch of the crumbling wall. "Ceddie, darling, don't cry. You are a brave little hero, I know, and heroes are never afraid to die." From the tail of her eye she watched Merode. He seemed to realise from these words to the child that she was reconciled to the inevitable, and with an air of satisfaction he put the pistol back into his pocket and walked beside her. She kept straight on with her soothing words; and, in the half-shadow, neither Merode nor Lanisterre could see that one hand was lost in the folds of her skirt.

"Ceddie, darling, let Miss Lorne be able to tell mummie that her little man was a hero; that he died, as heroes always die, without a fear or a weakening to the very last. I'll stand by you, precious; I'll hold your hand; and, when the time comes—"

It came then! The gateless archway was reached at last; and the thing she had been planning all along now became possible. With one sudden push she sent the boy reeling down the incline into the dry water-course, flashed round sharply, and before Merode really knew how the thing happened, she was standing with her back to the arch and a revolver in her levelled hand.

"Throw up your arms—throw them up at once, or, as God hears me, I'll shoot!" she cried. "Run, Ceddie—run, baby! He shan't follow you—I'll kill him if he tries!"

"You idiot!" began Merode, and made a lurch toward her. But the pistol barked, and something white-hot zigzagged along his arm and bit like a flame into his shoulder.

"Up with your hands—up with them!" she said in a voice that shook with excitement as he howled out and made a reeling backward step. "Next time it will be the head I aim at, not the arm!" Then, lifting up her voice in one loud shriek that made the echoes bound, she called with all her strength; "Help, somebody—for God's sake help! Scream, Ceddie—scream! Help! Help!"

And lo! as she called, as if a miracle had been wrought, out of the darkness an answering voice called back to her, and the wild, swift notes of a motor horn bleated along the lonely road.

"I'm coming—I—Cleek!" that voice rang out. "Hold your own—hold it to the last, Miss Lorne, and God help the man who lays a finger on you!"

"Mr. Cleek! Mr. Cleek, oh, thank God!" she flung back with all the rapture a human voice could contain. "Come on, come on! I've got him— got that man Merode, and the boy is safe, the boy is safe! Come on! come on! come on!"

"We're a-comin', miss, you gamble on that—and the lightnin's a fool to us!" shouted Dollops in reply. "Let her have it, Gov'nor! Bust the bloomin' tank. Give her her head; give her her feet; give her her blessed merry-thought if she wants it! Hurrah! hurrah! hurrah!"

And then, just then, when she most needed her strength and her courage, Ailsa's evaporated. The reaction came and with the despairing cries of Merode and Lanisterre ringing in her ears, she sank back, weak, white, almost fainting—and, leaning against the side of the archway, began to laugh and to sob hysterically. Merode seized that one moment and sprang to the breach.

Realising that the game was all but up, that there was nothing for him now but to save his own skin if he could, he called out to Lanisterre to follow him, then plunged into the mill, swung over the lever which controlled the sluice gates, and, darting out by the back way, fled across the waste.

But behind him he left a scene of indescribable horror, and the shrill screaming of a little child told him when that horror began. For as the sluice gates opened a sullen roar sounded; on one side the diverted millstream, and on the other the river, rose as two solid walls of water, rushed forward and—met; and in the twinkling of an eye the old water-course was one wild, leaping, roaring, gyrating whirlpool of up-flung froth and twisting waves that bore in their eddying clutch the battling figure of a drowning child.

Even before he came in sight of it the roaring waters and the fearful splash of their impact told Cleek what had been done. He could hear Ailsa's screams; he could hear the boy's feeble cries, and a moment later, when the whizzing motor panted up through the moonlight and sped by the broken wall, there was Ailsa, fairly palsied with fright, clinging weakly to the crumbling arch and uttering little sobbing, wordless, incoherent moans of fright as she stared down into the hell of waters; and below, in the foam, a little yellow head was spinning round and round and round, in dizzying circles of torn and leaping waves.

"Heavens, Gov'nor!" began Dollops in a voice of appalling despair; but before he could get beyond that, Cleek's coat was off, Cleek's body had described a sort of semi-circle, and—the child was no longer alone in the whirlpool!

Battling, struggling, fairly leaping, as a fish leaps in a torrent, one moment half out of the water, the next wholly submerged, Cleek struck from eddy to eddy, from circle to circle; until that little yellow head was within reach, then put forth his hand and gripped it, pulled it to him, and in another moment he was whirling round and round the whirlpool's course with the child clutched to him and his wet, white face gleaming wax-like over the angle of his shoulder.

They had not made the half of the first circle thus before Dollops had leaped to the bending willows, had scrambled up the rough trunk of the nearest of them, and, pushing his weight out upon a strong and supple bough, bent it downward until the half of its strongest withes were deep in the whirling waters.

"Grab 'em, Gov'nor—grab 'em when you come by!" he sang out over the roar of the waters. "They'll hold you, sir—hold a dozen like you; and if—Well played! Got 'em the first grab! Hang on! Get a tight grip! Now then, sir, hand over hand till you're at the bank! Good biz! Good biz! Blest if you won't be goin' in for the circus trade next! Steady does it, sir—steady, steady! Goal, by Jupiter! Now then, hand me up the nipper—I should say the young gent—and in two minutes' time—Right! Got him! 'Ere you are, Miss Lorne—lay hold of his little lordship, will you? I've got me blessed hands full a keepin' to me perch whilst the guv'nor's a-wobbling of the branch like this. Good biz! Now then, sir, another 'arf a yard. That's the call! Hands on this bough and foot on the bank there. One, two, three—knew you'd do it! Safe as houses, Gawd bless yer bully heart!"

And then as Cleek, wet, white, panting, dragged himself out of the clutch of the whirlpool and lay breathing heavily on the ground:

"By gums, Gov'nor," Dollops added as he looked down on the whirling waters, "what an egg-beater it would make, wouldn't it, sir? Ain't got such a thing as a biscuit about yer, have you? Me spine's a rasping holes in me necktie, and I'm so flat you could slip me into a pillar box and they'd take me home for a penny stamp."

But Cleek made no reply. Wet and spent after his fierce struggle with the whirling fury he had just escaped, he lay looking up into Ailsa's eyes as she came to him with the sobbing child close pressed to her bosom and all heaven in her beaming face.

"It is not the 'funeral wreath' after all, you see, Miss Lorne," he said. "It came near to being it; but—it is not, it is not. I wonder, oh, I wonder!"

Then he laughed the foolish, vacuous laugh of a man whose thoughts are too happy for the banality of words.

CHAPTER XXIII

It was midnight and after. In the close-curtained library of Chepstow House, Cleek, with his little lordship sleeping in his arms, sat in solemn conclave with Lady Chepstow, Captain Hawksley, and Maverick Narkom; and while they talked, Ailsa, like a restless spirit, wandered to and fro, now lifting the curtains to peep out into the darkness, now listening as if her whole life's hope lay in the coming of some expected sound. And in her veins there burned a fever of suspense.

"So you failed to get the rascals, did you, Mr. Narkom?" Cleek was saying. "I feared as much; but I couldn't get word to you sooner. We injured the machine in that mad race to the mill, and of course we had to come at a snail's pace afterwards. I'm sorry we didn't get Margot—sorrier still that that hound Merode got away. They are bound to make more trouble before the race is run. Not for her ladyship, however, and not for this dear little chap. Their troubles are at an end, and the sacred son will be a sacred son no longer."

"Oh, Mr. Cleek, do tell me what you mean," implored Lady Chepstow. "Do tell me how—"

"Doctor Fordyce, at last!" struck in Ailsa excitedly, as the door-bell and knocker clashed and the butler's swift footsteps went along the hall. "Now we shall know, Mr. Cleek—oh, now we shall know for certain!"

"And so shall all the world," he replied as the door opened and the doctor was ushered into the room. "I don't think you were ever so welcome anywhere or at any time before, doctor," he added with a smile. "Come and look at this little chap. Bonny little specimen of a Britisher, isn't he?"

"Yes; but my dear sir, I—I was under the impression that I was called to a scene of excitement; and you seem as peaceful as Eden here. The constable who came for me said it was something to do with Scotland Yard."

"So it is, doctor. I had Mr. Narkom send for you to perform a very trifling but most important operation upon his little lordship here."

"Upon Cedric!" exclaimed Lady Chepstow, rising in a panic of alarm. "An operation to be performed upon my baby boy? Oh, Mr. Cleek, in the name of Heaven—"

"No, your ladyship, in the name of Buddha. Don't be alarmed. It is only to be a trifling cut—a mere re-opening of that little wound in the thigh which you dressed and healed so successfully at Trincomalee. You made a mistake, all of you, that night when the boy was shot. The native poor Ferralt saw skulking along with the gun was not a mere tribesman and had not the very faintest thought of discharging that weapon at your little son, or, indeed, at anybody else in the world. He was the High Priest Seydama, guardian of the Holy Tooth—the one living being who dared by right to touch it or to lay hands upon the shrine that contained it. Fearful, when the false rumour of that intended loot was circulated, that infidel eyes should look upon it, infidel hands profane the sacred relic, he determined to remove it from Dambool to the rock-hewn temple of Galwihara and to enshrine it there. For the purpose of giving no clue to his movements, he chose to abandon his priestly vestments, to disguise himself as a common tribesman, and, the better to defeat the designs of any who might penetrate that disguise and endeavour to take the sacred relic from him and hold it for ransom, he hid the Holy Tooth in the barrel of a gun. That gun was in his hands, your ladyship, when Ferralt rushed out and brained him."

"In his hands? Oh, Mr. Cleek, then—then—" Her voice all but failed her as a sudden realization came. "That relic, that fetish! If it was in that gun at that time, then it is now—"

"Embedded in the fleshy part of the boy's thigh," said Cleek, finishing the sentence for her. "Inclosed, doubtless, in a sac or cyst which Mother Nature has wrapped round it, the tooth is there—in your little son's body; and for five whole years he has been the living shrine that held it!"

It was quite true—as events rapidly and completely proved.

Ten minutes later, the trifling operation was concluded; the boy lay whimpering in his mother's arms and the long-lost relic was on the surgeon's palm.

"Take it, Captain Hawksley," said Cleek, lifting it between his thumb and forefinger and carrying it to him. "There is a man in Soho—one Arjeeb Noosrut—who will know it when he sees it; and there is a vast reward. Five lacs of rupees will pay off no end of debts, my friend; and a man with that balance at his banker's can't be thought a mere fortune-hunter when he asks for the hand of the woman he loves."

The Captain didn't ask for *his*, however—he simply jumped up and grabbed it.

"By George, you're a brick!" he said, with something uneven in his voice—something that was like laughter and tears all jumbled up together;

then he glanced over at Lady Chepstow, and flushed, and floundered, and stammered confusedly, but went on shaking Cleek's hand all the time. "It's ripping of you—it's bully, dear chap, but—I say, you know, it isn't fair. It's jolly uneven. *You* found out. You ought at least to have a share in the reward."

"Not I," said Cleek, with an airy laugh. "Like the fellow who was born with a third leg, 'I have no use for it,' Captain. But if you really want to give any part of it away, bank a thousand to the credit of my boy Dollops to be turned over to him when he's twenty-one. And you might make Mr. Narkom, and, if she will accept the post, Miss Lorne, his trustees."

Miss Lorne faced round and looked at him; and even from that distance he could see that her mouth was moving tremulously and there was something shining in the corner of her eye.

"I accept that position with pleasure, Mr. Cleek," she said. "It is the act of a man and—a gentleman. Thank you! Thank you." And came down the long length of the room with her hand outstretched to take his.

CHAPTER XXIV

He took it with that grave courtesy, that gentle dignity of bearing which at times distinguished his deportment and was, indeed, as puzzling to her as it was to Mr. Maverick Narkom. It came but rarely, that peculiar air, but it was very noticeable when it did come, although the man himself seemed totally oblivious of it. Miss Lorne noticed it now, just as she had noticed it that day in the train when she had said banteringly: "I am not used to Court manners. Where, if you please, did you acquire yours?"

"I can't say how deeply indebted I feel—you must imagine that, Miss Lorne," he said, bending over the hand that lay in his, with an air that made Lady Chepstow lift her eyebrows and look at him narrowly. "It is one of the kindest things you could do for the boy and—for me. I thank you very, very much indeed. My thanks are due to you, too, Captain; for I feel that you will gladly do the favour I have asked."

"Do it? Yes, like a shot, old chap. What a ripping fellow you are!"

"I'm a tired one at all events," replied Cleek. "So, if you—and the ladies"—bowing to them—"will kindly excuse me, I'll be off home for a needed rest. Lady Chepstow, my very best respects. I feel sure that his little lordship will be quite all right in a day or two, although I shall, of course, be glad to learn how he progresses. May I? Perhaps Miss Lorne might be persuaded to send me a word or two through—Mr. Narkom."

Lady Chepstow was still looking at him as she had been from the moment he had taken Ailsa's hand. Now she put out her own to him.

"Why wait for written reports, Mr. Cleek? Why not call in person and see?" she asked. "It will be more satisfactory than writing; and you will be welcome always."

"I thank your ladyship," he said gravely—though all the soul of him rioted and laughed and longed to shout out for sheer joy. "It is a privilege I shall be happy to enjoy."

But afterward, when he came to take his leave, a dearer one was granted him; for Ailsa herself accompanied him to the door.

"I couldn't let the butler show you out, Mr. Cleek," she said, as they stood together in the wide entrance hall. "I couldn't let you go until I had said something that is on my mind—something that has been pricking my conscience all evening. I want to tell you that from this night on I am going to forget those other nights: that one in the mist at Hampstead, that other on the stairway at Wyvern House—forget them utterly and entirely, Mr. Cleek. Whatever you may have been *once*, I know that now you are indeed a man!"

Then gave him her hand again, smiled at him, and sent him home feeling that he was as near to the threshold of heaven as any mortal thing may hope to be.

Followed a time of such happiness as only they may know who having lived in darkness first know that there is such a thing as Light; followed days and weeks that went like magic things, blest to the uttermost before they go. For now he was a welcome visitor at the house that sheltered her; now the armour of reserve had dropped from her, and they were finding out between them that they had many tastes in common.

It was in August when the first interruption to this happy state of affairs occurred and they came to know that separation was to be endured again. Lady Chepstow, planning already for a wedding that was to take place in the early winter, decided to spend the last few months of her widowhood at her country house in Devonshire, and retired to it taking her servants, her little son, and her son's governess with her.

For a day or two, Cleek "mooned" about—restless, lonely despite Dollops's presence, finding no savour in anything; and it came as a positive relief when a call from The Yard sent him to a modest little house in the neighbourhood of Wandsworth Common. The "call" in question took the shape of a letter from Mr. Narkom.

"My dear Cleek," it ran, "a most amazing case—probably *the* most amazing you have yet tackled—has just cropped up. The client is one Captain Morrison, a retired Army officer living solely on his half pay. His daughter is involved in the astonishing affair. Indeed, it is at her earnest appeal that the matter has been brought to my notice. As the Captain is in too weak a state of health to journey any distance, I am going to ask you to meet me at No. 17, Sunnington Crescent, Wandsworth—a house kept by one Mrs. Culpin, widow of one of my Yard men, at three o'clock this afternoon. Knowing your reluctance to have your identity disclosed, I have taken the liberty of giving you the name you adopted in the Bawdrey affair, to wit: 'George Headland.' I have also taken the same precaution with regard to the Morrisons, leaving you to disclose your identity or not, as you see fit."

Glad enough for anything to distract his thoughts from the brooding state of melancholy into which they had sunk, Cleek looked up a time-table, caught the 2:47 train from Victoria Station; and Narkom, walking into Mrs. Culpin's modest little drawing-room at two minutes past three, found him standing in the window and looking thoughtfully out at the groups of children romping on the near-by common.

"Well, here I am at last, you see, my dear fellow," he said, as he crossed the room and shook hands with him. "Ripping day, isn't it? What are you doing? Admiring the view or taking stock of Mrs. Culpin's roses?"

"Neither. I was speculating in futures," replied Cleek, glancing back at the sunlit common, and then glancing away again with a faintly audible sigh. "How happy, how care-free they are, those merry little beggars, Mr. Narkom. What you said in your letter set my thoughts harking backward, and ... I was wondering what things the coming years might hold for them and for their parents. At one time, you know, Philip Bawdrey was as innocent and guileless as any of those little shavers; and yet, in after years he proved a monster of iniquity, a beast of ingratitude, and—Oh, well, let it pass. He paid, as thankless children always do pay under God's good rule. I wonder what his thoughts were when his last hour came."

"It did come, then?"

"Yes. Got playing some of his games with those short-tempered chaps out in Buenos Ayres and got knifed a fortnight after his arrival. I had a letter from Mrs. Bawdrey yesterday. His father never knew of—well, the other thing; and never will now, thank God. The longer I live, Mr. Narkom, the surer I become that straight living always pays; and that the chap who turns into the other lane gets what he deserves before the game is played out."

"Ten years of Scotland Yard have enabled me to endorse that statement emphatically," replied Narkom. "'The riddle of the ninth finger' was no different in that respect from nine hundred other riddles that have come my way since I took office. Now sit down, old chap, and let us take up the present case. But I say, Cleek; speaking of rewards reminds me of what I wrote you. There's very little chance of one in this affair. All the parties connected with it are in very moderate circumstances. The sculptor fellow, Van Nant, who figures in it, was quite well-to-do at one time, I believe, but he ran through the greater part of his money, and a dishonest solicitor did him out of the rest. Miss Morrison herself never did have any, and, as I have told you, the Captain hasn't anything in the world but his pension; and it takes every shilling of that to keep them. In the circumstances, I'd have made it a simple 'Yard' affair, chargeable to the Government, and put one of the regular staff upon it. But—well, it's such an astounding, such an unheard-of-thing, I knew you'd fairly revel in it. And besides, after all the rewards you have won you must be quite a well-to-do man by this time, and able to indulge in a little philanthropy."

Cleek smiled.

"I will indulge in it, of course," he said, "but not for that reason, Mr. Narkom. I wonder how much it will surprise you to learn that, at the present moment, I have just one hundred pounds in all the world?"

"My dear fellow!" Narkom exclaimed, with a sort of gasp, staring at him in round-eyed amazement. "You fairly take away my breath. Why, you must have received a fortune since you took up these special cases. Fifty or sixty thousand pounds at the smallest calculation."

"More! To be precise, I have received exactly seventy-two thousand pounds, Mr. Narkom. But, as I tell you, I have to-day but one hundred pounds of that sum left. Lost in speculation? Oh, dear no! I've not invested one farthing in any scheme, company, or purchase since the night you gave me my chance and helped me to live an honest life."

"Then in the name of Heaven, Cleek, what has become of the money?"

"It has gone in the cause of my redemption, Mr. Narkom," he answered in a hushed voice. "My good friend—for you really *have* been a good friend to me, the best I ever had in all the world—my good friend, let us for only just this one minute speak of the times that lie behind. You know what redeemed me—a woman's eyes, a woman's rose-white soul! I said, did I not, that I wanted to win her, wanted to be worthy of her, wanted to climb up and stand with her in the light? You remember that, do you not, Mr. Narkom?"

"Yes, I remember. But, my dear fellow, why speak of your 'vanishing cracksman' days when you have so utterly put them behind you, and since lived a life beyond reproach? Whatever you did in those times you have amply atoned for. And what can that have to do with your impoverished state?"

"It has everything to do with it. I said I would be worthy of that one dear woman, and—I can never be, Mr. Narkom, until I have made restitution; until I can offer her a clean hand as well as a clean life. I can't restore the actual things that the 'vanishing cracksman' stole; for they are gone beyond recall, but—I can, at least, restore the value of them, and—that I have been secretly doing for a long time."

"Man alive! God bless my soul! Cleek, my dear fellow, do you mean to tell me that all the rewards, all the money you have earned—"

"Has gone to the people from whom I stole things in the wretched old days that lie behind me," he finished very gently. "It goes back, in secret gifts, as fast as it is earned, Mr. Narkom. Don't you see the answers, the acknowledgments, in the 'Personal' columns of the papers now and again? Wheresoever I robbed in those old days, I am repaying in these. When the score is wiped off, when the last robbery is paid for, my hand will be clean, and—I can offer it; never before."

"Cleek! My dear fellow! What a man! What a *man*! Oh, more than ever am I certain *now* that old Sir Horace Wyvern was right that night when he said that you were a gentleman. Tell me—I'll respect it—tell me, for God's sake, man, who are you? *What* are you, dear friend?"

"Cleek," he made reply. "Just Cleek! The rest is my secret and—God's! We've never spoken of the past since *that* night, Mr. Narkom, and, with your kind permission, we never will speak of it again. I'm Cleek, the detective— at your service once more. Now, then, let's have the new strange case on which you called me here. What's it all about?"

"Necromancy—wizardry—fairy-lore—all the stuff and nonsense that goes to the making of 'The Arabian Nights'!" said Narkom, waxing excited as his thoughts were thus shoved back to the amazing affair he had in hand. "All your 'Red Crawls' and your 'Sacred Sons' and your 'Nine-fingered Skeletons' are fools to it for wonder and mystery. Talk about witchcraft! Talk about wizards and giants and enchanters and the things that witches did in the days of Macbeth! God bless my soul, they're nothing to it. Those were the days of magic, anyhow, so you can take it or leave it, as you like; but this—look here, Cleek, you've heard of a good many queer things and run foul of a good many mysteries, I'll admit, but did you ever—in this twentieth century, when witchcraft and black magic are supposed to be as dead as Queen Anne—did you ever, my dear fellow, hear of such a marvel as a man putting on a blue leather belt that was said to have the power of rendering the wearer invisible and then forthwith melting into thin air and floating off like a cloud of pipe smoke?"

"Gammon!"

"Gammon nothing! Facts!"

"Facts? You're off your head, man. The thing couldn't possibly happen. Somebody's having you!"

"Well, somebody had *him*, at all events. Young Carboys, I mean— the chap that's engaged, or, rather was engaged, to Captain Morrison's daughter; and the poor girl's half out of her mind over it. He put the belt on in the presence of her and her father—in their own house, mind you—

walked into a bedroom, and vanished like smoke. Doors locked, windows closed, room empty, belt on the floor, and man gone. Not a trace of him from that moment to this; and yesterday was to have been his wedding-day. There's a 'mystery,' if you like. What do you make of that?"

Cleek looked at him for an instant. Then:

"My dear Mr. Narkom, for the moment I thought you were fooling," he said in a tone of deep interest. "But I see now that you are quite in earnest, although the thing sounds so preposterous, a child might be expected to scoff at it. A man to get a magic belt, to put it on, and then to melt away? Why, the 'Seven-league Boots' couldn't be a greater tax on one's credulity. Sit down and tell me all about it."

"The dickens of it is there doesn't seem to be much to tell," said Narkom, accepting the invitation. "Young Carboys, who appears to have been a decent sort of chap, had neither money, position, nor enemies, so that's an end to any idea of somebody having a reason for wishing to get rid of him; and, as he was devotedly attached to Miss Morrison, and was counting the very hours to the time of their wedding, and, in addition, had no debts, no entanglements of any sort, and no possible reason for wishing to disappear, there isn't the slightest ground for suspecting that he did so voluntarily."

"Suppose you tell me the story from the beginning, and leave me to draw my own conclusions regarding that," said Cleek. "Who and what was the man? Was he living in the same house with his fiancée, then? You say the disappearance occurred there, at night, and that he went into a bedroom. Was the place his home, as well as Captain Morrison's, then?"

"On the contrary. His home was a matter of three or four miles distant. He was merely stopping at the Morrison's on that particular night; I'll tell you presently why and how he came to do that. For the present, let's take things in their proper order. Once upon a time this George Carboys occupied a fair position in the world, and his parents—long since dead— were well to do. The son, being an only child, was well looked after—sent to Eton and then to Brasenose, and all that sort of thing—and the future looked very bright for him. Before he was twenty-one, however, his father lost everything through unlucky speculations, and that forced the son to make his own living. At the 'Varsity he had fallen in with a rich young Belgian—fellow named Maurice Van Nant—who had a taste for sculpture and the fine arts generally, and they had become the warmest and closest of friends."

"Maurice Van Nant? That's the sculptor fellow you said in the beginning had gone through his money, isn't it?"

"Yes. Well, when young Carboys was thrown on the world, so to speak, this Van Nant came to the rescue, made a place for him as private secretary and companion, and for three or four years they knocked round the world together, going to Egypt, Persia, India, *et cetera*, as Van Nant was mad on the subject of Oriental art, and wished to study it at the fountain-head. In the meantime both Carboys' parents went over to the silent majority, and left him without a relative in the world, barring Captain Morrison, who is an uncle about seven times removed and would, of course, naturally be heir-at-law to anything he left if he had anything to leave, poor beggar, which he hadn't. But that's getting ahead of the story.

"Well, at the end of four years or so Van Nant came to the bottom of his purse—hadn't a stiver left; and from dabbling in art for pleasure, had to come down to it as a means of earning a livelihood. And he and Carboys returned to England, and, for purposes of economy, pooled their interests, took a small box of a house over Putney way, set up a regular 'bachelor establishment,' and started in the business of bread-winning together. Carboys succeeded in getting a clerk's position in town; Van Nant set about modelling clay figures and painting mediocre pictures, and selling both whenever he could find purchasers.

"Naturally, these were slow in coming, few and far between; but with Carboys' steady two pounds a week coming in, they managed to scrape along and to keep themselves going. They were very happy, too, despite the fact that Carboys had got himself engaged to Miss Morrison, and was hoarding every penny he could possibly save in order to get enough to marry on; and this did not tend to make Van Nant overjoyed, as such a marriage would, of course, mean the end of their long association and the giving up of their bachelor quarters."

"To say nothing of leaving Van Nant to rub along as best he could without any assistance from Carboys," commented Cleek. "I think I can guess a portion of what resulted, Mr. Narkom. Van Nant did not, of course, in these circumstances have any tender regard for Miss Morrison."

"No, he did not. In point of fact, he disliked her very much indeed, and viewed the approaching wedding with extreme disfavour."

"And yet you say that nobody had an interest in doing Carboys some sort of mischief in order to prevent that wedding from being consummated, Mr. Narkom," said Cleek with a shrug of the shoulders. "Certainly, Van Nant would have been glad to see a spoke put in that particular wheel; though I freely confess I do not see what good could come of preventing it by doing away with Carboys, as he would then be in as bad a position as if the marriage had been allowed to proceed as planned. Either way he loses Carboys' companionship and assistance; and his one wish would be to preserve both. Well, go on. What next? I'm anxious to hear about the belt. Where and how does that come in?"

"Well, it appears that Miss Morrison got hold of a humorous book called 'The Brass Bottle,' a fantastic, farcical thing, about a genie who had been sealed up in a bottle for a thousand years getting out and causing the poor devil of a hero no end of worry by heaping riches and honours upon him in the most embarrassing manner. It happened that on the night Miss Morrison got this book, and read it aloud for the amusement of her father and lover, Carboys had persuaded Van Nant to spend the evening with them. Apparently he enjoyed himself, too, for he laughed as boisterously as any of them over the farcical tale, and would not go home until he had heard the end of it. When it was finished Miss Morrison tells me, Carboys, after laughing fit to split his sides over the predicament of the hero of the book, cried out: 'By George! I wish some old genie would take it into his head to hunt me up, and try the same sort of a dodge with me. He wouldn't find this chicken shying his gold and his gems back at his head, I can tell you. I'd accept all the Arab slaves and all the palaces he wanted to thrust on me; and then I'd make 'em all over to you, Mary dear, so you'd never have to do another day's worrying or pinching in all your life. But never you nor anybody else depend upon an Arab's gratitude or an Arab's generosity. He'll promise you the moon, and then wriggle out of giving you so much as a star—just as Abdul ben Meerza did with me.' And upon Miss Morrison asking what he meant by that, he replied, laughingly: 'Ask Van, he knew the old codger better than I—knew his whole blessed family, blow him!—and was able to talk to the old skinflint in his own outlandish tongue.'

"Upon Miss Morrison's acting on this suggestion, Van Nant told of an adventure Carboys had had in Persia some years previously. It appears that he saved the life of a miserly old Arab called Abdul ben Meerza at the risk of his own; that the old man was profuse in his expressions of gratitude, and, on their parting, had said: 'By the Prophet, thou shalt yet find the tree of this day's planting bear rich fruit for thee and thy feet walk upon golden stones.' But, in spite of this promise, he had walked away, and Carboys had never heard another word from nor of him from that hour until three nights ago."

"Oho!" said Cleek, with a strong, rising inflection. "And he did hear of him, then?"

"Yes," replied Narkom. "Quite unexpectedly, and while he was preparing to spend a dull evening at home with Van Nant—for the night was, as you must recollect, my dear fellow, a horribly wet and stormy one—a message came to him from Miss Morrison asking him to come over to Wandsworth without delay, as a most amazing thing had happened. A box marked 'From Abdul ben Meerza' had been delivered there, of all astonishing places. The message concluded by saying that as it was such a horrible night, the Captain, her father, would not hear of his returning, so begged him to bring his effects, and come prepared to remain until morning.

"He went, of course, carrying with him a small bag containing his pyjamas, his shaving tackle, and such few accessories as would be necessary, since, if he stopped, he must start from there to business in the morning; and on his arrival was handed a small leather case addressed as he had been told. Imagining all sorts of wonders, from jewels of fabulous value to documents entitling him to endless wealth, he unfastened the case, and found within it a broad belt of blue enamelled leather secured with a circular brass clasp, on which was rudely scratched in English the words, 'The wizards of the East grew rich by being unseen. Whoso clasps this belt about his waist may become invisible for the wishing. So does ben Meerza remember.'

"Of course, Carboys treated it as the veriest rubbish—who wouldn't? Indeed, suspected Van Nant of having played a joke upon him, and laughingly threw it aside; and, finding that he had taken an uncomfortable journey for nothing, got some good out of it by spending a pleasant evening with the Captain and his daughter. A room had been made ready for him— in fact, although he did not know it, Miss Morrison had given him hers, and had herself gone to a less attractive one—and in due time he prepared to turn in for the night. As they parted Miss Morrison, in a bantering spirit, picked up the belt and handed it to him, remarking that he had better keep it, as, after marriage, he might some time be glad to creep into the house unseen; and, in the same bantering spirit, he had replied that he had better begin learning how the thing worked in case of necessity, and taking the belt, clasped it round his waist, said good-night, and stepped into the room prepared for him. Miss Morrison and her father heard him close the door and pull down the blind, and—that was the last that was seen or heard of him.

"In the morning the bed was found undisturbed, his locked bag on a chair, and in the middle of the floor the blue leather belt; but of the man himself there was not one trace to be found. There, that's the story, Cleek. Now what do you make of it?"

"I shall be able to tell you better after I have seen the parties concerned," said Cleek, after a moment's pause. "You have brought your motor, of course? Let us step into it, then, and whizz round to Captain Morrison's house. What's that? Oh, undoubtedly a case of foul play, Mr. Narkom. But as to the motive and the matter of who is guilty, it is impossible to decide until I have looked further into the evidence. Do me a favour, will you? After you have left me at the Captain's house, 'phone up The Yard, and let me have the secret cable code with the East; also, if you can, the name of the chief of the Persian police."

"My dear chap, you can't really place any credence in that absurd assertion regarding the blue belt? You can't possibly think that Abdul ben Meerza really sent the thing?"

"No, I can't," said Cleek in reply. "Because, to the best of my belief, it is impossible for a dead man to send anything; and, if my memory doesn't betray me, I fancy I read in the newspaper accounts of that big Tajik rising at Khotour a couple of months ago, that the leader, one Abdul ben Meerza, a rich but exceedingly miserly merchant of the province of Elburz, was, by the Shah's command, bastinadoed within an inch of his life, and then publicly beheaded."

"By Jove! I believe you are right, my dear fellow," asserted Narkom. "I thought the name had a familiar sound—as if I had, somewhere, heard it before. I suppose there is no likelihood, by any chance, that the old skinflint could have lived up to his promise and left poor Carboys something, after all, Cleek? Because, you know, if he did—"

"Captain Morrison would, as heir-at-law, inherit it," supplemented Cleek, dryly. "Get out the motor, Mr. Narkom, and let's spin round and see him. I fancy I should like a few minutes' conversation with the Captain. And—Mr. Narkom!"

"Yes."

"We'll stick to the name 'George Headland,' if you please. When you are out for birds it doesn't do to frighten them off beforehand."

CHAPTER XXV

It did not take more than five minutes to cover the distance between Sunnington Crescent and the modest little house where Captain Morrison and his daughter lived; so in a very brief time Cleek had the satisfaction of interviewing both.

Narkom's assertion, that Miss Morrison was "half out of her mind over the distressing affair" had prepared him to encounter a weeping, red-eyed, heart-broken creature of the most excitable type. He found instead a pale, serious-faced, undemonstrative girl of somewhat uncertain age—sweet of voice, soft of step, quiet of demeanour—who was either one of those persons who repress all external evidence of internal fires, and bear their crosses in silence, or was as cold-blooded as a fish and as heartless as a statue. He found the father the exact antithesis of the daughter, a nervous, fretful, irritable individual (gout had him by the heels at the time), who was as full of "yaps" and snarls as any Irish terrier, and as peevish and fussy as a fault-finding old woman. Added to this, he had a way of glancing all round the room, and avoiding the eye of the person to whom he was talking. And if Cleek had been like the generality of people, and hadn't known that some of the best and "straightest" men in the world have been afflicted in this manner, and some of the worst and "crookedest" could look you straight in the eyes without turning a hair, he might have taken this for a bad sign. Then, too, he seemed to have a great many more wrappings and swaddlings about his gouty foot than appeared to be necessary—unless it was done to make his helpless state very apparent, and to carry out his assertion that he hadn't been able to walk a foot unassisted for the past week, and could not, therefore, be in any way connected with young Carboys' mysterious vanishment. Still, even that had its contra aspect. He might be one of those individuals who make a mountain out of a molehill of pain, and insist upon a dozen poultices where one would do.

But Cleek could not forget that, as Narkom had said, there was not the shadow of doubt that in the event of Carboys having died possessed of means, the Captain would be the heir-at-law by virtue of his kinship; and it is a great deal more satisfactory to be rich oneself than to be dependent upon the generosity of a rich son-in-law. So, after adroitly exercising the "pump" upon other matters:

"I suppose, Miss Morrison," said Cleek in a casual off-hand sort of way, "you don't happen to know if Mr. Carboys ever made a will, do you? I am aware, from what Mr. Narkom has told me of his circumstances, that he really possessed nothing that would call for the execution of such a document; but young men have odd fancies sometimes—particularly when they become engaged—so it is just possible that he might have done such a thing; that there was a ring or something of that sort he wanted to make sure of your getting should anything happen to him. Of course, it is an absurd suggestion, but—"

"It is not so absurd as you think, Mr. Headland," she interrupted. "As it happens, Mr. Carboys did make a will. But that was a very long time ago—in fact, before he knew me, so my name did not figure in it at all. He once told me of the circumstances connected with it. It was executed when he was about three-and-twenty. It appears that there were some personal trinkets, relics of his more prosperous days: a set of jewelled waistcoat buttons, a scarf-pin, a few choice books and things like that, which he desired Mr. Van Nant to have in the event of his death (they were then going to the Orient, and times there were troublous); so he drew up a will, leaving everything that he might die possessed of to Mr. Van Nant, and left the paper with the latter's solicitor when they bade good-bye to England. So far as I know, that will still exists, Mr. Headland; so"—here the faintest suggestion of a quiver got into her voice—"if anything of a tragical nature had happened to him, and—and the trinkets hadn't disappeared with him, Mr. Van Nant could claim them all, and I should have not even one poor little token to cherish in memory of him. And I am sure—I am very sure—that if he had known—if he had thought—"

"Mary, for goodness' sake, don't begin to snivel!" chimed in her father querulously. "It gets on my nerves. And you know very well how I am suffering! Of course, it was most inconsiderate of Carboys not to destroy that will as soon as you and he were engaged; but he knew that marriage invalidates any will a man may have made previously, and—well, you can't suppose that he ever expected things to turn out as they have done. Besides, Van Nant would have seen that you got something to treasure as a remembrance. He's a very decent chap, is Van Nant, Mr. Headland, although my daughter has never appeared to think so. But there's no arguing with a woman any way."

Cleek glanced at Narkom. It was a significant glance, and said as plainly as so many words: "What do you think of it? You said there was no motive, and, provided Carboys fell heir to something of which we know nothing as yet, here are *two*! If that will was destroyed, one man would, as heir-at-law, inherit; ditto the other man if it was not destroyed and not invalidated by marriage. And here's the 'one' man singing the praises of the 'other' one!"

"Collusion?" queried Narkom's answering look. "Perhaps," said Cleek's in response, "one of these two men has made away with him. The question is, which? and, also, why? when? where?" Then he turned to the Captain's daughter, and asked quietly: "Would you mind letting me see the room from which the young man disappeared? I confess I haven't the ghost of an idea regarding the case, Captain; but if you don't mind letting your daughter show me the room—"

"Mind? Good Lord, no!" responded the Captain. "All I want to know is, what became of the poor boy, and if there's any likelihood of his ever coming back alive. I'd go up with you myself, only you see how helpless I am. Mary, take Mr. Headland to the room. And please don't stop any longer than is necessary. I'm suffering agonies and not fit to be left alone."

Miss Morrison promised to return as expeditiously as possible, and then forthwith led the way to the room in question.

"This is it, Mr. Headland," she said as she opened the door and ushered Cleek in. "Everything is just exactly as it was when George left it. I couldn't bring myself to touch a thing until after a detective had seen it. Father said it was silly and sentimental of me to go on sleeping in a little box of a hall bedroom when I could be so much more comfortable if I returned to my own. But—I couldn't! I felt that I might possibly be unconsciously destroying something in the shape of a clue if I moved a solitary object, and so—Look! there is the drawn blind just as he left it; there his portmanteau on that chair by the bedside, and there—" Her voice sank to a sort of awed whisper, her shaking finger extended in the direction of a blue semi-circle in the middle of the floor. "There is the belt! He had it round his waist when he crossed this threshold that night. It was lying there just as you see it when the servant brought up his tea and his shaving-water the next morning, and found the room empty and the bed undisturbed."

Cleek walked forward and picked up the belt.

"Humph! Unfastened!" he said as he took it up; and Miss Morrison, closing the door, went below and left them. "Our wonderful wizard does not seem to have mastered the simple matter of making a man vanish out of the thing without first unfastening the buckle, it appears. I should have thought he could have managed that, shouldn't you, Mr. Narkom, if he could have managed the business of making him melt into thin air? Hur-r-r!" reflectively, as he turned the belt over and examined it. "Not seen much use, apparently; the leather's quite new, and the inside quite unsoiled. British manufactured brass, too, in the buckle. Shouldn't have expected that in a Persian-made article. Inscription scratched on with the point of a knife, or some other implement not employed in metal engraving. May I trouble you for a pin? Thank you. Hum-m-m! Thought so. Some dirty, clayey stuff rubbed in to make the letters appear old and of long standing. Look here, Mr. Narkom: metal quite bright underneath when you pick the stuff out. Inscription very recently added; leather, American tanned; brass, Birmingham; stitching, by the Blake shoe and harness machine; wizard — probably born in Tottenham Court Road, and his knowledge of Persia confined to Persian powder in four-penny tins."

He laid the belt aside, and walked slowly round the room, inspecting its contents before turning his attention to the portmanteau.

"Evidently the vanishing qualities of the belt did not assert themselves very rapidly, Mr. Narkom," he said, "for Mr. Carboys not only prepared to go to bed, but had time to get himself ready to hurry off to business in the morning with as little delay as possible. Look here; here are his pyjamas on the top of this chest of drawers, neatly folded, just as he lifted them out of his portmanteau; and as a razor has been wiped on this towel (see this slim line of dust-like particles of hair), he shaved before going to bed in order to save himself the trouble of doing so in the morning. But as there is no shaving-mug visible, and he couldn't get hot water at that hour of the night, we shall probably discover a spirit-lamp and its equipment when we look into the portmanteau. Now, as he had time to put these shaving articles away after using, and as no man shaves with his collar and necktie on, if we do not find those, too, in the portmanteau, we may conclude that he put them on again; and, as he wouldn't put them on again if he were going to bed, the inference is obvious—something caused him to dress and prepare to leave the house voluntarily. That 'something' must have manifested itself very abruptly, and demanded great haste—either that, or he expected to return; for you will observe that, although he replaced his shaving tackle in the portmanteau, he did not put his sleeping-suit back with it. While I am poking about, do me the favour of looking in the bag, Mr. Narkom; and tell me if you find the collar and necktie there."

"Not a trace of them," announced the superintendent a moment or two later. "Here are the shaving-mug, the brush, and the spirit-lamp, however, just as you suggested; and—Hallo! what have you stumbled upon now?" For Cleek, who had been "poking about," as he termed it, had suddenly stooped, picked up something, and was regarding it fixedly as it lay in the palm of his hand.

"A somewhat remarkable thing to discover in a lady's bed-chamber, Mr. Narkom, unless—Just step downstairs, and ask Miss Morrison to come up again for a moment, will you?" And then held out his hand so that Narkom could see, in passing, that a hempseed, two grains of barley, and an oat lay upon his palm. "Miss Morrison," he inquired as Mary returned in company with the superintendent, "Miss Morrison, do you keep pigeons?"

She gave a little cry, and clasped her hands together, as if reproaching herself for some heartless act.

"Oh!" she said, moving hastily forward toward the window. "Poor dears! How good of you to remind me. To think that I should forget to feed them for three whole days. They may be dead by now. But at such a time I could think of nothing but this hideous mystery. My pigeons—my poor, pretty pigeons!"

"Oh, then you do keep them?"

"Yes; oh, yes. In a wire-enclosed cote attached to the house just outside this window. Homing pigeons, Mr. Headland. George bought them for me. We had an even half dozen each. We used to send messages to each other that way. He would bring his over to me, and take mine away with him at night when he went home, so we could correspond at any moment without waiting for the post. That's how I sent him the message about the arrival of the belt. Oh, do unlock the window, and let me see if the pretty dears are still alive."

"It doesn't need to be unlocked, Miss Morrison," he replied, as he pulled up the blind. "See, it can be opened easily—the catch is not secured."

"Not secured? Why, how strange. I myself fastened it after I despatched the bird with the message about the belt. And nobody came into the room after that until George did so that night. Oh, do look and see if the pretty creatures are dead. They generally coo so persistently; and now I don't hear a sound from them."

Cleek threw up the sash and looked out. A huge wistaria with tendrils as thick as a man's wrist covered the side of the house, and made a veritable ladder down to the little garden; and, firmly secured to this, on a level with the window-sill and within easy reach therefrom, was the dovecote in question. He put in his hand, and slowly drew out four stiff, cold, feathered little bodies, and laid them on the dressing-table before her; then, while she was grieving over them, he groped round in all corners of the cote and drew forth still another.

"Five?" she exclaimed in surprise. "Five? Oh, but there should be only four, Mr. Headland. It is true that George brought over all six the day before;

but I 'flew' one to him in the early morning, and I 'flew' a second at night, with the message about the belt; so there should be but four."

"Oh, well, possibly one was 'flown' by him to you, and it 'homed' without your knowledge."

"Yes, but it couldn't get inside the wired enclosure unassisted, Mr. Headland. See! that spring-door has to be opened when it is returned to the cote after it has carried its message home. You see, I trained them, by feeding them in here, to come into this room when they were flown back to me. They always flew directly in if the window was opened, or gave warning of their presence by fluttering about and beating against the panes if the sash was closed. And for a fifth pigeon to be inside the enclosure—I can't understand the thing at all. Oh, Mr. Headland, do you think it is anything in the nature of a clue?"

"It may be," he replied evasively. "Clues are funny things, Miss Morrison; you never know when you may pick one up, nor how. I shouldn't say anything to anybody about this fifth pigeon if I were you. Let that be our secret for awhile; and if your father wants to know why I sent for you to come up here again—why, just say I have discovered that your pigeons are dead for want of food." And for a moment or two, after she had closed the door and gone below again, he stood looking at Mr. Narkom and slowly rubbing his thumb and forefinger up and down his chin. Then, of a sudden:

"I think, Mr. Narkom, we can fairly decide, on the evidence of that fifth pigeon, that George Carboys left this room voluntarily," returned Cleek; "that the bird brought him a message of such importance it was necessary to leave this house at once, and that, not wishing to leave it unlocked while he was absent, and not—because of the Captain's inability to get back upstairs afterward—having anybody to whom he could appeal to get up and lock it after him, he chose to get out of this window, and to go down by means of that wistaria. I think, too, we may decide that, as he left no note to explain his absence, he expected to return before morning, and that, as he never did return, he has met with foul play. Of course, it is no use looking for footprints in the garden in support of this hypothesis, for the storm that night was a very severe one and quite sufficient to blot out all trace of them; but—Look here, Mr. Narkom, put two and two together. If a message was sent him by a carrier pigeon, where must that pigeon have come from, since it was one of Miss Morrison's?"

"Why, from Van Nant's place, of course. It couldn't possibly come from any other place."

"Exactly. And as Van Nant and Carboys lived together—kept Bachelor Hall—and there was never anybody but their two selves in the house at any time, why, nobody but Van Nant himself could have despatched the bird. Look at that fragment of burnt paper lying in the basin of that candlestick on the washstand. If that isn't all that's left of the paper that was tied under the pigeon's wing, and if Carboys didn't use it for the purpose of lighting the spirit-lamp by which he heated his shaving-water, depend upon it that, in his haste and excitement, he tucked it into his pocket, and if ever we find his body we shall find that paper on it."

"His body? My dear Cleek, you don't believe that the man has been murdered?"

"I don't know—yet. I shall, however, if this Van Nant puts anything in the way of my searching that house thoroughly or makes any pretence to follow me whilst I am doing so. I want to meet this Maurice Van Nant just as soon as I can, Mr. Narkom, just as soon as I can."

And it was barely two minutes after he had expressed this wish that Miss Morrison reappeared upon the scene, accompanied by a pale, nervous, bovine-eyed man of about thirty-five years of age, and said in a tone of agitation: "Pardon me for interrupting, Mr. Headland, but this is Mr. Maurice Van Nant. He is most anxious to meet you, and father would have me bring him up at once."

Narkom screwed round on his heel, looked at the Belgian, and lost faith in Miss Morrison's powers of discrimination instantly. On the dressing-table stood Carboys' picture—heavy-jowled, sleepy-eyed, dull-looking—and on the threshold stood a man with the kindest eyes, the sweetest smile, and the handsomest and most sympathetic countenance he had seen in many a day. If the eyes are the mirror of the soul, if the face is the index of the character, then here was a man weak as water, as easily led as any lamb, and as guileless.

"You are just the man I want to see, Mr. Van Nant," said Cleek, after the first formalities were over, and assuming, as he always did at such times, the heavy, befogged expression of incompetence. "I confess this bewildering affair altogether perplexes me; but you, I understand, were Mr. Carboys' close friend and associate, and as I can find nothing in the nature of a clue here, I should like, with your permission, to look over his home quarters and see if I can find anything there."

If he had looked for any sign of reluctance or of embarrassment upon Van Nant's part when such a request should be made, he was wholly disappointed, for the man, almost on the point of tears, seized his hand, pressed it warmly, and said in a voice of eager entreaty: "Oh, do, Mr. Headland, do. Search anywhere, do anything that will serve to find my friend and to clear up this dreadful affair. I can't sleep for thinking of it; I can't get a moment's peace night or day. You didn't know him or you would understand how I am tortured—how I miss him. The best friend, the dearest and the lightest-hearted fellow that ever lived. If I had anything left in this world, I'd give it all—all, Mr. Headland, to clear up the mystery of this thing and to get him back. One man could do that, I believe, could and would if I had the money to offer him."

"Indeed? And who may he be, Mr. Van Nant?"

"The great, the amazing, the undeceivable man, Cleek. He'd get at the truth of it. Nothing could baffle and bewilder him. But—oh, well, it's the old, old tale of the power of money. He wouldn't take the case—a high-and-mighty 'top-notcher' like that—unless the reward was a tempting one, I'm sure."

"No, I'm afraid he wouldn't," agreed Cleek, with the utmost composure. "So you must leave him out of your calculations altogether, Mr. Van Nant. And now, if you don't mind accompanying us and showing the chauffeur the way, perhaps Mr. Narkom will take us over to your house in his motor."

"Mind? No, certainly I don't mind. Anything in the world to get at a clue to this thing, Mr. Headland, anything. Do let us go at once."

Cleek led the way from the room. Halfway down the stairs, however, he excused himself on the plea of having forgotten his magnifying glass, and ran back to get it. Two minutes later he rejoined them in the little drawing-room, where the growling Captain was still demanding the whole time and attention of his daughter, and, the motor being ready, the three men walked out, got into it, and were whisked away to the house which once had been the home of the vanished George Carboys.

It proved to be a small, isolated brick house in very bad condition, standing in an out-of-the-way road somewhere between Putney and Wimbledon. It stood somewhat back from the road, in the midst of a little patch of ground abounding in privet and laurel bushes, and it was evident that its cheapness had been its chief attraction to the two men who had rented it, although, on entering, it was found to possess at the back a sort of extension, with top and side lights, which must have appealed to Van Nant's need of something in the nature of a studio. At all events, he had converted it into a very respectable apology for one; and Cleek was not a little surprised by what it contained.

Rich stuffs, bits of tapestry, Persian draperies, Arabian prayer-mats— relics of his other and better days and of his Oriental wanderings—hung on the walls and ornamented the floor; his rejected pictures and his unsold statues, many of them life-sized and all of clay, coated with a lustreless paint to make them look like marble, were disposed about the place with an eye to artistic effect, and near to an angle, where stood (on a pedestal, half concealed, half revealed by artistically arranged draperies) the life-size figure of a Roman senator, in toga and sandals, there was the one untidy spot, the one utterly inartistic thing the room contained.

It was the crude, half-finished shape of a recumbent female figure, of large proportions and abominable modelling, stretched out at full length upon a long, low, trestle-supported "sculptor's staging," on which also lay Van Nant's modelling tools and his clay-stained working blouse. Cleek looked at the huge unnatural thing—out of drawing, anatomically wrong in many particulars—and felt like quoting Angelo's famous remark anent his master Lorenzo's faun: "What a pity to have spoilt so much expensive material," and Van Nant, observing, waved his hand toward it.

"A slumbering nymph," he explained. "Only the head and shoulders finished as yet, you see. I began it the day before, yesterday, but my hand seems somehow to have lost its cunning. Here are the keys of all the rooms, Mr. Headland. Carboys' was the one directly at the head of the stairs, in the front. Won't you and Mr. Narkom go up and search without me? I couldn't bear to look into the place and see the things that belonged to him and he not there. It would cut me to the heart if I did. Or, maybe, you would sooner go alone, and leave Mr. Narkom to search round this room. We used to make a general sitting-room of it at nights when we were alone together, and some clue may have been dropped."

"A good suggestion, Mr. Narkom," commented Cleek, as he took the keys. "Look round and see what you can find whilst I poke about upstairs." Then he walked out of the studio and searching every nook and corner, whilst Van Nant, for the want of something to occupy his mind and his hands, worked on the nymph, and could hear him moving about overhead in quest of possible clues.

For perhaps twenty minutes Cleek was away; then he came down and walked into the room looking the very picture of hopeless bewilderment.

"Mr. Narkom," he said, "this case stumps me. I believe there's magic in it, if you ask me; and as the only way to find magic is with magic, I am going to consult a clairvoyante, and if one of those parties can't give me a clue, I don't believe the mystery will ever be solved. I know of a ripping one, but she is over in Ireland, and as it's a dickens of a way to go, I shan't be able to get back before the day after to-morrow at the earliest. But—look here, sir, I'll tell you what! This is Tuesday evening, isn't it? Now if you and Mr. Van Nant will be at Captain Morrison's house on Thursday evening at seven o'clock, and will wait there until I come, I'll tell you what that clairvoyante says, and whether there's any chance of this thing being solved or not. Is that agreeable, Mr. Van Nant?"

"Quite, Mr. Headland. I'll be there promptly."

"And stop until you hear from me?"

"And stop until I hear from you—yes."

"Right you are, sir. Now then, Mr. Narkom, if you'll let the chauffeur whisk me over to the station, I'll get back to London and on to the earliest possible train for Holyhead so as to be on hand for the first Irish packet to-morrow. And while you're looking for your hat, sir—good evening, Mr. Van Nant—I'll step outside and tell Lennard to start up."

With that, he passed out of the studio, walked down the hall, and went out of the house. And half a minute later, when the superintendent joined him, he found him sitting in the limousine and staring at his toes.

"My dear Cleek, did you find anything?" he queried, as he took a seat beside him, and the motor swung out into the road and whizzed away. "Of course, I know you've no more idea of going to Ireland than you have of taking a pot-shot at the moon: but there's something on your mind. I know the signs, Cleek. What is it?"

The response to this was rather startling.

"Mr. Narkom," said Cleek, answering one question with another, "what's the best thing to make powdered bismuth stick—lard, cold cream, or cocoa butter?"

CHAPTER XXVI

If punctuality is a virtue, then Mr. Maurice Van Nant deserved to go on record as one of the most virtuous men in existence. For the little Dutch clock in Captain Morrison's drawing-room had barely begun to strike seven on the following Thursday evening when he put in an appearance there, and found the Captain and his daughter anxiously awaiting him. But, as virtue is, on most excellent authority, its own reward, he had to be satisfied with the possession of it, since neither Narkom nor Cleek was there to meet him.

But the reason for this defection was made manifest when Miss Morrison placed before him a telegram which had arrived some ten minutes earlier and read as follows: "Unavoidably delayed. Be with you at nine-thirty. Ask Mr. Van Nant to wait. Great and welcome piece of news for him.—NARKOM."

Van Nant smiled.

"Great and welcome news," he repeated. "Then Mr. Headland must have found something in the nature of a clue in Ireland, captain, though what he could find there I can't imagine. Frankly, I thought him a stupid sort of fellow, but if he has managed to find a clue to poor George's whereabouts over in Ireland, he must be sharper than I believed. Well, we shall know about that at half-past nine, when Mr. Narkom comes. I hope nothing will happen to make him disappoint us again."

Nothing did. Promptly at the hour appointed, the red limousine whizzed up to the door, and Mr. Narkom made his appearance. But, contrary to the expectations of the three occupants of the little drawing-room, he was quite alone.

"So sorry I couldn't come earlier," he said, as he came in, looking and acting like the bearer of great good news; "but you will appreciate the delay when I tell you what caused it. What's that, Mr. Van Nant? Headland? No, he's not with me. As a matter of fact, I've dispensed with his services in this particular case. Fancy, Miss Morrison, the muff came back from Ireland this evening, said the clairvoyante he consulted went into a trance, and told him that the key to the mystery could only be discovered in Germany, and he wanted me to sanction his going over there on no better evidence than that. Of course, I wouldn't; so I took him off the case forthwith, and set out to get another and a better man to handle it. That's what delayed me. And now, Mr. Van Nant"—fairly beaming, and rubbing his palms together delightedly—"here's where the great and welcome news I spoke of comes in. I remembered what you said the other day—I remembered how your heart is wrapped up in the solving of this great puzzle—what you said about it being a question of money alone; and so, what do you think I did? I went to that great man, Cleek. I laid the matter before him, told him there was no reward, that it was just a matter of sheer humanity—the consciousness of doing his duty and helping another fellow in distress—and, throw up your hat and cheer, my dear fellow, for you've got your heart's desire: Cleek's consented to take the case!"

A little flurry of excitement greeted this announcement. Miss Morrison grabbed his hand and burst into tears of gratitude; the Captain, forgetting in his delight the state of his injured foot, rose from his chair, only to remember suddenly and sit down again, his half-uttered cheer dying on his lips; and Van Nant, as if overcome by this unexpected boon, this granting of a wish he had never dared to hope would be fulfilled, could only clap both hands over his face and sob hysterically.

"Cleek!" he said, in a voice that shook with nervous catches and the emotion of a soul deeply stirred, "Cleek to take the case? The great, the amazing, the undeceivable Cleek! Oh, Mr. Narkom, can this be true?"

"As true as that you are standing here this minute, my dear sir. Not so much of a money grabber as that muff Headland wanted you to believe, is he—eh? Waived every hope of a reward, and took the case on the spot. He'll get at the root of it—Lord, yes! Lay you a sovereign to a sixpence, Mr. Van Nant, he gets to the bottom of it and finds out what became of George Carboys in forty-eight hours after he begins on the case."

"And when will he begin, Mr. Narkom? To-morrow? The next day? Or not this week at all? When, sir—when?"

"When? Why, bless your heart, man, he's begun already—or, at least, will do so in another hour and a half. He's promised to meet us at your house at eleven o'clock to-night. Chose that place because he lives at Putney, and it's nearer. Eleven was the hour he set, though, of course, he may arrive sooner; there's no counting on an erratic fellow like that chap. So we'll make it eleven, and possess our souls in patience until it's time to start."

"But, my dear Mr. Narkom, wouldn't it be better, or, at least, more hospitable if I went over to meet him, in case he does come earlier? There's no one in the house, remember, and it's locked up."

"Lord bless you, that won't bother him! Never travels without his tools, you know—skeleton keys, and all that—and he'll be in the house before you can wink an eye. Still, of course, if you'd rather be there to admit him in the regulation way—"

"It would at least be more courteous, Mr. Narkom," Miss Morrison interposed. "So great a man doing so great a favour—Oh, yes, I really think that Mr. Van Nant should."

"Oh, well, let him then, by all means," said Narkom. "Go, if you choose, Mr. Van Nant. I'd let you have my motor, only I must get over to the station and 'phone up headquarters on another affair in five minutes."

"It doesn't matter, thank you all the same. I can get a taxi at the top of the road," said Van Nant; and then, making his excuses to Miss Morrison and her father, he took up his hat and left the house. As a matter of fact, it was only courtesy that made him say that about the taxi, for there is rarely one to be found waiting about in the neighbourhood of Wandsworth Common after half-past nine o'clock at night, and nobody could have been more surprised than he when he actually did come across one, loitering about aimlessly and quite empty, before he had gone two dozen yards.

He engaged it on the spot, jumped into it, gave the chauffeur his directions, and a minute later was whizzing away to the isolated house. It was eight minutes past ten when he reached it, standing as black and lightless as when he left it four hours ago, and, after paying off the chauffeur and dismissing the vehicle, he fumbled nervously for his latchkey, found it, unlocked the door, and went hurriedly in.

"Have you come yet, Mr. Cleek?" he called out, as he shut the door and stood in the pitch-black hall. "Mr. Cleek! Mr. Cleek, are you here? It is I—Maurice Van Nant. Mr. Narkom has sent me on ahead."

Not a sound answered him, not even an echo. He sucked in his breath with a sort of wheezing sound, then groped round the hall table till he found his bedroom candle, and, striking a match, lit it. The staircase leading to the upper floors gaped at him out of the partial gloom, and he fairly sprang at it—indeed, was halfway up it when some other idea possessed him, brought him to a sudden standstill, and, facing round abruptly, he went back to the lower hall again, glimmering along it like a shadow, with the inadequate light held above him, and moving fleetly to the studio in the rear.

The door stood partly open, just as he had left it. He pushed it inward and stepped over the threshold.

"Mr. Cleek!" he called again. "Mr. Cleek! Are you here?"

And again the silence alone answered him. The studio was as he had seen it last, save for those fantastic shadows which the candle's wavering flame wreathed in the dim corners and along the pictured walls. There, on its half-draped pedestal, the Roman senator stood—dead white against the purple background—and there, close to the foot of it, the great bulk of the disproportionate nymph still sprawled, finished and whitewashed now, and looking even more of a monstrosity than ever in that waving light.

He gave one deep gulping sigh of relief, flashed across the room on tiptoe, and went down on his knees beside the monstrous thing, moving the candle this way and that along the length of it, as if searching for something, and laughing in little jerky gasps of relief when he found nothing that was not as it had been—as it should be—as he wanted it to be. And then, as he rose and patted the clay, and laughed aloud as he realised how hard it had set, then, at that instant, a white shape lurched forward and swooped downward, carrying him down with it. The candle slipped from his fingers and clattered on the floor, a pair of steel handcuffs clicked as they closed round his wrists, a voice above him said sharply: "You wanted Cleek I believe? Well, Cleek's got you, you sneaking murderer. Gentlemen, come in! Allow me to turn over to you the murderer of George Carboys! You'll find the body inside that slumbering nymph!"

And the last thing that Mr. Maurice Van Nant saw, as he shrieked and fainted, the last thing he realised, was that lights were flashing up and men tumbling in through the opening windows; that the Roman senator's pedestal was empty, and the figure which once had stood upon it was bending over him—alive!

And just at that moment the red limousine flashed up out of the darkness, the outer door whirled open and Narkom came pelting up.

"He took the bait, then, Cleek?" he cried, as he saw the manacled figure on the floor, with the "Roman senator" bending over and the policemen crowding in about it. "I guessed it when I saw the lights flash up. I've been on his heels ever since he snapped at that conveniently placed taxi after he left Miss Morrison and her father."

"You haven't brought them with you, I hope, Mr. Narkom? I wouldn't have that poor girl face the ordeal of what's to be revealed here to-night for worlds."

"No, I've not. I made a pretext of having to 'phone through to headquarters, and slipped out a moment after him. But, I say, my dear chap"—as Cleek's hands made a rapid search of the pockets of the unconscious man, and finally brought to light a folded paper—"what's that thing? What are you doing?"

"Compounding a felony in the interest of humanity," he made reply as he put the end of the paper into the flame of the candle and held it there until it was consumed. "We all do foolish things sometimes when we are young, Mr. Narkom, and—well, George Carboys was no exception when he wrote the little thing I have just burned. Let us forget all about it—Captain Morrison is heir-at-law, and that poor girl will benefit."

"There was an estate, then?"

"Yes. My cable yesterday to the head of the Persian police set all doubt upon that point at rest. Abdul ben Meerza, parting with nothing while he lived, after the manner of misers in general, left a will bequeathing something like £12,000 to George Carboys, and his executor communicated that fact to the supposed friend of both parties—Mr. Maurice Van Nant; and exactly ten days ago, so his former solicitor informed me, Mr. Maurice Van Nant visited him unexpectedly, and withdrew from his keeping a sealed packet which had been in the firm's custody for eight years. If you want to know why he withdrew it—Dollops!"

"Right you are, Gov'nor."

"Give me the sledge-hammer. Thanks! Now, Mr. Narkom, look!" And, swinging the hammer, he struck at the nymph with a force that shattered the monstrous thing to atoms; and Narkom, coming forward to look when Cleek bent over the ruin he had wrought, saw in the midst of the dust and rubbish the body of a dead man, fully clothed, and with the gap of a bullet-hole in the left temple.

Again Cleek's hands began a rapid search, and again, as before, they brought to light a paper, a little crumpled ball of paper that had been thrust into the right-hand pocket of the dead man's waistcoat, as though jammed there under the stress of strong excitement and the pressure of great haste. He smoothed it out and read it carefully, then passed it over to Mr. Narkom.

"There!" he said, "that's how he lured him over to his death. That's the message the pigeon brought. Would any man have failed to fly to face the author of a foul lie like that?"

"Beloved Mary," the message ran, "come to me again to-night. How sweet of you to think of such a thing as the belt to get him over and to make him stop until morning! Steal out after he goes to bed, darling. I'll leave the studio window unlocked, as usual. With a thousand kisses.

"Your own devoted,

"MAURICE."

"The dog!" said Narkom fiercely. "And against a pure creature like Mary Morrison! Here, Smathers, Petrie, Hammond, take him away. Hanging's too good for a beastly cur like that!"

* * * * *

"How did I know that the body was inside the statue?" said Cleek, answering Narkom's query, as they drove back in the red limousine toward London and Clarges Street. "Well, as a matter of fact, I never did know for certain until he began to examine the thing to-night. From the first I felt sure he was at the bottom of the affair, that he had lured Carboys back to the house, and murdered him; but it puzzled me to think what could possibly have been done with the body. I felt pretty certain, however, when I saw that monstrous statue."

"Yes, but why?"

"My dear Mr. Narkom, you ought not to ask that question. Did it not strike you as odd that a man who was torn with grief over the disappearance of a loved friend should think of modelling any sort of a statue on that very first day, much less such an inartistic one as that? Consider: the man has never been a first-class sculptor, it is true, but he knew the rudiments of his art, he had turned out some fairly presentable work; and that nymph was as abominably conceived and as abominably executed as if it had been the work of a raw beginner. Then there was another suspicious circumstance. Modelling clay is not exactly as cheap as dirt, Mr. Narkom. Why, then, should this man, who was confessedly as poor as the proverbial church mouse, plunge into the wild extravagance of buying half a ton of it—and at such a time? Those are the things that brought the suspicion into my mind; the certainty, however, had to be brought about beyond dispute before I could act.

"I knew that George Carboys had returned to that studio by the dry marks of muddy footprints, that were nothing like the shape of Van Nant's, which I found on the boards of the verandah and on the carpet under one of the windows; I knew, too, that it was Van Nant who had sent that pigeon. You remember when I excused myself and went back on the pretext of having forgotten my magnifying glass the other day? I did so for the purpose of looking at that fifth pigeon. I had observed something on its breast feathers which I thought, at first glance, was dry mud, as though it had fallen or brushed against something muddy in its flight. As we descended the stairs I observed that there was a similar mark on Van Nant's sleeve. I brushed against him and scraped off a fleck with my finger-nails. It was the dust of dried modelling clay. That on the pigeon's breast proved to be the same substance. I knew then that the hands of the person who liberated that pigeon were the hands of someone who was engaged in modelling something or handling the clay of the modeller, and—the inference was clear.

"As for the rest; when Van Nant entered that studio to-night, frightened half out of his wits at the knowledge that he would have to deal with the one detective he feared, I knew that if he approached that statue and made any attempts to examine it I should have my man, and that the hiding-place of his victim's body would be proved beyond question. When he did go to it, and did examine it—Clarges Street at last, thank fortune; for I am tired and sleepy. Stop here, Lennard; I'm getting out. Come along, Dollops. Good-night, Mr. Narkom! 'And so, to bed,' as good old Pepys says."

And passed on, up the street, with his hand on the boy's shoulder and the stillness and the darkness enfolding them.

CHAPTER XXVII

For the next five or six weeks life ran on merrily enough for Cleek; so merrily, in fact, that Dollops came to be quite accustomed to hear him whistling about the house and to see him go up the stairs two steps at a time whenever he had occasion to mount them for any purpose whatsoever.

It would not have needed any abnormally acute mind, any process of subtle reasoning, to get at the secret of all this exuberance, this perennial flow of high spirits; indeed, one had only to watch the letter box at Number 204, Clarges Street, to get at the bottom of it instantly; for twice a week the postman dropped into it a letter addressed in an undoubtedly feminine "hand" to Captain Horatio Burbage, and invariably postmarked "Lynhaven, Devon."

Dollops had made that discovery long ago and had put his conclusions regarding it into the mournfully-uttered sentence: "A skirt's got him!" But, after one violent pang of fierce and rending jealousy, was grateful to that "skirt" for bringing happiness to the man he loved above all other things upon earth and whose welfare was the dearest of his heart's desires. Indeed, he grew, in time, to watch as eagerly for the coming of those letters as did his master himself; and he could have shouted with delight whenever he heard the postman's knock, and saw one of the regulation blue-grey envelopes drop through the slit into the wire cage on the door.

Cleek, too, was delighted when he saw them. It was nothing to him that the notes they contained were of the briefest—mere records of the state of the weather, the progress of his little lordship, the fact that Lady Chepstow wished to be remembered and that the writer was well "and hoped he, too, was." They were written by *her*—that was enough. He gave so much that very little sufficed him in return; and the knowledge that he had been in her mind for the five or ten minutes which it had taken to write the few lines she sent him, made him exceedingly happy.

But she was not his only correspondent in these days—not even his most frequent one. For a warm, strong friendship—first sown in those ante-Derby days—had sprung up between Sir Henry Wilding and himself and had deepened steadily into a warm feeling of comradeship and mutual esteem. Frequent letters passed between them; and the bond of fellowship had become so strong a thing that Sir Henry never came to town without their meeting and dining together.

"Gad! you know, I can't bring myself to think of you as a police-officer, old chap!" was the way Sir Henry put it on the day when he first invited him to lunch with him at his club. "I'd about as soon think of sitting down with one of my grooms as breaking bread with one of that lot; and I shall never get it out of my head that you're a gentleman going in for this sort of thing as a hobby—never b'Gad! if I live to be a hundred."

"I hope you will come nearer to doing that than you have to guessing the truth about me," replied Cleek, with a smile. "Take my word for it, won't you?—this thing is my profession. I don't do it as a mere hobby: I live by it—I have no other means of living *but* by it. I am—what I am, and nothing more."

"Oh, gammon! Why not tell me at once that you are a winkle stall-keeper and be done with it? You can't tell a fish that another fish is a turnip—at least you can't and expect him to believe it. Own up, old chap. I know a man of birth when I meet him. Tell me who you are, Cleek—I'll respect it."

"I don't doubt that—the addition is superfluous."

"Then who are you? What are you, Cleek? Eh?"

"What you have called me—'Cleek.' Cleek the detective, Cleek of the Forty Faces, if you prefer it; but just 'Cleek' and nothing more. Don't get to building romances about me merely because I have the *instincts* of a gentleman, Sir Henry. Just simply remember that Nature *does* make mistakes sometimes; that she has been known to put a horse's head on a sheep's shoulders and to make a navvy's son look more royal than a prince. I am Cleek, the detective—simply Cleek. Let it go at that."

And as there was no alternative, Sir Henry did.

It made no difference in their friendship, however. Police officer or not, he liked and he respected the man, and made no visit to town without meeting and entertaining him.

So matters stood between them when on a certain Thursday in mid September he came up unexpectedly from Wilding Hall and 'phoned through to Clarges Street, asking Cleek to dine with him that night at the Club of the Two Services.

Cleek accepted the invitation gladly and was not a little surprised on arriving to find that, in this instance, dinner was to be served in a little private room and that a third party was also to partake of it.

"Dear chap, pardon me for taking you unawares," said Sir Henry, as Cleek entered the private room and found himself in the presence of a decidedly military-looking man long past middle life, "but the fact is that immediately after I had telephoned you, I encountered a friend and a—er—peculiar circumstance arose which impelled me to secure a private room and to—er—throw myself upon your good graces as it were. Let me have the pleasure, dear chap, of introducing you to my friend, Major Burnham-Seaforth. Major, you are at last in the presence of the gentleman of whom I spoke—Mr. Cleek."

"Mr. Cleek, I am delighted," said the Major, offering his hand. "I have heard your praises sung so continuously the past two hours that I feel as if I already knew you."

"Ah, you mustn't mind all that Sir Henry says," replied Cleek, as he shook hands with him. "He makes mountains out of millstones, and would panegyrize the most commonplace of men if he happened to take a fancy to him. You mustn't believe all that Sir Henry says and thinks, Major."

"I shall be happy, Mr. Cleek, if I can really hope to believe the half of it," replied the Major, enigmatically—and was prevented from saying more by the arrival of the waiter and the serving of dinner.

It was not until the meal was over and coffee and cigars had been served and the too attentive waiter had taken his departure that Cleek understood that remark or realised what it portended. But even then, it was not the Major who explained.

"My dear Cleek," said Sir Henry, lowering his voice and leaning over the table, "I hope you will not think I have taken a mean advantage of you, but I have brought the Major here to-night for a purpose. He has, in fact, come to consult you professionally; and upon my recommendation. Do you object to that, or may I go on?"

"Go on by all means," replied Cleek. "I fancy you know very well that there is nothing you might ask of me that I would not at least attempt to do, dear chap."

"Thanks very much. Well then, the Major has come, my dear Cleek, to ask you to help in unravelling a puzzle of singular and mystifying interest. Now you may or may not have heard of a Music Hall artiste—a sort of conjurer and impersonator combined—called Zyco the Magician, who was once very popular and was assisted in his illusions by a veiled but reputedly beautiful Turkish lady who was billed on the programmes and posters as 'Zuilika, the Caliph's Daughter.'"

"I remember the pair very well indeed," said Cleek. "They toured the Music Halls for years, and I saw their performance frequently. They were among the first, I believe, to produce that afterwards universal illusion known as 'The Vanishing Lady.' As I have not heard anything of them nor seen their names billed for a couple of years past, I fancy they have either retired from the profession or gone to some other part of the world. The man was not only a very clever magician, but a master of mimicry. I always believed, however, that in spite of his name he was of English birth. The woman's face I never saw, of course, as she was always veiled to the eyes after the manner of Turkish ladies. But although a good many persons suspected that her birthplace was no nearer Bagdad than Peckham, I somehow felt that she was, after all, a genuine, native-born Turk."

"You are quite right in both suspicions, Mr. Cleek," put in the Major agitatedly. "The man *was* an Englishman; the lady *is* a Turk."

"May I ask, Major, why you speak of the lady in the present tense and of the man in the past? Is he dead?"

"I hope so," responded the Major fervently. "God knows I do, Mr. Cleek. My every hope in life depends upon that."

"May I ask why?"

"I am desirous of marrying his widow!"

"My dear Major, you cannot possibly be serious! A woman of that class?"

"Pardon me, sir, but you have, for all your cleverness, fallen a victim to the prevailing error. The lady is in every way my social equal—in her own country my superior. She *is* a caliph's daughter. The title which the playgoing public imagined was of the usual bombastic, just-on-the-programme sort, is hers by right. Her late father, Caliph Al Hamid Sulaiman, was one of the richest and most powerful Mohammedans in existence. He died five months ago, leaving an immense fortune to be conveyed to England to his exiled but forgiven child."

"Ah, I see. Then, naturally, of course—"

"The suggestion is unworthy of you, Sir Henry, and anything but complimentary to me. The inheritance of this money has had nothing whatever to do with my feelings for the lady. That began two years ago, when, by accident, I was permitted to look upon her face for the first, last, and only time. I should still wish to marry her if she were an absolute pauper. I know what you are saying to yourself, sir: 'There is no fool like an old fool.' Well, perhaps there isn't. But—" he turned to Cleek—"I may as well begin at the beginning and confess that even if I did not desire to marry the lady I should still have a deep interest in her husband's death, Mr. Cleek. He is—or was, if dead—the only son of my cousin, the Earl of Wynraven, who is now over ninety years of age. I am in the direct line, and if this Lord Norman Ulchester, whom you and the public know only as 'Zyco the Magician,' were in his grave there would only be that one feeble old man between me and the title."

"Ah, I see!" said Cleek, in reply; then, seating himself at the table, he arranged the shade of the lamp so that the light fell full upon the Major's face while leaving his own in the shadow. "Then your interest in the affair, Major, may be said to be a double one."

"More, sir—a triple one. I have a rival in the shape of my own son. He, too, wishes to marry Zuilika—is madly enamoured of her, in fact; so wildly that I have always hesitated to confess my own desires to him for fear of the consequences. He is almost a madman in his outbursts of temper; and where Zuilika is concerned—Perhaps you will understand, Mr. Cleek, when I tell you that once when he thought her husband had ill-used her, he came within an ace of killing the man. There was bad blood between them always—even as boys—and, as men, it was bitterer than ever because of *her*."

"Suppose you begin at the beginning and tell me the whole story, Major," suggested Cleek, studying the man's face narrowly. "How did the Earl of Wynraven's son come to meet this singularly fascinating lady, and where?"

"In Turkey—or Arabia—I forget which. He was doing his theatrical nonsense in the East with some barn-storming show or other, having been obliged to get out of England to escape arrest for some shady transaction a year before. He was always a bad egg—always a disgrace to his name and connections. That's why his father turned him off and never would have any more to do with him. As a boy he was rather clever at conjuring tricks and impersonations of all sorts—he could mimic anything or anybody he ever saw, from the German Emperor down to a Gaiety chorus girl, and do it to absolute perfection. When his father kicked him out he turned these natural gifts to account, and, having fallen in with some professional dancing-woman, joined her for a time and went on the stage with her.

"It was after he had parted from this dancer and was knocking about London and leading a disgraceful life generally that he did the thing which caused him to hurry off to the East and throw in his lot with the travelling company I have alluded to. He was always a handsome fellow and had a way with him that was wonderfully taking with women, so I suppose that that accounts as much as anything for Zuilika's infatuation and her doing the mad thing she did. I don't know when nor where nor how they first met; but the foolish girl simply went off her head over him, and he appears to have been as completely infatuated with her. Of course, in that land, the idea of a woman of her sect, of her standing, having anything to do with a Frank was looked upon as something appalling, something akin to sacrilege; and when they found that her father had got wind of it and that the fellow's life would not be safe if he remained within reach another day, they flew to the coast together, shipped for England, and were married immediately after their arrival."

"A highly satisfactory termination for the lady," commented Cleek. "One could hardly have expected that from a man so hopelessly unprincipled as you represent him to have always been. But there's a bit of good in even the devil, we are told."

"Oh, be sure that he didn't marry her from any principle of honour, my dear sir," replied the Major. "If it were merely a question of that, he'd have cut loose from her as soon as the vessel touched port. Consideration of self ruled him in that as in all other things. He knew that the girl's father fairly idolised her; knew that, in time, his wrath would give way to his love, and, sooner or later, the old man—who had been mad at the idea of any marriage—would be moved to settle a large sum upon her so that she might never be in want. But let me get on with my story. Having nothing when he returned to England, and being obliged to cover up his identity by assuming another name, Ulchester, after vainly appealing to his father for help on the plea that he was now honourably married and settled down, turned again to the stage, and, repugnant though such a thing was to the delicately-nurtured woman he had married, compelled Zuilika to become his assistant and to go on the boards with him. That is how the afterwards well-known music-hall 'team' of 'Zyco and the Caliph's Daughter' came into existence.

"The novelty of their 'turn' caught on like wild fire, and they were a success from the first, not a little of that success being due to the mystery surrounding the identity and appearance of Zuilika; for, true to the traditions of her native land, she never appeared, either in public or in private, without being closely veiled. Only her 'lord' was ever permitted to look upon her uncovered face; all that the world at large might ever hope to behold of it was the low, broad forehead and the two brilliant eyes that appeared above the close-drawn line of her yashmak. Of course she shrank from the life into which she was forced; but it had its reward, for it kept her in close contact with her husband, whom she almost worshipped. So, for a time, she was proportionately happy; although, as the years passed by and her father showed no inclination to bestow the coveted 'rich allowance' upon his daughter, Ulchester's ardour began to cool. He no longer treated her with the same affectionate deference; he neglected her, in fact, and, in the end, even began to ill-use her.

"About two years ago, matters assumed a worse aspect. He again met Anita Rosario, the Spanish dancer, under whose guidance he had first turned to the halls for a livelihood, and once more took up with her. He seemed to have lost all thought or care for the feelings of his wife, for, after torturing her with jealousy over his attentions to the dancer, he took a house adjoining my own—on the borders of the most unfrequented part of the common at Wimbledon—established himself and Zuilika there, and brought the woman Anita home to live with them. From that period matters went from bad to worse. Evidently having tired of the stage, both Ulchester and Anita abandoned it, and turned the house into a sort of club where gambling was carried on to a disgraceful extent. Broken-hearted over the treatment she was receiving, Zuilika appealed to me and to my son to help her in her distress—to devise some plan to break the spell of Ulchester's madness and to get that woman out of the house. It was then that I first beheld her face. In her excitement she managed, somehow, to snap or loosen the fastening which held her yashmak, and it fell—fell, and let my son realise, as I realised, how wondrously beautiful it is possible for the human face to be!"

"Steady, Major, steady! I can quite understand your feelings—can realise better than most men!" said Cleek with a sort of sigh. "You looked into heaven, and—well, what then? Let's have the rest of the story."

"I think my son must have put it into her head to give Ulchester a taste of his own medicine—to attempt to excite his jealousy by pretending to find interests elsewhere. At any rate, she began to show him a great deal of attention—or, at least, so he says, although I never saw it. All I know is that she—she—well, sir, she deliberately led *me* on until I was half insane over her, and—that's all!"

"What do you mean by 'that's all'? The matter couldn't possibly have ended there, or else why this appeal to me?"

"It ended for me, so far as her affectionate treatment of me was concerned; for in the midst of it the unexpected happened. Her father died, forgiving her, as Ulchester had hoped, but doing more than his wildest dreams could have given him cause to imagine possible. In a word, sir, the caliph not only bestowed his entire earthly possessions upon her, but had them conveyed to England by trusted allies and placed in her hands. There were coffers of gold pieces, jewels of fabulous value—sufficient, when converted into English money, as they were within the week, and deposited to her credit in the Bank of England, to make her the sole possessor of nearly three million pounds."

"Phew!" whistled Cleek. "When these Orientals do it they certainly do it properly. That's what you might call 'giving with both hands,' Major, eh?"

"The gift did not end with that, sir," the Major replied with a gesture of repulsion. "There was a gruesome, ghastly, appalling addition in the shape of two mummy cases—one empty, the other filled. A parchment accompanying these stated that the caliph could not sleep elsewhere but in the land of his fathers, nor sleep *there* until his beloved child rested beside him. They had been parted in life, but they should not be parted in death. An Egyptian had, therefore, been summoned to his bedside, had been given orders to embalm him after death, to send the mummy to Zuilika, and with it a case in which, when her own death should occur, *her* body should be deposited; and followers of the prophet had taken oath to see that both were carried to their native land and entombed side by side. Until death came to relieve her of this ghastly duty, Zuilika was charged to be the guardian of the mummy and daily to make the orisons of the faithful before it, keeping it always with its face towards the East."

"By George! it sounds like a page from the 'Arabian Nights,'" exclaimed Cleek. "Well, what next? Did Ulchester take kindly to this housing of the mummy of his father-in-law and the eventual coffin of his wife? Or was he willing to stand for anything so long as he got possession of the huge fortune the old man left?"

"He never did get it, Mr. Cleek—he never touched so much as one farthing of it. Zuilika took nobody into her confidence until everything had been converted into English gold and deposited in the bank to her credit. Then she went straight to him and to Anita, showed them proof of the deposit, reviled them for their treatment of her, and swore that not one farthing's benefit should accrue to Ulchester until Anita was turned out of the house in the presence of their guests and the husband took oath on his knees to join the wife in those daily prayers before the caliph's mummy. Furthermore, Ulchester was to embrace the faith of the Mohammedans that he might return with her at once to the land and the gods she had offended by marriage with a Frankish infidel."

"Which, of course, he declined to do?"

"Yes. He declined utterly. But it was a case of the crushed worm, with Zuilika. Now was *her* turn; and she would not abate one jot or tittle. There was a stormy scene, of course. It ended by Ulchester and the woman Anita leaving the house together. From that hour Zuilika never again heard his living voice, never again saw his living face! He seems to have gone wild with wrath over what he had lost and to have plunged headlong into the maddest sort of dissipation. It is known—positively known, and can be sworn to by reputable witnesses—that for the next three days he did not draw one sober breath. On the fourth, a note from him—a note which he was *seen* to write in a public house—was carried to Zuilika. In that note he cursed her with every conceivable term; told her that when she got it he would be at the bottom of the river, driven there by her conduct, and that if it was possible for the dead to come back and haunt people he'd do it. Two hours after he wrote that note he was seen getting out of the train at Tilbury and going towards the docks; but from that moment to this every trace of him is lost."

"Ah, I see!" said Cleek reflectively. "And you want to find out if he really carried out that threat and did put an end to himself, I suppose? That's why you have come to me, eh? Frankly, I don't believe that he did, Major. That sort of a man never commits suicide upon so slim a pretext as that. If he commits it at all, it's because he is at the end of his tether—and our friend 'Zyco' seems to have been a long way from the end of his. How does the lady take it? Seriously?"

"Oh, very, sir, very. Of course, to a woman of her temperament and with her Oriental ideas regarding the supernatural, *et cetera*, that threat to haunt her was the worst he could have done to her. At first she was absolutely beside herself with grief and horror; swore that she had killed him by her cruelty; that there was nothing left her but to die, and all that sort of thing; and for three days she was little better than a mad woman. At the end of that time, after the fashion of her people, she retired to her own room, covered herself with sackcloth and ashes, and remained hidden from all eyes for the space of a fortnight, weeping and wailing constantly and touching nothing but bread and water."

"Poor wretch! She suffers like that, then, over a rascally fellow not worth a single tear. It's marvellous, Major, what women do see in men that they can go on loving them. Has she come out of her retirement yet?"

"Yes, Mr. Cleek. She came out of it five days ago, to all appearances a thoroughly heart-broken woman. Of course as she was all alone in the world, my son and I considered it our duty, during the time of her wildness and despair, to see that a thoroughly respectable female was called in to take charge of the house and to show respect for the proprieties, and for us to take up our abode there in order to prevent her from doing herself an injury. We are still domiciled there, but it will surprise you to learn that a most undesirable person is there also. In short, sir, that the woman Anita Rosario, the cause of all the trouble, is again an inmate of the house; and what is more remarkable still, this time by Zuilika's own request."

"What's that? My dear Major, you amaze me! What can possibly have caused the good lady to do a thing like that?"

"She hopes, she says, to appease the dead and to avert the threatened 'haunting.' At all events, she sent for Anita some days ago. Indeed, I believe it is her intention to take the Spaniard with her when she returns to the East."

"She intends doing that, then? She is so satisfied of her husband's death that she deems no further question necessary. Intends to take no further step toward proving it?"

"It has been proved to her satisfaction. His body was recovered the day before yesterday."

"Oho! then he is dead, eh? Why didn't you say so in the beginning? When did you learn of it?"

"This very evening. That is what brings me here. I learned from Zuilika that a body answering the description of his had been fished from the water at Tilbury and carried to the mortuary. It was horribly disfigured—by contact with the piers and passing vessels—but she and Anita—and—and my son—"

"Your son, Major? Your son?"

"Yes!" replied the Major in a sort of half-whisper. "They—they took him with them when they went, unknown to me. He has become rather friendly with the Spanish woman of late. All three saw the body; all three identified it as being Ulchester's beyond a doubt."

"And you? Surely when you see it you will be able to satisfy any misgivings you may have?"

"I shall never see it, Mr. Cleek. It was claimed when identified and buried within twelve hours," said the Major, glancing up sharply as Cleek, receiving this piece of information, blew out a soft, low whistle. "I was not told anything about it until this evening, and what I have done—in coming to you, I mean—I have done with nobody's knowledge. I—I am so horribly in the dark—I have such fearful thoughts and—and I want to be sure. I must be sure or I shall go out of my mind. That's the 'case,' Mr. Cleek—tell me what you think of it."

"I can do that in a very few words, Major," he replied. "It is either a gigantic swindle or it is a clear case of murder. If a swindle, then Ulchester himself is at the bottom of it and it will end in murder just the same. Frankly, the swindle theory strikes me as being the more probable; in other words, that the whole thing is a put-up game between Ulchester and the woman Anita; that they played upon Zuilika's fear of the supernatural for a purpose; that a body was procured and sunk in that particular spot for the furtherance of that purpose; and if the widow attempts to put into execution this plan—no doubt instilled into her mind by Anita—of returning with her wealth to her native land, she will simply be led into some safe place and then effectually put out of the way for ever. That is what I think of the case if it is to be regarded in the light a swindle; but if Ulchester is really dead, murder, not suicide, is at the back of his taking off, and—Oh, well, we won't say anything more about it just yet awhile. I shall want to look over the ground before I jump to any conclusions. You are still stopping in the house, you and your son, I think you remarked? If you could contrive to put up an old army friend's son there for a night, Major, give me the address. I'll drop in on you to-morrow and have a little look round."

CHAPTER XXVIII

When, next morning, Major Burnham-Seaforth announced the dilemma in which, through his own house being temporarily closed, he found himself owing to the proposed visit of Lieutenant Rupert St. Aubyn, son of an old army friend, Zuilika was the first to suggest the very thing he was fishing for.

"Ah, let him come here, dear friend," she said in that sad, sweetly modulated voice which so often wrung this susceptible old heart. "There is plenty of room!—plenty, alas now—and any friend of yours can only be a friend of mine. He will not annoy. Let him come here."

"Yes, let him," supplemented young Burnham-Seaforth, speaking with his eyes on Señorita Rosario, who seemed nervous and ill-pleased by the news of the expected arrival. "He won't have to be entertained by us if he only comes to see the pater; and we can easily crowd him aside if he tries to thrust himself upon us—a fellow with a name like 'Rupert St. Aubyn' is bound to be a silly ass." And when, in the late afternoon, "Lieutenant Rupert St. Aubyn," in the person of Cleek, arrived with his snubnosed manservant, a kit-bag, several rugs and a bundle of golf sticks, young Burnham-Seaforth saw no reason to alter that assertion. For, a "silly ass"—albeit an unusually handsome one with his fair, curling hair and his big blonde moustache—he certainly was; a lisping "ha-ha-ing" "don't-cher-knowing" silly ass, whom the presence of ladies seemed to cover with confusion and drive into a very panic of shy embarrassment.

"*Dios!* but he is handsome, this big, fair lieutenant!" whispered the Spaniard to young Burnham-Seaforth. "A great, handsome fool—all beauty and no brains, like a doll of wax!" Then she bent over and murmured smilingly to Zuilika: "I shall make a bigger nincompoop of this big, fair sap-head than Heaven already has done before he leaves here, just for the sake of seeing him stammer and blush!"

Only the sad expression of Zuilika's eyes told that she so much as heard, as she rose to greet the visitor. Garbed from head to foot in the deep violet-coloured stuff which is the mourning of Turkish women, her little pointed slippers showing beneath the hem of her frock, and only her dark, mournful eyes visible between the top of the shrouding yashmak and the edge of her sequined snood, she made a pathetic picture as she stood there waiting to greet the unknown visitor.

"Sir, you are welcome—you are most welcome," she said in a voice whose modulations were not lost upon Cleek's ears as he put forth his hand and received the tips of her little, henna-stained fingers upon his palm. "Peace be with you, who are of his people—he that I loved and mourn!" Then, as if overcome with grief at the recollection of her widowhood, she plucked away her hand, covered her eyes, and moved staggeringly out of the room. And Cleek saw no more of her that day; but he knew when she performed her orisons before the mummy case—as she did each morning and evening—by the strong, pungent odour of incense drifting through the house and filling it with a sickly scent.

Her absence seemed to make but little impression upon him, however; for, following up a well-defined plan of action, he devoted himself wholly to the Spanish woman, and both amazed her and gratified her vanity by allowing her to learn that a man may be the silliest ass imaginable and yet quite understand how to flirt and to make love to a woman. And so it fell out that instead of "Lieutenant Rupert St. Aubyn" being elbowed out by young Burnham-Seaforth, it was "Lieutenant St. Aubyn" who elbowed *him* out; and without being in the least aware of it, the flattered Anita, like an adroitly hooked trout, was being "played" in and out and round about the eddies and the deeps until the angler had her quite ready for the final dip of the net at the landing point.

All this was to accomplish exactly what it *did* accomplish, namely, the ill temper, the wrath, the angry resentment of young Burnham-Seaforth. And when the evening had passed and bedtime arrived, Cleek took his candle and retired in the direction of the rooms set apart for him, with the certainty of knowing that he had done that which would this very night prove beyond all question the guilt or innocence of one person at least who was enmeshed in this mysterious tangle. He was not surprised, therefore, at what followed his next step.

Reaching the upper landing he blew out the light of his candle, slammed the door to his own room, noisily turned the key, and shot the bolt of another, then tiptoed his way back to the staircase and looked down the well-hole into the lower hall.

Zuilika had retired to her room, the Major had retired to his, and now Anita was taking up her candle to retire to hers. She had barely touched it, however, when there came a sound of swift footsteps and young Burnham-Seaforth lurched out of the drawing-room door and joined her. He was in a state of great excitement and was breathing hard.

"Anita—Miss Rosario!" he began, plucking her by the sleeve and uplifting a pale, boyish face—he was not yet twenty-two—to hers with a look of abject misery. "I want to speak to you—I simply must speak to you. I've been waiting for the chance, and now that it's come—Look here! You're not going back on me, are you?"

"Going back on you?" repeated Anita, showing her pretty white teeth in an amused smile. "What shall you mean by that 'going back on you'—eh? You are a stupid little donkey, to be sure. But then I do not care to get on the back of one—so why?"

"Oh, you know very well what I mean," he rapped out angrily. "It is not fair the way you have been treating me ever since that yellow-headed bounder came. I've had a night of misery—Zuilika never showing herself; you doing nothing, absolutely nothing, although you promised— you *know* you did!—and I heard you, I absolutely heard you persuade that St. Aubyn fool to stop at least another night."

"Yes, of course you did. But what of it? He is good company—he talks well, he sings well, he is very handsome and—well, what difference can it make to you? You are not interested in *me, amigo*?"

"No, no; of course I'm not. You are nothing to me at all—you—Oh, I beg your pardon; I didn't quite mean that. I—I mean you are nothing to me in that way. But you—you're not keeping to your word. You promised, you know, that you'd use your influence with Zuilika; that you'd get her to be more kind to me—to see me alone and—and all that sort of thing. And you've not made a single attempt—not one. You've just sat round and flirted with that tow-headed brute and done nothing at all to help me on; and—and it's jolly unkind of you, that's what!"

Cleek heard Anita's soft rippling laughter; but he waited to hear no more. Moving swiftly away from the well-hole of the staircase he passed on tiptoe down the hall to the Major's rooms, and, opening the door, went in. The old soldier was standing, with arms folded, at the window looking silently out into the darkness of the night. He turned at the sound of the door's opening and moved toward Cleek with a white, agonised face and a pair of shaking, outstretched hands.

"Well?" he said with a sort of gasp.

"My dear Major," said Cleek quietly. "The wisest of men are sometimes mistaken—that is my excuse for my own short-sightedness. I said in the beginning that his was either a case of swindling or a case of murder, did I not? Well, I now amend my verdict. It is a case of swindling *and* murder; and your son has had nothing to do with either!"

"Oh, thank God! thank God!" the old man said; then sat down suddenly and dropped his face between his hands and was still for a long time. When he looked up again his eyes were red, but his lips were smiling.

"If you only knew what a relief it is," he said. "If you only knew how much I have suffered, Mr. Cleek. His friendship with that Spanish woman; his going with her to identify the body—even assisting in its hurried burial! These things all seemed so frightfully black—so utterly without any explanation other than personal guilt."

"Yet they are all easily explained, Major. His friendship for the Spanish woman is merely due to a promise to intercede for him with Zuilika. She is his one aim and object, poor little donkey! As for his identification of the body—well, if the widow herself could find points of undisputed resemblance, why not he? A nervous, excitable, impetuous boy like that— and anxious, too, that the lady of his heart should be freed from the one thing, the one man, whose existence made her everlastingly unattainable— why, in the hands of a clever woman like Anita Rosario such a chap could be made to identify anything and to believe it as religiously as he believes. Now, go to bed and rest easy, Major. I'm going to call up Dollops and do a little night prowling. If it turns out as I hope, this little riddle will be solved to-morrow."

"But how, Mr. Cleek? It seems to me that it is as dark as ever. You put my poor old head in a whirl. You say there is swindling; you hint one moment that the body was not that of Ulchester, and in the next that murder has been done. Do, pray, tell me what it all means—what you make of this amazing case."

"I'll do that to-morrow, Major; not to-night. The answer to the riddle— the answer that's in my mind, I mean—is at once so simple and yet so appallingly awful that I'll hazard no guess until I'm sure. Look here"—he put his hand into his pocket and pulled out a gold piece—"do you know what that is, Major?"

"It looks like a spade guinea, Mr. Cleek."

"Right; it is a spade guinea—a pocket piece I've carried for years. You've heard, no doubt, of vital things turning upon the tossing of a coin. Well, if you see me toss this coin to-morrow, something of that sort will occur. It will be tossed up in the midst of a riddle, Major; when it comes down it will be a riddle no longer."

Then he opened the door, closed it after him, and, before the Major could utter a word, was gone.

CHAPTER XXIX

The promise was so vague, so mystifying, indeed, so seemingly absurd, that the Major did not allow himself to dwell upon it. As a matter of fact, it passed completely out of his mind; nor did it again find lodgment there until it was forced back upon his memory in a most unusual manner.

Whatsoever had been the result of what Cleek had called his "night prowling," he took nobody into his confidence when he and the Major and the Major's son and Señorita Rosario met at breakfast the next day (Zuilika, true to her training and the traditions of her people, never broke morning bread save in the seclusion of her own bed-chamber, and then on her knees with her face towards the east) nor did he allude to it at any period throughout the day.

He seemed, indeed, purposely, to avoid the Major, and to devote himself to the Spanish woman with an ardour that was positively heartless, considering that as they two sang and flirted and played several sets of singles on the tennis court, Zuilika, like a spirit of misery, kept walking, walking, walking through the halls and the rooms of the house, her woeful eyes fixed on the carpet, her henna-stained fingers constantly locking and unlocking, and moans of desolation coming now and again from behind her yashmak as her swaying body moved restlessly to and fro. For to-day was memorable. Five weeks ago this coming nightfall Ulchester had flung himself out of this house in a fury of wrath, and this time of bitter regret and ceaseless mourning had begun.

"She will go out of her mind, poor creature, if something cannot be done to keep her from dwelling on her misery like this," commented the housekeeper, coming upon that restless figure pacing the darkened hall, moaning, moaning—seeing nothing, hearing nothing, doing nothing but walk and sorrow, sorrow and walk, hour in and hour out. "It's enough to tear a body's heart to hear her, poor dear. And that good-for-nothing Spanish piece racing and shrieking round the tennis court like a she tom-cat, the heartless hussy. Her and that simpering silly that's trotting round after her had ought to be put in a bag and shaken up, that they ought. It's downright scandalous to be carrying on like that at such a time."

And so both the Major and his son thought too, and tried their best to solace the lonely mourner and to persuade her to sit down and rest.

"Zuilika, you will wear yourself out, child, if you go on walking like this," said the Major solicitously. "Do rest and be at peace for a little time at least."

"I can never have peace in this land—I can never forget the day!" she answered drearily. "Oh, my beloved! Oh, my lord, it was I who sent thee to it—it was I, it was I! Give me my own country—give me the gods of my people; here there is only memory and pain, and no rest, no rest ever!"

She could not be persuaded to sit down and rest until Anita herself took the matter into her own hands and insisted that she should. That was at tea-time. Anita, showing some little trace of feeling now that Cleek had gone to wash his hands and was no longer there to occupy her thoughts, placed a deep, soft chair near the window, and would not yield until the violet-clad figure of the mourner sank down into the depths of it and leaned back with its shrouded face drooping in silent melancholy.

And it was while she was so sitting that Cleek came into the room and did a most unusual, a most ungentlemanly thing, in the eyes of the Major and his son.

Without hesitating, he walked to within a yard or two of where she was sitting, and then, in the silliest of silly tones, blurted out suddenly: "I say, don't you know, I've had a jolly rum experience. You know that blessed room at the angle just opposite the library—the one with the locked door?"

The drooping, violet figure straightened abruptly, and the Major felt for the moment as if he could have kicked Cleek with pleasure. Of course they knew the room. It was there that the two mummy cases were kept, sacred from the profaning presence of any but this stricken woman. No wonder that she bent forward, full of eagerness, full of the dreadful fear that Frankish feet had crossed the threshold, Frankish eyes looked within the sacred shrine.

"Well, don't you know," went on Cleek, without taking the slightest notice of anything, "just as I was going past that door I picked up a most remarkable thing. Wonder if it's yours, madam?" glancing at Zuilika. "Just have a look at it, will you? Here, catch!" And not until he saw a piece of gold spin through the air and fall into Zuilika's lap did the Major remember that promise of last night.

"Oh, come, I say, St. Aubyn, that's rather thick!" sang out young Burnham-Seaforth indignantly, as Zuilika caught the coin in her lap.

"Blest if I know what you call manners, but to throw things at a lady is a new way of passing them in this part of the world, I can assure you."

"Awfully sorry, old chap, no offence, I assure you," said Cleek, more asinine than ever, as Zuilika, having picked up the piece and looked at it, disclaimed all knowledge of it, and laid it on the edge of the table without any further interest in it or him. "Just to show, you know, that I—er—couldn't have meant anything disrespectful, why—er—you all know, don't you know, how jolly much I respect Señorita Rosario, by Jove! and so—Here, señorita, you catch, too, and see if the blessed thing's yours." And, picking up the coin, tossed it into her lap just as he had done with Zuilika.

She, too, caught it and examined it, and laughingly shook her head.

"No—not mine!" she said. "I have not seen him before. To the finder shall be the keep. Come, sit here. Will you have the tea?"

"Yes, thanks," said Cleek; then dropped down on the sofa beside her, and took tea as serenely as though there were no such things in the world as murder and swindling and puzzling police-riddles to solve.

And the Major, staring at him, was as amazed as ever. He had said, last night, that when the coin fell the answer would be given—and yet it had fallen, and nothing had happened, and he was laughing and flirting with Señorita Rosario as composedly and as persistently as ever. More than that; after he had finished his second cup of tea, and immediately following the sound of someone just beyond the verandah rail whistling the lively, lilting measures of "There's a Girl Wanted There"—the "silly ass" seemed to become a thousand times sillier than ever; for he forthwith set down his cup, and, turning to Anita, said with an inane sort of giggle, "I say, you know, here's a lark. Let's have a game of 'Slap Hand,' you and I—what? Know it, don't you? You try to slap my hands, and I try to slap yours, and whichever succeeds in doing it first gets a prize. Awful fun, don't you know. Come on—start her up."

And, Anita agreeing, they fell forthwith to slapping away at the backs of each other's hands with great gusto, until, all of a sudden, the whistler outside gave one loud, shrill note, and—there was a great and mighty change.

Those who were watching saw Anita's two hands suddenly caught, heard a sharp, metallic "click," and saw them as suddenly dropped again to the accompaniment of a shrill little scream from her ashen lips, and the next moment Cleek had risen and jumped away from her side—clear across to where Zuilika was; and those who were watching saw Anita jump up with a pair of steel handcuffs on her wrists, just as Dollops vaulted up over the verandah rail and appeared at one window, whilst Petrie appeared at another, Hammond poked his body through a third, and the opening door gave entrance to Superintendent Narkom.

"The police!" shrilled out Anita in a panic of fright. "*Madre de Dios*, the police!"

The Major and his son were on their feet like a shot; Zuilika, with a faint, startled cry, bounded bolt upright, like an imp shot through a trap-door; but before the little henna-stained hands could do more than simply move, Cleek's arms went round her from behind, tight and fast as a steel clamp, there was another metallic "click," another shrill cry, and another pair of wrists were in gyves.

"Come in, Mr. Narkom; come in, constables," said Cleek, with the utmost composure. "Here are your promised prisoners—nicely trussed, you see, so that they can't get at the little popguns they carry—and a worse pair of rogues never went into the hands of Jack Ketch!"

"And Jack Ketch will get them, Cleek, if I know anything about it. Your hazard was right. I've examined the caliph's mummy-case; the mummy itself has been removed—destroyed—done away with utterly—and the poor creature's body is there!"

And here the poor, dumfounded, utterly bewildered Major found voice to speak at last.

"Mummy-case! Body! Dear God in heaven, Mr. Cleek, what are you hinting at?" he gasped. "You—you don't mean that she—that Zuilika—killed him?"

"No, Major, I don't," he made reply. "I simply mean that he killed her! The body in the mummy-case is the body of Zuilika, the caliph's daughter! This is the creature you have been wasting your pity on—see!"

With that he laid an intense grip on the concealing yashmak, tore it away, and so revealed the close-shaven, ghastly-hued countenance of the cornered criminal.

"My God!—Ulchester—Ulchester himself!" said the Major in a voice of fright and surprise.

"Yes, Ulchester himself, Major. In a few more days he'd have withdrawn the money, and got out of the country, body and all, if he hadn't been nabbed, the rascal. There'd have been no tracing the crime then; and he and the Señorita here would have been in clover for the rest of their natural lives. But there's always that bright little bit of Bobby Burns to be reckoned with. You know: 'The best laid schemes of mice and men,' *et cetera*—that bit.

But the Yard's got them, and—they'll never leave the country now. Take them, Mr. Narkom, they're yours!"

* * * * *

"How did I guess it?" said Cleek, replying to the Major's query, as they sat late that night discussing the affair. "Well, I think the first faint inkling of it came when I arrived here yesterday, and smelt the overpowering odour of the incenses. There was so much of it, and it was used so frequently—twice a day—that it seemed to suggest an attempt to hide other odours of a less pleasant kind. When I left you last night, Dollops and I went down to the mummy-chamber, and a skeleton key soon let us in. The unpleasant odour was rather pronounced in there. But even that didn't give me the cue, until I happened to find in the fireplace a considerable heap of fine ashes, and in the midst of them small lumps of gummy substance, which I knew to result from the burning of myrrh. I suspected from that and from the nature of the ashes that a mummy had been burnt, and as there was only one mummy in the affair, the inference was obvious. I laid hands on the two cases and tilted them. One was quite empty. The weight of the other told me that it contained something a little heavier than any mummy ought to be. I came to the conclusion that there was a body in it, injected full of arsenic, no doubt, to prevent as much as possible the processes of decay, the odour of which the incense was concealing. I didn't attempt to open the thing; I left that until the arrival of the men from The Yard, for whom I sent Dollops this afternoon. I had a vague notion that it would not turn out to be Ulchester's, and I had also a distinct recollection of what you said about his being able to mimic a Gaiety chorus-girl and all that sort of thing, and the more I thought over it, the more I realized what an excellent thing to cover a bearded face a yashmak is. Still, it was all hazard. I wasn't sure—indeed, I never was sure—until tea-time, when I caught this supposed 'Zuilika' sitting at last, and gave the spade guinea its chance to decide it."

"But, Mr. Cleek, how could it have decided it? That's the thing which amazes me most of all. How could the tossing of that coin have decided the sex of the wearer of those garments?"

"My dear Major, it is an infallible test. Did you ever notice that if you throw anything for a man to catch in his lap, he pulls his knees together to *make* a lap in order to catch it; whereas a woman—used to wearing skirts and, thereby, having a lap already prepared—immediately broadens that lap by the exactly opposite movement, knowing that whatever is thrown has no chance of slipping through and falling to the floor. When I tossed the coin to Ulchester, he instinctively jerked his knees together. That settled it, of course. And now, if you won't mind my saying it, I'm a bit sleepy and it is about time I took myself off to home and bed."

"But not at this late hour, surely? You will never catch a train."

"I shan't need one, Major. They are holding a horse and trap ready for me at the stables of the 'Coach and Horses.' Mr. Narkom promised to look out for that, and—I beg pardon? No, I can't stop over night. Thank you for the invitation, but Dollops would raise half London if I didn't turn up after promising to do so."

"I should have thought you might have simplified matters and obviated that by keeping the boy when you had him here," said the Major. "We could easily have found a place to put him up for the night."

"Thanks very much, but I wouldn't interrupt the course of his studies for the world," replied Cleek. "I've found an old chap—an ex-schoolmaster, down on his luck and glad for the chance to turn an honest penny—who takes him on every night from eight to ten; and the young monkey is so eager and is absorbing knowledge at such a rate that he positively amazes me. But now, really, it must be good-night. The boy will be waiting and I must hear his lessons before I go to bed."

"Not surely when you are so tired as you say?"

"Never too tired for that, Major. It makes me sleep better and sounder to know that the lad's getting on and that I've cheated the Devil in just one more instance. Good-night and good luck to you. It's a bully old world after all, isn't it, Major?" Then laughed and shook hands with him and fared forth into the starlight, whistling.

CHAPTER XXX

Who feeds on Hope alone makes but a sorry banquet; and for the next few weeks Hope was all—or nearly all—that came Cleek's way.

For some unexplained reason, Miss Lorne's letters—never very frequent, and always very brief—had, of late been gradually growing briefer: as if written in haste and from a mere sense of duty and at odd moments snatched from the call of more absorbing things; and, finally, there came a dropping off altogether and a week that brought no message from her at all.

The old restlessness, the almost outlived sense of personal injury and rebellion against circumstances, took hold of Cleek again when that time came; and the soul of him drank deep of the waters of bitterness.

So, then, it was all to be in vain, was it, this long struggle with the Devil of Circumstances, this long striving for a Goal? And after all, "Thou shalt not enter" was to be written over the gateway of his ambition? He had been lifted only to be dropped again, redeemed only to let him see how vain it was for the leopard, even though he achieved the impossible and changed his spots, to be other than a leopard always; how impossible it was for a man to override the decrees of Nature or evade the edicts of Providence? That was what it meant, eh?

To a nature such as his, Life was always a picture drawn out of perspective. There was never any Middle Distance; never any proper gradation. It was always either the Highest Heights or the Lowest Depths; the glare of fierce light or the black of deepest darkness. He could not plod; he must either fly or fall; either loll at the Gates of Paradise or groan in the depths of Hell. And the failure of Ailsa Lorne's letters sent him to the darkest and most hopeless corner of it.

Not that he blamed her—wholly; but that he blamed that Fate which had so persistently dogged him from childhood on. For now that the letters had ceased altogether, he recalled things which otherwise would have been forgotten; and, his sense of proportion being distorted, made mountains out of sand dunes.

In one of those letters, he recollected, she had spoken of meeting unexpectedly an old friend whom she had not seen since the days of his boyhood; in another, she had casually remarked, "I met Captain Morford again to-day and we spent a very pleasant half hour together," and in a third had written, "The Captain promised to call and take tea to-day but didn't. I rather fancy he divines the fact that Lady Chepstow does not care for him. Indeed, she dislikes him immensely. Why, I wonder? Personally, I think him exceedingly pleasant, and there are things in his character for which I have the deepest respect and admiration."

And out of these trifling circumstances—lo! the darkest corner that darkest Hell contained.

So that was how it was to end, was it? That was the card which Fate had all along kept up her sleeve while she stood off laughing at his endeavours, his hopes, his struggles against the inevitable? In the end, another man was to appear, another man was to win her, and the dream was to turn out nothing more than a dream after all.

Once again the voices of the Wild called out to the Caged Wolf; once again, the old things beckoned and the new things lost their savour and the Devil said, as before, "What is the use? What *is* the use?" and the Savage cried out to be stripped and flung back into the wilderness as God made him, and called and called and called for an end to the things that stank in his nostrils and for the fierce companionship of his kind. And but that Time had staled these things a little and blunted the keen edge of them so that they could not endure for long, and there was Dollops and the lessons and Dollops' future to recollect, the Wolf and the Savage and the Devil might not have hungered in vain.

Followed a period of intense depression when all things seemed to lose their savour and when Narkom, amazed, said to himself that the man had come to the end of his usefulness and had lost every attribute of the successful criminologist. For the next three cases he brought him Cleek botched in a manner that would have disgraced the merest tyro. Two, he failed utterly to solve, although the solutions were eventually worked out by the ordinary forces of the Yard; and in the third he let his man get away under his very nose and convey Government secrets to a foreign Power. It was but natural that these three dismal failures should find their way to the newspapers and that, in the hysterical condition of modern journalism, they should be flung out to the world at large with all the ostentation of leaded type and panicky scare heads, and that learned editors should discourse knowingly of "the limitations of mentality" and "the well-authenticated cases of the sudden warping of abnormal intelligences resulting in the startling termination of amazing careers," or snivel dismally over "the complete collapse of that imaginative power which, hitherto, had been this detective's greatest asset, and which now, on the principle that however deep a well may be if a force-pump be put into it it must some time suck gravel, seemed to have come to its end."

These things, when Cleek heard of them, affected him not at all. He seemed not to care whether his career was ended or not, whether the world praised or censured. Neither his pride nor his vanity was stirred even to the very smallest degree.

But Narkom, loyal still, took these gloomy prophecies and editorial vapourings much to heart and strove valiantly to confound the man's detractors and to put the spur to the man himself. He would not believe that the end had come, that his mental powers had run suddenly against a dead wall beyond which there was no possibility of proceeding. Something was weighing upon his mind and damping his spirits that was all; and it must be the business of those who were his friends to take steps to discover what that something was and, if possible, to eliminate it. He therefore sought out Dollops and held secret conclave with him; and Dollops dolefully epitomized the difficulty thus: "A skirt—that's what's at the bottom of it, sir. No letter at all these ten days past. She's chucked him, I'm afraid." And with this brief preface told all that he was able to tell; which, after all, was not much.

He could only explain about the letter that used to come off and on in the other days and which brought such a flow of high spirits to the man for whom it was intended; he could only say that it was addressed in a woman's hand and bore always the one postmark; and when Narkom heard what that postmark was and recollected where Lady Chepstow's country seat lay, and who was with her, he puckered up his lips as if he were about to whistle and made two slim arches with his uplifted eyebrows.

"Sir, if only you could sneak off and run down there without his knowing of it—it wouldn't do to write a letter, Mr. Narkom: he'd be on to that before you could turn round, sir," the boy ventured hopefully; "but if only you could run down there and give her a tip what she's a doing of and what she's a chuckin' away, what a Man she's a throwin' down, maybe, sir, maybe—"

"Yes, 'maybe,'" agreed the superintendent, after a moment's reflection. "At any rate it's worth a trial." And went, forthwith.

Not that it was a prudent thing to do; not that it is wise for any man at any time to interfere, even with the best intentions, with the course of another man's love affairs; and, finally, not that it was at all necessary or had any influence whatsoever upon the events which succeeded the step. Indeed, he might have spared himself the trouble, for he had barely covered a fifth of the distance when the country post was delivered in London, and Cleek, rocketing up in one sweep from the Pit to the Gateway, stood laughing huskily with a letter from Ailsa in his hand.

He ripped off the envelope and read it greedily.

"Dear Friend," she wrote, "I cannot imagine what you must think of my silence; but whatsoever you do think cannot be half so terrible as the actual cause of it. I have been in close touch with misery and death, with things so appalling that heart and mind have had room to hold nothing else. Indeed, I am still so horribly nervous and upset that I scarcely know how to think coherently much less write. I can only remember that you once said that if ever I needed your help I was to ask; and oh, Mr. Cleek, I need it very very much indeed now. Not for myself—let me find time to add that—but for a dear, dear friend—the friend I have so often written about: Captain Morford—who is involved in an affair of the most distressing and mysterious character and whose only hope lies, I feel, in you. Will you come to the rescue, for my sake? That is what I am asking. Let me say, however, that there is no possibility of a reward, for the captain is in no position to offer one; but I seem to feel that that will not weigh with you. Neither can I ask you to call at the house, for, as I have already told you, Lady Chepstow does not care for the Captain and under those circumstances it would be embarrassing to ask him there to meet you. So then, if no other case intervenes, and you really *can* grant me this great favour, will you be in the neighbourhood of the lich-gate of Lyntonhurst Old Church at nine o'clock in the morning of Thursday, you will win the everlasting gratitude of, Your sincere friend—AILSA LORNE."

Would he be there? He laughed aloud as he put the question to himself. A Bradshaw was on his table. He caught it up, found that there was a train that could be caught in thirty-five minutes' time, and clapped on his hat and—caught it.

That night he slept at the inn of the Three Desires—which, as you may possibly know, lies but a gunshot beyond the boundary wall of the glebe of Lyntonhurst Old Church—slept with an alarm clock at his head and every servant at the inn from the boots to the barmaid tipped a shilling to see that he did not oversleep himself.

He was up before any of them, however—up and out into the pearl-dusk of the morning before ever the alarm-clock shrilled its first note, or the sun's sheen slid lower than the spurs of the weather-cock on the spire of

Lyntonhurst Old Church—and twice he had walked past the big gates and looked up the still avenue to the windows of the huge house whose roof covered her before Lyntonhurst Old Church spoke up through the dawn-hush and told the parish it was half-past four o'clock.

By five, he had found a pool cupped in the beech woods with mallows and marsh marigolds and a screen of green things all round it and a tent of blue sky over the sun-touched tree tops; and had stripped and splashed into it and set all the birds to flight with the harsher song of human things; by seven he was back at the Three Desires; by eight he had shaved and changed and breakfasted and was out again in the fields and the leafy lanes, and by nine he was at the lich-gate of the church.

CHAPTER XXXI

She was there already; sitting far back at the end of one of the narrow wooden side benches with the shadow of the gate's moss-grown roof and of the big cypress above it partly screening her, her shrinking position evincing a desire to escape general observation as clearly as her pale face and nervously drumming hand betrayed a state of extreme agitation.

She rose as Cleek lifted the latch and came in, and advanced to meet him with both hands outstretched in greeting and a rich colour staining all her face.

"I knew that you would come—I was as certain of it as I am now this minute," she said with a little embarrassed laugh, then dropped her eyes and said no more, for he had taken those two hands in his and was holding them tightly and looking at her with an expression that was half a reproach and half a caress.

"I am glad you did not doubt," he said, with an odd, wistful little smile. "It is good to know one's friends have faith in one, Miss Lorne. I had almost come to believe that you had forgotten me."

"Because I did not write? Oh, but I could not—indeed I could not. I have been spending days and nights in a house of mourning—Lady Chepstow gave me leave of absence; and my heart was so full I did not write even to her. I have been trying to soothe and to comfort a distracted girl, a half-crazed old man, a bereft and horribly smitten family. I have been doing all in my power to put hope and courage into the heart of a despairing and most unhappy lover."

"Meaning Captain Morford?"

"Yes. He has been almost beside himself. And since this last blow fell.... Oh, I had been so sure that it would not, that between us all we would manage to avert it; yet in spite of everything it did fall—it did!—and if I live to be a hundred I shall never forget it."

"Calm yourself, Miss Lorne. You are shaking like a leaf. Try to tell me plainly what it is that has happened; what the danger is that threatens this—er—Captain Morford."

"Oh, nothing threatens *him*, personally," she replied. "He says he could stand it better if it were only that; and I believe him—I truly do. The thing that nearly drives him out of his mind is the thought that one day she—the girl he loves—the girl he is to marry—the girl for whose dear sake he stands ready to give up so much—the thought that one day *her* turn will come, that one day she, too, will be stricken down as mother and brothers have been is almost driving him frantic."

"Mother and brothers?—*brothers*?" Cleek looked up sharply, and there was a curious break in his voice, a yet more curious brightening of his eyes. "Miss Lorne, am I to understand that this Captain Morford is engaged to a girl who has *brothers*?"

"Yes. That is—no. She has 'brothers' no longer. There is only one left living now, Mr. Cleek, only one. Ah, think of it! of that whole family of six persons, but three are left: Miriam, Flora, and Ronald."

"Miriam, Flora, and ... Miss Lorne, will you tell me please the name of the lady to whom Captain Morford is engaged?"

"Why Miriam Comstock, of course—did I forget to mention it?"

"I think so," said Cleek; and shook out a little jerky laugh, and stood looking at her foolishly; not quite knowing what to do with his feet and hands. But suddenly—"Oh come, let's have the case—let's have it at once," he broke out impetuously. "Tell me what it is, what I'm to do for this Captain Morford, and I'll do it if mortal man can."

"And no mortal man can if you cannot—I've faith enough in you for that," she began, then stopped short and sucked in her breath, and crept back to the extreme end of the lich-gate and stood shaking and very pale. Someone had come suddenly round the angle of the church and was moving up the road that ran past the gate.

"Please—no—let me get away as quickly as possible," she said in a swift whisper as Cleek, startled by the change in her, made an eager step forward. "It is known that I have been with them—the Comstocks—and it is all so mysterious and awful.... Oh, who can tell whose hand it may be? who may be spying? or what? It is best that I should give no hint that assistance has been asked for; best that nobody should see me talking with *you*—Mr. Narkom says that it is."

"Mr. Narkom?"

"Yes. He was in the neighbourhood accidentally. He called last night. I told him and he was glad that I had sent for you. He is over there, on the other side of the churchyard. Oh, please will you go to him? Captain

Morford is within easy call and has agreed to come when he is wanted. Do go, do go quickly, Mr. Cleek. There's someone coming up the road and I am horribly frightened."

"But why? It is merely a farm labourer," said Cleek, glancing through the open side of the lich-gate and down the road. "You can see that for yourself."

"Yes, but—who knows? who can tell? There is no clue to the actual person and he is so cunning, so crafty—Oh, please, will you go? Afterward, if you like, we can meet here again. To-day I am too frightened to stay."

He saw that she was in a state of extreme nervous terror; that it would be cruel to subject her to any further suffering, and without one more word, walked past her into the Churchyard and made his way over the green ridge that rose immediately behind the building and down the slope beyond until he came to the extreme other side. And there in the shade of a thickly grown spinney, he found Mr. Marverick Narkom sitting with his back against a beech-tree smoking a nerve-soothing cigar and expectantly awaiting him.

"My dear fellow, I never was so glad," he said, tossing away his smoke and jumping up as Cleek appeared. "Happy coincidence my motoring down here—eh, what? Wife in these parts visiting. Rum, my turning up just after Miss Lorne had written you and at a time when we both are needed, wasn't it?"

"Very," said Cleek, pulling out a cigarette and stretching himself full length upon the ground. "Would as soon have expected to run foul of a specimen of the Great Auk endeavouring to rear a family in the neighbourhood of Trafalgar Square. Well, what's it now, Mr. Narkom?— I'm told you know the details. A match please, if you have one. Thanks very much. Now then let's have the facts. What sort of a case is it?"

"The knottiest in all my experience, the strangest that even you have ever handled," replied the Superintendent, impressively. "It's a murder— three murders, in fact, with a possible fourth and a fifth in the near future if the diabolical rascal who is at the bottom of it isn't pulled up sharp and his amazing *modus operandi* discovered.

"The case will interest you, my dear chap; it is so startlingly original in its methods of procedure, so complex, so weird, and so appallingly mysterious. Conceive if you can, my dear fellow, an individual so supernaturally cunning that he not only kills without a trace, but kills in the presence of watchers—kills whilst the victim is in the very arms of those watchers! And yet escapes, unseen, unknown, without a clue to tell when, where, or how he entered the room or left it; when, where, or how he struck the blow, or why; yet did strike it, despite the sleepless vigil of a man who not only sat up all night with the victim, but held him in his arms to be sure that nobody could get at him; nobody so much as approach him without his guardian's knowledge!"

Cleek twitched round sharply and sat up, leaning upon his elbow and looking at Narkom as though he doubted his sanity.

"Let me have that again!" he said in sharp, crisp tones. "A man killed whilst another man held him—held him in his arms—and watched over him, and yet the other man saw nothing of the murderer? Is that what you said?"

"That's it, precisely. Only I must tell you that, in the instance when the victim was held in the arms of the person watching him, it was not a man that was killed, but a boy. There had been a man killed, however, four weeks previously in the same house, in the same mysterious manner, and by the same unknown agency. A month earlier a woman, too, had been done to death there in the same way. The man was the brother of that boy, and the woman was the mother of both."

Cleek moved so quickly that he might fairly have been said to flash from a sitting to a standing position, and then began to feel round in his pockets for his cigarette case with a nervous sort of haste, which Narkom knew and understood.

"Ah," he said, in a tone of satisfaction, "I thought the case would interest you. You've been down in the dumps lately and needed something to buck you up a bit. I told Captain Morford that this would be sure to do it. Heard of him, haven't you? Extremely nice chap. Home on leave from Bombay. Only recently got his captaincy. Grandson and heir to that fine old snob, Sir Gilbert Morford, who's known everywhere as 'The Titled Teapot.' You know, 'Morford & Morford's Unrivalled Tea.' Knighted for something or other—the Lord knows what or why—and puts on more side over his tin-plate title than Royalty itself. The Captain is a decent sort, however. He'll give you the full particulars of this astounding case. Wait a bit. I'll call him"—pausing a moment to put the first two fingers of each hand into his mouth and blow out a shrill, ear-splitting whistle. "That'll fetch him! He'll be here before you can say Jack Robinson!"

He wasn't, of course; but you couldn't have said it half a hundred times before he was; or, at least, before Cleek, startled by a rustling of the boughs, glanced round and saw a tall, fairish young man who had no more the appearance of a soldier than a currant has of a gooseberry. He looked more like a bank clerk than anything else that Cleek could think of at the minute, and a none too prepossessing bank clerk at that, for Nature had not been any too lavish of her gifts as regards personal attractiveness, seeming to prefer to make up for her miserliness in the bestowal of good looks by an absolute prodigality in the gifts of ears—ears as big as an oyster-shell and so prominent that they seemed even larger than they were, and that is saying a great deal.

Still, unprepossessing as the man was, there was a certain charm of manner about him and a certain attractiveness in his voice Cleek discovered when he was introduced to him and found himself being "sized up," so to speak, by a pair of keen grey eyes.

"Now let us have the details of the case, if you please, Captain," said Cleek, coming to the point of the interview with as little beating about the bush as possible. "Mr. Narkom has given me a vague idea of the nature of it, but I want something more than that, of course. I am told that three persons in one family have been done to death in a most mysterious manner, and without any clue to the assassin or his motive; indeed that the hand which strikes strikes even in the presence of others, yet remains unknown and invisible. Frankly, I never heard of but one instance which at all resembles this or—No, Mr. Narkom, it is nothing that ever came your way, no affair that has happened since you and I first met, sir. It was a long time ago—eight or ten years, to be exact—and a good many miles from England. The cases were somewhat similar, judging from the scanty outline you have given me, and—What's that? No, the criminal was never apprehended. He got away, and his methods were never generally known. Even if they had been, they were not those which any desperado might have emulated, any tyro practised. They required a certain knowledge of anatomy, chemical action—even surgery. I don't believe that ten people in the world knew about the thing at that time. I stumbled upon what I believed was the solution of the mystery whilst I was taking a course of chemistry for—well, for the purpose of demonstrating the possibility of manufacturing precious stones of a size and weight to make them a profitable—er—speculation. The science in medicine was not so advanced in those days as it is now, and when I ventured to suggest to certain doctors what I believed to have been the cause of the mysterious deaths and the *modus operandi* of the murderer, I simply got laughed at for my pains. I felt pretty certain of my facts, however, and pretty certain of the man who was guilty. Pardon? No, not alive now; that fellow had his brains blown out in a bar-room brawl before I left New Zealand."

"New Zealand?" struck in Captain Morford agitatedly. "I say, that's a rum go, isn't it, Mr. Narkom. New Zealand is where the Comstocks come from—or, rather, the father and mother did."

"By Jove! Cleek, that looks suspicious, old chap," chimed in Narkom. "Don't think, do you, that there can possibly be any connection between the two cases? In other words, that that fellow you suspected in New Zealand didn't really die after all?"

"Shortly, the chemist? Not a doubt about his death, Mr. Narkom. I was in the bar-room when he was killed. Three bullets went through his head, and he was as dead as Napoleon Bonaparte by the time he struck the floor. The methods may be the same, but not the man—there is not the ghost of possibility of there being any connection between the two. But let us give the Captain a chance to explain the case. When, where, and how did these mysterious murders begin, Captain, if you please?"

"At Lilac Lodge, over Windsor way," replied the Captain, trying to answer all three questions at once. "They started about a week after the Comstocks went to live there. And the thing was so appalling, the place seemed so certainly under a curse, that although he had paid a good round sum for it, and had spent a pot of money having the house decorated and the garden laid out just as Miriam and her mother fancied it—Miriam is Miss Comstock, my fiancée, Mr. Cleek—nothing would induce Mr. Harmstead to stop in it another hour after the second murder occurred."

"Mr. Harmstead! Who is Mr. Harmstead, Captain?"

"The late Mrs. Comstock's bachelor uncle—a very rich old chap, who was once a sheep-farmer in New Zealand, and afterwards in Australia. Mrs. Comstock hadn't seen him since she was a very little girl until he came to England some few months ago to settle down and to take care of her children and her."

"How did it happen that she hadn't seen him in all that time? I take it there must have been some good reason, Captain?"

"Yes, rather. You see it was like this: The Harmsteads—Mrs. Comstock was a Harmstead by birth, and Uncle Phil was her father's only brother—the Harmsteads had never been well to-do as a family: indeed none of them but dear old Uncle Phil ever had a hundred pounds they could call their own, so when Miss Harmstead's father died, which was about eight months after his brother left New Zealand and went to Australia, she married a young joiner and cabinet-maker, George Comstock, to whom she had long been engaged, and a few weeks later, fancying there would be a better chance for advancement in his trade in England than out there, Mr. Comstock sold out what few belongings he had in the world and brought his wife over here."

"Oh, I see. Then of course she had no opportunity of seeing her uncle until he came here?"

"No, not a ghost of one. She corresponded with him for a time, however—wrote him after the first child was born—and christened 'Philip' in honour of him. In those days it used to take six months to get a letter to Australia, and another six to get word back, so the baby was more than a year old when Uncle Phil wrote that if he didn't marry in the meantime and have a son of his own—which was very unlikely—he would make young Phil his heir and come out after him, too, one of these fine days."

"One moment. Was the person you allude to as 'Young Phil' one of the sons that was murdered?"

"Yes. He was the first victim, poor, chap!"

"Oh, I see!" said Cleek. "I see! So there is money in the background, eh? Well go on. What next? Hear any more from Uncle Phil after that?"

"Oh, yes—for a long time. Miriam and Flora were born, and word of their arrival in the world was sent out to him before the final letter for years and years reached them. In that letter he wrote that he was doing better and better every year, and getting so rich that he didn't have time to do anything but just stop where he was and 'gather in the shekels.' There'd be enough for all when he did come, however, and he was altering his will so that in case anything should happen to young Phil—'which God forbid,' he wrote—the girls would come next, and so on to all the heirs of his niece. After that letter years went by, and never another one. They, thinking that he had married after all—for in his last letter he had spoken of a young widow who had lately been engaged to fill the post of housekeeper at his ranch—gave up all hope when after three times writing no reply came, and finally desisted entirely. He says, however, that it was just the other way about. That he did write—wrote six or seven times—but could get no reply; and as he afterwards found the housekeeper in question a designing and deceitful person, and shipped her off about her business, he makes no doubt that she received and destroyed Mrs. Comstock's letter to him and burnt his to her, hoping, no doubt, to inveigle him into marrying her."

"Quite likely, if she were a designing woman," commented Cleek. "But go on, please. What next?"

"Oh, years of hardship, during which Mr. Comstock died and his widow had to earn their own living unaided. Young Phil got a post as bookkeeper, Flora taught music and painting, Mrs. Comstock did needlework, and Miriam became a governess in the family of a distant connection of my grandfather, Sir Gilbert Morford. That's where and how I met her, Mr. Cleek, and—Well, that's another story!" his cheeks reddening and a flash of fire coming into his eyes. "My grandfather says he will 'chuck me out neck and crop' if I marry her; but it does not matter—I will!"

"Yes, you will—if the cut of that chin stands for anything," commented Cleek. "Well, to get on: the Comstocks were down in the deeps, and no hope of hearing any more from Australia and Uncle Phil, eh? What next?"

"Why, all of a sudden he dropped in on them, bless his bully old heart!—and then good-bye to hard times and any more struggling for them. He'd been in England searching for them for seven months before he found them; but when he did find them there was a time! Inside of ten hours, the whole world was changed for them. Made the boys and the girls give up their positions and come home to live with him and their mother, poured money out by the handful, bought Lilac Lodge and fitted it up like a little palace, dressed his niece and her daughters like queens, and settled down with them to what seemed about to be a life of glorious and luxurious ease, and in the midst of all this peace and plenty, brightness and hope, the first blow fell. Mrs. Comstock, going to bed at night in perfect health, was found in the morning stone-dead! Of course, as no doctor could give a death certificate when none had been in attendance upon her, the Law stepped in, the coroner held an inquest, an autopsy was decided upon, and the result of it was a deeper and more amazing mystery than ever. She had died—but from what? Every organ was found to be in a thoroughly healthy condition. The heart was sound, the lungs betrayed no sign of an anesthetic, the blood and kidneys not the faintest trace of poison—everything about her was perfectly normal. She had not died through drugs, she had not died through strangulation, suffocation, electrical shock, or failure of the heart. She had not been stabbed, she had not been shot, she had not succumbed to any mortal disease—yet there she was, stone-dead, slain by something which no one could trace and for which Science could find no name."

Narkom opened his lips to speak, but Cleek signalled him to silence, and stood studying the Captain from under down-drawn brows, looking and listening and thoughtfully rubbing his thumb and forefinger up and down his chin.

CHAPTER XXXII

"Of course the family was horribly shocked and upset by this sudden and mysterious interruption to the dream of peace," went on the Captain; "but nothing was left but to accept the verdict of 'Death from unknown causes,' and to believe it the will of God. The body was buried a few days later, and, comforting each other as best they could, the sorrowing uncle and heart-broken nieces and nephews settled down to living their lives without the one who had been the sunshine of the home, and whose loss seemed the greatest blow that could have been dealt them. A month passed and they were just beginning to forget details of the tragedy when a second and equally mysterious and horrifying one occurred, and the eldest son of the dead woman—Philip—was stricken down precisely as his mother had been, and, as his horrified brother, sisters, and uncle now recalled, like her, on the tenth day of the month!"

"Hum-m-m!" said Cleek, reflectively. "Rather significant, that. It was, I assume, that circumstance which first suggested the idea of something more than mere chance being at the back of these sudden and mysterious deaths?"

"That and one other circumstance. The condition of the bedclothing, Mr. Cleek, showed that in Philip's case there had been something in the nature of a struggle before he had succumbed to the Power which had assailed him. In other words, he had not been, as doubtless the poor mother had, so infinitely inferior in point of strength to the murderer as to be absolutely powerless in the wretch's grip from the very first instant of the attack. He had fought for his life, poor fellow, but it must have been a brief fight and death itself almost instantaneous; for although the bedclothing was tangled round his feet in a manner which could only have occurred in a struggle, he did not live long enough to get off the bed itself or slide so much as one foot to the floor. He died as his mother had died, and the verdict of the doctors and of the coroner's jury was the same: 'Death from unknown causes'!"

"Hm-m-m!" said Cleek again. "And were all the symptoms—or, rather, the absence of symptoms—the same?"

"Precisely. All the organs were discovered to be in a normal condition, the blood was untainted by any suggestion of either mineral or animal poison, the heart was sound, the lungs healthy—there was neither an internal disturbance nor an external wound, unless one could call a 'wound' a slight, a very slight, swelling upon the left side of the neck; a small thing, not so big as a sixpence."

"And appearing very much like the inflammation resulting from the bite of a gnat or a spider, Captain?"

"Exactly like it, Mr. Cleek. In fact, the doctors fancied at first that it was the result of his having been bitten by some poisonous insect, and were for accounting for his death that way. But, of course, the entire absence of poison in the blood soon put an end to that idea, so it was certain that whatever he died from, it was not from a bite or a sting of any sort."

"Clever chaps, those doctors," commented Cleek with a curious one-sided smile. "However, they were quite correct in that, I imagine, poison, either animal, vegetable, or mineral, was not the means of destruction. Still, I should have thought that at this second post-mortem the likeness of the son's case to that of the mother's would have impelled them to extra vigilance, and resulted in a much more careful searching, and minute examination of the viscera. If my theory is correct, I do not suppose they would have found anything in the contents of the thorax or the abdomen, but it is just possible that analysis of the matter removed from the cranial cavity might have revealed a small blood-clot in the brain."

The Captain twitched up his eyebrows and stared at him in open-mouthed amazement.

"Of all the—By Jove! you know, this beats me! To think of your guessing that!" he said. "As a matter of fact, that's precisely what they did do, Mr. Cleek. But as they couldn't arrive at any conclusion nor trace a probable cause of its origin they were more in the dark than ever. Selwin, the local practitioner, was for putting it down as a case of apoplexy on the strength of that small blood-clot, but as there was an entire absence of every other symptom of apoplectic conditions the other doctors scouted the suggestion as preposterous—pointed out the generally healthy state of the brain and of the heart, lungs, arterial walls, et cetera, as utterly refuting such a theory— and in the end the verdict on the son was the verdict given on the mother: 'Death from unknown causes'; and he was buried as she had been buried, with the secret of the murder undiscovered."

"And then what, Captain?"

"What I have already told you, Mr. Cleek. Nothing under God's heaven would or could persuade Mr. Harmstead to let his nieces and their two surviving brothers remain another hour in that house of disaster. He removed them from it instantly—fled the very neighbourhood, hired a house down here—at Dalehampton; a dozen miles or so on the other side of the Tor, yonder—and carried them there to live. The family now consisted of Miriam and Flora, the two girls, Paul, a boy of thirteen—old Mr. Harmstead's special pride and pet—and Ronald, a little chap of eleven. In this new home they hoped and prayed to be free from the horrible visitant who had made the memory of the old one a nightmare to them, but—they couldn't forget, Mr. Cleek, what the Tenth of each month had taken from them, and grew sick with dread at the steady approach of the Tenth of this one."

"And as this is the Twelfth," said Cleek, "the day before yesterday *was* the Tenth. Did anything happen?"

"Yes," replied the Captain, his voice dropping until it was little more than a whisper. "I tried to cheer them; Miss Lorne tried to cheer them. We sat with them, tried to make them think that our presence there would act as a shield and a guard—and tried to think so ourselves. But old Mr. Harmstead took even stronger measures. 'Nothing shall touch Paul—nothing that lives and breathes,' he said, desperately. 'I'll take him into my room; I'll sit up with him in my arms all night!'"

"And did so?"

"Yes. At twelve o'clock, Miss Lorne, Miss Comstock, and I went in to say good-night to him. He was sitting in a deep chair with the boy fast asleep in his arms—sitting and looking all about him with the dumb agony of a trapped mouse. I'll never forget how he clutched the boy to him nor the cry he gave when the door opened to admit us, the sob of relief when he saw it was only us. His cry and his movement awoke the boy, but he dropped off to sleep again before I left, and was breathing healthily and peacefully. The last look I had at the picture as I went out, Mr. Cleek, the dear old chap was holding his pet in his arms and smiling down into his boyish face. So he was still sitting, Miss Comstock tells me, when she came down this morning. 'Look,' he said to her, 'I watched him—I held him—the tenth day is past and the death didn't get him, my bonnie!' Then called her to his side and shook the little fellow to awaken him. It was then only that he discovered the truth. The boy was stone-dead!"

CHAPTER XXXIII

"There, Mr. Cleek," resumed the Captain, after he could master his emotion. "That is the case—that is the riddle I am praying to Heaven that you may be able to solve. What the mysterious power is, when, where, or how it got into the room and got at the boy, God alone knows. Mr. Harmstead will swear that he never let the little fellow out of his arms for one solitary instant between the time of our leaving him just after midnight, and Miss Comstock's coming in in the morning. He admits, however, that twice during that period he fell asleep, but it was only for a few minutes each time; and long years of being constantly alert for possible marauders—out there in the wilds of Australia—have tended to make his sleep so light that anything heavier than a cat's footfall wakes him on the instant. Yet last night something—man or spirit—came and went, and he neither heard nor saw either sound or shape from midnight until morning. One thing I must tell you, however, which may throw some light upon the movements of the appalling thing. Whereas Mr. Harmstead not only closed, but locked, both of the two windows in the room, and pinned the thick plushette curtains of them together—as Miss Comstock and I saw them pinned when we left the room last night—when those curtains came to be drawn this morning one of the windows was found to be partly open, and there was a smear of something that looked like grease across the sill and the stone coping beyond."

"Of course, of course!" commented Cleek enigmatically. "Provided my theory is correct, I should have expected that. A thing that comes and goes through windows must, at some period, leave some mark of its passage. Of course that particular window opened upon a balcony or something of that sort, didn't it?"

"No, it is a perfectly unbroken descent from the window sill to the ground. But there's a big tree close by, and the branches of that brush the pane of glass."

"Ah! I see! I see! All the soap dishes in the house left filled last night and found filled this morning, captain?"

"Good heavens! I don't know. What on earth can soap dishes have to do with it, man?"

"Possibly nothing, probably a great deal—particularly if there's found to be a cake of soap in each. But that we can discover later. Now one word more. Was that same minute swelling—the mark like a gnat's bite—on the neck of the boy's body, too? And had it been on that of the mother's as well?"

"I can't answer either question, Mr. Cleek. I don't remember to have heard about it being remarked in the case of Mrs. Comstock's death; and the murder of little Paul was such a horrible thing and so upset everybody that none of us thought to look."

"An error of judgment that; however, it is one easily rectified, since the body is not yet interred," said Cleek. "Ever read Harvey's 'Exercitatio Anatomica de Motu Sanguinis,' Captain?—the volume in which William Harvey first gave to the world at large his discovery regarding the circulation of the blood."

"Good heavens, no! What would I be doing reading matters of that kind? I'm not a medico, Mr. Cleek—I'm a soldier."

"I know. But, still—well, I thought it just possible that you might have read the work, or, at least, heard something regarding the contents of the volume. Men who have a hobby are rather given to riding it and boring other people with discussions and dissertations upon it; and I seem to think that I have heard it said that Sir Gilbert Morford's greatest desire in the time of his youth was to become a medical man. In fact, that he put in two or three years as a student at St. Bartholomew's, and would have qualified, but that the sudden death of his father compelled him to abandon the hope and to assume the responsibilities of the head of the house of Morford & Morford, tea importers, of Mincing Lane."

"Yes; that's quite correct. He bitterly resented the compulsion—the 'pitchforking of a man out of a profession into the abomination of trade,' as he always expresses it—but of course, he was obliged to yield, and the 'dream of his life' dropped off into nothing but a dream. But the old love and the old recollection still linger, and, although he no longer personally follows either trade or profession, he keeps up his laboratory work, subscribes to every medical journal in Christendom, and if you want to tickle his vanity or to get on the right side of him all you have to do is to address him as 'doctor.' With all due respect to him, he's a bit of a prig, Mr. Cleek, and hates people of no position—'people of the lower order,' as he always terms them—as the gentleman down under is said to hate holy water."

"So that he, naturally, would move heaven and earth to prevent his grandson and heir from marrying a young woman of that class? I see!" supplemented Cleek. "The dear gentleman would like the name of Morford to go down to posterity linked to duchesses or earls' daughters, and surrounded by a blaze of glory. Ah, it's a queer world, Captain. There is no bitterer hater of the 'common herd' than the snob who has climbed up from it! The snob and the sneak are closely allied, Captain, and men of that stamp have been known to do some pretty ugly things to uphold their pinchbeck dignity, and to keep the tinsel of the present over the cheap gingerbread of the past."

"Good God, man! You don't surely mean to suggest—"

"Gently, gently, Captain. Your indignation does you credit; but it is never well to have a shot at a rabbit before he's fairly out of the hole, and you are sure that it isn't the ferret you sent in after him. Anything in the way of a conveyance handy, Mr. Narkom?"

"Yes—the limousine. I came down in it yesterday. It's over at the Rose and Crown."

"Good! Then perhaps Captain Morford will meet us there in a half hour's time. Meanwhile, I've got a few things to throw into my kit-bag, and as that's over at the Three Desires, perhaps you won't mind coming along and giving me a hand. Then we'll run over to that house at Dalehampton and have a look at the body of that poor little shaver as expeditiously as possible. Will you come?"

"Yes, certainly," said Narkom; and having given a few necessary directions to the Captain walked on and followed Cleek. He knew very well the suggestion that he should do so was merely an excuse to have a few words with him in private—for no man would be likely to need another man's assistance in simply putting a few things into a bag—and he was rather puzzled to account for Cleek's desire to say anything to him which the Captain was not to hear. However, he kept his curiosity in check and his tongue behind his teeth until they were on the other side of the lich-gate and in the road leading to the Three Desires.

"There's something you want to say to me, isn't there?" he inquired. "Something you want attended to on the quiet?"

"Yes," admitted Cleek, tersely. "There's a public telephone station a mile or two on the other side of this place—I saw it this morning when I was out tramping. Slip off down there, ring up the head of the Dalehampton Constabulary, and tell him to have a man at the house ready to pop up when wanted. I'll be long enough over my supposed 'packing' to cover the time of your going and returning without the Captain's knowledge."

"Without—Good Heaven! My dear Cleek, you were serious, then? You meant it? You—you really believe that suspicion points to Sir Gilbert Morford?"

"Not any more than it points to Sir Gilbert Morford's grandson, Mr. Narkom."

"Good Lord! To him? To that boy? Why, man alive, what possible motive could he have for bringing grief and anguish to Miss Comstock when he's willing to give up a fortune to marry her?"

"Ah, but don't forget that another fortune descends to all the heirs, male and female alike, of the late Mrs. Comstock, Mr. Narkom, and that if the Captain's fiancée becomes, in course of time, the only surviving child of that unfortunate lady, the Captain's sacrifice will not be such an overpowering hardship for him, after all."

"Great Scott! I never thought of that before, Cleek—never."

"Didn't you? Well, don't think too much of it now that you have. For circumstantial evidence is tricky and treacherous, and he mayn't be the man, after all!"

"Mayn't be? What a beggar you are for damping a man's ardour after you've fanned it up to the blazing point. Any light in the darkness, old chap? Any idea of what—and how?"

"Yes," said Cleek, quietly. "If there's a mark on that poor little shaver's neck, Mr. Narkom, I shall know the means. And if there's soap on the window sill I shall know the man!" And then, having reached the doorway of the inn, he dived into it and went up the staircase two steps at a time.

CHAPTER XXXIV

The little house of Dalehampton was something more than a mere house of grief, they found, when the long drive came to an end and Cleek and his two companions entered it, for the very spirit of desolation and despair seemed to have taken up its abode there; and, like an Incarnate Woe, Miss Comstock paced through the hush and darkness, hour in and hour out, as she had been doing since daybreak.

"My darling, you mustn't—you really mustn't, dear. You'll lose your mind if you brood over the thing like this," said the Captain, flying to her the very instant they arrived; and, disregarding the presence of his two companions, caught her in his arms and kissed her. "Miriam, dearest, don't! It breaks my heart. I know it's awful; but do try to have strength and hope. I am sure we shall get at the bottom of the thing now—sure that there will be no more—that this is truly the end. These gentlemen are from Scotland Yard, dearest, and they say it surely will be."

"Heaven knows I hope so," replied Miss Comstock, acknowledging the introduction to Cleek and Narkom by a gentle inclination of the head. "But indeed, I can't hope, Jim—indeed, I cannot, gentlemen. The tenth of next month will take its toll as the tenth of this one has done. I feel persuaded that it will. For who can fight a thing unseen and unknown?"

Her grief was so great, her despair so hopeless, that Cleek forbore attempting to assuage either by any words of sympathy or promise. He seemed to feel that hers was an anguish upon which even the kindliest words must fall only as an intrusion, and the heart of the man—that curiously created heart, which at times could be savage even to the point of brutality, and again tender and sympathetic as any woman's—went out to her in one great surge of human feeling. And two minutes later—when all the Law's grim business of inquiry and inquest had been carried out by Narkom, and she, in obedience to his expressed desire, led them to the room where the dead boy lay—that wave of sympathetic feeling broke over his soul again. For the gentle opening of the door had shown him a small, dimly lit room, a kneeling figure, bent of back and bowed of head, that leant over a little white bed in a very agony of tearless woe.

"He can hardly tear himself away for an instant—he loved him so!" she said in a quavering whisper to Cleek. "Must we disturb him? It seems almost cruel."

"I know it," he whispered back; "but the place must be searched in quest of possible clues, Miss Comstock. The—the little boy, too, must be examined, and it would be crueller still if he were to stay and see things like that. Lead him out if you can. It will be for a few minutes only. Tell him so—tell him he can come back then." And turned his face away from that woeful picture as she went over and spoke to the sorrowing old man.

"Uncle!" she said softly. "Uncle Phil! You must come away for a little time, dear. It is necessary."

"Oh, I can't, Mirry—I can't, lovie, dear!" he answered without lifting his head or loosening his folded hands. "My bonnie, my bonnie, that I loved so well! Ah, let me have him while I may, Mirry—they'll take him from me soon enough—soon enough, my bonnie boy!"

"But, dearest, you must. The—the Law has stepped in. Gentlemen from Scotland Yard are here. Jim has brought them. They must have the room for a little time. There—there's the window to be examined, you know; and if they can find out anything—"

"I'll give them the half of all I have in the world!" broke in the old man with a little burst of tears. "Tell them that. The half of everything—everything—if they can get at the creature. If they can find out. But"—collapsing suddenly, with his elbows on his knees and his face between his hands—"they can't, they can't; nobody can! It kills and kills and kills; and God help us! we all shall go the same way! It will be my turn, too, some time soon. I wish it were mine now. I wish it had been mine long ago—before I lost my bonnie own!"

"Takes it hard, poor old chap, doesn't he?" whispered Narkom, glancing round and getting something of a shock when he saw that Cleek, who a moment before had appeared to be almost on the verge of tears, was now fumbling in his coat pockets, and, with indrawn lips and knotted brows, was scowling—absolutely scowling—in the direction where Captain Morford stood, biting his lips and drumming with his finger nails upon the edge of the washstand. But Cleek made no reply. Instead, he walked quickly across to the Captain's side, stretched forth his hand, took up a tablet of soap, turned it over, laid it down again, stepped to the window, stepped back, and laid a firm hand on the young man's shoulder.

"Captain," he said suddenly, in sharp, crisp tones, that sounded painfully harsh after the old man's broken cries, "Captain, there's a little game of cards called 'Bluff,' and it's an excellent amusement if you don't get caught at it. We shan't have to go any further with the search for clues in this case; but I think I shall have to ask you, my friend, a few little questions in private, and in the interests of a gentleman called Jack Ketch!"

This unexpected outburst produced something like a panic. Miss Comstock, hearing the words, cried out, put both hands to her temples, as though her head were reeling; old Mr. Harmstead straightened suddenly and flung a look of blank amazement across the room; and the Captain, twitching away from the man who gripped him, went first deathly white and then red as any beet.

"Good God!" he gulped. "You—I—Look here, I say now, what does this mean? What the dickens are you talking about?"

"Bluff, Captain! Simply 'bluff'!" responded Cleek serenely. "And as I said before, it's a clever little game. Stand where you are—keep an eye on him, Mr. Narkom. What I've got to say to you, my friend, we'll talk about in private, and after I have assisted Miss Comstock to lead her uncle out of the room."

With that he swung away from the Captain's side and went over to that of the old man.

"Come, Mr. Harmstead, let me help you to rise," he began; then stopped as the old man put up a knotted and twisted hand in supplication and protested agitatedly: "But—but, sir, I do not want to go. Good Heaven! What can you be hinting against that poor, dear boy? Surely you do not mean—you cannot mean—"

"That the little game of 'Bluff' has worked, Dr. Finch, and you'll never draw a revolver on me," rapped in Cleek, giving him a backward push that carried him to the floor, and in the twinkling of an eye he had pounced upon him like a cat and was saying, as he snapped the handcuffs upon his wrists: "Got you, you brute-beast; got you tight and fast! Do you remember Hamilton, the medical student, in New Zealand, eight years ago? Do you? Well, that's the man you're dealing with now!"

The man, struggling and kicking, biting and clawing like any other cornered wild cat, flung out a cry of utter despair at this, and collapsed suddenly; and in the winking of an eye Cleek's hands had flashed into the two pockets of the dressing-gown the fellow was wearing, and flashed out again with a revolver in one and a shining nickel thing in the other.

"Got your 'bark,' doctor, and got your 'bite' as well!" he said, as he rose to his feet. "You'd have put a bullet through me at the first word, wouldn't you, but for that little 'bluff' of suspecting and arresting another man?

Captain, look to Miss Comstock—I think she has fainted. You wanted the murderer of Mrs. Comstock and her children, didn't you? Well, here he is, the rascal!"

"Good God! Then it—it's not a mistake? You mean it—mean it? And Uncle Phil! You accuse Uncle Phil?"

"Uncle Nothing!" flung back Cleek with a sort of laugh—and, hazarding a guess which afterwards was proved to be the truth—"I'll lay my life, Captain, that when you apply to the Australian authorities you will find that old Mr. Philip Harmstead is in his grave; that he was attended in his last illness by one Dr. Frederick Finch, to whom his fortune would revert in the event of Mrs. Comstock and her children dying. Finch is the fellow's name—isn't it, doctor, eh?"

"Finch?" repeated the Captain. "Good Heaven! Why that was the name of the woman who was old Mr. Harmstead's housekeeper—you know, the widow I told you about to-night."

"Oho!" said Cleek. "That's possibly where the threads join and this little game begins. Or perhaps it may really be said to begin again where Shorty, the chemist, died, and the celebrated Spofford mystery ended—eh, doctor? Look here, Captain, look here, Mr. Narkom, you remember what I told you this morning about that case in New Zealand which so strongly resembled this one? That was the Spofford mystery. Do you remember what I said about hitting upon a theory and offering it to the medical fraternity, only to get laughed at for my pains? Well, it was to this man, Dr. Frederick Finch, I advanced that theory, and it was Dr. Frederick Finch who jeered at it, but has now made deadly use of it, the hound. Do you want to know how he killed his victims, and what he used? Look at this thing that you saw me take from the pocket of his dressing-gown. It is a hypodermic syringe, but there is nothing in it—there never has been anything in it. Air was his poison—air his shaft of death; and he killed by injecting it into the veins of his victims. The result of air coming into contact with the circulating blood of a human being is the formation of a blood-clot, and death is instantaneous the instant the clot reaches either the brain or the heart! That was his method. But thank God it's done with for ever now, and the next tenth day of the month will pass over this stricken family and leave it unscathed!"

* * * * *

"How did I know the man?" said Cleek, answering Narkom's query, as they came down the Tor-side afoot and forged on in the direction of Lyntonhurst Old Church—whither Captain Morford and the limousine had long ago preceded them—with the low-dropped sun behind them and lengthening shadows streaming on before. "Well, as a matter of fact, I never did know him until I actually touched him. I was certain of the method, of course; but the man—no. I got my first suspicion of 'Uncle Phil' when I heard him speak. I knew I had heard that voice somewhere, and I realised that it was much too young a voice for a man who appeared—and must be, if he were the real 'Uncle Phil'—extremely old; but it was only when I saw his hand, and the peculiar knotted and twisted little finger that I really knew who he was. What's that? The soap? Well, of course I knew that if, as I suspected, someone in the house was the real culprit, an attempt would be made to make it look as though the criminal entered from without, so naturally the window would be opened, and something of some sort would be smeared on the sill—something that wouldn't blow away and wouldn't wash off in the event of a sudden rainstorm coming up. Soap would do—and soap is always handy in a bedroom. I knew whose hand had made the smear as soon as I looked at the cake of soap in 'Uncle Phil's' room—it was badly rubbed on one side where it had been scraped over the stone coping and along the outer edge of the sill where—Pardon me: this is the turning—I leave you here. Pick me up at the inn of the Three Desires in an hour's time, please, and we'll motor back to town together. So long!"

And swung round into the branching lane and down the green slope, and round under the shadow of Lyntonhurst Old Church to the quiet country road and the lich-gate where Ailsa Lorne was waiting.

CHAPTER XXXV

She was sitting in the very same place she had occupied when first he saw her this morning, with the cypress tree and the roof making shadows above and about her; and now, as then, she rose when she heard the latch click and came toward him with hands outstretched and eyes aglow and little gusts of colour sweeping in rose waves over throat and cheeks.

"Oh, to think that you have solved it! To think that it is the end! And to think that it was he—that dear, kind 'uncle' of whom they all were so fond!" she said. "I could scarcely believe it when Captain Morford brought the news. It made me quite faint for the moment—it was so unexpected, so horrible!"

"And after all, there was nothing to fear from that farm labourer who frightened you so this morning, you see," he smiled, holding her two hands in his and looking down at her from his greater height. "Yet I find your crouching back in the shadow as if you were still frightened to be seen. Are you?"

"A little," she admitted. "You see, the road is a public one. People are always passing, and—How good it was of you to come all this long distance out of your way. Indeed, I am very, very grateful, Mr. Cleek."

"Thank you," he said gravely. "But you need not be. Indeed, the gratitude should be all on my side. I said I would come if ever you wanted me, and you gave me an opportunity to keep my word. As for it being out of my way to come here, it is but a little distance to the Three Desires and a long one to Lady Chepstow's place, so it is you, not I, that have 'gone out of the way!' It was good of you to give me this grace—I should have been sorry to go back to town without saying good-bye."

"But need you go so soon?" she asked. "Lady Chepstow will feel slighted, I know, if she hears that you have been in the neighbourhood and have not called. She is a friend, you know, a warm, true friend—always grateful for what you did, always glad to see you. Why not stop on a day or two and call and see her?"

A robin flicked down out of the cypress tree and perched on the gate top, looked up at Cleek with bright, sharp eyes, flung out a wee little trill, and was off again.

"I'm afraid it is out of the question—I'm afraid I'm not so deeply interested in Lady Chepstow as, perhaps, I ought to be," said Cleek, noticing in a dim subconscious way that the robin had flown on to the church door and perched there, and was in full song now. "Besides, she does not know of me what you do. Perhaps, if she did.... Oh, well, it doesn't matter. Thank you for coming to say good-bye, Miss Lorne. It was kind of you. Now I must emulate Poor Jo, and 'move on' again."

"And without any reward!" said Ailsa with a smile and a sigh. "Without expecting any; without asking any; without wanting any!"

He stood a moment, twisting his heel round and round in the gravel of the pathway, and breathing hard, his eyes on the ground, and his lips indrawn. Then, of a sudden—"Perhaps I did want one. Perhaps I've always wanted one. And hoped to get it some day perhaps from—you!" he said. And looked up at her as a man looks but once at one woman ever.

She had come a step nearer; she was standing there with the shadows behind her and the light on her face, warm colour in her cheeks, and a smile on her lips and in her eyes. She spoke no word, made no sound; merely stood there and smiled and, somehow, he seemed to know what the smile of her meant and what the bird's note said.

"Miss Lorne—Ailsa," he said, very, very gently, "if some day ... when all the wrongs I did in those other days are righted, and all that a man can do on this earth to atone for such a past as mine has been done ... if then, in that time, I come to you and ask for that reward, do you think, oh, do you think that you can find it in your heart to give it?"

"When that day dawns, come and see," she said, "if you wish to wait so long!"

EPILOGUE

THE AFFAIR OF THE MAN WHO HAD BEEN CALLED HAMILTON CLEEK

"Note for you, sir—messenger just fetched it. Addressed to 'Captain Burbage,' so it'll be from The Yard," said Dollops, coming into the room with a doughnut in one hand and a square envelope in the other.

Cleek, who had been sitting at his writing-table, with a litter of folded documents, bits of antique jewellery, and what looked like odds and ends of faded ribbon lying before him, swept the whole collection into the table drawer as Dollops spoke and stretched forth his hand for the letter.

It was one of Narkom's characteristic communications, albeit somewhat shorter than those communications usually were—a fact which told Cleek at once that the matter was one of immense importance.

"My dear Cleek," it ran. "For the love of goodness don't let anything tempt you into going out to-night. I shall call about ten. Foreign government affair—reward simply enormous. Look out for me. Yours, in hot haste—MAVERICK NARKOM."

"Be on the lookout for the red limousine," said Cleek, glancing over at Dollops, who stood waiting for orders. "It will be along about ten. That's all. You may go."

"Right you are, Gov'nor. I'll keep my eyes peeled, sir. Lor'! I do hope it's summink to do with a restaurant or a cookshop this time. I could do with a job of that sort—my word, yes! I'm fair famishin'. And, beggin' pardon, but you don't look none too healthy yourself this evening, Gov'nor. Ain't et summink wot's disagreed with you, have you, sir?"

"I? What nonsense! I'm as fit as a fiddle. What could make you think otherwise?"

"Oh, I dunno, sir—only—Well, if you don't mind my sayin' of it, sir, whenever you gets to unlocking of that draw and lookin' at them things you keep in there—wotever they is—you always gets a sort of solemncholy look in the eyes; and you gets white about the gills, and your lips has a pucker to 'em that I don't like to see."

"Tommy rot! Imagination's a splendid thing for a detective to possess, Dollops, but don't let yours run away with you in this fashion, my lad, or you'll never rise above what you are. Toddle along now, and look out for Mr. Narkom's arrival. It's after nine already, so he'll soon be here."

"Anybody a-comin' with him, sir?"

"I don't know—he didn't say. Cut along, now; I'm busy!" said Cleek. Nevertheless, when Dollops had gone and the door was shut and he had the room to himself again, and, if he really did have any business on hand, there was no reason in the world why he should not have set about it, he remained sitting at the table and idly drumming upon it with his finger tips, a deep ridge between his brows and a far-away expression in his fixed, unwinking eyes. And so he was still sitting when, something like twenty minutes later, the sharp "Toot-toot!" of a motor horn sounded.

Narkom's note lay on the table close to his elbow. He took it up, crumpled it into a ball, and threw it into his waste basket. "A foreign government affair," he said with a curious one-sided smile. "A strange coincidence, to be sure!" Then, as if obeying an impulse, he opened the drawer, looked at the litter of things he had swept into it, shut it up again and locked it securely, putting the key into his pocket and rising to his feet. Two minutes later, when Narkom pushed open the door and entered the room, he found Cleek leaning against the edge of the mantelpiece and smoking a cigarette with the air of one whose feet trod always upon rose petals, and who hadn't a thought beyond the affairs of the moment, nor a care for anything but the flavour of Egyptian tobacco.

"Ah, my dear fellow, you can't think what a relief it was to catch you. I had but a moment in which to dash off the note, and I was on thorns with fear that it would miss you; that on a glorious night like this you'd be off for a pull up the river or something of that sort," said the superintendent, as he bustled in and shook hands with him. "You are such a beggar for getting off by yourself and mooning."

"Well, to tell you the truth, Mr. Narkom, I came within an ace of doing the very thing you speak of," replied Cleek. "It's full moon, for one thing, and it's primrose time for another. Happily for your desire to catch me, however, I—er—got interested in the evening paper, and that delayed me."

"Very glad, dear chap; very glad, indeed," began Narkom. Then, as his eye fell upon the particular evening paper in question lying on the writing-table, a little crumpled from use, but with a certain "displayed-headed" article of three columns length in full view, he turned round and stared at Cleek with an air of awe and mystification. "My dear fellow, you must be under the guardianship of some uncanny familiar. You surely must, Cleek!"

he went on. "Do you mean to tell me that is what kept you at home? That you have been reading about the preparations for the forthcoming coronation of King Ulric of Mauravania?"

"Yes; why not? I am sure it makes interesting reading, Mr. Narkom. The kingdom of Mauravania has had sufficient ups and downs to inspire a novelist, so its records should certainly interest a mere reader. To be frank, I found the account of the amazing preparations for the coronation of his new Majesty distinctly entertaining. They are an excitable and spectacular people, those Mauravanians, and this time they seem bent upon outdoing themselves."

"But, my dear Cleek, that you should have chosen to stop at home and read about that particular affair! Bless my soul man, it's—it's amazing, abnormal, uncanny! Positively uncanny, Cleek!"

"My dear Narkom, I don't see where the uncanny element comes in, I must confess," replied Cleek with an indulgent smile. "Surely an Englishman must always feel a certain amount of interest in Mauravian affairs. Have the goodness to remember that there should be an Englishman upon that particular throne. Aye, and there would be, too, but for one of those moments of weak-backed policy, of a desire upon the part of the 'old-woman' element which sometimes prevails in English politics to keep friendly relations with other powers at any cost. Brush up your history, Mr. Narkom, and give your memory a fillip. Eight-and-thirty years ago Queen Karma of Mauravania had an English consort and bore him two daughters, and one son. You will perhaps recall the mad rebellion, the idiotic rising which disgraced that reign. That was the time for England to have spoken. But the peace party had it by the throat; they, with their mawkish cry for peace—peace at any price!—drowned the voices of men and heroes, and the end was what it was! Queen Karma was deposed—she and her children fled, God knows how, God knows where—fled and left a dead husband and father, slain like a hero and an Englishman, fighting for his own, and with his face to the foe. Avenge his death? Nonsense, declared the old women. He had no right to defy the will of Heaven, no right to stir up strife with a friendly people and expect his countrymen to embroil themselves because of his lust for power. It would be a lasting disgrace to the nation if England allowed a lot of howling, bloodthirsty meddlers to persuade it to interfere.

"The old women had their way. Queen Karma and her children vanished; her uncle Duke Sforza came to the throne as Alburtus III., and eight months ago his son, the present King Ulric, succeeded him. The father had been a bad king, the son a bad crown-prince. Mauravania has paid the price. Let her put up with it! I don't think in the light of these things, Mr.

Narkom, there is any wonder that an Englishman finds interest in reading of the affairs of a country over which an Englishman's son might, and ought to, have ruled. As for me, I have no sympathy, my friend, with Mauravania or her justly punished people."

"Still, my dear fellow, that should not count when the reward for taking up this case is so enormous—and I dare say it will not."

"Reward? Case?" repeated Cleek. "What do you mean by that?"

"That I am here to enlist your services in the cause of King Ulric of Mauravania," replied Narkom, impressively. "Something has happened, Cleek, which, if not cleared up before the coronation day—now only one month hence, as you must have read—will certainly result in his Majesty's public disgrace, and may result in his overthrow and death! His friend and chief adviser, Count Irma, has come all the way from Mauravania, and is at this moment downstairs in this house, to put the case in your hands and to implore you to help and to save his royal master!"

"His royal master? The son of the man who drove an Englishman's wife and an Englishman's children into exile—poverty—misery—despair?" said Cleek, pulling himself up. "I won't take it, Mr. Narkom! If he offers me millions, I'll lift no hand to help or to save Mauravania's king!"

The response to this came from an unexpected quarter.

"But to save Mauravania's queen, monsieur? Will you do nothing for her?" said an excited and imploring voice. And as Cleek, startled by the interruption, switched round and glanced in the direction of the sound, the half-dosed door swung inward and a figure, muffled to the very eyes, moved over the threshold into the room. "Have pardon, monsieur—I could not but overhear," went on the newcomer, turning to Narkom. "I should scarcely be worthy of his Majesty's confidence and favour had I remained inactive. I simply had to come up unbidden. *Had* to, monsieur"—turning to Cleek— "and so—" His words dropped off suddenly. A puzzled look first expanded and then contracted his eyes, and his lips tightened curiously under the screen of his white, military moustache. "Monsieur," he said, presently putting into words the sense of baffling familiarity which perplexed him. "Monsieur, you then are the great, the astonishing Cleek? You, monsieur? Pardon, but surely I have had the pleasure of meeting monsieur before? No, not here, for I have never been in England until to-day; but in my own country—in Mauravania. Surely, monsieur, I have seen you there?"

"On the contrary," said Cleek, speaking the simple truth. "I have never set foot in Mauravania in all my life, sir. And as you have overheard my words you may see that I do not intend to even now. The difficulties of Mauravania's king do not in the least appeal to me."

"Ah, but Mauravania's queen, monsieur—Mauravania's queen."

"The lady interests me no more than does her royal spouse."

"But, monsieur, she must—she really must—if you are honest in what you say, and your sympathies are all with the deposed and exiled ones—the ex-queen Karma and her children. Surely, monsieur, you who seem to know so well the history of that sad time cannot be ignorant of what has happened since to her ex-Majesty and her children?"

"I know only that Queen Karma died in France, in extreme poverty, befriended to the last by people of the very humblest birth and of not too much respectability. What became of her son I do not know; but her daughters, the two princesses, mere infants at the time, were sent, one to England, where she subsequently died, and the other to Persia, where, I believe, she remained up to her ninth year, and then went no one seems to know where."

"Then, monsieur, let me tell you what became of her. The late King Alburtus discovered her whereabouts, and, to prevent any possible trouble in the future, imprisoned her in the Fort of Sulberga up to the year before his death. Eleven months ago she became the Crown Prince Ulric's wife. She is now his consort. And by saving her, monsieur, you who feel so warmly upon the subject of the rights of her family's succession, will be saving her, helping Mauravania's queen, and defeating those who are her enemies."

Cleek sucked in his breath and regarded the man silently, steadily, for a long time. Then:

"Is that true, Count?" he asked. "On your word of honour as a soldier and a gentleman, is that true?"

"As true as Holy Writ, monsieur. On my word of honour. On my hopes of heaven!"

"Very well, then," said Cleek quietly. "Tell me the case, Count. I'll take it."

"Monsieur, my eternal gratitude. Also the reward is—"

"We will talk about that afterward. Sit down, please, and tell me what you want me to do."

"Oh, monsieur, almost the impossible," said the Count despairfully. "The outwitting of a woman who must in very truth be the devil's own daughter, so subtle, so appalling are the craft and cunning of her. That, for one thing. For another, the finding of a paper, which, if published—as the woman swears it shall be if her terms are not acceded to—will be the signal for his Majesty's overthrow. And, for the third"—emotion mastered him; his voice choked up and failed; he deported himself for a moment like one afraid to let even his own ears hear the thing spoken of aloud, then governed his cowardice and went on—"For the third thing, monsieur," he said, lowering his tone until it was almost a whisper, "the recovery—the restoration to its place of honour before the coronation day arrives—of that fateful gem, Mauravania's pride and glory—'the Rainbow Pearl!'"

Cleek clamped his jaws together like a bloodhound snapping and over his hardening face there came a slow-creeping, unnatural pallor.

"Has that been lost?" he said in a low, bleak voice. "Has he, this precious royal master of yours, this usurper—has he parted with that thing—the wondrous Rainbow Pearl?"

"Monsieur knows of the gem, then?"

"Know of it? Who does not? Its fame is world-wide. Wars have been fought for it, lives sacrificed for it. It is more valuable than England's Koh-i-noor, and more important to the country and the crown that possess it. The legend runs, does it not, that Mauravania falls when the Rainbow Pearl passes into alien hands. An absurd belief, to be sure, but who can argue with a superstitious people or hammer wisdom into the minds of babies? And *that* has been lost—that gem so dear to Mauravania's people, so important to Mauravania's crown?"

"Yes, monsieur—ah, the good God help my country!—yes!" said the Count brokenly. "It has passed from his Majesty's hands; it is no longer among the crown jewels of Mauravania—a Russian has it."

"A Russian?" Cleek's cry was like to nothing so much as the snarl of a wild animal. "A Russian to hold it—a Russian?—the sworn enemy of Mauravania—the race most hated of her people! God help your wretched king, Count Irma, if this were known to his subjects."

"Ah, monsieur, it is that we dread—it is that against which we struggle," replied the Count. "If that jewel were missing on the coronation day, if it were known that a Russian holds it—Dear God! the populace would rise—rise, monsieur, and tear his Majesty to pieces."

"He deserves no better!" said Cleek, through his close-shut teeth. "To a Russian—a Russian! As heaven hears me, but for his queen—Well, let it pass. Tell me, how did this Russian get the jewel, and when?"

"Oh, long ago, monsieur—long ago; many months before King Alburtus died."

"Was it his hand that gave it up?"

"No, monsieur. He died without knowing of its loss, without suspecting that the stone in the royal parure is but a sham and an imitation," replied the count. "It all came of the youth, the recklessness, the folly of the crown prince. Monsieur may have heard of his—his many wild escapades—his thoughtless acts, his—his—"

"Call them dissipations, Count, and give them their real name. His acts as crown prince were a scandal and a disgrace. To whom did he part with this gem—a woman?"

"Monsieur, yes! It was during the time he was stopping in Paris—incognito to all but a trusted few. He—he met the woman there, became fascinated with her—bound to her—an abject slave to her."

"A slave to a Russian? Mauravania's heir and—a Russian?"

"Monsieur, he did not know that until afterward. In a mad freak—there was to be a masked ball—he yielded to the lady's persuasions to let her wear the famous Rainbow Pearl for that one night. He journeyed back to Mauravania and abstracted it from among the royal jewels—putting a mere imitation in its place so that it should not be missed until he could return the original. Monsieur, he was never able to return it at any time, for, once she had got it, the Russian made away with it in some secret manner and refused to give it up. Her price for returning it was his royal father's consent to ennoble her, to receive her at the Mauravanian Court, and so to alter the constitution that it would be possible for her to become the crown prince's wife."

"The proposition of an idiot. The thing could not possibly be done."

"No, monsieur, it could not. So the crown prince broke from her and bent all his energies upon the recovery of the pearl and the keeping of its loss a secret from the king and his people. Bravos, footpads, burglars—all manner of men—were employed before he left Paris. The woman's house was broken into, the woman herself waylaid and searched, but nothing came of it—no clue to the lost jewel could be found."

"Why then did he not appeal to the police?"

"Monsieur, he—he dared not. In one of his moments of madness he—she—that is—Oh, monsieur, remember his youth! It appears that the woman had got him to put into writing something which, if made public, would cause the people of Mauravania to rise as one man and to do with him as wolves do with things that are thrown to them in their fury."

"The dog! Some treaty with a Russian, of course!" said Cleek indignantly. "Oh, fickle Mauravania, how well you are punished for your treasonable choice! Well, go on, Count. What next?"

"Of a sudden, monsieur, the woman disappeared. Nothing was heard of her, no clue to her whereabouts discovered for two whole years. She was as one dead and gone until last week."

"Oho! She returned, then?"

"Yes, monsieur. Without hint or warning she turned up in Mauravania, accompanied by a disreputable one-eyed man who has the manner and appearance of one bred in the gutters of Paris, albeit he is well clothed, well-looked after, and she treats him and his wretched collection of parakeets with the utmost consideration."

"Parakeets?" put in Narkom excitedly. "My dear Cleek, couldn't a parakeet be made to swallow a pearl?"

"Perhaps; but not this one, Mr. Narkom," he made reply. "It is quite the size of a pigeon's egg, I believe; is it not, Count?"

"Yes, monsieur, quite. To see it is to remember it always. It has the changing lights of the rainbow, and—"

"Never mind that; go on with the story, please. This woman and this one-eyed man appeared last week in Mauravania, you say?"

"Yes, monsieur; and with them a bodyguard of at least ten servants. Her demand now is that his Majesty make her his morganatic wife; that he establish her at the palace under the same roof with his queen; and that she be allowed to ride with them in the state carriage on the coronation day. Failing that, she swears that she will not only publish the contents of that dreadful letter, but send the original to the chief of the Mauravanian police and appear in public with the Rainbow Pearl upon her person."

"The Jezebel! What steps have you taken, Count, to prevent this?"

"All that I can imagine, monsieur. To prevent her from getting into close touch with the public, I have thrown open my own house to her, and received her and her retinue under my own roof rather than allow them to be quartered at an hotel. Also, this has given me the opportunity to have her effects and those of her followers secretly searched; but no clue to the letter, no clue to the pearl has anywhere been discovered."

"Still she must have both with her, otherwise she could not carry out her threat. No doubt she suspects what motive you had in taking her into your own house, Count—a woman like that is no fool. But tell me, does she show no anxiety, no fear of a search?"

"None, monsieur. She knows that my people search her effects; indeed, she has told me so. But it alarms her not a whit. As she told me two days ago, I shall find nothing; but if I did it would be useless, for, on the moment anything of hers was touched, her servants would see that the finder never carried it from the house."

"Oho!" said Cleek, with a strong rising inflection. "A little searching party of her own, eh? The lady is clever, at all events. The moment either pearl or letter should be removed from its hiding-place her servants would allow nobody to leave the house without being searched to the very skin?"

"Yes, monsieur. So if by any chance you were to discover either—"

"My friend, set your mind at rest," interposed Cleek. "If I find either, or both, they will leave the house with me, I promise you. Mr. Narkom—" he turned to the superintendent—"keep an eye on Dollops for me, will you? There are reasons why I can't take him—can't take anybody—with me in the working out of this case. I may be a couple of days or I may be a week—I can't say as yet; but I start with Count Irma for Mauravania in the morning. And, Mr. Narkom!"

"Yes, old chap?"

"Do me a favour, please. Be at Charing Cross station when the first boat-train leaves to-morrow morning, will you, and bring me a small pot of extract of beef—a very small pot, the smallest they make—not bigger than a shilling nor thicker than one if they make them that size. What's that? Hide the pearl in it? What nonsense! I don't want one half big enough for that. Besides, they'd be sure to find it when they searched me if I tried any such fool's trick as that. Dollops isn't the only creature in the world that gets hungry, my friend, and beef extract is very sustaining, very, I assure you, sir."

II

"A beautiful city, Count—an exceedingly beautiful city," said Cleek, as the carriage which had been sent to meet them at the station rolled into the broad Avenue des Arcs, which is at once the widest and most ornate thoroughfare the capital city of Mauravania boasts. "Ah, what a heritage! No wonder King Ulric is so anxious to retain his sovereignty; no wonder this—er—Madame Tcharnovetski, I think you said the name is—"

"Yes, monsieur. It is oddly spelled, but it is pronounced a little broader than you give it—quite as though it were written Shar-no-vet-skee, in fact, with the accent on the third syllable."

"Ah, yes. Thanks very much. No wonder she is anxious to become a power here. Mauravania is a fairyland in very truth; and this beautiful avenue with its arches, its splendid trees, its sculpture, its—Ah! *cocher*, pull up at once. Stop, if you please, stop!"

"Oui, monsieur," replied the driver, reining in his horses and glancing round. "*Dix mille pardons, M'sieur*, there is something amiss?"

"Yes; very much amiss—from the dog's point of view," replied Cleek, indicating by a wave of the hand a mongrel puppy which crouched, forlorn and hungry, in the shadow of an imposing building. "He should be a Socialist among dogs, that little fellow, Count. The mere accident of birth has made him what he is, and that poodled monstrosity the lady yonder is leading the pet and pride of a thoughtless mistress. I want that little canine outcast, Count, and with your permission I will appropriate him, and give him his first carriage ride." With that, he stepped down from the vehicle, whistled the cur to him, and taking it up in his arms, returned with it to his seat.

"Monsieur, you are to me the most astonishing of men," said the Count, noticing how he patted the puppy and settled it in his lap as the carriage resumed its even rolling down the broad, beautiful avenue. "One moment upholding the rights of birth, the next rebelling against the injustice of it. Are your sympathies with the unfortunate so keen, monsieur, that even this stray cur may claim them?"

"Perhaps," replied Cleek enigmatically. "You must wait and see, Count. Just now I pity him for his forlornity; to-morrow—next day—a week hence—I may hold it a better course to put an end to his hopeless lot by chloroforming him into a painless and peaceful death."

"Monsieur, I cannot follow you—you speak in riddles."

"I deal in riddles, Count; you must wait for the solution of them, I'm afraid."

"I wish I could grasp the solution of one which puzzles me a great deal, monsieur. What is it that has happened to your countenance? You have done nothing to put on a disguise; yet, since we left the train and entered the landau, some subtle change has occurred. What is it? How has it come about? The night before last, when I saw you for the first time, your face was one that impressed me with a sense of familiarity—now, monsieur, you are like a different man."

"I am a different man, Count. Like puppy, here, I am a waif and a stray; yet, at the same time, I have my purpose and am part of a carefully-laid scheme."

The Count made no reply. He could not comprehend the man at all, and at times—but for the world-wide reputation of him—he would have believed him insane. Not a question as to the great and important case he was on, but merely incomprehensible remarks, trifling fancies, apparently aimless whims! Two nights ago a pot of beef extract; to-day a mongrel puppy; and all the time the hopes of a kingdom, the future of a monarch resting in his hands!

For twenty minutes longer the landau rolled on; then it came to a halt under the broad *porte cochère* of the Villa Irma, and two minutes after that Cleek and the Count stood in the presence of Madame Tcharnovetski, her purblind associate, and her retinue of servant-guards.

A handsome woman, this madame, a woman of about two-and-thirty, with the tar-black eyes and the twilight coloured tresses of Northern Russia; bold as brass, flippant as a French cocotte, steel-nerved and calm-blooded as a professional gambler. It had been her whim that all the women of the Count's family should be banished from the house during her stay; that the great salon of the villa—a wondrous apartment, hung in blue and silver, and lit by a huge crystal chandelier—should be put at her disposal night and day; that the electric lights should be replaced with dozens of wax candles (after the manner of the ballrooms of her native Russia), and that her one-eyed companion, with his wicker cage of screeching parakeets, should come and go when and where and how he listed, and that an electric alarm bell be connected with her sleeping apartment and his.

"Your hirelings will tamper with his birds and his effects in the night—I know that, Monsieur le Comte," she had said when she demanded this. "He is a nervous fellow, this poor Clopin; I wish him to be able to ring for help if you and your men go too far."

Clopin was sitting by the window chattering to his birds when Cleek entered, and a glance at him was sufficient to decide two points: first, he was not disguised, nor was his partial blindness in any way a sham, for an idiot could have seen that the droop of the left eyelid over the staring, palpably artificial eye which glazed over the empty socket beneath was due to perfectly natural causes; and, second, that the man was indeed what the Count had said he resembled, namely, a gutter-bred outcast.

"French!" was Cleek's silent comment upon him. "One of those charlatans who infest the streets of Paris with their so-called 'fortune-telling birds,' who, for ten centimes, pick out an envelope with their beaks as a means of telling you what the future is supposed to hold. What has made a woman like this pick up a fellow of his stamp? Hum-m-m! Puppy, I think you are a good move," stroking the ears of the mongrel dog; "a very much better move than a cage of useless parakeets that are meant to throw suspicion in the wrong direction and have a seed-cup so large and so obviously overfilled that it is safe to say there is nothing hidden in it and never has been! And madame has a fancy for waxlights," his gaze travelling upward to the glittering chandelier. "Hum-m-m! How well they know, these women whose beauty is going off, that waxlights show less of Time's ravages than gas or electricity. Candles in the chandelier; candles in the sconces, candles on the mantelpieces. This room should be very charming when it is lighted at night."

It was—as he learned later. Just now things not quite so charming filled the bill, for madame was jeering at him in a manner not to be understood.

"A police spy—that is what you are, monsieur!" she said, coming up to him and impudently snapping her fingers under his nose. "Such a fool, this white-headed old dotard of a Count, to think that he can take me in with a silly yarn about going to visit a nephew and bringing him back here to stay. Monsieur, you are a police spy. Well, good luck to you. Get what the Mauravanian king wants, if—you—can!"

"Madame," replied Cleek, with a deeply deferential bow and with an accent that seemed born of Paris, "madame, that is what I mean to do, I assure you."

"Ah, do you?" she answered, with a scream of laughter. "You hear that, Clopin? You hear that, my good servitors? This silly French noodle is going to get the things in spite of us. Oho, but you have a fine opinion of yourself, monsieur. You need work fast, too, pretty boaster, I can tell you. For the royal jewellers will require the Rainbow Pearl very soon to fix it in its place in the crown for the coronation ceremony, and if that thing his Majesty holds is offered to them, how long, think you, will it be before all Mauravania knows that it is an imitation? Look you," waxing suddenly vicious, "I'll make it shorter still, the time you have to strive. Monsieur le Comte, take this message to his Majesty from me: If in three days he does not promise to accede to my demands and give me a public proof of it over his royal seal, I leave Mauravania—the pearl and letter leave with me, and they shall not come back until I return with them for the coronation."

"For the love of God, madame," said the Count, "don't make it harder still. Oh, wait, wait, I beseech you!"

"Not an hour longer than I have now said!" she flung back at him. "I have waited until I am tired of it, and my patience is worn out. Three days, Count; three days, monsieur with the puppy dog; three days, and not an instant longer, do you hear?"

"Quite enough, madame," replied Cleek, with a courtly bow, "I promise to have them in two!"

She threw back her head and fairly shook with laughter.

"Of a truth, monsieur, you are a candid boaster!" she cried. "Look you, my good fellows, and you too, my poor dumb Clopin, pretty monsieur here will have the letter and the pearl in two days' time. Look to it that he never leaves this house at any minute from this time forth that you do not search him from top to toe. If he resists—ah, well, a pistol may go off accidentally, and things that Mauravania's king would give his life to keep hidden will come to light if any charge of murder is preferred. Monsieur the police spy, I wish you joy of your task."

"Madame, I shall take joy in it," Cleek replied. "But why should we talk of unpleasant things when the future looks so bright? Come, may we not give ourselves a pleasant evening? Look, there is a piano, and—Count, hold my puppy for me, and please see that no one feeds him at any time. I am starving him so that he may devour some of Clopin's parakeets, because I hate the sight of the little beasts. Thank you. Madame, do you like music? Listen, then: I'll sing you Mauravania's national anthem: 'God guard the throne; God shield the right!'" and, dropping down upon the seat before the open instrument, he did so.

* * * * *

That night was ever memorable at the Villa Irma, for the detective seemed somehow to have given place to the courtier, and so merry was his mood, so infectious his good nature, that even madame came under the spell of it. She sang with him, she even danced a Russian polka with him; she sat with him at dinner, and flirted with him in the salon afterward; and when the time came for her to retire, it was he who took her bedroom candle from the shelf and put it into her hand.

"Of a truth, you are a charming fellow, monsieur," she said, when he bent and kissed her hand. "What a pity you should be a police spy and upon so hopeless a case."

"Hopeless cases are my delight, madame. Believe me, I shall not fail."

"Only three days, remember, *cher ami*—only three days!"

"Madame is too kind. I have said it: two will do. On the morning of the third madame's passport will be ready and the Rainbow Pearl be in the royal jeweller's hands. A thousand pleasant dreams—*bon soir!*" And bowed her out and kissed his hand to her as she went up the stairs to bed.

III

Thrice during the next twenty-four hours Cleek, who seemed to have become so attached to the mongrel dog that he kept it under his arm continually, had reason to leave the house, and thrice was he seized by madame's henchmen, bundled unceremoniously into a convenient room, and searched to the very skin before he was suffered to pass beyond the threshold. And if so much as a pin had been hidden upon his person, it must have been discovered.

"You see, monsieur, how hopeless it is!" said the Count despairfully. "One dare not rebel: one dare not lift a finger, or the woman speaks and his Majesty's ruin falls. Oh, the madness of that boast of yours! Only another twenty-four hours—only another day—and then God help his Majesty!"

"God has helped him a great deal better than he deserves, Count," replied Cleek. "By to-morrow night at ten o'clock be in the square of the Aquisola, please. Bring with you the passports of madame and her companions, also a detachment of the Royal Guard, and his Majesty's cheque for the reward I am to receive."

"Monsieur! You really hope to get the things? You really do?"

"Oh, I do more than 'hope,' Count—I have succeeded. I knew last night where both pearl and letter were. To-morrow night—ah, well, let to-morrow tell its own tale. Only be in the square at the hour I mention, and when I lift a lighted candle and pass it across the salon window, send the guard here with the passports. Let them remain outside—within sight, but not within range of hearing what is said and done. You are alone to enter—remember that."

"To receive the jewel and the letter?" eagerly. "Or, at least, to have you point out the hiding-place of them?"

"No; we should be shot down like dogs if I undertook a mad thing like that."

"Then, monsieur, how are we to seize them? How get them into our possession, his Majesty and I?"

"From my hand, Count; this hand which held them both before I went to bed last night."

"Monsieur!" The Count fell back from him as if from some supernatural presence. "You found them? You held them? You took possession of them last night? How did you get them out of the house?"

"I have not done so yet."

"But can you? Oh, monsieur, wizard though you are, can you get them past her guards? Can you, monsieur—can you?"

"Watch for the light at the window, Count. It will not be waved unless it is safe for you to come and the pearl is already out of the house."

"And the letter, monsieur—the damning letter?"

Cleek smiled one of his strange, inscrutable smiles.

"Ask me that to-morrow, Count," he said. "You shall hear something, you and madame, that will surprise you both," then twisted round on his heel and walked hurriedly away.

And all that day and all that night he danced attendance upon madame, and sang to her, and handed her bedroom candle to her as he had done the night before, and gave back jest for jest and returned her merry badinage in kind.

Nor did he change in that when the fateful to-morrow came. From morning to night he was at her side, at her beck and call, doing nothing that was different from the doings of yesterday, save that at evening he locked the mongrel dog up in his room instead of carrying him about. And the dog, feeling its loneliness, or, possibly, famishing—for he had given it not a morsel of food since he found it—howled and howled until the din became unbearable.

"Monsieur, I wish you would silence that beast or else feed it," said madame pettishly. "The howling of the wretched thing gets on my nerves. Give it some food for pity's sake."

"Not I," said Cleek. "Do you remember what I said, madame? I am getting it hungry enough to eat one—or perhaps all—of Clopin's wretched little parakeets."

"You think they have to do with the hiding of the paper or the pearl, cher ami? Eh?"

"I am sure of it. He would not carry the beastly little things about for nothing."

"Ah, you are clever—you are very, very clever, monsieur," she made answer, with a laugh. "But he must begin his bird-eating quickly, that nuisance-dog, or it will be too late. See, it is already half-past nine; I retire to my bed in another hour and a half, as always, and then your last hope he is gone—z-zic! like that; for it will be the end of the second day, monsieur, and your promise not yet kept. Pestilence, monsieur," with a little outburst of temper, "do stop the little beast his howl. It is unbearable! I would you to sing to me like last night, but the noise of the dog is maddening."

"Oh, if it annoys you like that, madame," said Cleek, "I'll take him round to the stable and tie him up there, so we may have the song undisturbed. Your men will not want to search me of course, when I am merely popping out and popping in again like that, I am sure?"

Nevertheless they did, for although they had heard and did not stir when he left the room and ran up for the dog, when he came down with it under his arm and made to leave the house, he was pounced upon, dragged into an adjoining apartment by half a dozen burly fellows, stripped to the buff, and searched, as the workers in a diamond mine are searched, before they suffered him to leave the house. There was neither a sign of a pearl nor a scrap of a letter to be found upon him—they made sure of that before they let him go.

"An enterprising lot, those lackeys of yours, madame," he said, when he returned from tying the dog up in the stable and rejoined her in the salon. "It will be an added pleasure to get the better of them, I can assure you."

"Oui! if you can!" she answered, with a mocking laugh. "Clopin, cher ami, your poor little parakeets are safe for the night—unless monsieur grows desperate and eats them for himself."

"Even that, if it were necessary to get the pearl, madame," said Cleek, with the utmost sang-froid. "Faugh!" looking at his watch, "a good twenty minutes wasted by the zealousness of those idiotic searchers of yours. Ten minutes to ten! Just time for one brief song. Let us make hay while the sun lasts, madame, for it goes down suddenly in Mauravania; and for some of us—it never comes up again!" Then, throwing himself upon the piano-seat, he ran his fingers across the keys and broke into the stately measures of the national anthem. And, of a sudden, while the song was yet in progress, the clock in the corridor jingled its musical chimes and struck the first note of the hour.

He jumped to his feet and lifted both hands above his head.

"Mauravania!" he cried. "Oh, Mauravania! For you! For you!" Then jumped to the mantelpiece, and catching up a lighted candle, flashed it twice across the window's width, and broke again into the national hymn.

"Monsieur," cried out madame, "monsieur, what is the meaning of that? Have you lost your wits? You give a signal! For what? To whom?"

"To the guards of Mauravania's king, madame, in honour of his safe escape from you!" he made reply; then twitched back the window curtains until the whole expanse of glass was bared. "Look! do you see them—do you, madame? His Majesty of Mauravania sends Madame Tcharnovetski a command to leave his kingdom, since he no longer has cause to fear a wasp whose sting has been plucked out."

Her swift glance flashed to the fireplace, then to the corner where Clopin still sat with his jabbering parakeets, then flashed back to Cleek, and—she laughed in his face.

"I think not, monsieur," she said, with a swaggering air. "Truly, I think not, my excellent friend."

"What a pity you only think so, madame! As for me—Ah, welcome, Count, welcome a thousand times. The paper, my friend; you have brought it? Good! Give it to me. Madame, your passport—yours and your associates'. You leave Mauravania by the midnight train, and you have but little time to pack your effects. Your passport, madame, and—your bedroom candle. Oh, yes, the paper is still round it—see!" slipping off a sheet of note paper that was wrapped round the full length of the candle from top to bottom, "but if you will examine it, madame, you will find it is blank. I burned the real letter the night before last when I put this in its place."

"You what?" she snapped; then caught the tube-shaped covering he had stripped from the candle, uncurled it, and—screamed.

"Blank, madame, quite blank, you see," said Cleek serenely. "For one so clever in other things, you should have been more careful. A little pinch of powder in the punch at dinner-time—just that—and on the first night, too! It was so easy afterward to get into your room, remove the real paper, and wrap the candle in a blank piece while you slept."

"You—you dog!" she snapped out viciously. "You drugged me?"

"Yes, madame; you and the one-eyed man as well! Oh, don't excite yourself—don't pull at the poor wretch like that. The glass eye will come out quite easily, but—I assure you there is only a small lump of beeswax in the socket now. I removed the Rainbow Pearl from poor Monsieur Clopin's blind eye ten minutes after I burnt the letter, madame, and—it passed out of this house to-night! A clever idea to pick up a one-eyed pauper, madame, and hide the pearl in the empty socket of the lost eye, but—it was too bad, you had to supply a glass eye to keep it in, after the lid and the socket had withered and shrunk from so many years of emptiness. It worried the poor man, madame; he was always feeling it, always afraid that the lump behind would force it out; and, what is an added misfortune for your plans, the glass shell did not allow you to see the change when the pearl vanished and the bit of beeswax took its place. Madame Tcharnovetski, your passport. I know enough of the King of Mauravania to be sure that your life will not be safe if you are not past the frontier before daybreak!"

* * * * *

"Get up, Count," he said, with a little shaky laugh. "I appreciate the honour, but—your fancy is playing you a trick. I tell you I never set foot in Mauravania before, my friend."

"I know—I know. How should you. Majesty, when it was as a child at Queen Karma's breast Mauravania last saw—Don't leave like this! Majesty! Majesty! 'God guard the right'—the pearl and the kingdom are here."

"Wrong, my good friend. The kingdom is there—where you found me—in England; and so, too, is the pearl. For there is no kingdom like the kingdom of love, no pearl like a good woman. Good night, Count, and many thanks for your hospitality. You are a little upset to-night, but no doubt you will be all right again in the morning. I will walk to the station and—alone, if it is all the same to you."

"Majesty!"

"Dreams, Count, dreams. The riddle is solved, my friend. Good luck to your country and—good-bye!"

And, setting his back to the palace and the lights and the fluttering flag, and his face to the land that held her, turned and went his way—to the West—to England—and to those things which are higher than crowns and better than sceptres and more precious than thrones and ermine.

"Monsieur le comte—no! I thank you, but I cannot wait to be presented to his Majesty, for I, too, leave Mauravania to-night, and, like Madame yonder, return to other and more promising fields," said Cleek, an hour later, as he stood on the terrace of the Villa Irma and watched the slow progress down the moonlit avenue of the carriage which was bearing Madame Tcharnovetski and her effects to the railway station. "Give me the cheque, please; I have earned that, and—there is good use for it. I thank you, Count. Now do an act of charity, my friend: give the little dog in the stable a good meal, and then have a surgeon chloroform him into a peaceful and merciful death. They will find the Rainbow Pearl in his intestines when they come to dissect the body. I starved him, Count—starved him purposely, poor little wretch, so that he could be hungry enough to snap at anything in the way of food and bolt it instantly. To-night, when I went up to take him out to the stable, a thick smearing of beef extract over the surface of the pearl was sufficient; he swallowed it in a gulp! For a double reason, Count, there should be a cur quartered on the royal arms of this country after to-night."

His voice dropped off into silence. The carriage containing madame had swung out through the gateway, and its shadow no longer blotted the broad, unbroken space of moonlit avenue. He turned and looked far out, over the square of the Aquisola, along the light-lined esplanade, to the palace gates and the fluttering flag that streamed against the sky above and beyond them.

"Oh, Mauravania!" he said. "An Englishman's heritage! Dear country, how beautiful! My love to your Queen—my prayers for you."

"Monsieur!" exclaimed the Count, "monsieur, what juggle is this? Your face is again the face of that other night—the face that stirs memory yet does not rivet it. Monsieur, speak, I beg of you. What are you? Who are you?"

"Cleek," he made answer. "Just Cleek! It will do. Oh, Mauravania, dear land of desolated hopes, dear grave of murdered joys!"

"Monsieur!"

"Hush! Let me alone. There are things too sacred; and this—" His hands reached outward as if in benediction; his face, upturned, was as a face transfigured, and something that shone as silver gleamed in the corner of his eye. "Mauravania!" he said. "Oh, Mauravania! My country—my people—good-bye!"

"Monsieur! Dear Heaven—*Majesty!*"

Then came a rustling sound, and when Cleek had mastered himself and looked down, a figure with head uncovered knelt on one knee at his feet.